The Wrath

by

Kristina Schram

*Mischief*Maker*Media*

Published by Mischief Maker Media (USA)

First printing: September, 2013

Cover Design, Interior, and Technical Expertise: GorKee

ISBN: 978-1-939397-04-1

Visit Kristina Schram on the World Wide Web at:
www.KristinaSchram.com

Acknowledgements

I want to thank a few amazing people for making this book happen. My husband, Dan, is my biggest supporter and has made publishing this book a reality. He actually read it, too, even though thrillers, Dilbert, and computer code are more his style than paranormal romance. I will love you always, Dan!

I tend to use the same readers for all my books and they have been diligent, uncomplaining, and insightful. Thank you Heather Duane, Elizabeth Schram, Kendra DeCota, Gordon Unzen, and Dan Unzen. You have made this book so much better!

To my readers… Thanks for being so awesome and supportive of my endeavors. I hope that my writing continues to improve as long as I can tap keys, so that I can keep the stories coming, and you happily entertained.

Chapter One

✳

The Man on the Train

The window seat called to me and I seized on it like a talisman. I wanted to believe that the little haven it created would shelter me. It was an illusion that I needed, for the simple reason that this journey I'd embarked upon was not safe. Not in the least.

Still, here I was in England, safely seated, with train schedule clutched in one slightly trembling hand, the cryptic letter that had started it all, folded and worn from many failed attempts to interpret its message, tucked in the front pocket of my new slacks. I felt nervous and a little bit frightened, but also mildly triumphant, even a bit rebellious. Instead of retreating, as was my typical response to challenges, this time I had dived forward. Of course, I'd only done so because *this time* I felt in my heart that if I didn't follow my mysterious quest through to its end, I wouldn't recover from the failure.

Besides, my mother wouldn't have let me return home. And when I thought about it, nor did I especially want to go back. I was embarking on an adventure of a lifetime. For too long I had lived at the periphery of life, hiding out in the shadows cast by the brighter and more beautiful. I'd wasted altogether too much time ducking humankind.

"Is this seat taken?"

The voice startled me, its deep resonance breaching my port as ruthlessly as a torpedo. The train, on its way to Newton Abbot, had stopped just outside London. The passengers, all of whom had been waiting impatiently on the platform, swiftly boarded the train—a rush of businessmen and women in dark suits, teenagers sporting ear buds and texting with frantic thumbs, and the requisite horde of tourists, bedecked in practical clothes and cameras.

I glanced to my left and then up, straight into the most challenging eyes I'd ever seen—eyes that dared me to say yes, to say anything at all. I hadn't the breath to speak so I shook my head. No, the seat was not taken. With a brusque nod, the man slipped into the chair opposite me, next to the window. He was six or seven inches taller than my five-foot-seven frame, his legs as long as a distance runner's. He took up a lot of room and with nowhere else to go I felt myself pushing back into my seat.

After a bit of maneuvering, we now sat knee to knee, or more accurately, knee to shin, with only an inch or two to separate us. His closeness made me feel prickly inside. Several itchy spots broke out along my back, none of which I could reach gracefully. First I tried to ignore them. When that failed, I attempted to relieve the itch without using my hands, which only made me look like a goon as I wiggled and rubbed my back against the seat as surreptitiously as I could, while hoping no one noticed.

Moments later a crowd of boisterous tourists entered our car and pushed their way into seats. Talking loudly, their presence and my itching back left me no space to study my seatmate, no time to wonder, did I register in his thoughts at all? How very aggravating, especially when all I wanted to do was look at the man who was taking up all my space, and scratch my back, of course.

A large man, uneasily dressed in a navy blue, off-the-rack, polyester business suit with shiny elbows, breathily took the seat beside me. The scent of fried fish and the salty tang of sweat engulfed me soon after he sat. His girth, like too many scoops of ice cream piled on a cone, spilled over the armrest, into my sanctum. Itches forgotten, I scooted over toward the window to avoid his hefty elbow swinging like a pendulum as he attempted to stow his battered briefcase below his seat. My knees banged against the passenger opposite me, yet he made no effort to move out of the way.

The businessman straightened up with a sigh. "Do yeh happen to know what time it is, Miss?" An innocent, entirely normal question to ask of a person, yet I avoided his eyes as though he'd just asked me for my phone number, focusing instead on a drop of sweat sliding down his ample cheek and past a mole the size of a pencil eraser on his jaw. "I lost me watch yesterday and now I don't know whether I'm coming or going."

I shook my head. "I'm in the same boat as you, I'm afraid," I told him with an apologetic shrug. "Or is it train?" My attempt at a joke appeared to fall flat and I hurried on, "I'm not sure I have the right hour. I've just come over from the States. I meant to check at Paddington, but I just made the train myself." I glanced at my new wristwatch, silver and gold, a going-away present from my father. "I think it might be around 1:00."

In unison, we looked toward our neighbor across from us, expectantly. Feeling our gaze, he reluctantly peered over his paper. His heavy lids gave an annoyed flicker, then he slipped a long-fingered hand into the pocket of his gray tweed jacket to pull out an impressive silver pocket watch. Pressing a button at the top, the face popped open.

"2:05," he corrected me, barely glancing my way. The face closed and the watch was promptly hidden away again, quick as a mouse. He was English, then, his ethnicity coming through loud and clear in a mere three syllables.

Before I changed my watch over to the correct time, I made sure to memorize the initials I'd seen engraved on his watch…N.A.T. The letters should be easy to remember. Add a 'G' at the beginning and you'd have the tiny, flying pests that swarmed a person on humid summer days in Minnesota, and which had a surprisingly nasty bite considering their size. The man seated across from me, hidden behind his paper, was as annoying as those little bugs. Except, unlike the gnat, he didn't swarm a person, nor did he bite. At least for the moment. He was infuriating in his elusiveness—the newspaper serving as his shield against common people like myself.

"Really?" the big man wheezed good-humoredly. "Well, I'll be buggered. That's a first. I'm right on time!" He beamed, his full, red cheeks like bulbs. "I don't ride the train much, but me car's in the garage, and I hate riding the bus as much as I hate not having pudding for dinner. No room to stretch yer legs on these things."

"The chairs are very close together…" I put forth.

"Too right." He blotted at his face with a stained, vaguely pink handkerchief. "So ye're from the States, are yeh?" I bobbed my head. "Which part?"

"That depended on my parents," I told him.

"Army brat, eh?"

"Actor brat," I amended. There was a reason I knew about Minnesota summers. We once stayed in Minneapolis for five months—my parents were in a play at the Guthrie Theater—bugging out just before winter set in.

He gave a shout of laughter. "And now ye're here."

"And now I'm here."

He pushed back against his seat, chuckling. The chair tried to maintain its uprightness, then gave in, leaning backward like a sapling in the wind. "Well, be a luv and wake me at Newbury. I'm whacked." A moment later, he was snoring softly; his cavernous nostrils above a mustache the color of ginger quivering delicately.

Newbury Station didn't come quickly enough. While I liked the man, I soon tired of fighting off his elbow. The appendage took up a surprising amount of space, crowding me against the cold glass. When we finally rolled to a stop nearly half an hour later, I nudged the man. He snorted, then stared at me blankly. "This is your stop."

"Right!" he cried, moving quickly to grab his scuffed, brown briefcase. His fingernails, short and square and surrounded by doughy flesh, were buffed to a high shine. Crappy suit, lovely manicure. Go figure. "Well, goodbye to you." He nodded at our fellow passenger, who didn't look up to respond. My new friend winked at me. "Good luck with that one," it said.

Watching him squeeze his way down the narrow aisle, I was surprised to discover that the car had emptied like fish from a net. I had been abandoned. I frantically consulted my schedule. The next stop wasn't due for quite some time.

So it was just me, and the Impenetrable Wall. Super.

After ten minutes of fidgeting with the zipper on my purse and staring out the window, I finally gave in. I could no longer deny myself another peek at NAT, though I'm not sure why I felt so curious about someone so supercilious. At the moment, he was reading his paper, by all appearances thoroughly engrossed in its contents. But as my gaze slid over toward him, he shifted and my eyes dashed back toward the window, spooked like a child. I didn't want him to catch me ogling him. I had some pride, deeply buried, which resurrected now and again. Besides, I felt quite sure his big head didn't need any more flattery filling it—I imagine it was on the verge of exploding as it was.

A minute later, I tried again. I couldn't help it. Not looking at him was like trying not to goggle at a car wreck. His paper had his full attention and I thought he must be reading about a murder to warrant such scrutiny. More likely, though, it was probably only the stock report, all that talk of mergers and pork bellies making his cold, little heart go pitta-pat.

The paper drooped and dipped to neck level and my eyes zoomed back in. He was in his late-twenties, I calculated, maybe ten years older than myself. He had dark hair, freshly cut, worn close to the scalp on the sides and longer on top, and brown, deep-set eyes. Slightly curved lips, the lower a bit plumper than its mate, punctuated his pale skin. His ears were a bit on the large side, which his haircut didn't bother to hide; his long nose boasted a bump centered in the middle of its slope. All in all, his features were reasonably attractive, I conceded. He wore a dark, heather-gray blazer over a light blue oxford, the two colors bringing out the best in each other. Except for his ink-stained fingers, he looked expensive. He was someone my mother would call, 'the right sort of person.'

Naturally, I disliked him.

Without warning, the paper gave a bow. He was folding it, putting it away. My eyes quickly slid back to the window, taking refuge in the green fields.

"What are you looking at?" The words, coming a minute later, couldn't have been more unexpected. My eyes jumped back to him.

"You," I said, realizing as soon as the word leaped out of my mouth that the retort had sounded much better in my head. I cringed. Out loud it sounded purposely childish. I sighed and my fingers automatically laced together, as though seeking solace, and I felt hot and cold all at once. Sophistication has never been my forte.

A dark eyebrow rose. "I meant, before. Out there." He nodded at the window. "What do you see in all that?"

"I guess I see my future," I blurted out, once again forgetting to think before I spoke. My mother hated it when I was cryptic like this, but sometimes I couldn't help myself. My future *was* what I was seeing, or at least thinking about. Unfortunately, my honesty often came out sounding flippant, as though I were playing games with people.

"And what does your future hold?" His smile was condescending; he might just as well have inserted "my dear" at the end of the question. To him I was just a way to pass the time, like a cat toying with his four-legged—less than sublime, but it will have to do—dinner.

Knowing I was about to be dismissed, I plowed ahead anyway. "It holds grief," I replied in my best gypsy fortuneteller voice. I pointed at the raindrops starting to spot the thick windowpane and my finger absently traced one's wayward path down to the sill. Based on the fact that my past had been full of trouble, going mainly by the name Silvia Filmore, also known as my mother, it was a good answer. "But I think it also holds endless possibilities." I gestured at the broad expanse of moor that stretched on forever, into the distance. My greatest wish was to have a life of choices and paths to take, without being steered—forced—down them. So far, my wish has remained only that—a wish.

He nodded, thoughtful, his dark eyes on mine. "Pain and possibilities. That sounds like a good life to me, Madame Gypsy." He ran a finger around the back of his collar as though to loosen its hold. I had the fleeting impression that he wore formal clothes out of habit, and perhaps might have chosen something altogether more comfortable if he put any thought into it.

I laughed in surprise, the sound echoing as loudly as a crow's caw. "Pain is good?"

"Pain is growth." He stopped, his wide brow crumpling, as though warring thoughts fought beneath its thin layer of skin. "Or it can be. Some people do the wrong thing with their pain."

"Maybe they only do what they know best. It's not wrong, just all they know."

His expression was wry, almost grim. "Then they should try harder to know more."

I leaned forward. "Geniuses know a lot and look at how they suffer."

"They know facts, not necessarily themselves."

"Or maybe they know themselves too well," I answered back, enjoying this. "They know they have a dark side."

"Perhaps," he conceded. His fingers tapped a slow beat against the armrest; the sound like drums before an execution.

The rain started to pelt the glass in earnest, blurring the view. "Which one are you?" I ventured. "Self-aware, or unenlightened?"

He shrugged. "I don't know, probably somewhere in-between. You?" He leaned forward as though truly interested in what I had to say. We were very close now; I could smell his cologne and it made me think of spring and new beginnings.

I felt a tiny thrill flutter in my stomach. Could he really be interested in my opinion? How exciting and unexpected. The problem was, I wasn't sure how to answer his question. Before this conversation I would've said that I knew myself too well. My character was a topic I'd thoroughly dissected and found wanting at every inspection. The constant search exhausted me. Each time I hoped to find something redeeming—something that made me who I was, unique and worthy of notice—and each time, I failed. I could do a lot of things reasonably well—Mother had made sure of that—but nothing I did was my *own*.

"I'm starting to realize that I don't know myself at all." I frowned, wishing I could take the revealing words back. I wasn't used to sharing. On the few dates I'd been on, and with the few, temporary friends I'd had, I never spoke of myself at a depth more personal than my favorite band or what I liked on my pizza. I think I was afraid to go deeper, afraid of people's judgment—worse, afraid they would find there was nothing there.

He stared at me, studying me. He was entirely aware of my presence, I realized. I stared back at him. Typically I would have looked away, down at my feet, back out the window. But not today. There was too much at stake, though I had no idea what was at stake, or why I felt this way. Maybe it was the foreign country, maybe because I might never see him again.

"Where are you headed?" he asked, still looking at me. He leaned his aristocratic head back against the chair, away from me, his chin raised, his deep, brown eyes pensive. I pulled back, too, wishing fervently that I knew what he was thinking so I could say what he wanted to hear.

"Filmore Estate in Ellwood," I told him. "Near Dartmoor."

He sat up, his knees pulling away from mine. "Pardon?"

I frowned, pulling out the directions from my pants pocket. "Filmore Estate in Ellwood. It says right here." I held up the piece of paper for him to see. He snatched it out of my hand.

Face drawn, he handed the directions back to me after reading them, and shook his head. "You can't go there."

My heart beat a little harder. "What do you mean I can't go there? Is there something wrong?"

"There's something wrong all right." His dark eyes were wary, almost angry, the tips of his excessive ears reddening.

I waited. "Could you explain?" I asked when he said nothing more.

He shook his head, turning to look out the window at the rain. "I can't believe this. Of all the bloody rotten luck."

He was scaring me. I leaned toward him again, imploring. "Please tell me what's wrong. Are my aunts hurt? Insane? What?"

There was a groan. His profile was hard, a shadow of stubble just beginning to mark his jaw. "They're your *aunts*? Not just friends you call aunt? A quaint custom your family practices?"

"According to my mother, we are truly related. What is all this?"

"I can't say," he mumbled, searching about for his things. He grabbed his neatly folded newspaper and black leather briefcase, and stood up nearly hitting his head on the overhang. "If you'll excuse me, I cannot stay here. Not with you."

I fell back against my chair with a thump, stunned, and watched as he ducked low to exit the swaying car. After he disappeared, I wished, childishly, that on the way out he'd hit his perfect head. Then he'd have something to remember me by. Because it wouldn't be my name he'd recall.

He hadn't bothered to ask what it was.

Chapter Two

*

The Letter

My parents had done very little to prepare me for life, which is odd considering they're both in the entertainment business. Being their only child, I should, by all rights, be a spoiled, precocious brat—world weary and terribly bored with everything, and everybody. While I'm grateful that I'm not that kind of person, I wouldn't have minded being better prepared to handle NAT's storming off instead of staring at his retreating back like an overgrown idiot.

Simply put, I'd never learned how to deal with life's curveballs. Generally, I either ducked out of the way when one of them came roaring at me, or I avoided walking onto the playing field in the first place. My limited experience socializing with other people, and lack of siblings, had left me a bit defenseless, especially when it came to standing up for myself. It didn't help that my mother was so skilled at giving orders, and I was so good at following them.

"Take French, Evie," she ordered. "It'll make you seem smarter." I took French. "Don't wear those pants. They make you look fat, and you certainly don't need that on top of everything else." I threw out the pants.

One time I dared to ask, "Am I really stupid and fat?" and her snide response, delivered in her best Hollywood actress voice was, "Compared to what, darling?" After that, I pretty much gave up.

Maybe I should have made more of a protest when she insulted me, but I could never quite muster the courage for it. Not only was it easier to do as I was told, it was safer. Besides, I wasn't sure what I wanted to do or be in place of Mother's 'suggestions' so I went along with them.

And I hated myself for it.

The inevitable result, of course, was that I began to believe what my mother said. It didn't matter that I wasn't *really* stupid or fat, what mattered was that I thought I was. Perception, I've learned, is a hard illusion to rout, especially when established at the age of three when my toddler potbelly earned me a ban on public swimming pools for the summer.

Appearance is everything to my parents. My mother is a theater actress and my father works in television under the slightly altered name, Edmund More. Eight years ago, when I was ten, he landed a part in a popular soap opera. He was an instant hit, and we finally settled down in New York City, close to his studio. Before that, we went where the work was, typically staying in small cities with decaying theaters (the Guthrie being a rare exception) for as long as the show was a success. My parents could not be without adulation.

My childish adoration was not enough for them so when I became a teenager I transferred my affections to various actors at the Crenshaw where my mother now performs, still hoping for her big break. With its faded grandeur, dizzying catwalks, worn, red velvet seats, and the smell of sawdust and powder makeup, the Crenshaw was more like a home to me than my real one. I love it there.

Earlier in the spring I had made plans to work backstage over the summer building sets, but Mother had other ideas. She had introduced the topic while applying black mascara to the long, curled lashes surrounding her artificially blue eyes. I had the blue eyes; hers were actually brown. "You're going to England, Evie," she said in a tone that brooked no argument. "Your father and I need to get away."

"From what?" I asked, clasping my hands together. Whenever I was around my mother my fingers transformed into ten nervous snakes, each one weaving and winding through the other nine, searching for a hiding place.

"From…" She paused and wiped at an eyelash thick with tarry goop. "Well, from work and all that."

While I might not be able, in the presence of strangers, to put more than three words together to form a sensible sentence, I wasn't entirely stupid. She meant to say, "Away from you, Evie. You bore us to tears."

"Why England?" I questioned, tugging at a curl of chestnut hair. I felt like I was twelve again, not an adult of eighteen years. Mother had a way of reversing time whenever I was around her. Scientists should study the woman. She'd astound them.

"Oh, Evie!" she groaned. "You and your questions. Your father has some relatives living there…" She pulled at the skin around her eyes, tightening it like a drum.

"And…?" I prompted. She had a habit of starting sentences and not finishing them. She thought everyone should be able to read her mind.

"Oh, I don't know. I think they want to see you. You *are* half English, remember, which does explain a few things," she muttered darkly.

How could I forget? My mother was always reminding me of my British ancestry. She used my ethnicity as an excuse to her friends for my less than stunning looks, my once crooked teeth, which were now braces free—thank God—and for my reserved nature. Strangely, she never did the same for my father, who was British through and through. Probably because he was incredibly good-looking and immeasurably charming.

"It'll be good for you," she continued, slicking Vaseline on her teeth to keep her lips from sticking to them—she'd worked the pageant circuit before she met my father (once winning runner-up for Miss New York) and knew all the tricks. "A trip to Europe before you go off to college. Everyone's doing it these days."

"I thought you and father wanted to get away from work. So why am I the one who's leaving?"

"I made that up. I thought it would persuade you to go."

I sighed. What did it matter? Why did I care that my mother didn't want me around? It wasn't like we were one of those close-knit families who went for Sunday drives or on picnics together. I was used to being alone. I was used to summoning up company like ghosts at a séance. And though my daydreamed relationships were often insubstantial and never enough, I had adjusted to this way of life and found it, if not terribly rewarding, at least livable.

"So that's it? This is something everyone my age is doing, so I should do it, too?"

She sighed angrily and banged the Vaseline down on the dressing table. From a drawer in her jewelry box, she pulled out a folded piece of paper. She handed it to me, not once looking me in the eye, then returned to her ablutions. The stationery, ivory and of thick stock, bore an elaborate coat of arms emblazoned across the top. My father's family coat of arms.

Attero pro vos es pessum ire. This phrase was written on a scroll, which unfurled beneath a colorful shield. "Destroy before you are destroyed," my mother translated when I asked, delivered with a roll of her wide blue eyes that looked younger than they should. Amazing what a little plastic surgery can do. "It's a nice way of saying, it's okay to be a bully."

"What do you mean?" I asked, as I plopped down on the nearby divan and stared at the shield. The design was ostentatious, with its lions and tigers and bears, oh my, and banners a-waving.

"Let's just say your ancestors dealt with conflict by getting rid of anyone who did not agree with them."

"You're sure we're not talking about your side of the family?" This sounded much more like the Peachams—Mother's maiden name—than the Filmores. My father avoided conflict like he would a pack of angry, plague-carrying orangutans. But my mother...she both welcomed and embraced it.

I studied the banner again. To learn that I came from a long line of bullies was disturbing. I hated bullies and had experienced my fair share of them. To discover that my own flesh and blood practiced such tactics was discouraging, to say the least. I'd rather hear that my ancestors were King Arthur-like, fair and noble and kind, not King Henry the Eighth-like, mean and petty and cowardly...not to mention, murderous.

"We have supporters," I pointed out, looking for the saving grace in all of this. "Only the nobility get supporters."

Mother, using a delicate, painted nail, traced the two figures standing on either side of the shield, holding it up, supporting it. "Yes, you come from nobility." She said it with distaste and I stared at her in wonder.

Her coated eyelashes drooped disdainfully at me. "What? Do you think I like all that pomp and circumstance? The snobbery and judgment?"

"Uh, yeah. You live for that stuff."

She sighed. "I only pretend to, Evie. For the audience." She flared out her fingers like a fan, checking her pale pink manicure for chips.

She was lying, but neither of us felt the need to pursue it. She only disliked snobbery and judgment when it found her lacking. Otherwise, she used it like a warrior used his sword.

I began to read the letter, wrapping a curl around and around my index finger like spaghetti on a fork. My eyes traveled down to the precise penmanship of the letter's author. The letter was addressed to my father.

Dear Edmund,

I never knew you could act. But I should have guessed that about you. I also should have known you would change your name.

Well, you can hide no longer. You must return. You got what you wanted and now it's our turn. Don't make us come and fetch you, dear Edmund...

Remember the Augustine affair? Of course, you do. How could you forget? I don't believe you'd want that little incident to come back to haunt you, would you? So come at once...and leave your wife behind.

Your sisters, Priscilla and Kelli

Mother was staring out the window, her freshly plumped lips pursed. "What is this all supposed to mean?" I asked for the second time in the space of a minute. I turned the paper over as though hoping to find the answers on the other side. The back was blank, like my mother's expression.

"You must go find out," she said, fluffing the dark hair around her face.

For once, I was happy to follow her orders. I had thought it over and come to believe that traveling to England was what I wanted to do. My father had been born in Dartmoor, living there until he was eighteen, and I thought it would be interesting to see the country of my ancestors, even if they were bullies. And reading such classics as *The Lion, the Witch and the Wardrobe* and *I Capture the Castle* had instilled in me a belief that England was a magical and romantic place. Maybe there I could become the person I wanted to be.

Despite Mother's less than rational reason for sending me, and father's obvious, though unexplained, reluctance to see his sisters, I wanted to go.

I was desperate to go.

I left New York City at night, as most sane people do who wish to fly across the Atlantic Ocean, departing without anyone seeing me off. I know it's normal to say goodbye to loved ones setting off on a journey—I've seen people do it. But my father pleaded an early morning shooting schedule and my mother said point-blank that she didn't feel like making the trip to the airport and back. Taxis gave her wrinkles.

Oh, the times I've been tempted to poison her apple martini.

Before leaving, I spent many joyful hours shopping for what I imagined would make the perfect English wardrobe—a tweed blazer, soft sweaters for layering, a pair of forest green Wellingtons, and sturdy walking boots. I packed and repacked everything to fit in my suitcases, including the books I'd bought on Dartmoor, where the family estate was located, devouring them each night before I fell asleep.

On bus rides to and from the mall, I tried to interpret the letter, finally accepting after hours of thorough, mind boggling examination that only my father and his sisters were meant to understand its meaning. When I tried to pin him down about it, he would flutter away like a moth, keeping just out of reach. He didn't seem to appreciate the fact that I was doing him a favor, traveling hundreds of miles to solve a problem—*his* problem.

"Must practice my lines, Evalina," he'd say, waving a white script at me like a surrender flag. Only he didn't surrender to my demands, he merely retreated—behind the heavy mahogany door of his study, as he usually did when I tried to connect with him. Since I was a child, I'd taken on the silly belief that if I could only get him to look at me, then he'd finally *see* me and reach out to me. He never did. Yet I've never stopped trying to get him to look.

In the end I discovered nothing useful, other than that the old lock to his study was impossible to pick and his sisters were odd. And the latter revelation came through Mother.

My aunts didn't know I was coming. Mother was supposed to call and let them know, but I'm quite certain she never did. She always left the administrative side of life to me, or to other professionals—father's personal assistant, an accountant, the dry cleaners. The rest I could handle, but I wasn't about to call two strangers and ask them what their letter could possibly mean and if it was okay if I came in my father's place. My mind refused.

Anyway, they wouldn't want to hear from *me*. They were expecting their brother, not his daughter. And since they were upset with him for not doing something he was supposed to do and wanted him to make amends, I was betting I was going to be a poor substitute.

At various times during the days leading up to my trip, I thought about what the aunts would say when I showed up on their doorstep. And I wondered why they didn't invite my mother. Because they didn't like her? What had she done to get on their bad side (although she probably just opened her mouth)? And what was the Augustine affair?

There were so many questions it made my head spin.

~

Weeks after first reading the letter, it still spun. Unsettled, I scrubbed at the train window's grimy surface with my sleeve, then leaned my burning forehead against the cool glass. Fingerprints and round nose smudges dotted the dusty pane at varying heights, but I didn't notice them. I was staring at my reflection, which showed flushed cheeks and pale skin, brimming blue eyes and a runny nose that I quickly wiped with the checkered handkerchief I kept in my pants pocket.

Why did he have to be so rude?

I sighed deeply, watching the rain angrily pelt the reflected oval of my face.

Because you're the type of girl people feel they can be rude to, I told myself. *You let them.*

My fingers curled into fists and I felt a terrible rage building in my chest. I wanted to smash that insipid image of myself, to shout and wail and curse the world. I wanted to hurt others as much as they had hurt me. Yet I did not move. No, I did as I have always done and shoved the seething ball of fire deep down inside me, crushing it like an overripe tomato.

Unfortunately I couldn't do the same to NAT. In fact, there really wasn't much I could do about him at all. I certainly wasn't going to follow the bastard and berate him for being rude. Despite serving as my mother's whipping girl for nearly two decades, I had maintained— *clung to*—a certain modicum of dignity. Or was it just a natural antipathy toward shaming experiences that kept me rooted to my seat?

He never came back.

Oh, why did I bother to hope that he would? Even the faithful dog can learn after so many inescapable, uncontrollable electric shocks, to give up trying. He learns *helplessness*. Well, not all dogs do. Some of them never quit. I wondered which one I would rather be—the dog who gives up on life after too much punishment, or the one who keeps hope alive even after getting kicked in the stomach time and again?

Both options sounded rather stupid to me.

My anger dissipated for the moment and I picked nervously at a fingernail as rural England passed me by. I spent the rest of the train trip brooding about my lack of good looks, my mother's criticisms, my father's distance, and NAT, that awful man who possessed the power to hurt me, even though I didn't know him, nor did he know me.

I was angry, and I was hurt. But through it all, and thank Heaven for this part of me, I drank in the scenery like draughts of champagne. I stored it away; I remembered it. The moors were amazing and I wished fervently that I were like them—wild, free, too beautiful to deny.

Chapter Three

*

Filmore

At last the train pulled into Newton Abbot. Here it dispelled several passengers, including myself and my new Louis Vuitton luggage, which Mother had bought to impress the aunts. Their letter telling Father to leave his wife at home had pierced even my mother's thick skin.

NAT was nowhere to be seen.

An old man in a flat cap slouched behind the wheel of the last remaining taxi, a beat-up, black VW belching smoke from both the tailpipe and the driver's window, which was cracked open a couple inches. Spotting me, he climbed out, a chewed-up cigar clenched between visibly decaying teeth, and motioned vigorously to me. I walked toward him mutely, succumbing to his imperious gestures. Once at the car, he tore my luggage from my hands and slammed it into the trunk like garbage bags. "You'll take me to Ellwood?" I ventured to ask, and he grunted. I assumed that was a yes.

As I climbed into the smoky interior I had a feeling that the man's taxi company was a one-vehicle enterprise, and that he probably didn't get much business beyond spineless simpletons like myself. I gingerly sat on the cracked vinyl seat reminiscent of thin ice while the driver slammed his body behind the wheel, muttering to himself. The car smelled of stale smoke, body odor, and fried onions. I tried not to breathe through my nose. I tried not to breathe at all, but I started to get dizzy and gave up.

The engine fought the driver's efforts to start it, but eventually roared to life. Before we'd traveled twenty feet, the grizzled man launched into a diatribe about the state of his country's government—parliament and the latest prime minister and what a crap job he was doing—steering with only one hand as he jabbered at me via the rearview mirror. He possessed the stereotypical British teeth (as I once had)—crooked and overlapping, with slightly protruding uppers, likely stained from the tobacco he kept pouched in his cheek. He looked like a lopsided, slightly rabid squirrel.

Not understanding much of what he was talking about, I merely listened as he ranted, nodding occasionally when he seemed to demand some sort of response. Jetlagged and unable to see much of anything through the dirty windows, I found myself sliding into sleep. A jerk woke me as the car shuddered to a stop. We had arrived.

"You'll be getting out here." The driver gestured at the window.

I blinked a few times as I scanned the vast landscape. *Here* was the middle of nowhere—rolling hills, copses of trees, and little else, certainly no houses. Where were we?

"Is this Ellwood?" I asked timidly.

"This is as far as I go," he barked. "That'll be thirty pounds." He was cheating me. I knew the cost from my research, but I handed the money over all the same. He took it, muttering the whole while about idiotic Americans and our daft foreign policy and how rude we were, only he didn't just say rude, there were a few expletives beforehand, and afterward, too.

I wanted to protest that I hadn't meant to fall asleep, that I would be happy to hear more about how bloody useless the euro was, *please, oh, please*, but again I said nothing. Despite my good intentions, and despite years of practice pacifying Mother, once I began to speak, I wasn't always as placating as I meant to be. In this case, I decided it was best that I kept my opinions to myself. Besides, it was terribly isolated out here and though I knew some self-defense, I didn't rate my odds high on using the hammer strike against a cranky, old man. I determined to keep quiet and be on my way as soon as possible.

The trunk popped open like a toothless shout and I hurried toward it, anxious to be away from this foul and smelly man and his equally foul and smelly car. He didn't move from his seat, apparently inviting me to handle my own suitcases, if I wanted to keep them. I did. I'd brought several of my favorite books along, ones I'd had for years—*Castle D'or*, *Tamsin*, *The Secret Garden*, and a compendium of Jane Austen. I didn't want to lose them, especially not to a horrid lug like him.

Two large suitcases, a backpack, and my purse were left sitting on the dirt lane as the black taxi whipped around and tore off, leaving me in a cloud of acrid smoke. Dazed and coughing, I watched it speed away, a bullet of decreasing size, until it disappeared over a hill.

Glancing at my watch, I saw that it was close to five o'clock, hours from sunset. But the rain clouds lurking overhead made it seem later than it was, casting their shadows over the land like black smudges on canvas. The clouds were heavy and full, sure to burst at any time. A cold wind buffeted against me, throwing my curls into my face. I shivered. I had better get moving.

I turned about in a circle, the world spinning around me dizzily, then stopped and gazed wildly about. The countryside was delicious to look at—dark green moors strewn with rocky valleys and hills, large clumps of trees sprouting here and there like black mushrooms, a stream bubbling over a jagged rock bed. I had the presence of mind to appreciate that if I had to be lost, this would be a good place to be lost in, at least while there was still light. I felt sure there was magic to be found here.

The trouble was, I was standing, ironically enough, at a crossroads and didn't know which way to go. Before me, the small country lane split in two like a snake's tongue and I hadn't the slightest clue which direction to take. One road was unmistakably more well-traveled than the other, the grass down the middle nearly non-existent from being perpetually mowed by cars' underbellies. The other road, narrow and scruffy, led down a slight hill and disappeared into a copse of trees. For the next two or three minutes, I looked dully back and forth between the two and pushed hair out of my face. Jet lag was hitting hard now and I simply couldn't think.

"I'll take the road less traveled," I finally decided, laughing lightly. I imagined my mother gasping in shock at the very idea of it and smiled to myself as I set off.

It wasn't long before I realized that my suitcases were heavy and awkward and I didn't want to carry them anymore. I was close to the large stand of trees now, which, from this perspective, looked less like a copse and more like a forest. Figuring it would be easier to hide my luggage amongst the trees, I dragged the cases the last couple hundred yards, into the dark woods. I'd come back for them later.

Several yards in, I spotted a distinctive gray boulder, easily recognizable for when I returned, and shoved the two cases behind it. Feeling better, I continued on my way through the ever-darkening wood. The quiet, like a sentient being, quickly surrounded me, and I felt a bit like Little Red Riding Hood. And maybe Gretel, too.

Despite my efforts hauling the luggage, I soon grew chilled. The temperatures for this part of England averaged mid-sixties in June and were likely dropping with every passing minute. All my research was about to pay off, though. I had packed two sweaters in my carry-on backpack for just such a scenario.

After setting my pack on the ground, I pulled out a pale blue cardigan (maybe not so English, I realized, after seeing all the dark-garbed natives, but very pretty) and pulled it on, immediately feeling warmer.

Ahead of me, the path sloped downward into a valley. The trees in the wood stood on thick, dark brown trunks and wore large leaves like cloaks. Some grew tall and straight, others were short and twisted. A misty gray fog filled in the remaining spaces like spilled milk. I started to walk, often glancing over my shoulder as though watching eyes followed me. *Little Red's wolf.* I moved faster. There might be magic here, but now a darkness infused it, and I didn't want to be caught in this place when night fell.

Eventually the trees began to thin, allowing in enough light to brighten the woods. Hope returned. In the distance, tiny cottages of pale gray stone, with thatched roofs supporting gargoyle-like chimneys, popped into view. I caught sight of a turret rising up toward the sky and my spirits rose with it. To see the church was heartening. Even though my research on Ellwood had yielded very little information beyond a bland description and a few photos of the centuries-old church, I knew this was it.

The path left the woods and leveled out, transforming itself once more into a road. At this point, I realized that the village was farther away than I had first thought from higher up on the hill. I kept walking, hoping I didn't have much farther to go.

Not long afterward I spotted a drive off to my right, bordered by trees and marked by a sign so white it glowed. On it the word FILMORE was stamped in bold, black letters. I *was* in the right place! To see my last name, written in such lovely script, was encouraging, though I didn't expect much from the house itself. Father spoke little of it, so Mother determined from his lack of enthusiasm that the place must be one of those cramped country cottages burdened with low ceilings, yellowed by smoke stains, and ragged wallpaper, likely smelling of damp and age. She was only guessing, of course, as there weren't any photographs to go by.

My father wouldn't talk much about his childhood, either. I knew he had two sisters, Priscilla and Kelli, and that his parents were long since dead, killed in a car accident while driving home from church. Looking around, I wondered how on earth that had happened. The narrow lane that continued onward was not built for racing, and anyone who lived here would know that. To push a car to that kind of speed could only have been intentional. The reality of what this meant made me shiver.

At last it was hitting home that my father, so charming and larger than life on television, was a very secretive man.

After pulling in a fortifying breath, I faced the dirt drive to Filmore and began to march down it. Soon, another hill confronted me, the other side of the valley, perhaps, and I struggled upward. Before long I heard rushing water and upon rounding a curve in the road, spotted a brook. A stone bridge, arches like bowlegged cowboys standing side by side, was just wide enough for a single car to pass.

The sun was setting, creating a slow sinking shadow over the land, and a gentle rain began, striking against my cheek. I sighed. Quite stupidly I had left my umbrella and raincoat in my suitcase. The lane leveled out once again and I met with another curve in the road. As I rounded it, I saw Filmore for the first time.

Shocked, I stumbled to a halt. This was no decrepit country cottage. A towering manor, it sat regally as a haughty blueblood, with the green of the lawn spread about it like a velvet skirt. Numb and cold, I stood in the rain and stared at the magnificent stone structure in awe.

Like the ringing of an ancient bell, a loud barking began to reverberate from within the manor's walls. It was a terrible and desperate noise, and it made me nervous. When I was eight, a large dog had slipped his leash and chased after me. Once his apologetic owner had the dog's collar firmly in his grasp, he explained that Mosie was only trying to say hello. Even though I hadn't been hurt, and Mosie and I eventually became friends, I could never entirely forget the terror I'd felt when he'd been chasing me. I could handle being around dogs, but I always remained a little bit wary of them, especially the big ones.

And this one sounded big. I stayed where I was, hovering close to the edge of the woods in case I should need to run into them, all the while thinking I might possibly have found the hound of the Baskervilles himself.

A moment later, the grand front door opened wide to reveal a tall, thin figure, dressed in black, slim and appealing, with enviously long legs. One hand, pale and slight, incongruously gripped a shotgun; the other firmly grasped the collar of an Irish wolfhound that kept trying to break free.

At least, I hoped the hand was firmly grasping.

"Who are you, and what do you want?" The voice was clipped and sure, very upper crust, sharply British.

"I, uh, I'm, um..."

"Spit it out. I haven't got all day to be staring at you standing in the rain."

"My name is Evalina Filmore," I finally managed. Water dripped from my chin and traveled down the front of my white blouse like icy snakes. I shivered and could barely push out the words through chattering teeth. "My father sent me. He's your brother."

"I assumed that hearing your name. No need to say more than necessary."

"Right," I responded. "Of course."

"Where is the taxi? Didn't trust coming this far in, I imagine. Figures," she muttered. "Well, grab your luggage and come in."

I lifted my purse and backpack. "I've already got them."

"What about those behind you, then?"

I turned around. Sitting at the edge of the woods, innocent as could be, were my two abandoned suitcases.

Chapter Four

✳

The Aunts

A shiver shook my spine. "But I left them in the woods! Behind a rock."

"What woods? You were dropped off in the village, weren't you?"

Turning back around to face my aunt, I slowly shook my head. "I was on the moors." I pointed back behind me. "I took the road that led through the woods and followed it here."

We were standing about twenty feet from each other, yet I could see her slender body stiffen. "You followed the Wrath's Path?"

I shrugged. "If that's what the path through the woods is called, then yes." Not exactly a welcoming name, I thought to myself, but deliciously wicked, all the same. "The taxi driver dumped me off up on the moors, said he'd gone far enough."

"But your luggage…" She indicated the bags with her gun, seemingly ready to shoot them if they made a wrong move. "You *must* have carried them…" Her voice trailed away as the idea occurred to her that hauling them all that distance would've been quite an undertaking. "Get inside," she ordered suddenly. "Move…*now.*"

Startled by the urgency in her voice, I quickly ran and grabbed my bags. Hands full, I scurried toward her, awkward as a porcupine, as she scanned the area behind me, not bothering to help. The shaggy, black wolfhound, whose head rose parallel to my aunt's chest, sniffed at me as I passed by, though thankfully he had quit trying to attack me.

Once inside, I took three steps, but could go no further as I peered upward in awe. Built in the Gothic style, the grand hall's ceilings soared high as a cathedral's. Replete with ornate carvings and arched windows, along with the requisite dark corners and spooky nooks, there was such a feeling of history here, so strong and entrenched, that the past could easily serve as the mortar holding the stones together.

The Filmores must have thought themselves very grand to build a house like this. But then, they had once been nobility. Father briefly, and reluctantly, explained to Mother that some time in the seventeenth century, after picking the wrong side to support during one of the countless rebellions against the monarchy, the family had lost its title. What a pity. I would've liked to have been a spoiled member of the aristocracy.

My luggage had grown too heavy to hold onto and I set it down on the stone floor. A cold, wet nose replaced one of the warm leather handles and I nearly jumped out of my shoes.

"It looks as though Bones likes you." Rather than sounding pleased, my aunt's tone was rather miffed. "She's my dog. She's very loyal, you see. Very protective."

I didn't reply, only nodded stiffly, not wanting to make any sudden movements around such teeth. My aunt stood two or three inches taller than me, which meant that the top of Bones' head sat level with my chin. Bones was one big dog.

"I cannot say that I am pleased to see you," she went on.

Taking refuge in silence, I didn't respond. If I'd spoken I might have said, "I think the feeling is mutual."

She stood close to me now, and in the light from the dusty chandelier overhead, I could better make out what she looked like. It was strange. While she wasn't unattractive, she was not as beautiful as I had first thought. Her white-blond hair was short, bobbed in a chic cut that made her look capable and modern. The little makeup she wore was expertly applied, highlighting pale blue eyes and downplaying her broad nose. She wasn't very old, I was surprised to see, not sure why I'd expected her to be ancient. Like my father, who was thirty-eight and looked thirty, she had aged well.

Even though she wasn't the most attractive person, she came across as someone who was. Priscilla was the sort of woman men would find compelling. She was elegant, thin, and classy, and her movements, like her demeanor, were quick and polished, efficient to the extreme. I had a feeling that when Priscilla wanted something, she got it. In short, she was everything I wished I could be. Except, maybe a bit prettier so I could get my mother off my back.

"When is your father coming?"

Ugly prickles of anxiety made me squirm and the cold water dripping down my back only added to my discomfort. "Um, as far as I know, he's not."

A pale eyebrow lifted, disbelieving me. "Oh?"

"It's his work, you see. He couldn't get time off, so I came instead. He sends his warmest regards, of course." He hadn't. My words, strange and uneasily spoken, made me sound like a character in a play, speaking someone else's lines. Sometimes I could act. Sometimes I couldn't.

"Warmest regards?"

She was on to me. "He really couldn't come," I said again, since I had nothing else left in the arsenal to fend her off. My mother could talk her way out of a one-way ticket to hell. I couldn't talk my way out of a cardboard box.

"This won't do," she said, speaking half to herself. "He was to come. *Himself*! That was the bargain!"

"I'm sorry, Aunt Priscilla," I apologized, though I had no idea why I was taking on his offense.

She reached down to pluck a twig from Bones' fur. "Never mind." She straightened up, her features bland, unreadable. "You must meet your Aunt Kelli."

Urgh. Before meeting someone new I really wanted to get out of my wet clothes and have time to think about what had happened outside with my suitcases.

"Dinner is at eight. She rarely misses a meal. You'll meet her then."

Relieved, I glanced down at my watch. Half past *seven*? I frowned. How long had I been on that path? I thought I'd entered the woods around five o'clock, but it must have been later. Jetlag was making my brain fuzzy. I felt like the time my mother had given me a shot of whiskey for a sore throat, when I was only ten and still innocent.

"Come along. I'll show you to your room."

We climbed the grand spiral staircase and I kept my eyes on my aunt the whole way. From this angle she no longer looked so sophisticated, more like an undernourished child. A strange part of me wanted to tie her to a chair and shove donuts in her mouth. My suitcases thumped on the steps and several times the dog glanced back at me, though I wasn't sure if he was keeping an eye on me for security purposes, or was curious about how I might taste.

The door to my room was on the second floor, down a long hallway, on the right. Aunt Priscilla, who had easily outpaced me as I struggled with my suitcases, stood waiting for me outside the dark room. When I grew near, she flicked on a light switch and stepped inside. I followed after her.

"How long do you plan on staying, Evalina?" she asked, moving to the window to look out. Her arms folded crisply across her flat chest as she studied her reflection with an assessing eye.

"Mother thought you'd want me for the summer." I set the suitcases on the floor.

"That long?"

"Maybe I'll just stay a week," I decided, clasping my hands together nervously. "I don't want to put you out."

"Don't be in such a rush," she said slowly. "Now that you're here, maybe we can make this work to our advantage."

"Make what work?"

"Your father never told you anything?"

I shook my head. "My father never tells me anything."

She gave a wry laugh. "That sounds like Edmund all right, but I suppose that will make my job easier."

"What job is that?" I tried again, though my voice quivered a little. Aunt Priscilla was hard to talk to, and even harder to question.

"Just some family matters that need to be cleared up. He isn't here, so I guess you'll have to do his dirty work." She turned to look at me finally, a small smile lifting the corners of her mouth, yet failing to reach her eyes. I wondered what kind of family matters would make her look so sour. "Why don't you change, then join us downstairs in half an hour. Bones will show you the way to the dining room." The dog gazed mournfully after Priscilla as she left the room.

My cold-thickened fingers fumbled with the tiny buttons of my soggy cardigan as I pondered how I felt about my aunt. She hadn't been very welcoming, but then, she hadn't thrown me out, either. Or let her dog eat me.

Giving me a dispassionate look, Bones dropped down in front of a brick fireplace, the length of his body taking up the entire faded hearthrug. Being stared at can be unsettling under the best of circumstances, but when the culprit doing the staring has sharp incisors, it can be downright frightening. I promptly turned away.

As I peeled off my sweater, I looked around the room Priscilla had chosen for me. It was quite small, likely reserved for lesser guests. Pink peonies the size of oranges and faded as sun-bleached bones decorated the peeling wallpaper. The furniture was dark. There was an overstuffed, wing-backed chair of deep green, a looming mahogany armoire, and a matching sturdy desk tucked into the corner. If this room had been meant for Father, he wasn't exactly getting the warm welcome from his sisters. He was used to ritz now—he would hate this room. I, on the other hand, liked it immensely. The gothic atmosphere suited my mood perfectly.

Bones' great unnerving eyes never left me as I moved about unpacking my bags, stacking books on the walnut bedside table, spreading out my damp clothes over the back of a chair to dry. When I flung open the wardrobe's doors, lavender, dust, and age greeted me like old friends. Before tucking my clothes and shoes inside, I inhaled deeply, feeling strangely excited.

After changing into a navy blue turtleneck sweater and cream-colored corduroys, and toweling my curls dry with an NYU sweatshirt, I said in a fake, hearty voice, "Well, Bones, where to now?" He blinked at me a couple times, seemingly assessing my level of intelligence. A dismissive snort told me the result, and it wasn't in my favor. I had a pretty good feeling I'd just been insulted. "Don't look at me like that. According to Aunt Priscilla, you're supposed to like me."

Ignoring this, he slowly struggled to his monstrous feet and padded over to the door. Once outside the room, we trotted along the hallway and down the curving stairs, our pace increasing with each step. When I heard the ringing of silver striking stone, I realized what his hurry was. It was time for his supper, too.

Without slackening his pace, he led me into a massive, high-ceilinged room. A giant chandelier, glowing dimly, hung above a glossy oak table that could seat twenty people. The table was set for two, one on each end. Bones headed for a door on the other side of the room, past a dead, black fireplace big enough to park in.

As he neared the door, it swung partly open, revealing a thin rectangle of bright light. Still moving fast, he barreled through the opening, narrowly avoiding knocking over a tiny woman entering the room. Her hands, swollen and heavily veined, gripped a silver serving tray bearing a set of dinnerware. The little woman was peering down at the tray and mumbling to herself.

The words, barely audible before, suddenly became clear as the door swung shut behind her. "I dunna ken why I stay in this devil house. Do this, Bessie. Fetch that! I might be a servant, but I'm no slave. I should up and leave 'em to themselves. See what happens to the Missus High and Mighty, then!"

She was a scrawny thing, stooped and worn as a rug. Her claw-like hands clutched the tray with a ferocity that spoke of possessiveness, though as she neared my end of the table, I spotted another reason for her intense concentration. Her swollen knuckles and oddly slanted fingers bore the unmistakable signs of arthritis. She was afraid to drop the tray.

She stopped suddenly and looked up. "Are you like yer father, lass?"

"Not at all," I breathed, wondering how she'd known who I was, or even that I was here in this room. She hadn't once looked up; I was sure of it. "Or do you mean, do I look like him?"

The old woman, who had called herself Bessie, set the tray on the table too fast and a resounding clang echoed through the room. "Are you like him inside?" she asked, as she unloaded the tray. The forks and knives, more than necessary, slowly lined up on either side of the delicate blue and white plate. A carafe of blood red liquid grasped in a shaky hand filled a crystal glass, which towered over the knives and spoons.

"No," I answered, though I wasn't really sure. I knew so little about my father, I truly had no idea whether I was like him or not. "Did you know him?"

"I did. Too bad he dinna come back."

"Why?" I whispered.

The old servant slowly turned to look at me. Her bland, gray eyes, all red-rimmed and drooping skin, had come to life. "You should leave, little one. Get yerself out of this cursed place."

I gulped, feeling strangely light-headed and distant from her even though she stood only a few feet from me, smelling of muscle balm and tea. "What do you mean?"

"I mean—"

Footsteps sounded behind us. Someone was coming. The fire in the old woman's eyes blinked out and she turned to go, taking the tray with her.

"Dinner is almost ready, isn't it, Bessie?" Priscilla asked, entering the dining room through the same door Bones had brought me through. The old woman nodded, but didn't turn around. In a gray dress, shapeless as a sack, and stained bedroom slippers, she shuffled back toward the swinging door, to what I assumed was the kitchen.

"You've met our servant," Priscilla noted, passing by me like a wraith. "She's a bit touched in the head, as you've probably already figured out. But she's loyal."

I begged to differ, at least about the loyalty part, but kept my thoughts to myself. I had the feeling that if Bessie could get away with it, she'd burn this house down, preferably with the sisters in it, and roast marshmallows over its embers. I wondered why. Priscilla was brusque, but seemed kind enough. Maybe Kelli was the problem.

"Sit down," Priscilla invited, nodding at the place Bessie had just set. I was to be seated exactly in the middle of the table, my back to the gaping fireplace, facing a series of four windows stretching ten feet high. There was nothing to be seen outside in the evening dusk. Luckily the daytime would afford me a view, whatever it might be, that wouldn't involve having to look anyone in the eye. I could be grateful for that at least. Though I was going to have trouble with my chair. It weighed a ton and I struggled clumsily to scoot far enough forward to reach my plate.

"It seems Kelli has made her escape," Priscilla commented, as she easily took the grand chair at the head of the table, the one closest to the kitchen door. With a snap, she unrolled her white linen napkin and laid it across her lap. I followed her example. I knew basic etiquette—Mother had seen to that—but not to this extent.

"Escape from what, Aunt Priscilla?" I asked, anxiously smoothing the edges of the napkin while nervously counting the spoons and forks.

"Not from prison, if that's what you're thinking."

That wasn't what I'd been thinking *at all*, but it was an interesting way to put it. "Then from what?"

"She fancies herself the heroine of a bad romantic novel. Every once in a while she feels the need to run off, wanting to see if she's missed, I suppose. She always returns a few hours later. She's not very good with her own company." She checked a silver watch draped expensively around her pale, bony wrist. "I wonder how long she's been gone this time."

"Maybe we should go look for her," I suggested. "She could be hurt."

Priscilla laughed coolly. "Oh, she's fine. She doesn't need our help, or encouragement. I've learned that much over the years."

"You're right. I certainly don't need your help." The sultry voice came from near the swinging door to the kitchen, which strangely, wasn't swinging. At the back of my mind I wondered how she'd entered the dining room without us knowing, or had she steadied the door to eavesdrop? "I'm here, aren't I?"

Priscilla didn't bother turning around. "This is your niece, Kelli, come instead of our brother. What do you think of that?"

"If you mean to shock me, Prissy, it can't be done. I've already heard the news from Bessie." The redhead sashayed toward me in black ballet slippers. She had a curvy figure, which her flowing, pale green dress, nipped in at the waist and low-cut at the bodice, did little to hide. Long, dark red hair hung loosely down her back. From a distance, she was no more than twenty. As the span between us shortened, she aged to a woman over thirty, each step adding years to her face.

Still, she gave off an aura of youth. It may have been the mischievous smile on her ruby lips, the saucy swish of her fertility goddess hips. Or maybe it was her creamy skin, unlined and flushed.

She might sound quite lovely, described this way, but my aunt was actually rather plain upon closer inspection. Her mouth was a touch too wide, bracketed by dissatisfied half moons; her nose was round and snub and perpetually lifted in contempt. Her green eyes, full of discontent, were set a little too far apart. Like her sister, she gave off the illusion of beauty, a deception that could not be sustained.

Had my father been adopted, I wondered, or just the lucky one—the one who'd won the aesthetic gene pool race?

She passed by me with a breeze, pretending lack of interest. She smelled of musk and cigarette smoke, recklessness and wine. "She looks nothing like her father," she announced, as she took her seat. Despite her indifferent attitude, she had been studying me as I had her.

"Of course not," Priscilla agreed. "Even if she did, it doesn't matter. We needed *him*." I wondered if there was business with the house that could only be resolved by my father, something to do with his inheritance, perhaps.

Kelli shrugged. "Maybe she'll be enough for our purposes."

Priscilla narrowed her arctic blue eyes. "I've been considering that. It's worth a try, anyway."

The kitchen door banged open and a wobbly silver cart made an appearance, followed by a limping Bessie. She looked glum as she served us soup. Green soup. I stared down at my bowl, uncertain what to do next. Kelli suffered no such apprehension. She dove in immediately, her spoon clinking against the side of the delicate soup bowl as she ate. I toyed with mine for a moment, searching for eyeballs, I suppose, before taking the plunge. To the shock of my palate, which had been expecting something entirely different, the soup turned out to be cold. Despite my hunger, I set down my spoon. I'm quite sure the soup wasn't meant to be cold, like vichyssoise or cucumber soup, but time had done its damage.

"So how is Eddie?" Kelli asked, taking a slurp of the swampy soup, then plunging her spoon back in for more. She looked almost feral as she ate. "Pompous as ever?"

"My father isn't pompous," I defended him. "Not toward me, anyway." He was only disconnected toward me, never pompous.

"She came through the Wrath's Path," Priscilla announced, watching Kelli closely. She had been waiting to share this news for some time, I realized.

"What?" Kelli cried, her green eyes flashing at her sister. Her hand faltered and the spoon fell into the soup with a plop. She turned on me. "How?"

I looked back and forth between them. Priscilla looked sleekly satisfied at getting a reaction out of her sister. Kelli looked surprised, and angry.

"Um, I cut through the woods," I told her. "The path led me here."

"No one goes that way," she insisted. A small dribble of soup clung to the corner of her mouth. "Not even me, and I'll do just about anything." I didn't doubt that.

"Is it supposed to be haunted?" I asked, not really meaning it seriously. "Are there wolves?" I added, a little more soberly.

Kelli shook her head. "Neither." She took a gulp of wine, then wiped away a tiny red river spilling from the corner of her mouth and down her chin. "I can't think why the driver would have left you there. There's nothing about, not even—"

"Just don't go that way again," Priscilla interrupted. "Go to the village, walk the grounds of the house, but stay out of those woods. For your own safety…"

"Okay," I readily agreed. I felt no particular inclination to enter them again anyway. Not after I'd lost a couple hours. Not after my luggage had grown legs and followed me. I was surprised Priscilla hadn't mentioned that little detail to Kelli. Most likely she'd tell her later, when I wasn't around.

After the soup disaster, the food improved a little. I managed to appease my complaining stomach with a bit of glutinous mashed potatoes and lots of bread and butter. The bread was the best part of the meal, and I had a sneaking suspicion Bessie had bought it at a store. I made a mental note to find out which one.

Both sisters finished eating well before I did—Priscilla only picked at her meal, Kelli devoured everything, even the fat from the roast beef. Bessie had refilled the wine carafe once and it now stood empty; Kelli appeared to take her beverage consumption very seriously.

"How was your flight?" Priscilla asked politely after a few minutes of silence.

"Fine. Long," I added, not wanting to sound rude.

"And the drive? Your taxi driver—what did he look like?" she wondered.

"Old, I guess, and he had crooked teeth and smoked a cigar."

"How unpleasant for you," she said, but she was smiling.

Bessie brought in dessert and after she left, Priscilla cleared her throat—she even did that elegantly—looking not at me as she spoke, but at her sister. "Stay as long as you like, Evalina," she invited. "I think you'll work out very well. Don't you agree, Kelli?"

Kelli lifted up her wine glass. "Here, here." She smiled mischievously at me. "Stay as long as you like, Niece. It'll be great fun!"

Chapter Five

✳

Dead, Dead, Dead

The aunts left the table together with orders from Priscilla to get myself off to bed as soon as I was done eating. No doubt I looked bushed. I certainly felt it.

Like the potatoes, dessert was simply too sticky to be palatable. How had Bessie managed to mess up apple pie? I was glad she wasn't too offended by my lack of appetite as she cleared away my plate. "Get along to bed, child," she shooed. "You're too tired to even eat."

I looked at her through bleary eyes. "Do you still think I should leave, um...?" I paused. "What do I call you?"

"Bessie'll do," she replied. "And I think lots of stuff. Though no one ever heeds me opinion, I daresay."

"I will. Leave, that is. If you truly think I should go."

Her rheumy eyes narrowed in thought. "I dunna think there's any goin' back now. Best to let it all play out. But keep yer eyes peeled and yer ears to the ground."

Both suggestions sounded rather uncomfortable. I sighed and pushed away from the table, my mind spinning from fatigue. Had what she said made any sense? I wasn't sure. "Good night, Bessie," I called over my shoulder, as I staggered from the room. Behind me there was a grunt, which I took as a goodnight in return.

Somehow I managed to climb the curving staircase to my room without falling down the stairs. In the attached bathroom, whose narrow door I discovered lodged in the corner of the room, I splashed my face with ice-cold water, which, despite my attempts, never warmed up. Back in my bedroom, I changed into one of my new nightgowns, and once snuggled beneath a thick quilt, plummeted into a deep sleep.

~

I awoke the next morning, refreshed yet disoriented. I glanced around the bright room, blinking. My eyes settled on my luggage and my memory returned in a burst. I was in England, staying with my aunts, living an adventure, and I wasn't quite sure what I thought of it. But despite all that had gone wrong, from NAT to the taxi man, I was strangely happy to be here.

The bedside clock told me I'd slept through a great portion of the morning. I didn't like wasting time sleeping, but since I felt much better, I figured my long winter's nap was worth it. After rolling out of bed and taking a luxurious bath in the claw foot tub (the water had finally warmed up), I dressed in jeans and my brown leather walking boots, and pulled on a pink fleece pullover that, according to my mother, brought out the color in my cheeks. After checking my reflection in the bathroom mirror, I headed downstairs in search of a phone.

Up until now the thought of calling my parents and telling them I'd arrived safely had not occurred to me. I wasn't being callous. Once I became a teenager my mother informed me that there was no need to check in with her like I always did—said the police would inform her if I went astray. She might have been joking, but I took her at her word without any recourse on her part. I didn't particularly like her hands-off approach to parenting, but I was used to it. And I was really only calling now because I hoped she might know what my aunts wanted me to do.

I met Bessie coming out of the dining room carrying a tin bucket and a dirty mop. She wore the same outfit as yesterday—drab dress, handkerchief wrapped around her head, slippers. I was to discover that this was pretty much her standard uniform, though the dress and handkerchief color varied every three or four days. "You'll be wantin' to eat, I suppose." She didn't look happy about it.

"When do you usually eat lunch?"

"Dinner? Not 'til one o'clock." That was an hour and a half away. "Tea at four, dinner at eight. You missed yer breakfast."

"I can wait for lunch," I told her. "I don't want to put you to extra trouble."

Her annoyance waned and her expression settled down from a scowl to a frown. Judging by the pattern of wrinkles webbing her face, I had a feeling that, at the very least, she was always frowning. "If you're hungry, you can make yerself a piece. Look about a bit. You're bound to find somethin' that suits you."

"A piece of what?"

The scowl returned. "You call it a sandwich, I suppose." She snorted through pinched nostrils. "Talkin' with you is going to be quite a chore, I can see."

"Sorry."

She waved the mop at me. "Och. Pay me no mind. Me rheumatism is actin' up again."

"Oh. Well, I can make lunch for everyone."

She shook her head. "No use for that. Their highnesses be out for the day. Both went their separate ways."

"Then I can help you with the cleaning."

"Ta, but I work faster on me own. You get yerself somethin' to eat and look about. Best to know yer surroundings." Her tired eyes were both suspicious and curious as she regarded me. "Run along, now."

I did as she directed, making my way through the dining room and into the kitchen. The room, though spacious, was like a cave, dark and full of nooks and crannies. Dried herbs hung from hooks drilled into the beams of the ceiling and big, black kettles squatted atop the ancient stovetop like fossilized gnomes. A long stone sink sat beneath the only window in the room. A grungy wooden table, the top a foot thick and legs the size of my calves, filled in the middle of the room. I smelled potatoes and earth and vegetable soup and my stomach growled.

The refrigerator was old, but large and stuffed with food. The sisters didn't go without, I noticed. Inside its dark bulk, I discovered a ham hock, but no mayo. I ended up slathering two thick slices of bread with creamy, white butter found in a crock and slipping pieces of ham in between. A hunk of cheddar, a mottled apple, and a bottle of fizzy mango juice, and I was set to go.

After cleaning off a dusty picnic basket found stuck in a cobwebby corner, I packed it with my lunch and a couple napkins. The phone call to Mother would have to wait. This house was too dark and brooding to stay inside any longer. I didn't like hearing the grandfather clock in the front hall ticking all through the house, marking time, like a bomb waiting to go off.

I also didn't like that, despite my promise to myself, I couldn't stop thinking about NAT—his dark eyes, the hint of stubble darkening his firm jaw, his long, ink-stained fingers. There was an aura of mystery about him that intrigued me, though I wished I could forget about him. Having fallen for the wrong guy too many times in my life, I knew better than to get involved with his type. I must learn from my past experiences. I must dash him from my mind, quickly and ruthlessly.

Standing in the dimly lit kitchen, picnic basket gripped firmly in hand, I tried very hard to do just that. But he wouldn't stay gone. In fact, in the cool darkness, memories of him rooted even more deeply in my mind—I could even recall the sound of his voice, low and intelligent, almost caressing.

Damn.

My only choice was to get outside and try to outrun my thoughts. I quickly headed for the main door and let myself out. Once outside, I crossed the lawn, marching toward the woods that grew on the far side of the house. Despite the rain yesterday, the afternoon was hazy and golden and the light breeze was fresh and warm on my skin. As I neared the line of trees, I heard the sound of rushing water. Somehow I had missed it when I'd arrived in the rain, tired and out of sorts. Curious, I tracked the babbling to its source, a rocky stream that ran along the edge of the woods.

Downstream, I calculated, must lead to the bridge. I'd already been that way, so I decided to follow the water upstream. I trudged along for some time, intent only on moving forward. The house soon disappeared from view, replaced by trees on both sides of the stream. I wondered if this part of the woods was what Priscilla had warned me against, or was I safe here?

Either way, I couldn't seem to make myself turn back...the landscape was too beautiful. More than likely Priscilla was just being an anxious aunt, determined to protect her charge. I felt sure she was overreacting, but out of respect for her, I would be careful.

On my right the woods began to lighten and the way grew littered with stones as the path headed upward toward open sky. Another forty yards along, I left the trees and climbed the rocky knoll. Before long, a swift rise of earth transformed the stream into a powerful waterfall. I climbed to its crest and sat on a flat stone, gazing around at a view, which would inspire even the worst grump—perhaps even Bessie—to smile.

From my vantage point I could see the village down below, the buildings like bird eggs and the hills and trees encircling them, the nest. Thatched roofs and colorful gardens, the white church spire and black and white sheep crowding the road, could all be seen and admired. Now this was glorious England!

From where I sat, the woods did not look dangerous, as Aunt Priscilla implied they were. Still, I did feel uneasy about them. I was pretty sure I'd only spent, at most, half an hour tromping through them yesterday, but my watch said differently, that it had been two and a half hours. And since my watch matched the time on the grandfather clock and the one on my bedside table, I knew it was accurate. Had I fallen asleep in the woods? Had I been hit so hard with jetlag that I'd entirely lost my senses? That didn't seem likely. And what about the strange arrival of my suitcases? How had they turned up at the house without anyone seeing who'd delivered them?

None of it made sense.

In an effort to diffuse the strange feeling in my chest, I inhaled deeply of the fresh English air. Here in this magical place lingered the timeless scent of sun-warmed earth and sweet honeysuckle. The heather was not due to bloom for another month or so, but I imagined what it would be like when it did—a profusion of pink, purple, and white flowers blanketing the moors, smelling like heaven.

Feeling better, I opened the picnic basket and attacked my lunch with gusto. After swallowing the last bit of ham sandwich, I finished off the fizzy mango. Lowering the bottle, I spotted a figure on a dark horse burst from the line of trees on the other side of the stream, about a half-mile from where I sat. The sun was bright and I shaded my eyes to watch. Moving as one, rider and horse flowed across the landscape like the shadow of a cloud. I could almost hear the hoof beats over the roar of the water; feel them in my chest.

I wondered who the rider was. A neighbor? The devil himself? He certainly looked like a fiend, riding so carelessly, so swiftly. I felt a shiver tap down my spine as I watched him gallop like the wind. I liked speed, especially when I was feeling chaotic and out of sorts. It made it more difficult for my troubles to catch me. Perhaps he felt the same way.

With a crick threatening in my neck, I turned away to relieve it. When I turned back, the horse had stopped and the rider was looking in my direction. I had thought he couldn't see me, galloping like he was, but now he seemed to be staring straight at me. Self-consciously, I lifted my hand in a half-wave, hoping I wasn't trespassing. He did not return the greeting, though I was sure he'd seen it. He merely spurred his horse on, moving away from where I sat.

Biting my lip, I began to shove the remains of my lunch back into the picnic basket as fast as I could. Finished packing, I hurried away from the waterfall, not bothering to see if the rider was still out there. I wanted to look, but I had to maintain a bit of dignity as I crept away.

Feeling a little reckless, instead of following the stream back, I headed across the moor, down toward the forest. I wouldn't enter it, though, I decided, but would follow along its edge.

The going was rough, bits of rock sticking up like thorns, and I had to focus on where I placed my feet. I didn't notice the wind picking up, nor catch the sky darkening as a mist blew over the land. When I did glance up at last, I found myself surrounded by a malevolent white mass. Before I could think what to do, the fog swallowed me whole.

I froze. *All you have to do is go back to the stream and follow it home*, I told myself over the pounding of my heart. The path would be treacherous, and I would be traveling it nearly blind, but it was the only way back to the manor that I knew.

Despite the danger, I turned to head back toward the stream, but immediately realized my precarious situation. I couldn't see the water, nor could I hear it. Swallowing hard, I slowly turned back around. Then, as though possessed, I ran, and the picnic basket banged painfully against my leg. Despite my intentions to avoid the forest, I soon found myself within its confines.

Once I realized what I'd done, I stopped and looked around, breathing hard. Nothing was familiar, and even if it were, I couldn't see anything in the thick fog. Fighting an urge to panic and run again, I kept moving forward, but at a slower pace now as branches slapped at my face and thick moss shifted beneath my feet.

Just when I was beginning to lose hope of finding my way home, the fog lifted and the way cleared before me. I could see again. I found I was standing in a yard, but it wasn't Filmore's. It wasn't a yard exactly, either, more like a garden, vast and tempestuous and filled with large-leafed plants, massive shrubs, and ivy—everywhere ivy. It was so alive, yet almost too much so, seemingly choking on its own lawless growth.

A stone manor suddenly appeared before me, rising up like a cliff. Despite its magnificence, it appeared to serve merely as a backdrop to the lush garden, almost invisible unless you looked a certain way.

The mist still lurked amongst the trees, thick as smoke, and I realized I would have to stay in this strange place until it cleared. Mouth dry, I headed toward the stone building. Ivy covered the high walls, effectively bearding the house's blank face. Perhaps someone lived here who knew their way around and could guide me home, or at the least give me a warm place to wait. The day had grown damp, my fingertips felt cold as snow.

"Hello?" I called softly, not entirely sure I wanted to be heard. There was something disturbing about this place. "Is anyone here?"

When no one answered, I followed a winding trail through the grasping garden, up to the house. The path was covered with white gravel, which crunched beneath my feet with every step, like tiny bones. I tried to walk softly; the thought of crushing some creature's skull beneath my boots was horrifying.

At last I reached the stairs and climbed them, each step echoing like a death knoll. Standing before an enormous, black door, my cold fingers curled into fists. It was hard to stay calm. I'll admit I'm morbid and fanciful by nature, but I was not imagining the sensation of watching eyes. It was the same vibe I'd felt while walking the Wrath's Path to reach Filmore. I was sure of it.

To my surprise, the door was open, revealing a dark crack into an unknown realm. Feeling as though I was about to take a step into another world, I pushed on the door and it opened silently. I took a hesitant step inside, then another. The house was still and my steps on the hardwood floor made a knocking sound, as though someone were trapped beneath it, looking for escape.

My pulse pushed against my skin and I wanted desperately to bolt. Images of mausoleums and prisons, oubliettes and gallows, flooded my mind. I should not be here. Yet I felt compelled to stay.

"Hello?" I called again, and my timid voice floated upward like dust motes in a sunbeam. My eyes followed the sound toward the high ceiling, as though they could see the letters imprinted in the air. Glass windows encircled the highest floor, and a dome, its curved walls covered by a darkly painted scene, acted as a cruel crown.

Despite my fear, I felt myself drawn to the picture, my neck stiffening as I stared raptly upward. In the center of the mural was a larger than life figure, muscular and full of power, dressed in a white garb similar to a Roman toga. A glowing orb surrounded him. The god-like man's face was severe; his cheeks were suffused with the blood of righteous indignation. His accusing finger pointed to another, less imposing figure, encompassed by his own muted halo of light.

Down on his knees, the smaller figure's bruised hands laced together in a prayerful pose, as though begging for mercy. From out of the darkness, a disembodied hand reached out to grab the back of the man's torn shirt, its action arrested just before seizing hold. The effect was so powerful that I wanted to warn him, but the cry lodged in my throat.

A footstep sounded behind me and I turned around, startled out of my reverie. A stranger, tall and formidable, filled the doorway, then stalked toward me. That's all I took in before I spun away, looking for a means to escape.

"You're not leaving?" he asked. His voice sounded unusual to me, lilting, yet full of authority.

I went still. My back was to him and I'd never felt more exposed in my life, as though I were standing naked onstage. I didn't hear any more footsteps, but still my skin prickled and my breath came in short pants. "I-I'm sorry," I pushed out. "I didn't mean to trespass. I got lost and…and I was cold."

"Turn around so I can see you." After a moment's hesitation, I did what he asked, as though I had no choice in the matter. "That's better." He took a step toward me. I took a matching step back, into the shadows, until he stood alone in the pale light from the glass windows overhead. The light caught glints of golden hair. It was wavy, with little wings flaring outward. He glanced up at the painting and I saw that his eyes were blue and green and gray, all at once, like an ocean in a storm. Long, dark lashes, silky and seductive, fringed them. His jaw was firm, his cheekbones high. He was classically beautiful.

Too bad for him, I didn't trust the beautiful. Much as I wanted to be one of them myself.

"He should've waved back," he remarked casually, bringing those stormy eyes to rest on mine. I blinked, trying to break the bewildering spell I seemed to be under. "I saw him. I was watching, you see."

"It doesn't matter," I answered softly. "Maybe I was trespassing." The words came automatically, but what I should've been demanding to know was, why had he been watching me?

"I would've been angry. Why aren't you angry?" He seemed genuinely puzzled.

"Is this your place?" I asked. I did not want to talk about my anger. Talking about it would make it real, turn it into a live thing.

"It is. In a manner of speaking."

"Do you live here alone?" I was continuing to make polite conversation because I didn't know what else to do. I was trespassing and he was blocking my way. He had me trapped. And he seemed to know that.

"Mostly."

"It's so quiet and empty. It seems as though no one lives here."

There was a glint in his ocean eyes—a warning. "That would be true, too."

He was playing games with me, it seemed, but I didn't feel up to playing. I only wanted to go home. "Can you show me the way back? I'm staying at Filmore Manor."

"I know where you're staying."

"Oh. I suppose in a village this size everyone knows everything about everybody. I've always lived in a city. I'm used to blending in." I was growing increasingly nervous, my tongue letting loose a series of inanities. My fingers laced together and gripped tight. He wouldn't stop looking at me—a lean, hungry look. No one had ever looked at me like that. I wanted to flee from him, yet a strange part of me wanted to stay and… What? Be eaten?

"I'll get you home. That is what you want, isn't it, Evalina?" He took a step forward, his hand held out to take mine.

"You know my name." I tucked my hands into my pockets, not wanting, yet wanting, almost desperately, to touch him.

"Of course, I do. But you do not know mine." He took another step toward me, hand still demanding.

"Have we met before?"

The eyes gleamed wickedly. "Oh, yes."

I shuddered. I didn't like that gleam. "Here?"

"Yes. Close by. I carried your bags for you."

"Yes, you did." How did I know this now, when I hadn't before? Dark shadows depressed my memory like weights. Still, I was certain of my knowledge.

"You won't let yourself remember," he accused. He was very close to me now. I could smell his scent...pine, fall leaves, rainstorm, and something hard to define, perhaps what power smelled like.

"I'm trying to. Did I hit my head?"

"Not that I saw. We talked about quite a bit, you and I."

I winced. What had I said? Had I shared too much? It wouldn't be the first time. When I was fourteen, I'd slipped into my parents' liquor cabinet and drank half a bottle of sherry. My parents were discussing sending me to yet another boarding school and I'd grown tired of feeling about as wanted as a case of head lice. When the bottle was empty, I staggered over to the Crenshaw and spilled my guts to Tom, one of the stagehands. He'd been quite nice about it, but I could never look him in the eye after that. I couldn't remember what all I'd said, but I had the feeling that whatever it was wasn't good. Maybe something like I had a huge crush on him and would happily have his babies.

The sensation I felt now was painfully similar. Something had happened, I couldn't remember it, but judging by the look on the stranger's face, it was maybe just a little bit wicked.

"Hmm." I was afraid of giving away more than I already had.

"Would you like to know what about?"

"I don't think I do."

"You talked about *him*," he said, ignoring my answer. "The man who was rude to you on the train. You talked about your father, too. You had a lot to say about the two of them. Now you are as quiet as the clouds. Have I offended you?"

"I don't remember talking to you," I said, wishing very much that I could. "It's a blank...mostly."

I hate him; I hate them all.

My eyes widened. Had I said *that* to this man? It sounded horrible; it sounded like my mother.

I will make them suffer until they are dead, dead, dead.

My stomach tightened. That wasn't my mother.

"I am not like them, Evalina," he whispered, brushing a strand of hair from my cheek.

"Who are you?" I groaned, my skin tingling. I shuddered involuntarily.

His hand pulled back and he straightened just as the sky opened up and the sun shone down onto his golden head. "I cannot tell you my name. Not yet." He was suddenly distant, growing more so in the light. "It is time for you to go. My beast will guide you."

A furry snout pushed against the door. Bones. "But that's my Aunt Priscilla's dog."

He laughed. "Of course he is. You must leave now. We will meet again."

Bones glanced over at the nameless man, then trotted up to me. I placed a shaking hand on his warm fur, tightened my grip on the basket with the other, and let him lead me away from this place. The door slammed behind me, but I didn't turn around.

I was too afraid of what I might see looking back at me.

Chapter Six

✳

Tea for Three

Bones kept me moving as he hurried through the misty woods. Upon entering the house, he disappeared and I can't say I was sad to see him go. After emptying the picnic basket and storing it away, I heard vacuuming noises and followed them. I found Bessie in one of the rooms, struggling with a dented vacuum cleaner that creaked and groaned as she rolled it back and forth. Despite her protests, I took over the job. I couldn't stand watching her suffer, swollen fingers not doing what she wanted them to do. Anyway, I wasn't being entirely altruistic. Doing the work for Bessie would keep my mind off what had happened in the woods. I really needed to stop thinking about the stranger, because every time I did, my mind swirled around and around and I would break into a cold sweat. The episode had been so outside my realm of experience that I needed to block it all out for a while.

When I was done vacuuming the first floor, I joined Bessie in the library to help her dust the hundreds of books, ranging from a volume of Keats' poetry, which looked brand new despite a thin layer of dust, to a much-read copy of *Torture Devices of the Middle Ages*. I swept a rag along the rich, dark wood and catalogued which books I wanted to borrow—*Haunted Britain and Ireland*, *Jane Austen's Letters*, Machiavelli's *The Prince*—while Bessie muttered and complained the whole time we worked. When I started singing "the sun will come out tomorrow," she cursed in Gaelic and her old eyes fluttered irritably.

Still, I was pretty sure I might have seen a spark of amusement in those eyes.

At three o'clock, I followed her into the kitchen to help prepare tea. "You need glasses," I told her, right before she was about to dump a heaping tablespoon of salt into the scone mix. She scowled, but thankfully held back.

"I can see just fine, missy," she grumped, her twisted hand quickly producing the right sized spoon—a ¼ teaspoon—and measuring out the correct amount. Setting the steel spoon on the counter, she reached for a dusty bottle sitting on a lopsided shelf above the stove.

"So are you trying to kill us then?"

"What are you goin' on about?"

"That's not vanilla. I think it might be poison." I leaned forward. "Yup. That's poison, all right—see the skull and crossbones, and the dead rodent?"

A callused finger rubbed at both eyes, then she held the bottle up to her nose. "Well, I'll be…" I swore she chuckled. I promptly decided it was time to take over.

"Here, let me." I'd learned to cook and bake when I was seven years old; my mother was useless in the kitchen. Taking charge, I ordered Bessie to sit down and rest her feet. I couldn't stand seeing that slumped-over body, seemingly on the verge of collapse, or those shaking hands, any longer. She ought to be sitting in front of a fire sipping hot tea and petting an impressively fat cat, not trying to maintain this massive house on her own.

"I'll lose me place."

"And that would be devastating…?"

She snorted. "Easy for you to joke. But I've got nothin' else and nowhere to go."

I shook my head. "You shouldn't be doing all this work by yourself. Isn't there any money for more help?"

"Oh, there be plenty of that," she replied.

"Are you sure?" I asked, mixing the batter. "We had very little growing up. My father didn't have a dime to his name until he made it big."

"Your aunts dunna work, in or outside the home, yet they buy whatever they please, whenever they please."

The oven, a gorgeous, cast-iron affair, was now bellowing heat like a dragon. I began shaping round bits of dough and placing them on a blackened cookie sheet. So there was family money, but my father hadn't seen any of it as far as I knew. What had happened? Some sort of family scandal? Marrying an American might have done it. Perhaps his parents, the ones who'd died in the car crash, had cut him out of their will. Typically, in families like this, the male inherits the estate. Trouble was, I wasn't sure if they'd died before or after he'd met Mother. And anyway, if he *were* cut out of the will, you'd think his sisters would want him to stay away. They wouldn't want him getting any ideas about contesting it.

The whole affair was odd…not as odd as my meeting with the stranger at the house in the woods, but mysterious all the same. I found myself growing curious. Maybe I should track down the family solicitor, ask some questions.

I slid the sheet of scones into the oven and turned to Bessie. "Why do the aunts want my father to come home?"

Bessie's slumped shoulders lifted and dropped. She had settled on a stool, looking rather happy about life at the moment. "It be a mystery to me. One day he were here, eighteen and full of the world, and the next he were gone without so much as a by your leave."

"And he never returned…"

"Somethin' odd happened." She nodded sagely at me. "You can be sure of that."

The kettle shrieked and I prepared the tea. Losing myself in the process, I worked in silence, readying the silver tray for three and getting out a plate and mug for Bessie. At four o'clock, as per Bessie's instructions, I carried the tray of tea into the front parlor. On its dull surface (I resolved to polish it later), sat a plate of freshly baked scones, a pot of cream that I had made myself, and a gleaming jar of raspberry jam. Before I left, I ordered Bessie, under pain of death, to sit and enjoy her tea. She mumbled about getting sacked, but I told her I'd take care of everything. Her derisive snort told me what she thought of my power to do much of anything, still she didn't move from her cozy spot.

While I waited for my aunts to arrive, I studied the small room, which overlooked a green expanse of lawn. Luscious landscape paintings covered the walls, beautiful woodwork gleamed throughout, and a tapestry of the family crest hung above the requisite fireplace, whose elaborately carved mantle was topped by delicate knick-knacks. The room was befitting a formal parlor, though not my taste at all.

I hate him; I hate them all.

Damnit, where had that come from? I was not vindictive by nature. Yes, I often found myself wanting to strangle my mother, but she gave me good reason to, and besides, I always refrained. But the frustrated anger and rage these words evoked were entirely new. I'm not sure I'd ever experienced true *rage*, or if I had, I didn't remember it; I *was* awfully good at repression. As far as I knew, my first time had been after meeting NAT on the train when I'd wanted to smash things, the second during my meeting with the stranger in the woods.

Remembering his vivid eyes, I sighed regretfully. I'd been hoping to suppress that experience. But what, I wondered, was I actually trying to block out, and why? I'd spoken to an attractive man; there was nothing wrong with that—I should be feeling pretty cocky actually. The problem was that I'd said things to him that I didn't remember saying. He knew about NAT and my father, so I'd obviously spoken about the two of them. But what had I actually said? It was the not knowing that I didn't like. If I could recall what I'd shared, I could at least go into damage control. Just thinking about it made me feel hot inside, as though I'd swallowed a fire snake. I knew now that I could no longer trust myself to keep my own secrets.

"Look at you, already here." Priscilla strode gracefully into the room. "Hungry?"

"Very. I took a walk and built up an appetite."

"We might as well start. Who knows when Kelli will show. She's often late."

I nodded and poured the tea. At my last boarding school, and the one where I'd stayed the longest—a whopping two years—I had a wonderful home-ec teacher, Mrs. Bonner, who loved everything to do with England. She was a big reason why making scones was easy for me. She'd also taught the class how to serve tea. She was a bit silly at times and a hopeless romantic, but I liked Mrs. Bonner very much, plus she always seemed to make an extra effort with me. She'd encouraged my love for England, something my father had never done, and I wished she could be here with me. She would've died and gone to English heaven, sitting in this lovely room, partaking in a spot of tea.

"Your father taught you how to do that, I suppose." Priscilla sounded reluctantly impressed.

"My father rarely speaks to me," I informed her, picking up my delicate teacup. Today we were having Earl Grey. I savored my first sip of the bitter brew, letting it flow down my parched throat—it felt strangely raw and sore, as though I'd been talking all day.

Or screaming.

Priscilla reached for a scone, eyeing it warily. "These don't look half bad." She spread a thin layer of cream on the biscuit, followed by a dollop of jam—it looked like a pink eye—and took a tentative bite. "These are actually rather good." She looked at me. "Did *you* make them?"

I froze. "Well, yes I did, Aunt Priscilla. Bessie has so much to do around here—this place really is massive, isn't it?—so I thought I'd help her out."

She studied me for a moment. "Don't waste your pity on Bessie. She has a roof over her head, plenty to eat, even if it *is* absolutely horrid, and a wage, to boot. Believe me, she does quite well for herself." She shook her head, seeing my skeptical look. "Oh, Evalina. Don't tell me Bessie has already taken you in. I thought Americans were more cynical than that." She gave me a tight smile that put my hackles up. In the past, I'd always avoided confrontation whenever feasibly possible. But this time, I couldn't stop the words from spilling out.

"If you mean that she's shown me a warm welcome," which wasn't quite true, "then, yes, I guess she has taken me in."

"Well," she replied carefully after taking a sip of tea, "I suggest you let her do her job. You are a guest here, *and* a Filmore. Besides, Bessie should know better than to let you do her work for her."

I bit my lip, feeling thoroughly put in my place.

"I'm *so* sorry I'm late," Kelli announced, as she breezed through the doorway, her violet skirt swishing like a lion's tail and her silver sandals clacking like castanets. She certainly didn't look sorry, more like the cat that caught the canary and swallowed it whole. She actually *liked* being late, I realized, because then she could make a dramatic entrance. She was like my mother that way. "I saw our neighbor this afternoon," she mentioned casually, plopping down into an overstuffed, pink velvet chair almost as voluptuous as its current occupant. "He stopped to talk to me. That's why I'm late. I was chatting with him."

Priscilla stiffened and her typically bland expression sharpened into a glimmer of interest. "What did you talk about? Did he ask about me?"

Kelli gave a little smile, the corners of her wide mouth stretching toward her earlobes, which today sported large, golden hoops. "Why, I believe the subject of Priscilla Filmore never came up."

Priscilla pulled back, realizing her mistake, and I felt the slightest bit sorry for her. Her inquisitiveness was a bit too eager. Since it didn't matter if *I* appeared eager, I leaned forward, curious to hear more.

"I can't believe he said much of anything about you, either," she snapped. Then, noting my intrigued gaze, quickly straightened out her anger-pinched features.

"He asked if we were expecting visitors." My stomach dropped—that would mean me. Was she talking about the stranger? Was he searching for me? I felt both excited and ill at the thought. "I told him we had one right now. Our dear, sweet niece." She gave me a searching, slightly sour look that effectively canceled out the 'dear' and 'sweet.' I had the distinct feeling that my Aunt Kelli didn't like me, but I wasn't sure why.

"What else did he say?"

"Oh, this, that, and another thing," Kelli replied vaguely, twirling a strand of red hair around a healthily plump finger, a secretive smile on her face.

I sensed right away that the neighbor had said little else of importance about *her* personally, otherwise Kelli would have repeated the conversation word for word, enjoying each and every second. She seemed to like antagonizing her sister.

"And how did you occupy yourself today, little niece of ours?" Kelli turned to me, her eyes brimming with amusement—what *did* she and the neighbor talk about to arouse such bliss? She took a bite of scone, with half of it disappearing into her mouth and the other half spilling crumbs down the front of her lilac blouse. While I wasn't sure I liked her, I did admire her bold outfits. I wished I could dress so vividly…like the poem where the woman declares that when she's an old woman she shall wear purple, 'but maybe I ought to practice a little now?'

"But Mother wouldn't like it," a prissy little voice—the part of me that gave a crap about what others thought of me—whispered cruelly in my ears, "making yourself stand out like that."

How I wanted to squash that little voice.

"She made the scones," Priscilla answered for me, her disapproval bleeding through every word.

Kelli eyed me with interest. "She cooks? Well, well, well…" The gleam in those wide-set eyes of hers was startlingly rapacious. "She really will have her uses, won't she?"

Priscilla sipped her tea. "She thinks Bessie is overworked."

Kelli guffawed, spewing another round of scone and raspberry jam onto her delicate teacup. I waited for her to wipe off the bits. She didn't. "Bessie has been trying to get out of work since Mummy and Daddy hired her when they got married. She's a lazy, old skank. And those slippers she wears!" She peered down at her raised feet, shod in expensive, silver sandals, toenails painted a fiery red. She either was very warm-blooded to wear sandals in such cool, wet weather, or very vain. "You'd think she was a slave or something!"

Priscilla smiled, saying nothing to defend Bessie. I could only stare at Kelli, her harsh words echoing in my mind. Had she really just called Bessie a skank? What a horrid name, and entirely undeserved. I thought about defending Bessie, then remembered how things like that turned out with my mother, and decided to stay quiet. I shoved a piece of scone into my mouth, which helped. I didn't want to make Bessie's life worse. I would have to find another way to help her.

I will make them suffer until they are dead, dead, dead.

I took a scalding gulp of tea, hoping to burn the frighteningly brutal words out of me. But I only ended up choking on the scone. No one exactly flew to my rescue—though Kelli did lean toward me, green eyes alight—and eventually I managed to swallow as I blinked back tears.

"Are you all right?" Priscilla finally asked. I nodded, clearing my throat. "I'll be going out tonight," she went on, slipping a bit of scone to Bones who had come to lie by her feet. He glanced over at me as he took the sweet bread, and I would swear he gave me a look that said, "If you value your life, human, don't say anything about me and the stranger."

I didn't plan to. The aunts had their mysteries and now I had one of my own.

Kelli eyed her sister with an expression that could only be called venomous. Its ferocity surprised me. "Oh, what a coincidence! I'm going out, as well."

Priscilla set down her teacup and saucer on the table beside her with more force than was necessary. For a moment I thought one—perhaps both—of the fragile ceramic pieces would shatter. But they silently held their own, as if used to the abuse.

Priscilla tucked a bit of white bob behind a petite ear. "With friends?"

"Just one." Kelli smiled at her sister, her full, ruby lips moist with tea.

"Jessica?"

Kelli threw back her head and laughed. "Wrong sex."

"One of the village boys, I suppose. You go through them like handkerchiefs, Kelli. It's disgusting. Your little escapades shame the family name." My eyes widened.

Sparks of fury shone in Kelli's, which she did nothing to suppress. "At least I live a little."

"Judging from the rumors," Priscilla sniffed, "you live a lot." My mouth dropped open.

Kelli stood abruptly and the crumbs sprinkling her purple skirt dropped to the floor like snow, the same floor I'd recently vacuumed. "You're just jealous because he wants *me*," she jabbed at her cleavage, "and can barely stand the sight of *you*!" She dropped back into her chair, winded from her exertions.

Priscilla's teeth ground inside her clenched mouth. "Really? Then why did he ask me to host the annual fundraiser booth for the upcoming Solstice Festival? He told me I was the only person who could do the job properly." She actually preened a little as she said this.

Kelli stomped her foot angrily and it came to me that they were both attracted to the same man. I wondered what his draw could be to charm such completely different women.

"He never did!"

"Oh, he did. And we won't be needing your services this year for the dunking booth. There's only so many times a person can stomach seeing you drenched from head to toe, looking like a cat in heat." Stunned by her ruthlessness, I dazedly wondered if cats in heat looked wet, though at this moment Kelli did look feline, and ready to launch herself at her sister, the proverbial rat, claws out, fur raised, hisses galore.

But she would have no chance to attack. The bout was over. Priscilla had won. She and Bones were out the door and down the hall before Kelli recovered her tongue. "I could kill her!"

"Then why don't you?" I asked, then clapped a hand to my mouth. Oh, dear Lord, where had that come from?

Her green eyes narrowed thoughtfully. "You're not quite the mug you put on. Perhaps Eddie's little girl has a backbone, after all."

"Aunt Kelli, I didn't really mean—"

She laughed, cutting me off. "Oh, don't back off now. I rather like you this way." She pulled out a cigarette and lit it with a hand still quivering with anger. She thrust the pack at me. I shook my head. "How would you suggest I go about it, then?"

"I was only kidding. I didn't really mean for you to kill her. I just..."

"You just what?" She was growing impatient with me. For a brief moment I had been interesting to her.

"Never mind." I quickly loaded the tray while Kelli watched me work. "I'll bring this to the kitchen."

"You know," she said, shaking the cigarette clenched between two plump fingers at me, her eyes squinting in the bluish smoke rising from it, "I might just take you up on your suggestion. And for the final touch, put the blame on you." When she saw my expression, she gave a hoarse laugh. "I'm just taking the piss, luv."

As I hurried away, desperate to escape her and her wretched laughter, I had the far-fetched and frightening impression that she meant every word she said.

Chapter Seven

✴

Miss Dunton's Teashop

I ended up leaving a message for my parents on their answering machine. Mother's outgoing message mentioned something about being off to the Cape for the weekend. She liked telling people where she was going so that she wouldn't miss out on anything, refusing to listen when I told her she was basically issuing an invitation for thieves to hit our apartment. Her response was that I was paranoid. Maybe she was right; we've never been robbed. Though I've been tempted to empty the place myself and sell everything on eBay, just to prove the woman wrong.

I spent some time unpacking a few toiletry items and snooping about my wing of the house. After finding nothing of interest, I joined Bessie in the kitchen for a small supper. As they had announced, Priscilla and Kelli were out for the evening. Neither had been clear about where they were going and I wondered where they would end up. Both were interested in the stranger, but I sensed that neither of them had a date with him, or someone would be gloating with great enthusiasm.

During the meal, Bessie was in a good mood...for her. With the aunts gone, she felt, as I did, the house breathing easier. After the dishes were done, she shuffled off to her room with a plate of oatmeal raisin cookies and a glass of her special homemade 'medicine' (no doubt mostly whiskey) to watch *Monarch of the Glen* re-runs.

Once in my own room, I pulled a white cotton nightgown over my head. Noting the pale light outside, I drifted over to the window. The sun had dipped behind the trees, leaving twilight behind and transforming the world outside into an irresistible fairyland—though its inhabitants were fireflies, not real fairies. I'd only ever seen fireflies in a park close to our apartment during the summer my parents worked for the Guthrie Theater in Minnesota. Being only nine years old at the time, I didn't remember much about the flying creatures other than that they glowed, but I thought the ones here in England seemed quite large, darting about as fast as hummingbirds. I watched them zip around, mesmerized by their zigzagging flights just inside the boundary of the woods.

And then I saw something that made my whole body go cold. With one small step, the stranger entered the swarm of fireflies, standing amidst them like a god. Bones stood by him, dark and daunting. The stranger peered up at my window, then lifted a hand, beckoning me to come down. A tingling sensation ran down my spine, warming my fingers and toes. I longed to obey.

But I daren't. Tomorrow I would ask Bessie about him, without giving away that we'd met, of course. I didn't want my aunts learning I'd gone into the woods after being told not to, and had met a strange man there, to boot. I'm not sure what they would do about my insubordination, but as I didn't want to leave England yet, I thought I'd better err on the side of caution.

For the moment, it was best to steer clear of him. He knew too much about me when I knew nothing about him. I stepped back behind the heavy brocade curtain, and for a long while, stood in the dark, willing him to go away.

When I at last peeked out the tall window, he was gone, as were the fireflies. Despite my resolve to avoid him, I was disappointed that he'd given up so easily. At the very least, he could have thrown a pebble or two at my window.

~

The next day started out bright and sunny, though by now I knew better than to trust the weather here. By afternoon, the elements would most likely turn to rain. I thought maybe today I'd visit the village; maybe track down the local busybody. Nearly every one of the gothic novels I'd read contained at least one gossip. There had to be some way for the heroine to learn things, as she was rarely clairvoyant, and sometimes downright obtuse.

I took a quick bath in the deep tub, dressed in brown cords, a camel-colored turtleneck, and a pair of walking shoes, and grabbed my mother's cast-off Burberry raincoat. My long, dark hair curled about my face and fell down my back in a soft cascade. Typically I felt dumpy, even itchy in my own skin, but for once I was pleased with my appearance.

Bessie was cleaning the oven with whip cream when I arrived in the kitchen for breakfast. "I'm setting up an appointment for you to see an eye doctor," I told her, taking the can, which had to be Kelli's, away from her. Kelli seemed like the type to enjoy whip cream in a can, and for more than just as a culinary delight.

Bessie grimaced at me. "I willna be puttin' none of those pieces of glass right on me eyeballs."

"Let's just start with good, old-fashioned spectacles," I said. "I think those will be plenty for you." I had visions of her poking out an eyeball with those untrustworthy fingers of her. Rummaging under the sink, I found the oven cleaner and started work. The old stove was a mess, inside and out. I spent most of my efforts scrubbing at several bits of charred something or other on the bottom of the stove, likely hunks of venison dating back to the 1700s.

"So, are there any neighbors close by?" I casually ventured, as I worked. This time Bessie hadn't needed to be coaxed into sitting down. She was relaxing in a rocking chair I'd found during my exploration yesterday, sipping—well, slurping—a second cup of tea. In between rinsing out my cleaning rags and scrub brush, I managed to finish off a cup myself, along with a couple biscuits.

Her eyes narrowed to slits. "There be none round here for a very long time."

"Really?" I tried hard not to show my surprise. "No neighbors?"

She cackled. "Not close by. Already lookin' for different company?"

I laughed lightly, glad she hadn't figured me out. "I guess so. It is a bit quiet and cut-off here. I'm used to living in a city."

She leaned her aged head back against a red and white gingham pad. "There used to be a big house back in the woods a ways. Mind, I've only heard stories about it. T'was here and gone before me time."

I pulled my head out of the oven. "Really? What happened to it?" My mind was spinning and not just from the fumes. Here and *gone*?

"The owners, the Allertons, I believe, made the mistake of buildin' where they shouldna built. Less than a year later, they moved out, leavin' the house to rot. The manor was a masterpiece, I've heard tell, and a right shame to let it go to waste, but they wouldna listen, and that's what you get when you turn a deaf ear."

Stunned and curious, I returned my upper half to the stove's inner recesses and started wiping up the black goop. I didn't want Bessie to see my face. "How long ago was that?"

"A hunnert years, give or take."

My head whipped back out, smacking into the side of the oven. *Damnit.* A *hundred* years, and supposedly abandoned? The house I'd visited looked neither that old, nor derelict. "And you're sure it's all gone."

Bessie cracked an eye. "What are you goin' on at? Of course, I'm sure it's all gone." She paused, her other eye emerging from beneath its saggy lid like a turtle popping its head out. "Mostly sure. Never checked, actually. Dunna dare."

"What do you mean, you don't dare? Has anyone dared?" I had to know.

She shrugged, setting down her cup and saucer with a clatter and pushing herself out of the chair. She left it rocking behind her as she carried her cup to the sink. "Not that I kennt." She wagged a crooked finger at me. "Now don't you be thinkin' of goin' explorin', either. Those woods baint be safe. Full of wild creatures and whatnot." I solemnly shook my head and she frowned. "I ken yer kind, Evie. Go into the village if you be wantin' somethin' to do."

"But what about the house? I can help you with cleaning upstairs."

She shook her head. "You've been a big enough help already. Besides, I dunna want the Misses Uppity and Trollop gettin' their knickers in a bunch. The one that wears 'em, anyway."

I grinned, though the image of the knickerless Trollop made me cringe a little. "I think I will," I decided, throwing away the blackened cleaning rags before scrubbing my greasy hands with pungent lye soap. "It'd be nice to explore for a bit."

She waved me off. "Go to Miss Dunton's for your midday. Tell her Bessie sent you."

"If you're sure…"

"Scalamabooch!" she scolded, practically pushing me out the door.

I was happy to go, actually. I was curious to see what the village of Ellwood was about. The scant information on the town, most of it gleaned from the author of a guidebook written for serious walkers, had intrigued me. I hadn't learned much from the author, but the sentence, "Ellwood is a mysterious backwoods village stuck somewhere between the nineteenth and twenty-first centuries, where the residents are reticent to the point of rudeness, and surely hiding something, perhaps inbreeding, perhaps treasure…" was a good warning of what to expect.

Grabbing my raincoat, I headed out the door. Already the skies had grown sullen, dark with unspilled rain. I was learning that the weather was very reliable here. Wait a few minutes and it will change. In the morning, from good to bad. In the afternoon, from bad to worse.

Unable to resist, I spent several minutes leaning over the side of the bridge watching the water slip beneath the arches. Today the stream was heather gray, froths of white punctuating the darkness like snowy kerchiefs tossed by young girls making wishes for true love. After squelching a silly desire to do the same, succeeding only after determining that I didn't have a kerchief, I continued down the muddy dirt lane. Before taking a right toward the village, I glanced at the woods, catching sight of what was supposedly the Wrath's Path. I had a hard time believing I'd passed so easily through it. The dark skies transformed the trees into death figures, black and old and waiting, and the trail looked shadowy and overgrown, barely a pathway at all.

I looked away, determined not to dwell on what might have happened there with the mystery man I'd met at his *supposedly* non-existent house. There must be some kind of misunderstanding, I decided, a story put out by the owner—the stranger, of course—to keep nosy Parkers and kids away. He was a hermit, I decided, an eccentric, very good-looking hermit.

The road to the village was quiet, even the birds were silent, and I met no one. Luckily the spire of the church in the distance and the low stone walls running parallel to the road kept me company along the way. Although I was alone, I felt, as I had in the woods, the heavy, prickly sensation of being watched. I suppose I had a right to my paranoia, if that's what it was. Not only was I staying in a strange land, but I was also a wary person. Living with my mother had ensured that. She often attacked without warning, bursting in from out of nowhere with guns blazing, and then disappearing as I stuttered out an ignored rebuttal. I secretly called her the Kamikaze Critic and had once even defiantly muttered the name under my breath when she'd put down a *much*-loved hat that I'd owned, ruining any pleasure I took in wearing it.

It would kill her to hear it, but she and the aunts were a lot alike. Maybe I'd bring it up the next time we talked on the phone.

Once I entered the village, I knew for certain that I was being watched, but only because my audience made no secret of his curiosity. A man herding sheep across the road stopped in his tracks and his brown, weathered face crinkled up as he studied me. Skirting a large mud puddle, I nodded shyly and said a soft "hello." He said nothing in reply, but he did return my nod after removing his cap.

His relentless study was nerve-wracking, but the nod had been reassuring. I passed the first of the thatched cottages, ivy-laden and surrounded by colorful flowers. The dwellings quickly multiplied on either side of the road. Women, tending to fenced-in vegetable gardens or dirty, fussy children, stopped what they were doing to watch me. One even nudged a neighbor who was bending to soothe her crying child and who might have missed seeing me if not for the warning.

I said hello to them in a quiet voice and like the old shepherd, they all nodded, but not a word was spoken in my presence, not even by the children, who also watched me pass by. They, too, looked as solemn as the adults, and curious, as well. There was even a degree of awe, I thought, on their little faces. I picked up a stray, blue ball that had slipped away from a redheaded boy, only about four years old, and tossed it back to him. He caught it, checked it over for possible damage, then cradled it to his thin chest like a precious baby.

The cottages eventually gave way to little businesses. On one side of the street patrons came and went from a quaint post office and a busy bar, or pub, as they call it in England. On my side of the road there was a bold flower shop painted a pale green, with bright blue shutters and cascading flower boxes, and a used bookstore, no doubt as dusty on the inside as its display window, which was papered with posters. *Shakespeare Art the King of Literature!* one proclaimed. A slender young man wearing thick glasses walked out of the store, his long nose nearly pinched between the covers of a book. Even he, as distracted as he was, stopped and looked at me, his eyes squinting over the square rims of his glasses. I gave a little wave and he blinked at me twice before raising a hesitant hand.

Farther along, the gleaming white church, upright and invincible against the dark sky and surrounded by tilted, moss-covered gravestones, rose up to greet me. Just past the bookstore, I spotted the delicate sign for Miss Dunton's Teashop and Bakery peeping at me. Painted on it were a wedding cake and a pansy-flowered teapot, and I knew immediately I would like the place. I walked faster, anxious to escape further scrutiny, and to see what the bakery was selling in terms of delectable treats. It was past my normal lunchtime and I was hungry.

I opened the door and stepped into the warm, cozy establishment. A little silver bell tinkled lightly above my head, its nearly breathless sound serving more as a greeting to the customer than as a warning to the shopkeeper. Several small tables, round and brightly painted, were spread around the room. Older women sharing gossip and a cup of tea occupied three of them. Next to the fireplace, where a fire crackled merrily, a variety of announcements on yellow, pink, or blue pieces of paper covered a corkboard. One large notice announced the Solstice Festival coming on Saturday, a week from today, and promising "fun for the whole family." I remembered then that Priscilla had mentioned running one of the booths. Based on the layout, the shop must have been a home at one time, and maybe still served as one on the second floor.

When the other patrons saw me enter the shop, the room fell silent. One poor woman's teacup hovered inches from her mouth, her hand trembling with the effort not to move. Not wanting to startle her I stopped where I was. Standing perfectly still, the scent of baking bread, lemony tea, and sweet frosting descended on me, and my stomach rumbled.

"You must be the American girl!" a hearty voice announced behind me. The declaration interrupted the spell, but did not entirely break it. The women moved, allowing themselves to set down a teacup or a scone, but they did not return to their gossiping. I was the main event at Miss Dunton's Teashop today and they were determined not to miss the show.

Still careful with my movements, I slowly turned around to face my greeter. "Is it that obvious?"

The woman laughed merrily. She was a round, little thing, cheery and bright. But for all her merry manner and plump form, there was a sharp gleam in her English blue eyes as she appraised me. I only caught it because I, of course, was appraising her, too.

"I'm Miss Dunton, the owner."

"Pleased to meet you." I bobbed an awkward curtsy—not something I usually did, but it somehow seemed appropriate with this woman. "I'm Evalina Filmore."

"I already know your name, dear. What I don't know is what brings a Filmore to my humble establishment." Her voice was suddenly cool.

"Bessie sent me," I said, the fingers of my right hand squeezing my left.

Quick as a flash, her demeanor changed. "Well then, I welcome you. Bessie doesn't take to many folk. If you're found wanting, she'll not give you the time of day. She isn't easy to fool, our Bessie."

I wasn't sure if I should feel flattered I'd gotten in Bessie's good graces or worried she'd find out my secrets. "She thought it would be good for me to see the village," I said. "So here I am."

"And what do you think of it so far?" The old ladies leaned forward as one, and I could almost hear the creaking of their bones.

"It's a beautiful village." There was a murmur of approval from the women.

"We like it."

"Though I wonder what makes my presence so interesting to everyone I meet."

The laughter again. High, bubbling, very amused. "The simple fact that you're new. We don't receive too many visitors here. Not like Newton Abbot or Plymouth. We like it that way, you see."

I nodded, understanding. Wherever my parents traveled when working for the theater, few places ever regarded strangers as a good thing.

Not at first, anyway. I had a feeling that here in Ellwood strangers would never break down that barrier.

"Your bread is amazing." I nodded at the glass shelves stacked with golden loaves of bread that looked exactly like what I'd filled up on my first night at Filmore.

Miss Dunton allowed herself a smile. "I bake it myself. But then, you knew that."

"I was hoping you did." I pressed an earnest hand to my chest. "Bessie served a loaf of sourdough my first night and it saved me from starvation."

"I'm pleased to hear that I saved your life." She nodded at a round table separate from the others, tucked away in a nook close to the front window where red and pink geraniums in colorful pots decorated the windowsill. "Come, join me in a cup. My treat." She slipped behind the counter as I headed for the table.

"As long as you don't let me forget to buy some of those cookies before I go," I said over my shoulder. Trays of them filled a long, low shelf inside the glass case, which also displayed a variety of beautifully frosted cakes fit for a wedding or a fairy soirée.

Her lips twitched. "I think you and I might get along, Miss Filmore."

"I do hope so, Miss Dunton," I said, as I sat down. "Because right now you're the only person in the village who seems willing to talk to me."

She laughed, a real laugh this time. "I suppose you don't know why that is." She poured fragrant lemon tea into two delicate teacups. A plate of scones appeared on the painted tray and she carried it to the table with efficiency. I expect, had she needed to, she could have hefted it with one hand and juggled with the other at the same time.

Not shy when it came to food, and feeling very hungry now, I took one of the scones and bit into it. Before I knew it I had devoured the best raisin scone I'd ever tasted. It was moist and warm, with a buttery cinnamon undertone. Miss Dunton drank her tea and watched, amused, as I took another one.

When I'd swallowed the last bit, I wiped my mouth with a snowy napkin and took a sip of the refreshing tea. The citric scent cleared my mind and my palate. "You are very good at your job, Miss Dunton," I told her appreciatively. "I suppose you won't share your scone recipe?" She only chuckled, as I'd expected her to. No baker worth her salt gives away her best recipes. "Okay, then maybe you can tell me why no one in the village will even say hi to me?"

She didn't bother to lower her voice; she could've whispered in my ear and the others would have heard her, they were so quiet. "Because you passed through the Wrath," she paused and took a sip of tea before fixing her bright blue eyes on me, "and lived to tell about it." Her fingers trembled slightly as she clutched the pink and white ceramic cup's delicate handle.

"You can't be serious."

"No one passes through those woods. Not the magistrate, not the Filmores or the Thorndikes, not even the Queen herself if she knew what was what. And, of course, we'd warn her. We love our Queen."

The tip of my tongue nervously swiped at a bit of cream on my upper lip that my napkin had missed. "How do you know I passed through the Wrath? I don't even know what it is. Maybe I went around it. Did someone actually see me there?" *Perhaps the stranger in the woods?*

"Not as far as I know. We heard about what happened from your aunt—that your taxi driver dropped you off at the wrong place. She looked jolly well pleased with herself when she told us the news."

"Which aunt told you?"

She peered at me over the gold rim of her cup. "Do you have to ask?"

No. "My Aunt Kelli, I imagine..." I said this slowly, realizing as I spoke that I never referred to my aunts as Aunt Priscilla or Aunt Kelli while thinking about them. I wondered why that was, though if pushed to answer, I'd have to say it had to do with the undercurrent I felt from them—a sense that they meant to make me do something that I wouldn't want to do, like sign away millions, renounce father's claim to Filmore Manor, or sacrifice a lamb.

"Priscilla tries not to speak to common folk if she can help it. Thinks she's too good for the likes of us. Kelli feels the same way, but she can't help herself. Good gossip is good gossip. She had to share it with someone. And who would care about such news, but us villagers?"

"Doesn't she have friends she could tell?" I remembered her mentioning some at tea, during her argument with Priscilla.

"Oh, sure. Of good family, too. But Kelli likes the spotlight, in case you haven't noticed." I had. "She'd want to tell anyone who'd listen. And for this, everyone had an ear to spare."

"But she didn't actually see me—"

"I'm told her sister passed along the details," Miss Dunton interrupted, sounding almost impatient with me. "That you passed through the Wrath, left your bags inside the woods, and then the luggage showed up at the Manor all of its own."

"Ah." I was right that Priscilla would tell Kelli what had happened with my bags. They might fight, but a strong bond united them. I wouldn't call it a sisterly one, though.

"The Wrath cannot be mistaken. Its territory runs the length of the entire woods from High Moor down to where Filmore sits right on the edge of it. The Wrath cannot be missed."

I took a deep breath to steady myself. "Okay, but *what* is the Wrath?"

She narrowed her eyes, considering how much to share with an outsider, and a Filmore at that. I tried very hard to look sweet and endearing. "The Wrath is a dangerous place. Steer clear of it in future. That's all you need to know." I suppressed a disappointed sigh. She might be the local gossip, but even she had her limits with strangers. Either that, or my sweet and endearing look wasn't as sweet and endearing as I thought it was.

She drained her cup of tea as though it were a much-needed shot of whiskey and abruptly stood. "The biscuits are on the house." Her chair scraped against the stone floor as she pushed back from the table.

Following her cue, I finished my tea and met her at the counter. Before I had a chance to ask more questions, a white paper bag heavy with biscuits, or cookies as I knew them, was in my left hand and the last scone from the plate in my right. Small, but surprisingly strong, Miss Dunton steered me toward the door. "Stop by again some time, Miss *Filmore*. You're good for business. Your kind always is..."

The bell jingled cheerily and I was outside in the light rain that had inevitably begun to fall, standing like an idiot, both hands clutching food, a stunned expression on my face. A beautiful Irish setter sniffed at my ankles, then glanced hopefully at the scone. Before I could feel nervous, a sharp, angry whistle signaled his unseen master's demand to come, and the dog ran off, disappointed. I felt bad for the poor thing. Given another thirty seconds to introduce ourselves, I would've tossed it some bits of scone.

Feeling embarrassed by my abrupt dismissal, I decided to end my adventure and head back home, scurrying like a dog with its proverbial tail tucked between its legs. But as I walked, something strange happened. The humiliation faded away and something more powerful took its place. Fury. It began to burn in my chest, warming my body despite the damp cold rolling over me. I had done nothing to deserve being stared at, having my questions avoided, and then being summarily dismissed like a child. And to imply that I was the only one who'd walked the Wrath's Path and escape unharmed... Really, I had expected better things of England.

This time, I refused to hang my head in shame. I had done nothing wrong, and I would face Miss Dunton's belittling behavior with courage. Head held high, I strode down the village road at a fast clip, thankful for once for the rain that had sent the women and children inside.

At the outskirts of town, where the trees began, I met the puddle I'd skirted earlier. It wasn't very wide but it spanned the road. I could easily jump it. I took a few steps back and began to run.

Just as I was about to lift off, a desperate voice cried out, "Sadie, get back here!" My head jerked up and at the same time my foot slipped. Instead of leaping forward as I'd planned, I fell, landing right in the middle of the puddle. Muddy water immediately soaked through my shoes and pants, even sneaking up under my raincoat in spots, and splotches of mud splattered my cheeks and forehead. The only saving grace was that my bag of cookies had landed on the grass where I had flung them in a desperate effort to keep them safe.

My scone, however, was not so lucky. The Irish setter I had met in the village was busily wolfing it down, practically swallowing it whole. I dragged myself out of the puddle and sat in a sopping heap at its edge. I suddenly wanted to cry. My anger dissipated, leaving me feeling confused and empty, cold and wet, too.

"Are you all right?"

I looked up and groaned. Peering down at me from atop his horse, which could have been the Black Stallion itself, was the man I had christened NAT. In his fitted, black riding jacket and black trousers tucked into matching leather riding boots, he looked like a noble hero. He sat there on his literal high horse, poised and in command, waiting for me to answer.

He looked amazing.

I was an absolute mess.

And I hated him for it.

Chapter Eight

＊

Thorndike

"Do I look all right?" I grumbled, trying ineffectually to de-mud myself with broad swipes at my arms and legs. It was a losing battle, especially since I also had to fend off the Irish setter that kept licking my face.

"She always gets a scone at Miss Dunton's Teashop," he explained. "Sit, Sadie!" he commanded, and she sat at the edge of the puddle, tongue hanging out as she panted happily.

"But she didn't get one today," I finished for him, realizing what had happened. He'd seen me coming out of the shop and had called off his dog to avoid meeting up with me. "Well, until now. I *would* have shared," I told her. She panted happily at me.

He winced. "Sorry about that. We were well on our way, but Sadie got it into her silly head to go back to the village to get her scone. She's a stubborn dog, aren't you, Sadie girl?" As though she knew she was in trouble, the beautiful red dog cocked her head to one side and gave me a winsome look. I decided to forgive her. Behind her, I spotted two more dogs, a chocolate lab and a golden retriever, nosing around my cookies, threatening to eat them. *That*, I could not forgive.

"Could you at least save my cookies for me?" I pointed a dripping finger at the white bag.

NAT slid down off his horse and plucked it up, just before the lab got hold of it. After slipping the paper sack into a saddlebag, he turned back to me and held out his hand. I took it. It was warm and smooth and dry, and I felt a sudden, naughty urge to yank him into the puddle. My grown-up side resisted, long enough for him to get better footing anyway, and I lost my chance.

He pulled me, slipping and sliding, to my feet. Wet and shivering in the open air, I wished, perversely, that I were sitting down again. The wind had a clear sweep at me now, nipping at my wet flesh. My urge to cry intensified.

"Come along," he said, sensing my surrender. "We'll get you home."

"I can make it on my own," I insisted. Oh, that was rich. I wasn't making it anywhere. At that moment, I felt as drained and empty as a whiskey jug on a cold night. But damned if I was going to let him know that.

"No, you can't." He pulled off his black jacket and wrapped the soft wool around my shoulders. Before I could thank him, he grabbed his horse's reins and began to walk. Despite my desire to lie down and die from embarrassment, I trailed after him. He whistled to the dogs and they joined us, jumping and sniffing. He bent low to pet each dog, strong, ink-stained fingers scrunching up their ears affectionately. They panted and gazed at him with adoration, and I knew that they were more Mosie and less Bones. Nate smiled at them, one corner of his mouth tilting upward. "Go on now, you brutes." They scampered off, chasing each other joyfully, the lab playfully nipping at the golden's ears.

"Not home!" he called to them when they zipped down a road I hadn't noticed on my way in, distracted by the shepherd and his sheep, most likely. The narrow dirt drive skirted the edge of the woods, soon disappearing around a corner. The dogs turned about with questioning looks, then excitedly joined us on the main road again, once more racing ahead. I now knew where he lived. Studying his horse for a moment, I also determined that he had to be the man on the moor—the one who hadn't returned my wave, the one who I'd thought might be the devil.

Sometimes I can be very astute.

"I suppose this meeting was unavoidable," NAT said after a couple minutes of silence.

"What a charming way to put it." The sarcastic response was out before I had a chance to nice it up.

"I mean, with such a small village..." He stopped.

"Your being rude to me on the train was avoidable." I held my breath and waited.

"I didn't mean it that way." When I glanced over at him his dark eyes were troubled. "It's just that...well, you took me by surprise."

I exhaled. "Yes, I like doing that to strangers. Especially if it makes them flee from my presence."

He sighed. "I'm trying to explain."

I crossed my arms, then uncrossed them, deciding I must look like a petulant child. "I'd prefer an apology, actually. Explanations are merely glorified excuses."

He glanced over at me, his walnut-colored eyes hooded like a falcon's. "Our families...the Filmores and the Thorndikes...we have a history."

"And..." I prompted. I was not impressed. This was not how you started an apology.

"We do not get along."

"Since when?"

"Since 1556."

"Oh." Okay, now I was impressed. "What happened?"

"I don't know."

Laughter burst out of me like a cannon shot. He frowned. The rain had stopped, leaving behind a misty web draping his black hair. At that moment, a ray of sunlight shot down through the racing clouds, exposing a patch of blue sky. *Beam him up, Scotty*, I thought irreverently. *No, don't.* Even though his perfection irritated me, I wanted to look at him some more.

That's when I noticed something that made my body go cold. There was a strange sort of similarity between the man I saw standing before me and the stranger, though I couldn't place my finger on where it lay.

I shivered. "I don't even know your name."

"Really?" He seemed surprised. "I know yours." It was my turn to be surprised, until I remembered how people living in small villages tend to know everything that's going on with everyone else, almost before it happens. "I'm Nathaniel Thorndike." He offered his name easily, as though bestowing a gift on me.

"Not Nat?" The name would be my own private joke.

He shook his head. "Funnily enough, those are my initials. The 'A' is for Augustus. I believe we must have had some Roman ancestors, but don't tell anyone." He gave me a sidelong glance that held an unexpected gleam of humor. "I'll go for Nate, though."

I smiled, deciding to be honest. "A gnat is an annoying bug."

His eyes glittered dangerously for a moment. "I know."

My eyebrows shot up. Oops. "So why the strange behavior?" I ventured. "In the train…on the moor."

"I'd really rather not talk about it." He scratched at a spot behind his ear and looked off into the distance.

"So you're just going to leave me to think something is wrong with me?"

"You think it's you? Bloody hell!"

"What did you expect me to think?"

The dogs, having cornered a brown hare, barked loudly, high-pitched yelps of excitement. They were very near the wood's edge. "Go on now!" he shouted at them. "Leave it be. That place is not for you."

If what Miss Dunton had said was true, then this was the Wrath. I looked over at Nate, wondering what he knew of it. Likely everything. But I doubted he'd share his knowledge with me, at least not if I asked him now. His horse was spooked, blowing wet air through widened nostrils, pawing at the ground, eyes wild and rolling, and Nate had to concentrate to keep a tight hold on the reins.

A short time after, we reached the bridge and the horse calmed down. The dogs, having gone for a short swim, joined us, dripping dark spots of water on the gray stone. The sound of each drop was surprisingly loud over the rush of water passing below our feet, louder even than the whiffing of my soaked pants. It seemed my hearing had suddenly magnified, a strange sensation that made my hair stand on end. As soon as we left the bridge behind, my hearing returned to normal, and I told myself that I must have been imagining things. Though I had a hard time believing my own words.

Just before we reached the green circle of lawn, Nate pulled on the horse's reins. "I'll leave you here, if you're all right to go on yourself."

"You're afraid of my aunts," I said bravely, as I studied his stiff expression. "That's what this is about."

"I'm not afraid of your aunts!" He looked horrified at the thought. "I'm not afraid of anyone. Not even..." He stopped and looked around him, searching the woods. "It's just that it's awkward. As I told you, our families don't get along."

"It's more than that, isn't it?" I wasn't sure where this courage to question him was coming from, but I liked it.

"Perhaps. At any rate, it certainly has nothing to do with you."

"Then why avoid me if it has nothing to do with me?"

He released a long and put-upon sigh. "It's complicated."

"Then explain it to me like I'm two."

A smile twitched his lips. "If I talk to you, then I'm going to have to talk to them more often than I want to. Is that simple enough?"

"Talking to someone means you have to talk to their family as well? That's a rule here in England?"

"A social one. Unwritten."

"Are they really so bad?" I paused. "Wait, don't answer that."

His brown eyes lit up, defrosting a bit. "Am I sensing dissension in the ranks?"

I retreated. Kelli was a bit rude, Priscilla somewhat aloof. My mother was worse than both of them put together. "They're not that bad, I guess."

"Give them more time." He looked down at the ground, as though weighing his future. "All right." He held out his free arm. "Shall we?"

I stared at him. "Shall we what?"

"Enter the lair..."

I laughed. He looked quite sincere, his lips thinned determinedly. "I believe you mean it."

"I won't be seen as a coward. Not to someone who's been through the—" He quickly attempted to cover what he'd been about to say. "Through the wringer, like you've been."

My eyes narrowed and not from the sunlight piercing a cloud and settling warmly upon my face. "That's not what you meant to say." He had meant to say the Wrath.

He shrugged, then pulled out his pocket watch, the silver one named NAT. "I have to get Heathcliff home." Heathcliff? If you would like me to come in with you, we'll have to hurry." His voice was polite, but he was already withdrawing from the conversation, from me, from this place.

"No," I answered, watching his face. Only a twitch at the corner of one dark eye showed his relief. "It's probably better that you don't. I'm very cold and not in the mood for a face-off, as entertaining as this one might be."

"You are wise."

"I'm self-protective." I pulled off the wool jacket and gave it to him.

He laid it over the saddle, then handed me the cookies. I took the bag using only the tips of my mud-dried fingers, so as not to get dirt all over the precious contents. "I'm sorry about your scone and this…" He indicated my sopping state.

"Well," I said over my shoulder, as I headed for the house, "you'll just have to make it up to me."

I didn't wait for his response—a time proven method I'd picked up from my mother for avoiding hearing what she didn't want to hear. At the door I glanced back to see him riding off, galloping swiftly down the driveway and disappearing around the bend, dogs following like a swarm of leggy bees, mud flying every which way.

Inside, the house seemed empty, yet listening. Someone, besides Bessie, was in the house. Glancing around and seeing no one, I hurried up to my room. A hot bath and a change of clothes buoyed my spirits, as did a thorough rehashing of my conversation with Nate as I rinsed the mud out of my pants in the tub. When I was through dissecting what had passed between us, I felt quite sure that I'd gotten the better of him.

Feeling pleased with myself, I was heading to the front parlor for tea when I heard voices coming down the hall. Priscilla and Kelli. Not thinking, I slipped into a side room, cluttered and dark, and shut the door. They stopped just outside the room where I was hiding and I cringed. Why had I ducked in here? What if they caught me eaves-dropping? I told myself to get a grip. It wasn't like they were going to murder me and make me into soup. *Don't be too sure about that*, a darker voice warned. *Oh, shut up*, I hissed at it.

"Our niece is awfully naïve, isn't she?" Kelli said and I flinched, the tips of my ears burning uncomfortably. She sounded so contemptuous. "That girl would believe I'm a saint if I told her." Priscilla snorted; Kelli ignored the implied jab. "Eddie really did a job on her."

"I believe it more likely he did nothing at all. He always shunts his re-sponsibilities onto other people. Like he did with us."

"Do you really think she'll work? In his place, I mean?"

There was silence. "She does have his blood in her. That should be enough. If it isn't, we're all in trouble."

What is going on? I wondered, feeling a little frightened. *What do they want from me?*

"Not me," Kelli said defiantly. "Eddie got away. I can, too."

"You'd lose everything."

"I'll be alive. That'll have to be enough."

"Not for me. I mean to finish what we started. Whatever the cost."

"Easy for you to say," Kelli grumbled. "You have nothing to lose."

"And you do?"

"I've got friends! People like me here! I'd be missed, you know."

"Only as a source of entertainment. Don't you know they laugh at you behind your back? Haven't you figured that out yet?"

"You're just jealous," Kelli accused, though her tone was sullen, per-haps from the knowledge that what Priscilla said might have an ounce of truth in it.

"Bessie will be coming with the tea soon," Priscilla changed the sub-ject. "I haven't seen Evie around today so I'm sure it will taste hellish as usual."

"Could we make her cook all the time? I did like those scones."

"Good lord! Do you have to lick your lips like that? You look abso-lutely common."

"I can't help it if I'm a naturally sensuous woman…"

"Which magazine did you get that out of?"

The conversation faded at that point and I was extraordinarily grate-ful for its end. Those two bickered quite a bit, and they could be very nasty to each other. No wonder Bessie looked so sour all the time, having to listen to them.

I waited a minute or two, then reluctantly joined the aunts in the par-lor. Kelli's head swung toward me as I entered the room, looking me over. She sat in the same chair as yesterday and her frog green eyes were suspicious. I immediately stiffened, readying myself for attack. I wasn't sure where this reaction was coming from, but I imagined it had something to do with her calling me awfully naïve. "Where were *you* today?"

I was just about to answer her, as I would normally do when someone ordered me to perform, but something inside me reared its rebel head. Putting Nate in his place was doing wonders for my ego. "I might ask the same of you, Aunt Kelli."

"No, you might not!" She scowled at me, her lush lips pouting, though her eyes looked a bit surprised. She hadn't expected the naïve young thing to fight back. "We're supposed to be looking after you and you simply disappeared without a word!"

"You're to tell us when you leave the house," Priscilla agreed, and I looked back and forth between the two of them.

"Seriously? I didn't really think it necessary to tell you about my every move. Besides, neither of you told me where you were going to be today. You simply left the house without a word to me. How was I supposed to tell you anything? You weren't here."

I wasn't just standing up for myself, I realized, I seemed to be deliberately poking them. What was the matter with me? Didn't I get enough abuse from my mother? I clamped my lips shut, hoping to stop any further inflammatory words from leaping out.

"I had important errands to run for the Solstice Festival," Priscilla stated, her voice unruffled. The force she was putting into petting Bones's head, however, belied her calm tone.

"I'm not explaining myself to this twit!" Kelli snorted angrily. The strange thought occurred to me that I liked her this way—upset and defensive. Now she might make mistakes.

Whoa. What was that about? This wasn't a showdown, a standoff between good guy and bad guy. I took a deep breath, trying to reconnect with myself. "I went into the village," I explained calmly. "I thought I'd look about. Bessie knew where I was."

"She didn't say," Kelli replied grumpily. "Honestly, Prissy," she appealed to her older sister, who frowned at her, a tiny crease splitting the narrow path of skin between her pale eyes. "We really ought to get rid of that old biddy."

"She serves our need," Priscilla responded, visibly working, though it took some effort, to relax her forehead muscles. Watching her, a memory forced its way into my mind.

Temper, temper, Evie! my mother would scold whenever I was feeling particularly cross and left out. *Scowling wrinkles the skin, so please refrain from doing so, especially at me.*

I sighed. Across an ocean and I could still hear her voice. The woman was relentless.

"But you're the one who's always going on about getting rid of her—" Kelli continued.

The door banged open and Bessie pushed her skinny behind backward through the opening. The silver serving trolley, dented and in need of a good polishing, came after her. Priscilla must see its decrepit state, I thought, but she said nothing on the subject. I realized that as much as she complained, she didn't truly want to get rid of Bessie. I wondered why. My suspicious side whispered that maybe she kept Bessie *because* she was old and nearly blind. The old servant would miss a lot of what might be going on in the house.

The thought made me shiver.

"So what did you do in the village?" Kelli demanded around a mouthful of biscuit. "If I have to put up with you being so high-handed about it, I might as well be entertained." When the taste finally reached her brain, the scowl on her ripe face faded. "You made these, didn't you?" She waved the pastry at me, more bits of flaky bread flying off onto my vacuumed floor. "I might just have to forgive you for sassing me." She grinned charmingly. She ran hot or cold, and unpredictably, like the water temperature in the manor.

I had made the biscuits yesterday and Bessie had simply re-warmed them in the oven, but I wasn't going to admit to doing anything. Bessie leaped in to rescue me, or more likely, her job. "Are you sayin' I canna cook, Miss Kelli?"

"She's saying nothing of the sort," Priscilla intervened, shooting Kelli a cold look. Kelli only shrugged and took a long slurp of tea from the cup Bessie had just filled, then stuffed the rest of the biscuit into her mouth. The charm she'd shown only moments earlier had fled, quick as a startled bird. Now she reminded me of a predator in mid-feed. A set of fangs and blood covering her muzzle would complete the picture. I looked away, feeling rather queasy.

After being sure she had made her point, Bessie left the room, tossing me a surreptitious wink as she went. I smiled inwardly. How nice it was to have someone on my side in this den of secrets.

When she was gone, Priscilla turned to me. "So what *did* you do in the village, Evalina?" She was as interested as Kelli, but did a slightly better job of concealing her curiosity.

"I took tea with the locals...at Miss Dunton's. We talked about old times, about the wealthy, upper-crust families that live around here. Like you guys, for example." Priscilla's face turned paler and stiffer with each word I spoke. I thought her cheekbones might actually fracture. "Oh, and the Thorndikes. They came up, too."

Yes, definitely poking.

The whole room froze, as though time had stopped and an ice age had set in. I, too, froze, teacup in mid-air. Not responding to utter panic is extremely difficult, though understanding why the sisters were reacting this way might help me to know what to do next. Were they afraid that I had learned something about their plans for me?

"And what did the *locals* have to say about us...and the Thorndikes?"

I almost admired how adeptly Priscilla separated herself from the little people simply by how condescendingly she uttered a single word. *Locals.* She might just as well have said, *Losers.*

"Oh, not much, actually." The room defrosted slightly. "Though I did meet a Thorndike today." The room swung from frigid to sultry with one tick of the clock. Kelli looked as though she was going to have a heart attack, thrashing about as she tried to sit up in the overly soft chair to gape at me. She looked almost savage.

Priscilla only looked wary. "And...?"

"*And!*" Kelli cried. "She talks to Nat and that's all you have to say about it?"

I tried to keep my expression neutral. "Is there something wrong, Aunt Priscilla?"

Priscilla managed to keep her head perfectly still as she said, "Why would you think that?"

"Well, Nate told me that there was something...well, just something between our families."

Kelli was positively foaming at the mouth. "How can *she* talk to Nat, when he barely talks to...well, anybody?"

Well, well. She called him Nat, which he hated, and she lived to tell about it. I wondered how she'd managed that. Not that I was jealous, mind you. "I *can* talk," I pointed out, "and he was able to respond to me, as well. I believe it's called a conversation." Yikes. I was beginning to sound more like my mother with every passing second. This place was working its evil sorcery on me.

She ignored my sarcasm. "What did he say?"

I wondered what to tell her that would bother her the most. "He said something about a feud between our families."

"He never did!"

"Yes, he did, and he said he didn't want to come into the house because of it." I was throwing poor Nate to the dogs, but it was *his* dog, after all, who'd stolen my scone. Sounded like ironic justice to me.

A muscle over Priscilla's left eye twitched as though something beneath her skin had snapped and flown loose. "Nathaniel is an old family friend. He was pulling your leg."

"Oh. Was that what it was, Aunt Priscilla?" I blinked my blue eyes innocently at her. "Leg pulling?"

"What else did he say?" Kelli demanded, leaning forward. Biscuit crumbs lay scattered like birdseed on the pale mounds surrounding her cleavage. A spot of strawberry jam on her left breast looked like a fresh wound.

"Kelli!" Priscilla hissed. "Act your age!"

It was at that precise moment when I understood their intense reaction to the Thorndike name. Nate was the man Kelli and Priscilla were fighting over. He was the one they both wanted. Yet he apparently wanted nothing to do with them.

How very interesting…

Chapter Nine

✳

The Invitation

I stood up. Now was the perfect time to make my exit, especially since I valued my life. I wasn't really all that hungry, anyway, having had tea at Miss Dunton's not that long ago. Plus, and more importantly, I wanted to make my aunts sweat. Well, Kelli, anyway. She *had* called me a twit.

"If you'll excuse me," I said to the two women who were taking turns glaring at me and at each other, "I have some letters to write." I set down my teacup and popped up from my chair like a jack-in-the-box.

Priscilla looked away from her sister and at me. I would swear I saw murder in those eyes right before the shutters came down, and I regretted my momentary rebellion. "I believe there's a storm coming this way, Evalina. You had best stay in the house for the rest of the day."

I shivered at the thought of being trapped in here with these two sparring sisters, feeling angry with myself for getting more involved than I needed to be. "Sure, Aunt Priscilla," I replied. "No problem." I turned to go.

"Evie!"

"Yes, Aunt Kelli?"

"What else did Nathaniel speak to you about?"

"Well, it was a long walk from the village. We talked about a lot of things, I guess. Mostly we laughed." I had to bite my tongue to keep from saying more, rerouting the giggle making its way up my throat. I was only making things worse for myself.

"You're making that up," Kelli pouted.

I gazed guilelessly at her. "Why would I do that, Aunt Kelli? He's very funny, you know. Well, you would know, being old friends. I'm not sure why he refused to come into the house, though. Are you two having a fight?"

Kelli actually growled and Bones sat up expectantly. "Nat and I are good mates. More than that I think, soon enough." She gave Priscilla a triumphant look. "I'm quite sure of it."

"Nathaniel Thorndike would never go for the likes of you, Kelli," Priscilla stated firmly. "He has the family name to think of, and you quite obviously don't fit the expectations for a Thorndike wife. And—"

"Well, I'll be going now," I interrupted, then hurried out the door before they could stop me. I had gotten myself in over my head—time to get myself out, and quick. Kelli looked ready to explode.

Once in my room, I mulled over what I'd just done. I'd purposely antagonized my aunts, but why? What did I expect to gain from poking at them? Well, I did get one thing from the experience. I knew for certain now that they didn't like me. Before I had thought that at least Priscilla was all right, but now I felt certain she didn't like me any more than Kelli did. And I'd done everything I could in those few short minutes in the parlor to encourage her dislike. Not smart. From now on, it was best to lay low and avoid contact with the two sisters until they cooled down.

I sighed and went to sit at the old desk, thinking I could write letters. But there was really only one letter to write. Mother and Father didn't expect one, and more likely didn't want one because then they might feel obligated to write back. After happily snooping through all the desk drawers, I settled down to writing a rambling letter to Mrs. Bonner, my old home-ec teacher, about my adventures, leaving out the more disturbing bits, of course.

I know you'll love it here, Mrs. Bonner, I wrote. *Everything really is as green as we saw in that movie,* Sense and Sensibility, *you showed for our holiday treat last year. The landscape practically drips with romance and the scones truly are to die for. I'm enjoying myself immensely, and I believe you would, too.* As I scribbled, I found myself falling into an archaic style of writing altogether fitting for a letter to Mrs. Bonner. *The village where I'm staying is full of odd characters and ancient buildings. I took tea at the local teashop and met the owner. She was thoroughly British and frightened me immensely. But I have since recovered. Then a dog stole my scone and I ended up in a very cold mud puddle and the local lothario had to rescue me.* How romantic that bit sounded, though I hadn't thought so at the time. At the end of the letter I encouraged her to make the trip herself. *I organized everything myself, quite easily actually, and found a good ticket price on the Internet. People rent out rooms in their homes for quite reasonable prices, I think you'll agree, including meals. Do give it a try, won't you?*

For her sake, I hoped she'd finally take the big step of making her dream come true. I also hoped the reality lived up to her expectations. My reality, on the other hand, was very different from what I'd been expecting. This was not turning out to be the dream vacation I'd been fantasizing about. Gothic, yes. Romantic? Definitely not. Well, okay, maybe just a tad. There was the stranger, and now Nate, who seemed determined to make things up to me. Letting him might turn out to be quite fun. I smiled to myself and began to hum a little tune.

According to my watch, dinner wouldn't be for another two hours so I sat in the large window seat behind the curtains and spent the time writing in my journal about my trip, the aunts and their 'plans' for me, meeting Nate, and finally, the stranger. In the margins next to each topic, I made a few sketches—the train, the village, Nate's horse, Heathcliff, and then Nate himself. Next to him, I drew the stranger, comparing their features detail by detail when I'd finished. I wasn't the best artist in the world, but I managed to capture enough to make them recognizable. Nate seemed remote and mysterious to me while the stranger appeared as mischievous and bright as a bewitching child. No matter how hard I tried, I could no longer see a resemblance between the two men and decided I'd been imagining things.

After staring at their images longer than was necessary, I locked my journal in my suitcase and grabbed the gothic romantic thriller, *Castle D'or*, to read in the window seat. My current setting heightened the dark atmosphere and suspenseful mystery of the story and I enjoyed it immensely.

Several chapters in, thunder rumbled in the distance, announcing the storm's impending arrival. I glanced up at the sky. Spilled ink spread over the tops of the lush trees surrounding the house and the room darkened. Lightning flashed high in the sky and I pulled back instinctively. But just as quickly, I leaned forward again. I had seen something in the blaze of light.

A man.

The stranger stood at the edge of the woods, facing the house, looking more like a ghost than a living being. He spotted my silhouette and raised his hand, beckoning to me. I glanced up at the roiling sky, then back at him and shook my head no. Too dangerous. I had no desire to become a statistic or to get pummeled by Mother Nature yet again today. One dousing was enough for me. Anyway, despite my 'mischievous boy' rendering, the stranger disturbed me, more so than the storm.

He beckoned again and I felt my will falter. This house was so oppressive sometimes; it would feel good to be free of its shackles. A brief walk in the woods would do me no harm, and might actually do me some good. All my life I'd preferred to follow a well-ordered routine, structured and safe, and I was finally realizing that such rigorous constraint might be why I'd never had much of a life. I rarely allowed my wild side to rule, to make choices for me, always using my good sense to dictate my every move. Did I really want to live that way? No—at least, not all the time. If I wanted to experience more of life, I would have to be more daring. I was tired of always being good. Good was dull. No wonder I bored Mother. I was boring.

No longer! I declared to myself. It was time I did something I would never have considered doing in the past. I was going to sneak out of the house.

In the end, I didn't have to sneak. No one was around to stop me. Priscilla most likely believed that simply telling me to stay put would be enough to make me stay put. She obviously had forgotten what restless teenagers can be like. Besides, I was also an adult now, and I could come and go as I pleased. I needed to remember that.

He was waiting for me just inside the boundaries of the forest. He stood there quietly, yet he still managed to manifest a presence that was alive, that simmered with emotion. He was the kind of person I suddenly wanted desperately to be. He wouldn't let others take advantage of him or insult him, and he most certainly would not care what people thought of him. He lived life according to his own rules.

And he *thrived.*

"You defied me the first time I called to you," was his terse greeting to me. His striking features floated above a long-sleeved, white shirt, buttoned and hanging loosely, the soft material framing a silver medallion that lay against his luminescent skin like a medal of honor.

"I did?"

"No one defies me." Even in the dusky light his beautiful face was striking; his lush lips and fevered cheeks glowed as though a fire blazed inside him. I thought that if I were to touch his skin it would be hot, that it might burn me. Yet at the same time, he seemed cold and distant. I couldn't make him out—his endless contrasts.

"That wasn't defiance. I simply come and go as I please." That sounded like something a plucky heroine right out of a Jane Austen novel would say. I liked it.

"Even at the risk of angering me?"

I breathed in the heavy air and lightning sparks slid down my throat. "At the risk of angering anybody." The time to stand up and be counted had arrived. Bad timing, though, I quickly realized. This was a man who would not like being thwarted. Still, in for a penny, in for a pound.

To my surprise, he laughed. "I cannot figure you out, Evalina. Others are so easy to read."

"What are looking to read in me?" I had no idea that I was hiding something.

"I want to know why I don't see fear in you."

I shrugged. "I guess I'm tired of being afraid."

"Others—I can taste their fear. It's so strong, it flavors the air."

"Why do others fear you?"

He scanned my face. "I would think that would be obvious."

I frowned. "Don't tell me you're a bully."

For the first time since I met him, I caught a hint of uncertainty in his eyes. "I do not need to be a bully, as you say, Evalina," he responded coolly. "I simply am. That is enough."

"You *are* a bully!" Announcing my opinion, I found, was startlingly easy to do. I liked the taste and feel of the words in my mouth. Like hot fudge on cold ice cream. "You use your power—however you got it—to get what you want without concern for other people's feelings. That's being a bully."

"Come with me. I want to show you something."

I stared at him. Had words come out of my mouth? Had he heard a single thing I'd said? "And if I don't want to?"

"I will draw your aunts' attention to your missing presence."

"How would you do that?"

"I have my ways."

Strangely enough, I didn't doubt that he *did* have his ways. At the same time, I promptly decided that I didn't want my aunts to know I was out here in the woods. Not that I was afraid of them, I just didn't want my time with the stranger to end. "All right, I'll go. Lead away." A frisson of nervous excitement fluttered inside my stomach. It felt like what I imagined hummingbird wings would feel like against my cheek.

He studied me for a few breathless moments, as though trying to figure me out, then turned and strode through the trees. He either had long legs or was following a path I could not see because it wasn't long before he left me behind in the darkening woods.

"Hello?" I called out, though not as loudly as I should have. I was foolish to have left the house to go with a strange man into the woods. Alone with him now, I felt the vulnerability of my position very keenly.

"I'm right here," he pointed out. I looked to my left. He was standing beside me.

"How did you get there?" I gasped. "You were way ahead of me!"

"Do you want to dwell on inanities or do you want to see what I have to show you?"

I wrapped my arms around myself, suddenly trembling. "I think I should go back."

He frowned. The movement arched his golden eyebrows into V's, making him look particularly devilish. "Why would you want to do that?"

"I'm not sure I should be here."

The frown flew away. He looked quite happy now. "You *are* scared."

Though I'd been afraid of him before, it wasn't fear of him now that was driving me away. There was something else, something hovering between us that caught hold of my sensible, rational side like a hook and made me rethink my presence here. "No, not quite. I admit I'm nervous about the storm, but I'm not scared of you."

"Damnit, you should be!"

I took a step back from him. A dead branch broke beneath my foot—a shotgun blast in the still wood. I bit my lip hard, tasting blood. "I'm going back to the house. If you try to stop me, I'll—"

He strode toward me, stopping only a few inches from where I stood. His gaze took in the blood on my lip, then he peered into my eyes. "You'll what?"

"I'll never speak to you again." It was a lame threat, but it was all I had. I turned to go and he did not follow.

"Now you won't get to see my surprise."

"I'll be back," I told him. "When you're ready to behave."

Spinning away from him, I hurried out of the woods, praying not to get lost. Behind me, his laughter rang out, but he didn't try to stop me. Once inside the house, heart beating fast and hard, I headed straight for the kitchen. I needed Bessie's no-nonsense presence to make me right again.

"Couldna stay away from me, could you?" Bessie cackled, as she stirred the contents in a cast-iron pot on the stove. The room was warm and pleasantly pungent with onion and garlic and I felt my clenched jaw relax even as the thunder crashed overhead.

"You've discovered my secret," I said with a grin. My lip smarted and I pulled out a white kerchief to dab at the blood. "Should you really be doing that?" I asked, as I approached her, folding the spotted white cotton into a square and tucking it into my pocket. "Remember how we talked about your malfunctioning vision and how you might end up poisoning us all?"

"I remember," she grumbled, her shoulders hunched secretively. "But I've yet to poison anyone."

"Hey, what's going on?" I demanded when she didn't turn around. "You're up to something, I can tell."

"You'd better not laugh," she warned, as she slowly shuffled about to face me. I blinked. A pair of ancient spectacles, which had probably been the first ever invented, sat on her humpy nose.

"Where did you get those?" I asked, struggling to maintain a straight face. If I thought she looked odd before…

"They're me da's old specs. He's dead so I figured he willna be needin' 'em anymore."

I choked back a hysterical urge to giggle. "I imagine you're right."

She went back to stirring, steam rising from the pot's mysterious depths like witchy imps. The brew smelled delicious…chicken and dumplings, I deduced. So Bessie could cook, after all.

"So you had to go and poke the beast, did you?" she spoke up.

I jumped, startled. How could she already know about the stranger, about our meeting in the woods? I glanced around the kitchen. The lone window didn't look out over the front lawn so how had she seen me? "I didn't mean to…"

"Oh, yes, you did. And you did a good job of it. I never laughed so hard in me life. Course I couldna do it out loud, listenin' at the door as I were. Did you really meet Nate Thorndike himself? He's harder to track down than a bogle. He keeps to himself, that one. Canna say I blame him."

I breathed a surreptitious sigh of relief. She didn't know about my sneaking out of the house. It seemed a silly thing to worry about, but I couldn't help feeling as though I'd done something wrong. "I'm not surprised," I remarked casually. "Being that he thinks he's better than everyone else."

"Now I wouldna be sayin' that." I looked at her, astonished. She didn't see my expression, busy as she was with her pot stirring, but she seemed to sense it. "Oh, aye. He's an elusive one, but he has his reasons for keepin' to himself."

"Such as…"

The door banged open. "What do you have on your face?" Kelli demanded, staring at Bessie.

"I might ask the same of you," Bessie growled, bending down to pull a loaf of bread from the oven. I felt a waft of warm air on my cheeks. It looked like real bread. Things were definitely improving around here.

"You're such a grump. I hope those ridiculous things help you with your cooking because they certainly don't improve your looks. Or is she doing all this?" She pointed a fat finger at me.

"I just got here."

She narrowed her vulpine eyes. "*Just* got here? Then where were you all this time? I just came from your room, and I checked everywhere else in this dump."

I gazed at her innocently. "I was in my room, and then I came down to the kitchen. We must have missed each other." Apparently, unable to wait until dinner to further grill me on my talk with Nate, Kelli had decided to track me down. She apparently had trouble delaying gratification, like a child. But I could handle children. Of course, I was also bigger than most of them. Kelli, on the other hand, easily outweighed me by a good twenty-five or thirty pounds.

"How long has she been here?" she demanded of Bessie.

Bessie shrugged. "I'm old. Time has no meanin' to me."

Kelli stewed. "Fine. Be that way." She turned on me like a lawyer cross-examining a witness. "I want to know what you talked about with Nat." Subtle, she was not.

I shrugged. "I don't really remember. The weather came up, I'm sure. Then we discussed the feud between the Thorndikes and the Filmores. I think that topic filled up the rest of the time."

Her full cheeks brightened. "What did he say about the feud? Did he tell you it was all a big mistake? It happened centuries ago, you know, and has nothing to do with our generation. Did he say that?"

"You look upset, Aunt Kelli," I murmured sympathetically—a tactic I used on my mother when she was being particularly trying.

Fury widened her nostrils, the same reaction my mother displayed. "I am not upset, I'm just curious!" Plump fists clenched, knuckles white, she tried visibly to calm down, though she wasn't doing a very good job at it. Her round face looked like a cherry tomato about to split from the heat of the sun.

"Well, he didn't want to come into the house, I remember that part."

She tried to laugh. "Nat is always making jokes. He's a real prankster, our Nattie! Isn't he, Bessie?" Bessie only scowled.

"Funny. He didn't strike me as the mischievous type."

"Did he mention me?" She waited avidly for my answer, and I began to feel as though I were the main course at a cannibal convention.

"By name?"

"Yes, by name, you git!" She stomped her sandal for emphasis.

"I only ask because at one point, he said, 'we just do not get along.' He could have been talking about you, Aunt Kelli, though he didn't actually say your name."

Really, I was enjoying this far too much.

A noise like a cat being strangled gurgled through her fleshy, red lips. "I'm going to kill him!"

"But I thought you two were an item. That *is* what you implied in the parlor, isn't it? When we were having tea?"

Bessie, who'd been laying low in order to listen in, snorted, unable to help herself. "An item? The chances of those two bein' together are about as high as me marryin' bonny Prince Charles. Now, if you two dunna mind, I'd like to serve dinner." She pushed the loaded cart toward the dining room.

I hurried ahead of her and held the door open. Kelli looked like she was on the verge of grabbing a butcher knife and plunging it through my chest, and I thought it would be a good idea to put something solid between us. As I sat down in my usual chair, Kelli stormed past me and flounced into hers, glaring at me from a distance as she gulped down a mouthful of wine. I pretended not to notice as I unfolded my crisp linen napkin and placed it over my lap, though my fingers were trembling and my throat felt tight. Served me right.

"He didn't really say that, did he?" she demanded, making me wonder if she was desperate, masochistic, or slow. Probably all three.

"Didn't really say what?" Priscilla asked, as she sauntered through the door on the other side of the room. When she sat at her usual place, back erect and expression blank as beach sand, Bones left her side to get his own dinner in the kitchen.

"She says Nat told her that he and I don't get along!" Kelli huffed.

"I didn't say *that*," I protested, as Bessie served me with tedious slowness, making no secret that she was listening to the conversation. By the satisfied look on her face, I judged she was enjoying the show.

"It's true, though, whoever said it," Priscilla pointed out. "Nathaniel finds you annoying, Kelli."

"And he thinks *you're* frigid."

Frantic to stifle a howl of laughter, I took a sip of water and it went down the wrong pipe. I started coughing and wheezing and Bessie had to beat me on the back until I recovered. When she determined that I would live, she served Kelli, who'd been watching me struggle to catch my breath with a morbid fascination. Distracted by the sight of what looked like edible food on her plate, she turned her attention away from me and dug in. When everyone was eating, Bessie shuffled back

to the safety of the kitchen. The moment she was out of sight, a muffled, metallic ring came from Priscilla's direction.

She looked down. "Who could be ringing at this hour?"

"You can't answer it," Kelli sneered. "You said no phone calls at the
table. Your rule, you know."

Priscilla opened the phone to see who it was. When she saw the
number on the screen, a self-satisfied smile lifted the corners of her
pale mouth. "I think this time we can make an exception." She pressed
a button, then brought the phone up to her ear. "Nathaniel..." she
positively purred, and I started nervously, realizing I thought it might
be my father calling. "What a pleasure!"

Her face flushed as she spoke. "Why, yes. I could do that. Oh, yes. I
mean, we could do that. I'd love to. Tomorrow evening then. Seven-
ish? I'll be there. And Nathaniel, I do look forward to it." She turned
off the phone, her expression coolly triumphant.

"What was that all about?" Kelli snapped. She had picked up a thick
slice of bread and was tearing it to pieces while Priscilla spoke on the
phone. She now proceeded to shove the chunks into her mouth.

"Nathaniel invited me to dinner tomorrow evening. He thought he
and I should talk."

"You said 'we' on the phone," Kelli accused around the gluey wad of
bread.

"Did I?" Priscilla frowned, her thin, upper lip curled in annoyance.
"Oh, yes. You two were invited, as well."

I sat up, startled. Nate had magically transformed from a man who
couldn't remain in the same train car with me to a welcoming neighbor
inviting us all to dinner. I thought he'd wanted nothing to do with me,
or Priscilla and Kelli. So why the sudden change of heart? Unless he'd
been teasing me about the feud. Come to think of it, for wanting to
avoid the aunts, it seemed he had an awful lot of contact with them.
Maybe he really did like them.

Kelli's eyes squinted cunningly. "I know what I'm going to wear.
That green number I have—the one that shows off my ass...ets to
their very best." She snickered lewdly.

Priscilla's pale orbs flicked upward in disgust. "Do you always have to
be so common?"

"That's not common, Prissy, that's common sense. I haven't met a
man yet who could resist the girls." She peered down at her ample
bosom. My eyes followed hers, then realized where they were going
and flew back to my soup. Like she needed more admirers of her
'girls.'

"What did he want to talk about?" I asked Priscilla.

"He didn't say…" She looked thoughtful as she spoke, no doubt pondering the mystery and finding its imagined resolution to her liking. Undoubtedly she believed Nate wanted to propose to her. Kelli probably cherished the same idea. She looked very smug at the moment, and perhaps even dreamy, fantasizing about the wedding dress she'd wear, how many flower girls to have, and only one bridesmaid, of course, to keep the attention fully focused on her and the *girls*.

Nate's invitation distracted them from making good on their implied threat to interrogate me about my conversation with him. Priscilla pushed food around her plate, the fork making metallic scrapes against the ceramic as she surreptitiously contemplated her bare left ring finger. Kelli ate with ever-increasing enthusiasm.

Neither one spoke much beyond saying 'yes' or 'no' to Bessie's next dish. She, of course, was immediately suspicious as she took in Kelli shining moonbeams from her eyes and Priscilla's unusual preoccupation. I mouthed to her that I'd tell her about it later. She had to be satisfied with that, though I noticed the last two courses came and went very quickly.

When Priscilla excused herself, Kelli hurried after her. Before she left the room, she whispered something to her sister and they both turned to look at me. Not a pleasant look—a very calculating one, in fact. I felt like the chicken about to get its head chopped off. I liked that look about as much as the chicken did.

Chapter Ten

✳

An Engagement

After the aunts left the dinner table, I realized that a long evening stretched before me. The storm had hit not long after Nate's call, so I couldn't go for a walk, and as far as I could tell, there was no communal television, so mindless entertainment wouldn't be my savior.

Not that I'd be able to focus on TV anyway; too many mysteries whirled around in my head. First of all, who was the stranger, and what had he wanted to show me this afternoon? Second, what was going on with Nate and his seeming change of heart? Third, what were the aunts up to? And finally, were all of them in on some kind of conspiracy to drive me crazy?

I'd seen the movie *Gaslight*—several times, in fact, since my mother forced me to watch the old film with her every time it came on the Movie Scene Channel—so I was mentally prepared for anything they might try. Still, I was alone here. There'd be no Inspector Cameron from Scotland Yard to save me. I was on my own.

To take my mind off my troubles, I thought I'd go help Bessie in the kitchen. Besides, she was surely about to burst if I didn't tell her what was going on. I finished my pudding, which was much better than the apple pie, and hurried into the kitchen.

"Nate invited us to dinner," I told her, as I set my dirty dishes on the counter and took over scrubbing the black pot, which looked like it hadn't been washed in a decade. I'd heard of seasoning the pot, but the thick layer of crud coating its bottom was taking it a little too far.

"Well, 'tis a miracle." She looked me up and down through her new specs as she dried a baking dish. "A man's mind is a mirk mirror, mind you. Perhaps he wants to be makin' it up to you."

"Making what up to me?"

"Whatever he did to make you so mad at him. A man's hat in his hand never did him no harm."

"Hmmm…" I replied noncommittally, mainly because I wasn't exactly sure what she was talking about.

Bessie cackled and picked up a pan to dry. As we worked, I asked her how she'd come to be here in England. She told me about her home in Scotland, how she'd been in service since age eleven, ever since her mother and father died in a farm accident. "Both got caught in a baler. It were awful to see, and all I could do to keep me sisters from seein' it, too." Her two older brothers went to work for an uncle, along with her two younger sisters, who were still moldable. The aunt didn't much care for Bessie, nor did Bessie much care for her.

"Tain't no one could mold me," she stated firmly and I believed her. She came to work for the Filmores after her long-time employer, a Mrs. Scott, passed away. Her husband, Mr. Scott, had no use for Bessie, but he was a kind man and put an ad in the paper for her. "He gave me excellent references and I were truly grateful to him for that." Unfortunately, he didn't realize what the Filmores, touring Scotland on their honeymoon, were truly like. They took care to hide their worst qualities. Bessie only learned their true nature her first night in England. "Mrs. Filmore locked me in me room for pullin' her hair while brushin' it. It were only a little tug, but she was a pulin' creature, I'm sorry to tell you. And she had herself a temper."

"I'm sorry you had to go through that, Bessie." Living with Priscilla and Kelli didn't seem to be any improvement in her lot, either. Just thinking about the name Kelli had called Bessie, and the accusations the aunts both made about the poor woman being lazy and shifty, made me furious. A person need only take one look at her and know she was a hard worker—the hours of back-breaking labor had leached the strength from her bones and etched deep lines into her face.

"It were a long time ago, bairn. Don't fuss yerself." She set the pan down on the stove and picked up another, her story seemingly forgotten.

"I was wondering, Bessie," I spoke into an extended silence that had fallen while we worked, "if you could tell me anything about my fath—" A loud jangling sound interrupted me. She looked confused for a moment, then scowled when the sound shrilled again.

"That be the devil himself." She scuttled over to a corner and lifted the black receiver of an old rotary phone to her ear. "What?" she barked into the mouthpiece. "She just might." She handed the phone to me, the long, curled cord stretching like a rubber band. "It's for you. I'm done here so I'll be headin' up to me room. There's a show on the telly I've been wantin' to see all week. It's an Agatha Christie murder mystery!" Her eyes glowed with anticipation, and I wished I could join her.

I lifted the heavy piece to my ear. "Hello?"

"Why won't you get a cell phone?"

"Hello, Mother." Bessie had to be clairvoyant. It *was* the devil herself. "How are you? I'm fine. Thank you for asking. My flight was good, the plane didn't crash anyway, and I made it here okay." I didn't bother explaining, *again*, that I didn't have a cell phone because I had no one to call, or who would want to call me.

"Well, I wouldn't be talking to you if you hadn't made it. Your father is worried."

"About me?" I felt both confused and suspicious. Something wasn't right here. He never worried about me.

"He wants to know what his sisters are saying about him."

Ah, mystery explained. "They're not telling me anything. They're as bad as he is."

"You need to find out."

"Find out what?"

"What they're planning."

"How do you know they're planning something?"

"Your father thinks they are."

"Is he the least bit worried about me?"

"You know how your father is…"

"Distant and unreachable?"

"Exactly."

"Well, are *you* worried about me?"

She snorted. "I raised you better than that."

"You didn't raise me, Mother, you heckled me."

"And look how well you turned out."

I wiped facetiously at an invisible tear. It was the closest thing to a compliment I'd ever received from her. "That's really nice, Mother. I can feel the love."

"You'd better. It's all you're going to get from me. Now," she went on, resuming a brusque air. "Be a dear and find out what those two wenches are up to."

"You think Dad doesn't know?"

I could see her shrugging on the other side of the Atlantic. "Humor him."

"That's what I've been doing all my life. I'm not sure I like being his sacrificial lamb. His sisters aren't exactly Aunt Bea material."

"Well, after being raised by me, you should know exactly how to handle them." Was there a slight quake in her voice?

"You weren't *that* bad," I forced out, feeling guilty.

She laughed. "You almost got that out without a hint of sarcasm in your voice, Evie." She took a drag on a cigarette—a deep rush of air pulled in, then pushed out again, right into my ear. She allowed herself one cigarette a day, which meant she could tell people she didn't smoke. "Just find out what they're up to, all right? I've got to go. I went to a party at the Brecht's the other night and wanted to give them a call to thank them for boring me to death. They're such snobs, but they have excellent connections in the business. Their son is a producer and he's putting together a new TV show. This might be my big break."

Poor mother. I admired her tenacity, but her blindness to reality was kind of sad. "I'll see what I can do." This was stated more for her benefit than my father's.

"Good. Ring my cell when you have something."

"Good luck with the producer."

"Oh, luck has nothing to do with it, my dear," she said in a Mae West drawl. "It's all in how you flaunt your goods."

"Goodbye, Mother." She was already gone.

I hung up the phone and stood staring at it for a moment, feeling strange. My father, who never gave away much of anything, other than when he was acting, was showing nerves. If he was worried enough to get Mother to appeal to me for help, he must be scared. The thought made my hands shake a little—at first from fear, then from anger.

First of all, he'd allowed me to go to England knowing his sisters were up to something, possibly something *dangerous*. I couldn't believe he would knowingly have done that to me. It seemed so thoughtless and cruel, as though he were the evil villain in a play rather than my father. I rubbed at my aching temples. Why had I spent my entire life trying to impress him, hoping desperately to have his attention on me, just for a token I could cherish later when I was alone? *What a stupid waste*, my thoughts flashed, *all that energy and worry. All for nothing!* I would never be able to do enough to please him because he couldn't be pleased. He didn't give a crap about me. All he cared about was his career, his fans, and my mother, likely in that order. I didn't even exist to him!

The truth of this shrieked in my ears. My fists curled into tight balls and my head filled with rage. I felt an overwhelming urge to scream, to release the crazed demons swarming inside my head.

Tired of fighting, I gave in. The roar started in my chest, nearly suffocating me in its hurry to escape. I wanted to start smashing things, expensive things.

Let it go, Evalina, a voice inside me pushed. *Show your power.* A wild howl shot up my rage-swollen throat and—

The phone clamored next to me and I swallowed the scream, leaving a painful lump in my throat.

"What is it now, Mother?" I hollered into the receiver, feeling a desperate urge to cry, but I swallowed that, too.

"Evie?" a voice murmured softly, and a sudden chill froze my anger. Was it the stranger calling me? "Is that you?"

"Who is this?" I demanded, my voice cracking. My emotional swing had made me dizzy. To steady myself, I stared at the old clock, minus its minute hand, hung on the wall in front of me. The remaining hand moved from second to second with a reassuring click, click, click.

"It's Nate." This time his voice came through strong and clear.

"Oh. I thought you were—"

"Your mother. Yes, I kind of got that."

"Sorry."

"Don't mention it."

"So why were you whispering?" I asked.

"Hm? I wasn't exactly…I mean, there was probably something wrong with my mobile. Bad connection, I'm sure." He paused. "Listen, I wanted to be sure you received my invitation to dinner."

"Yes, I did. My aunt passed it along."

"Priscilla likes her schedule so I knew if I called at dinnertime I'd catch her when others were around. I figured she couldn't pretend I asked only her, especially not with Kelli at the table. That woman can sniff out a lie like a wild pig hunting for truffles. Probably because she tells so many herself."

"I-I-" I was stunned. "I thought maybe you were only teasing me about not liking them…after you invited them to dinner."

"I told you I don't like being thought of as a coward. Since I didn't take you up on your challenge to come into the house, I decided to have them come into mine."

"This is about salvaging your pride, then." *And has nothing to do with me*, I finished in my head. I quickly blinked back tears. Self-pity, I was beginning to realize, along with the requisite weeping, was tiring, and at the moment I didn't have the energy to indulge in it.

"Put that way… Well, it makes me sound like a self-centered prig."

"Oh, dear. Does it?"

"No need to be sarcastic. I want to prove to you that I'm not afraid of your aunts."

"Why do you care?"

There was silence. "Because my dog stole your scone?"

I laughed lightly. "You could've just sent some scones."

"I wish I'd known that before I invited your aunts to dinner."

I couldn't help myself, I laughed again. "Well, now you're stuck with all three of us."

"I won't say I'm looking forward to it."

"I respect your honesty."

"I did want to ask you something, Evie. About what I've been hearing around the village." He sounded both wary and embarrassed.

"Yes?"

"I'm having trouble believing it myself. I think there's been some mistake. Very likely, actually."

"Spit it out, Nate." I flinched. I sounded exactly like my mother. Come to think of it, I was sounding more and more like her since coming to England.

"All right, then. Did you really brave the Wrath?"

I sighed. This again. "I really couldn't tell you, Nate. If it's that stretch of woods between the moors and the path to the village, then yes, I guess I did. Though I don't feel like I was braving anything. There wasn't any other way to go. The taxi driver dropped me off at what seemed to be the top of the world, giving me little choice. Well, there was a choice, but I was kind of jetlagged at the time, so I took the road less traveled." I was rambling.

"There's a reason it's not well-traveled, Evie."

"So I'm starting to gather. Why is that?"

"Strange things happen in those woods. People get hurt and then don't remember what happened, or if they do, they go mad with their knowledge, or they just plain disappear. Anyone who builds anything in the Wrath had better count on a battle, though nobody is fool enough to build there after what happened to the Allertons. The Wrath doesn't take kindly to interlopers and the villagers here respect that."

The heat of the kitchen suddenly grew stifling. "What happened to the Allertons?"

"They built a grand manor in the Wrath and after that came the trouble. Broken furniture, carpets stained with dirt and rotten tomatoes, spoiled food, a garden trampled to bits, cut up clothes, and shoves from out of nowhere. It soon became apparent that the Allertons were not wanted there."

"But who did it?" My voice came out a whisper.

"I couldn't say…"

Couldn't or wouldn't? "Sounds to me like something out of a storybook."

"This is no story, Evie."

No. I was learning that. "So the Wrath is a *place?*"

"In a manner of speaking."

"Are there any houses there now?"

There was a momentary silence, filled with Nate's mental gymnastics as he tried to suss out what I wanted to hear. "Not that I know of."

He was hiding something from me, but if I were to pursue what it was, I might give my own knowledge away. "Do you believe in the Wrath, Nate?"

"I didn't use to."

"Something made you change your mind."

"Yes." A succinct response in a tone that warned against pursuit.

"There must be some people who have had nothing happen to them when they went into the woods."

"None...until now. Which brings me back to my point. Are you sure you went through those woods?"

"I thought I did. It's all rather fuzzy. I entered them at five o'clock and didn't emerge until over two hours later. The problem is, it didn't seem like I was in the woods that long." I recalled the stranger's mentioning our conversation. According to him, I'd said a lot. I didn't pass this information along to Nate. I didn't want him to know about the stranger. I wasn't sure I could trust him. I wasn't sure about anything.

"Just don't go near those woods again," he ordered. I didn't respond; instead my teeth worked at the wound on my lower lip, inviting more blood to flow. I could taste it—salt and iron. "Do you hear me, Evie?" He had returned to his old, officious self.

"I still don't see why *I* shouldn't go into the woods. Aunt Priscilla told me the same thing, but nothing happened to me, so what do I have to worry about?"

"I have to agree with Priscilla about this." He coughed, as though simply speaking the words irritated his throat. At least, I hoped that's what was happening. I didn't want him to like Priscilla, or anybody, for that matter. "I want to know more, but I have... Well, I have an engagement to attend to. See you tomorrow?"

"Tomorrow," I agreed.

But tomorrow didn't work out.

Chapter Eleven

✳

Imprisoned

With uncommon energy, I spent the rest of the evening stewing about all the people in my life who felt they had a right to tell me what to do. The more I thought about how much people treated me like I was their own personal puppet, the angrier I grew.

Stay out of the woods, Evie.
Go to England, Evie.
Find out what your aunts are planning, Evie.
Come with me, Evalina.
All very infuriating.

My anger energized me, made me feel like a new person, and I stoked its flames. I would go into those woods whenever I wanted. I would find out what my aunts were planning, but for my sake, not for anyone else's. If my father wanted to know what they were up to, he could come here and find out for himself. And if the stranger wanted to impress me, he was going to have to try a lot harder.

My thoughts about Nate fell into a category all to themselves, mainly because after rehashing our conversation, I decided he angered me most of all—though not for any rational reason I could nail down. Maybe I just hated that he, like Priscilla, thought he could tell me what to do. I also didn't like that he'd invited the aunts to his house just to salvage his injured ego. Really, if he wanted to make things up to me, he could've invited me—alone. As far as I knew, he *did* like one of the aunts and was using me as a means to further his cause with her.

Urgh! I had a good mind not to go.

I fell asleep with visions of hatchets and knives dancing in my head. These hostile images set the mood for my dreams—the aunts performing satanic rituals over my body, Nate hunting me down, then trampling me under Heathcliff's hooves, all the while laughing evilly.

Thunder rumbled overhead and I sat up in bed to a dull, gray morning. Nine o'clock, my watch told me. I had slept in, but didn't feel the least bit rested. Nevertheless, I didn't want to go back to sleep, not knowing what I might return to. I could still see Nate's demonic face, hear his cold laughter.

A warm bath helped sort me out, but not as much as I would have liked. Dressing warmly, I donned gray wool pants and a black turtleneck that kept out the chill—though that was about all my outfit could do for me. A suit of armor would have been a better choice for how I felt today. When I wasn't in battle, I could simply go stand in a corner and watch the world go by.

My stomach protested against that option. I was hungry. Typically, heroines in gothic romances lost their appetites during times of trouble; mine only seemed to increase. I headed for the kitchen where I found a crumpled note, the handwriting tiny and cramped, on the table.

Gone to visit me great-Aunt Grear, a real pain in the arse, but who's got lots of money tucked away somewhere. Yer own aunts went shopping in Newton Abbot for fancy get-ups for the big dinner tonight. I expect to hear about everything when I get back. Though you can leave out the boring bits.

There was no signature, but there needn't be.

I was alone in the house, but for how long? I ate a quick breakfast of burnt toast and loads of butter and marmalade to soften the blow—I'd been daydreaming and the wonky toaster had made quick work of my bread. I figured I had at least a couple hours to see if I could find out what Priscilla and Kelli were up to. Most shops didn't open until ten o'clock and then the aunts would have to drive home, Newton Abbot being a good half hour away. There should be enough time for me to search through a couple rooms, maybe hunt down an attic. Attics could always be counted on for hiding treasures, and secrets. That's why I loved them.

Armed with a dented silver flashlight and a flathead screwdriver, both discovered on a dusty shelf over the stove, I went in search of Priscilla's room, the screwdriver held out before me like a sword, the flashlight lifted high in the air in case I needed to knock someone, or some-*thing*, over the head with it. Nobody was supposed to be home, but I wasn't taking any chances.

Back in the main hall, I picked a staircase opposite the one leading up to my room and followed it upward. The numerous steps led me to a different wing of the house, noticeable in that it overlooked the side yard and a pond choked with weeds. At the top of the landing, a single multi-paned window let in a bit of light despite the dark clouds. This part of the house was much more posh than where the aunts had put me up. This had to be where they lived.

A mixture of musk and sweet smoke beckoned seductively, like a siren's curved finger, from a bedroom off to my left. The door had been left wide open, as though its occupant had knocked it aside in her rush to leave. I stepped inside and the competing sensations of stagnating hopes and chaos overwhelmed me. Clothes of velvet, chenille, spandex, and see-through crepe were everywhere—hanging from the white bedposts, strewn on the fuchsia shag rug, draped over a bright pink, plush loveseat. This had to be Kelli's room. A big-screen TV sat in a corner of the room, the shelves below its perch packed with DVDs. Half-full bottles of perfume and lotion, gaudy costume jewelry, and used cotton balls covered the top of a large make-up table. Magazine photos of David Beckham bordered the edges of the massive lighted mirror backing the table, and posters of various American pop stars intermingling with newspaper cut-outs of the royal princes, Harry and William, plastered the pink wall, giving the room an aura of adolescence as though Kelli had never moved beyond her teen years.

If there were anything of relevance to find here, it wouldn't be easy to root out. I slowly backed out of the room, afraid that if I were to turn my back on its gaping maw, it would grab me and pull me back in. Kelli had secrets, but most likely her room hid only those of the human kind. Condoms in a bedside drawer, joints in her jewelry box, perhaps some kinky sex toys in the closet. Fascinating stuff, but not anything I had time, or frankly, the desire, to snoop for.

Out in the hallway, I glanced down the dark corridor, feeling almost silly in my caution. In my defense, there was a sense of *lurking* here; a crawling feeling that creatures resided within the walls, in corners, behind bookshelves, watching my every move. I was only being smart, I defended myself, not dramatic.

I began creeping down the gloomy hall, my rubber soles squeaking on the hardwood floor, when a low, deep growl stopped me in my tracks. Stretched out before one of the tightly closed doors lay what I had thought was a shadow, but turned out to be Bones. He did not look pleased to see me. When he bared his teeth, I stopped, my flashlight and screwdriver aimed in the direction of his oversized muzzle.

"Good doggie," I wheedled, as I slowly backed away. "I'll just be going this way." He blinked steadily at me as I made my retreat.

I decided to head back to the foyer and give another set of stairs a shot. This time I chose one tucked down a long hall, in an unlit back corner. It seemed the most likely way to the attic and my heartbeat quickened in anticipation.

My footsteps made dull thumps on the worn wooden stairs, which were narrow and cobwebby and smelled of dust. The beam of my flashlight was dull—naturally—but bright enough to give me the courage to continue. At the top of the stairs, I found a door. Its painted white knob wrestled against me briefly before giving way with a screech to reveal a large open space. I stepped into the room. The air was cold up here and perfumed by the odor of mothballs. I sneezed several times.

The sound of rain pattering on the roof registered in my mind as I looked around. Droopy cardboard boxes, battered steamer trunks, and broken antique furniture littered the wide-planked floor—a dumping ground for all things unwanted. Directly in front of me a battered trunk took center stage. Treasure! I rushed across the dusty floor and kneeled down in front of it. When I opened the heavy lid a strong dose of mothballs overwhelmed me, setting off another round of sneezing.

After blowing my nose, I leaned forward again. Inside, I found stacks of men's attire fashioned in a style dating back twenty years. My father's? I dug around a bit beneath the piles, but gave up after finding nothing unusual. Only clothes lived here. Nothing human remained in the old fabric. Certainly no clues.

Behind the trunk, three cardboard boxes and one wooden crate were lined up like soldiers. If I were to guess, I would say Priscilla had put them here, unable to resist setting them in order. One open box held a trove of trophies for first place in a variety of sports, like polo and equestrianism, even golf. Someone, possibly my father himself, had scratched his name into the wood on the bottom of each trophy. I stared at the box in disbelief. My father was athletic? He knew how to ride a horse? I simply couldn't believe it. When he was not at the studio, or out to dinner with mother, he never left the apartment, preferring to hide away in his den. I had no idea what he did in there, but it certainly wasn't polo.

The next box, full of clipped newspaper articles, confirmed the story. Page after page regaled the prowess of Edmund Filmore, golden boy of Ellwood. The strange thing was that none of the articles showed photographs of the golden boy. I wanted to see what my father looked like as a young man, but the contents didn't satisfy my curiosity, only made it stronger, in fact. Either there had never been a picture included with the story, or someone had cut each article in such a way as to exclude the photo.

I quickly moved on to the next box—a pale wood crate—my curiosity humming. Prying the cover loose with the screwdriver, I was thrilled to find photo albums, at least six or seven of them, nestled inside. I started with the largest one, which was also the most worn, its blue leather covering faded and cracked. When I opened the book, my eyes settled immediately on several pictures of two young girls, stuck fast to the yellowed page.

One of the girls was fair and thin, the other chubby and red-haired. The photos on this page appeared to all have been taken on the same day. In every picture, both subjects looked discontent, even at such a young age. *Prissy and Kelli, 10 and 7*, someone had jotted beneath the photo. Not the oldest album, then, but interesting all the same. I turned another page.

Edmund, aged 12, caught my eye the quickest. My father. But when my eyes flitted upward to see his face, my stomach flipped. Where his head should have been only a hole remained. Someone had cut his face out of the photo. I flipped forward several more pages. On each one I found the same disfiguration, again and again, done with a ruthless determination that frightened me. Someone in this house was bent on making sure my father disappeared from the family archives.

Each subsequent album showed the same peculiarity. My guess, based purely on the neatness of the vandalism, was Priscilla. But why? Why not just get rid of all the pictures of him? Why desecrate them? Priscilla didn't seem like the type to harbor such anger or to do something so useless.

Feeling like I'd just dug up someone's grave I closed the album and put it away, then nailed the lid back on the box as precisely as I could with the screwdriver's handle. It was hard; my hands were shaking.

The last cardboard box was a surprise. Several recent press releases, photo ops, and newspaper stories, all dating from the past few months, of my father as I knew him—the actor—lined the bottom of the box. Every photo had been allowed to remain in the clipping, though someone had taken a black pen and scribbled over his face with a ferocity that left the paper in tatters as though a wild beast had attacked it, claws fully extended. I shuddered as I pushed the paper away. Kelli, this time?

Why did the aunts hate my father so much? What had he done to them? Did it have something to do with the Augustine affair? I wondered if there was a way to find out more about that name, about my father's life in Ellwood. I had a feeling the information wouldn't reside here in the attic. No, treasure like that would be kept locked up. Which brought me back to Priscilla's room...she must have something in there that would tell me what I wanted to know.

Getting Bones out of the house was the only snag in my plans. Maybe the stranger would help me out with that. He seemed to believe he owned the dog. Rather grandiose thinking, in my opinion, but Bones appeared to go along with it.

I closed up boxes and checked to see the trunk was secure, then, flashlight and screwdriver in hand, scuffed up the floor on my way out so the dust wouldn't look too disturbed. Back in the kitchen I made myself lunch. While I ate, I watched the rain fall outside—a steady sheet from the heavens. The sound might have been more relaxing sans the leaky faucet, which possessed the kitchen like a poltergeist. The irritating dripping did not help my thought processes, jumbled as they were. Based on what I'd found in the attic, someone quite obviously wanted all signs of my father erased. Well, not every sign, only one, in fact. They had kept his possessions, his trophies and newspaper clippings, but they had destroyed his face.

Destroy the image; destroy the man.

The scary part…from what I could determine, my aunts now accepted me as a substitute for my father. If he owed them something, and hadn't come to return what he'd taken, then they would take it from me—cut it from me, if necessary, as they had done his image from paper. But what would they do when they found out that I didn't have what they wanted? Seek revenge? If that were the case, I would truly become my father's sacrificial lamb.

My first instinct was to hole up in my room and wait for our dinner outing at Nate's house tonight. My second and third instincts agreed with the first and I hurried up to my room to hide out. Efforts to light the laid-out fire proved successful and I spent the afternoon putting logs on the fire, eating my rescued cookies, reading Daphne du Maurier, and taking turns thinking about Nate and the stranger. When I finally emerged from my sugar and fantasy-induced stupor, I saw that it was five o'clock. A car door slamming outside my window pulled me out of bed and over to the window to take a look.

The aunts had returned, along with several colorful shopping bags. The rain had stopped, leaving a wet haze. They hurried through the light fog to the house, looking almost furtive in their swift movements. When I heard them coming up the stairs to my room, Kelli's heavy tread and Priscilla's brisk one, I got a funny feeling in my stomach.

"Evalina?" Priscilla called through the door. "Are you in there?"

I stayed where I was, by the window, my arms crossed over my chest in a defensive posture. "Yes," I replied. Then louder, "Yes, I'm here."

"Good. Kelli and I have decided that it would be best for you to stay in tonight. You're definitely coming down with something. We could see it last night at dinner, when you were coughing. Perhaps it's just a cold, but one can never be too careful."

"That wasn't coughing," I told her, my fingernails digging into my skin. "My water went down the wrong pipe, that's all. I'm perfectly fine, not sick at all."

"Denial," Kelli diagnosed. "You coughed during tea the other day, too. After we're gone you can get yourself some soup and crackers. We'll leave a tin of chicken noodle on the counter."

"But I'm not sick!" I protested, wondering what they were up to. Then I sneezed—remnants from my dusty outing in the attic.

"I think you've just proved our point," Priscilla stated firmly. A click sounded near the door—a key turning in the lock. "I'll check on you when I get home."

"Did you just lock the door?" I hurried over and twisted the knob. The door didn't budge. I rattled the knob again, then pushed on the hard surface, slapping my hands against it when it didn't budge.

"I did, for your own safety. You are my responsibility and I won't have you running about as ill as you are."

"How am I supposed to get my soup, then?" It was an idiotic thing to ask, I suppose, but I was desperate and my thoughts were none too coherent. I kicked at the door, feeling trapped.

"I think for one night you can go without a meal. Isn't it starve a cold, feed a fever?"

"It's the other way around!" I kicked at the door again.

"Well, then aren't you glad she's not your mummy?" Kelli snickered.

"This is insane! You can't just lock me in here!"

"We can," Kelli retorted, "and we did."

"I'll let you out tomorrow," Priscilla promised. "When you're no longer contagious. Neither Kelli nor I can afford to get sick and miss the Festival. Remember, this is for your own good. Now get some sleep. I'm sure you'll feel better in the morning."

"What? Wait, wait!" I grabbed the doorknob with both hands and pulled. "You can't do this! Hey! Please…let me out!"

"Ta, ta," Kelli called. "Be a good girl!" Her voice faded with each spoken word and the follow-up laughter she let loose finally slipped away into nothingness. They were gone.

A frantic and thorough search turned up neither secret passages nor other doors anywhere in the room. I was stuck here, caged like an animal in a zoo. I now remembered why I hated zoos.

"You can't treat me this way!" I cried in a panic, as I paced back and forth. "I'll burn the house down!" Tempting though the idea was, it was entirely impractical, being that I was trapped inside the very house I was considering burning down. I plopped down on the bed and cradled my throbbing head between my cold, clammy hands.

The car doors slamming outside an hour later signaled the aunts' departure. I hurried to the window and watched them go; a sleek black Ferrari whisked them down the drive. Damn them. They had really done it.

I will make them suffer until they are dead, dead, dead.

I welcomed the words this time, like old friends come to comfort me. Where before they had seemed disturbingly inhuman, they now made a frightening sort of sense. Why not get them before they got me? Whatever it was that people saw in me—that doormat quality, that victim aura—was going to have to be put to death.

Forehead pressed against the cold windowpane, I breathed a circle of fog onto the glass. With a quivering finger, I traced the letters, D-I-E. When I saw what I'd written, I quickly swiped it away with my shirtsleeve. What was I thinking? What was happening to me?

An image appeared where the letters had been. I leaned forward. My golden stranger had arrived, and he was motioning to me to come. Even though this time I really wanted to go to him, I could not. I was locked in my room like a prisoner, with no foreseeable way out. The window was too high above the ground, the door was locked, and I'd left my ax in the States.

I gazed at him, raising my hands in the air and shrugging to convey the unwilling message, "I can't come." Disappointed, I turned to glare at the door that was now my enemy. A second later, the lock clicked and the door swung open.

I was free.

Chapter Twelve

*

Gabriel

I did not question how the stranger had opened the door, if he had done so in the first place. Old houses, coupled with fires in fire-places drying out the wood...well, stranger things have happened. It didn't matter anyway. What mattered was that I was out of the house and running across the lawn, free as anyone.

This time I was ready to go with him wherever he should want to take me. I felt stronger now, more sure of myself. I could handle him. I could handle all of this. The rest of them had better hope they could handle me.

He stood, much like last time, just inside the woods. Each time we met, I noticed something else about him—his ever-changing ocean eyes and golden hair at our first meeting, his crisp white shirt and antique silver medallion at our second. I felt like with each visit he solidified and became more real. Today I noticed a small mole below his left eye, but otherwise his skin was smooth, devoid of age. He held a flute in his hand. It was a beautiful piece, carved out of a dark, rich wood, and shaped like a snake, the mouthpiece its head. He raised the flute to his lips, still moist from playing, and tapped out a little tune. My heart fluttered along with the notes, like a butterfly flitting from flower to flower.

He lowered it again. "Do you play?"

I shook my head regretfully. "My mother wanted me to learn an instrument, but I never found one that suited me. I was never good enough at anything I tried."

The flute disappeared into a leather pouch he wore at his hip. "You weren't going to come at first."

"My aunts locked me in my room."

"They did?"

"But I got out."

An eyebrow quirked upward. "Obviously. What I'd like to know is how you managed that."

"The key turned in the lock and the door opened."

Instead of looking smug, as I thought he would, he looked momentarily puzzled. "Your aunts must have unlocked the door before they left, or not locked it properly in the first place. Maybe they never locked it at all."

I studied him. Any of those things could have happened. But, while it made the least amount of sense, I had the feeling that *he* was the one who had done something to open the door. Yet, unless I believed in magic or that he had someone working for him, I was going to have to accept that he couldn't have done anything. He'd been standing at the edge of the woods, several hundred yards away from the house at the time the lock clicked and the door opened. No one could move that fast. Still, he was so sure of himself that I wanted to think he had rescued me; that I was important enough to save.

"If they did unlock the door—and yes, it was locked—it was done very quietly."

He took a step toward me. "Don't you hate them for doing that to you?"

I pulled my shoulders back. "I'm starting to."

His darkened features lit up, his sea eyes glowed bright green, then quivered to blue. "Good. Hatred is better than giving in, and engaging in battle always trumps retreat."

My heart beat a little harder. "Your motto is make war, not love?"

The secretive smile came again. "Not always. But if war is what it takes to win, then I will wage war. And woe be to those who do not heed my counsel."

I laughed. "How biblical of you."

The frown returned; his eyes stormed. "Are you ready to see what I wanted to show you?" His voice was nearly thunderous, his cheekbones painted with heat.

My chest constricted and my doubts returned, yet still I said, "I think so."

He relaxed. "Then come with me. This time you had better take my hand. It is so easy to get lost in these woods." He smiled, his cherry red lips almost sinful in their fullness.

He held out his hand to me. Long, tapered fingers, strong and assured, reached toward me, certain of their acceptance. My own hand floated slowly, hesitantly, out to meet him halfway. When our skin made contact, he grabbed hold of my outstretched hand like a trapdoor spider, startling me. My body flushed hot, then cold, and back to hot again. He gazed at me intently; his expression unsettled.

I swallowed hard. "Shall we go?" My voice came out barely a whisper.

His warm hand tightened its grip on mine. He did not answer, merely pulled me along after him. I ran to keep up, loath to lose our connection. His power surged through me, a steady throbbing in my veins. With him by my side, I could do anything.

After a few minutes of silence, we stopped walking. "Close your eyes," he whispered.

When I responded too slowly, his hand slipped up and covered my eyes for me, my nose and mouth, as well, so that his skin heated my lips. I breathed in the scent of him—musky patchouli and rich earth. My heart tap-danced with the thrill of this strange new world he was offering to me. My mind and body merged and rational thought was blown away.

When he took away his hand, the dizzying sensation of oneness heightened. Before me a wonderland of sparkling lights filled the misty woods. Spots of luminescence were everywhere, flitting and flickering like a fantastical city set against the night sky.

"Fireflies!" I cried in delight. "I saw them at the manor. I've only seen them once before, when we spent a summer in Minnesota. I loved that summer." I sighed wistfully, remembering the time I'd spent in the wild city park, when I'd fallen in love with nature. "English fireflies are bigger," I noted. "Much bigger, actually. It must be all the rain you get here. They grow like insects in a rainforest."

He threw me an amused look—almost father to child. "Something like that."

My joy faded. I hated being patronized; my mother was an expert at it. She reveled in treating me like a child. "Why did you do that?"

"Do what?" He looked genuinely confused.

"You looked at me like I was a silly child."

"I was merely enjoying your innocence."

I bit my lip in frustration, touching on the sore spot. I hadn't expected him to say that. Thrown off stride, I changed the subject. "I still don't know your name, you know."

"I am called many things," he said. "None of them flattering."

"Well, I need to call you something."

"What name would you give me?"

I thought about it, finally choosing a name I'd always liked. "Gabriel."

He threw back his head and laughed, a delightfully lively roar. He became human to me in that instant and I relaxed. Before this moment, I'd been wondering if he and I were of the same species. He seemed to me both worldly and otherworldly.

His eyes sparkled. "Yes, call me Gabriel. I would like that."

"I'd rather call you by your real name."

"Not just yet."

The thought occurred to me, not entirely whimsical, that he was wanted for a crime. He had that aura of trouble about him. "Gabriel, it is," I agreed.

"And you will be my Eve." He reached out to me, placing his hand on my arm. I shivered, feeling nearly lost in his touch. His power over me was complete; though I couldn't let him know this. I had to let him believe that I was free of his charm, and his power.

"Evie!" A voice called to me from a long way away. "*Evie!*" it came again.

Gabriel frowned. "Someone is braving the Wrath."

"I am. You are."

He blinked, his eyelids falling and rising slowly, rhythmically, making me sleepy. "I must go."

"Why? Who's coming?"

He smiled at me. "The one who does not know your name…" On those words, he turned to go. His tall silhouette blended into the shadows until I could no longer distinguish his form from the trees. I felt a strong desire to follow him, as though an invisible bond bound us together, yet I let him go.

"Evie!" The one who did not know my name was Nate, of course. But why was he here…in these woods? What had happened to his dinner date with the aunts?

"I'm over here," I called. When his figure broke through a line of trees, I felt strangely glad to see him. Chilled and shivering now, I just wanted to be back in my warm room, even though only moments before I'd thought of it as a prison.

"Good Lord, Evie!" he exclaimed. He set something on the ground and grasped my arms. "Where have you been? What are you doing here?"

"How did you know I was gone?" I gasped, stunned by his intense reaction.

He stared at me. It was then that I realized how dark the woods were—that Nate had brought along a kerosene lantern, which sat on the ground nearby emitting nose-stinging fumes. Strange how I hadn't noticed that night had come. "It's almost midnight." He examined me thoroughly; his hand brushed back my hair looking for signs of harm. "I thought you were sick."

I looked around me at the woods, disoriented. "The aunts locked me in my room," I managed to say. "They said I was sick, but I'm not sick." I paused. "Did you say midnight?"

"A quarter of. Why are you in the woods, Evie? Do you sleepwalk? Is that what happened?"

"No, I don't think so. I felt like getting some fresh air." Which was true. The air in a prison soon grows toxic, even if it's just in your head.

"You said the aunts locked you in?"

"They did, but one of them must have snuck up and unlocked the door before they left because it opened right up when I tried again later."

His eyes were skeptical, worried. "I thought I told you not to come into these woods."

"I was feeling rebellious."

His chin lowered, his face shadowed in the lamplight. "Evie, you need to look at me." He was still grasping my arms and now he peered into my eyes. "Is there something you're not telling me?"

"Can we go home now?" I asked, refusing to answer his question, refusing to meet his eyes. I didn't want to lie to him.

"I'm not sure you should go back to Filmore. I don't trust your aunts. They told me you were sick in bed with a cold. Flat out miserable, is what they said, actually. I must admit a part of me thought you were faking it."

He was guiding me through the woods now, moving fast and sure, his hand wrapped securely around my elbow, the other holding the lantern out in front of him. He kept looking about him as we walked. "Why would I be faking it? I wasn't, you know."

"Our meetings haven't exactly been a pleasure for you."

"You have a point there, and I must admit I did think of not going, but I decided I wanted to. If only to give you a hard time."

He laughed and squeezed my arm. "Your aunts did enough damage, thank you very much."

"I wish I could have seen that."

"I'm sure you do. Come to dinner tomorrow," he said. Impulsively, I felt.

"I'd rather avoid the aunts from here on out," I replied grimly.

"I'm not inviting your aunts."

"Just me?"

"Just you."

"You don't have any other...engagements?"

"I do, but plans can change."

"You don't have to do this, you know. You've proved your courage by inviting the aunts over for dinner. And I've forgiven your dog for stealing my scone."

He chuckled. "Good. But I want to make it up to you, missing tonight and all."

"That wasn't your fault."

"Maybe it was," he mumbled.

I wanted to ask him to explain, but we were at the house now. A bare bulb shone over the doorway and spread a half-circle of light twenty feet into the yard. Priscilla stood on the front steps, smoking a cigarette, a red firefly from this distance. A dark shadow lay next to her.

"You found her." She sounded relieved, which seemed odd. The firefly bobbed up, brightened, then was squashed.

"Safe and sound."

"What were you thinking, Evalina?" she scolded me. "Why did you go into the woods in the middle of the night? You must be delirious from your cold." She had reached us by then and grabbed my arm from Nate's grasp, her short, blunt nails digging into my skin. She smelled of cigarette smoke and brandy and desperation. She smelled like Kelli. "How did you get out?"

"You unlocked the door…" I subtly tried to pull away, but she kept her grip.

"Oh." She faltered, then rallied. "Oh, yes, I did. Before we left…in case of fire. I thought you were asleep by then and would be safe, that you wouldn't think of leaving the house."

"I must have been sleepwalking," I told her, avoiding Nate's questioning eyes.

"You must have been. No one goes into those woods by choice."

"Nate just did."

Her breathing quickened. "Yes, he did. Thank you, Nathaniel. You were very good to come. Nothing happened?"

"I'm fine, Priscilla." He was brusque. "But from now on, I see no reason to lock Evie in her room. Even if, as you claim, she is sick." He none too gently pulled me away from Priscilla's grasp, her nails leaving scratches on my arms.

"I was only doing what I thought best."

He stared at her for a few seconds before looking at me. "Are you sure you'll be all right, Evie?" His face lingered only inches from my own, his lamp illuminating the space between us like a stage light. His eyelashes arched darkly above his eyes; his cheekbones created hollows below. A drop of sweat rolled down the side of his jaw.

I slowly nodded, my eyes glued to his. "Yes, I'll be all right. I'll see you tomorrow?"

"I'll come pick you up."

"What are you two talking about?" Priscilla demanded.

Nate's eyes never left mine. "I want to make up for Evie missing dinner tonight."

"But she's *sick*, Nathaniel."

"I've miraculously recovered," I spoke up.

Bones growled, then started barking at the woods. "There's something out there," Priscilla breathed, backing up the stairs.

"You'd better go, Nate," I told him.

He gave me a searching look, quite aware that I was holding something back. His eyes followed mine to the trees. "We'll talk tomorrow. Oh," he walked over to his car, a mud-spattered red Jeep, of all things—I would never have pegged him as a Jeep guy—and pulled out a white bag, "I brought you these."

I took the familiar sack, which smelled delicious. "Thanks."

"Tomorrow, then?"

"Tomorrow."

He waited until I was at the doorway before he drove away. One last look at the woods assured me that we were right to go. Gabriel was standing at the edge, just inside the shadows, surrounded by fireflies.

I turned and went inside.

Priscilla and Kelli pounced on me as soon as I stepped into the foyer. "How did you get out?" Kelli growled.

I shrugged. "I just wished for it and it happened."

Her reaction was unexpected. She went pale and backed away from me. "Did you hear that, Prissy?"

"I heard it," Priscilla said coolly. "I'm glad to see you're feeling better, Evalina. I hope you don't suffer another attack tomorrow night."

"I wasn't ever sick, Aunt Priscilla."

One cool eyebrow lifted at the challenge. "Viruses can be so unpredictable, coming and going without warning. I wouldn't be surprised if you were deathly ill come dinner time tomorrow."

"Maybe I'll really die and spoil all your plans."

She jerked back, as though I'd swung at her. In my mind I had. "Go to bed," she ordered. "It's late."

Glancing repeatedly over my shoulder—not wanting to have my back to them—I headed up the stairs to my room. The two sisters, distinct opposites, stood watching me go, their bodies rigid, their expressions hard and calculating. "We need to move quickly," Kelli hissed, thinking

I was out of earshot. I didn't turn around when she said this, just kept marching up those interminable steps.

"For once I agree with you," Priscilla remarked in a bone chilling voice. "We must get what's ours, and soon."

The scary part... Unlike Kelli, I think Priscilla knew very well that I could hear her.

Chapter Thirteen

✳

The Dance

That night I didn't fall asleep for hours. Like a tiny boat, I tossed about on the sea that was my bed, surrounded by hungry sharks and the violent, unpredictable waves that made up my current predicament. I had come to the conclusion that my aunts were dangerous women, most especially to me. That we were related didn't matter; they felt nothing familial toward me—at most, only as a Cain and Abel scenario where I was poor Abel.

Maybe she'll be enough for our purposes.

She does have his blood in her.

I mean to finish what we started. Whatever the cost.

My mind wondered fancifully if they meant to sacrifice me to some kind of god. In a few days, Ellwood was hosting their Solstice Festival, which seemed a propitious time for sacrifices. I didn't entirely believe they'd actually murder me, but I also couldn't quite convince myself that they wouldn't either. After locking me in my room and lying to Nate, they seemed quite capable of doing just about anything.

I decided to stay on my guard while I determined what they meant to do, even though it was probably something quite mundane, like a blood test to prove paternity for an illegitimate child—nothing sinister, at all. Still, it wouldn't hurt to be watchful, to expect the worst. They weren't above locking me in my room again, even though they'd unlocked it not long after. Or so Priscilla had claimed. I thought I had tested the doorknob again after they'd left the house and found it locked, although it was possible the latch had gotten stuck.

I sighed and turned over. I tried thinking about my dinner tomorrow with Nate, but that didn't ease my restlessness. The bag he'd handed me contained scones, and having gone without supper, I ate two of them before crawling into bed. They were delicious and softened my stance on him quite a bit. Still, he confused me. At times he came across as an arrogant bastard, and at others, he seemed thoughtful and caring.

Eyes closed I recalled the feel of his strong fingers touching my skin, checking for wounds. He'd braved the woods to come looking for me, and I realized now how grateful I was to him for searching me out, risking his safety in doing so. Even Priscilla had been impressed by his courage. The odd part was that he'd entered and left the woods un-harmed. The day before he'd implied that no one but myself had en-tered the Wrath without consequence. I'd have to ask him about it at dinner.

Then there was Gabriel, the stranger in the woods. How did he fit into all this? He seemed to know everyone here, but did they know who he was? His name never came up in conversation, at least not in any in which I'd participated. Of course, Gabriel wasn't his real name, just an appellation I'd picked out of thin air. Or had I? Maybe he'd told me his name in the woods during the time I couldn't remember and was now having a bit of fun at my expense.

Whatever his name, no one—and I was pretty sure Kelli wouldn't be able to avoid talking about him—spoke of a gorgeous neighbor who wandered about the woods.

As I fell into a restless sleep, I speculated about when I would see him again.

~

In the morning, groggy and out of sorts, I stumbled to the door, half expecting to find it locked again. It *was* locked, but only on my side. While snooping through the desk the other day, I'd found a key, and last night had put it to use. Not that locking the door would do me any good if someone really wanted to get in. But I'd reasoned that the locked door would make enough noise to wake me in case someone tried to get at me and finish me off. I chuckled a little at how idiotically dramatic that sounded, then went to shower.

I found Bessie in the kitchen, kneading bread. "Heard you were boak."

"Huh?"

"Ailin'. You look all right to me." She peered at me over her father's old-fashioned glasses.

So the aunts were clinging to the illness story with all the might of a giant squid. "I'm not sick, and I never was. They didn't want me to go to dinner at Nate's so they locked me in my room."

"Figured it were somethin' like that. They're a right jealous lot, those two."

"Speaking of the devils incarnate, are they around?"

She shook her head. "There be a meetin' for the Solstice Festival for everyone involved in the plannin', Kelli included, though she does naught but make trouble. Priscilla's headin' the committee. She likes to claim Nate asked her to do it, but all he had for say in the matter was not to protest her pickin' herself for the job."

I smiled, pleased. I was happy the aunts were both out of the house, and hoped they'd stay gone until after Nate picked me up. I didn't want to be thrown in the dungeons. I wasn't sure I'd be rescued this time.

"I heard you were out in the Wrath again."

"Hmmm…" I murmured noncommittally. I didn't like the idea of facing Bessie's disapproval. But her next question surprised me.

"So what were it like out there?" She stole a sly glance at me.

I kept my expression neutral. "Dark, full of trees. Nothing special." Except for a strange man called Gabriel and lots of unusually large fireflies, but if she didn't already know about such things, I wasn't going to be the one to tell her. I liked Bessie a lot, but I couldn't trust her not to gossip.

"Folks be startin' to wonder about you."

"Wonder about me?" I echoed. "Wonder what?"

"How you've managed to face the Wrath twice and not get yerself hurt or taken."

I shrugged, wondering how they already knew about the second time, being that it had happened only just last night. No doubt Bessie had been the source. Good gossip was good gossip, I supposed, but she had just confirmed my decision to keep certain things to myself. "Maybe it's because I'm an American. Or maybe because I don't really believe there's anything wrong with the woods."

She regarded me skeptically, her gray eyes narrowed to red slits. "You think we're makin' it all up?"

"I don't think you made anything up. I think something perfectly natural happened—like someone fell into a hole and couldn't be found—and the story grew from there."

"It grew all right. A good ten folk have gone missin' in those woods. You encountered nothin' in there? Nothin' to frighten you?"

Ah, now that was a hard one to answer. "What would I meet?" I turned the question back on her. "What do you think is out there?"

"*Them*," she breathed.

Them? "Who's them?"

The life went out of her face. Perhaps she realized she had shared too much with a stranger, one who didn't hold with her beliefs. The phone rang, cutting off whatever answer she might have given, if any.

She wiped her hands on a pale blue towel, then scurried over to the phone. "What?" she barked into the receiver. "Oh, Eliza. Glad you called. Yes, she's right here."

But I was already backing out of the room, an orange and a banana nut muffin in hand. "I won't keep you," I called, scuttling out the door. Much as I wanted to know who *they* were, I didn't want to face any more questions from Bessie and whoever this Eliza was—no doubt a busybody from the village.

I headed outside, peeling my orange as I walked. The day was dry for the moment, though overcast. The sky hung so low I felt as though I could reach up and touch it. I strolled along the drive to the bridge, found a rock near the stream, and sat down to eat my breakfast. The air was chilly, but it was a relief compared to the rotting stillness of the manor.

When the warm muffin and cool orange slices were gone, I sat with empty hands and watched the water tumble by. My thoughts, jittery and jumpy as fleas, finally settled on the puzzle Bessie had evoked using the word, *them*. Who were these elusive beings? Wild animals? Eccentric villagers? A cult?

I tossed a smooth, round stone into the swirling water. Seven rings formed, then quickly dissipated in the current. Nate must know who *they* were. He'd warned me about the woods for a reason, though he, himself, wasn't afraid of it—unlike the other villagers. Lack of fear often means one of two things: Extreme stupidity, or knowledge. Nate wasn't stupid, so he must know something. Maybe he was even one of *them*.

I could ask Gabriel what he knew about *them*, but that would mean entering the woods to seek him out. After so many warnings from so many people, did I dare go again? And would he want me to pursue him? Up until now, he'd been the one to invite me into the woods. This last time he had only to beckon and I came running. This time would be different. I would be the one initiating the meeting. I would be taking charge. A rare feeling of confidence reared up inside me. I liked this idea very much.

I stood up on the rock and searched the surrounding woods for a place to start. A lovely stand of hemlocks farther up the stream caught my eye and I decided to begin my search there. Having a landmark and staying close to the water should keep me from getting lost, though I hoped I wasn't deluding myself in thinking this.

As soon as I entered the woods, the dim light from the sun nearly disappeared, swallowed up by shadows and secrets. The moss grew thick and green here, the stones were like moist pillows, the ground a downy blanket. I felt an uncanny urge to lie down and go to sleep. My top teeth crunched down hard on my lower lip and the pain instantly cleared my head. I took four or five hesitant steps into the forest, then stopped.

Before me, a dark brown pathway cut through the green moss, as though someone had dragged a giant stick through the dirt. The dark snake wound through the stand of trees, disappearing into the darkness beyond. I began to walk again, following the trail, wondering what I would see in this supposedly dangerous and haunted place. A wild hare, the elusive fox?

A wolf?

A movement to my right stayed my foot and I froze where I was, listening hard, hoping to see Gabriel. Gliding along beneath the rustle of a light breeze crept the unexpected sound of human speech. The hissing and chattering soon became intelligible and I caught the tail end of what appeared to be an argument.

"Look at her. She's perfect for what we want."

"Hmmm…" The other one sounded less sure. "She does look the right type."

"So let's take her."

At this point I began to inch backwards, easing my way toward the wood's edge. I hadn't gone that far into the trees, and only a few steps remained until I reached the tree line. Ready to run, I took several long strides, then whirled about. To my shock, I found that I'd been heading further into the woods, not out of it. Had I gotten turned around? I spun in a circle, only to discover that I was surrounded by an infinity of trees. The clearing was nowhere to be seen.

"Hello!"

I swung around, heart pounding in my throat. A young woman stood before me. She wore a pale green dress the color of lichen, and her long, brown hair was twisted into braids. Large brown eyes, brazen and presumptuous, studied me. She was quite pretty in a pouty sort of way.

"Uh, hi."

"I'm Gwyn. Come play a game with us."

"It's nice of you to offer, but I can't," I said in my most appeasing voice. "I was just heading home. Lunch time, you know." *Well-done, idiot*, I admonished myself. It wasn't even close to noon.

She frowned, then beckoned behind her. Several figures stepped out from the trees to encircle me. "I'm sorry, but you're going to have to play with us. We need another player. One of us left, you see."

I folded my arms stubbornly. "I really don't want to play. I have to go home."

There were about eleven of them surrounding me now—young men and women, almost evenly divided into two groups, all slender and fair, all youthful. And yet the expression on their lovely faces was wise and watchful as any adult. A hint of something not quite human in their eyes winked out at me, though I was sure it was only my imagination.

"It's a fun game," one of them told me. She had curly hair the color of nearly ripe strawberries. "We need just one more player. Oh, do please say you'll play!" This girl, with her wide, innocent blue eyes and surplus of freckles, was more appealing than the other one—the bossy Gwyn. I almost felt inclined to say yes to her.

"My aunts will be wondering where I am."

Nudged from behind by Gwyn, one of the young men took a reluctant step toward me. He looked like a Greek Adonis, hair as blond as a sun-drenched cloud, eyes the color of spring leaves. "It's a dance," he said. The numbers rearranged themselves and I saw that there were twelve of us in all.

"You want me to dance with you?" He ducked his head, looking away. He was a reluctant partner, I thought, acting as though he didn't want anything to do with me, or any of this.

"Can you sing, too?" Gwyn demanded. "That would be splendid."

"Not according to my mother."

The others laughed and I felt better. They seemed like normal kids, like myself, only incredibly attractive. Eerily so, in fact.

"Just one dance," the red-haired girl assured me.

"I don't think she can!" Gwyn challenged. "Not like us." She did a little pirouette. She was quite good.

"All right," I agreed, unable to resist the challenge, and also because I enjoyed dancing. I'd had more than a few dance lessons myself, courtesy of Mother. Without her constant criticism, I might have continued them. But one day I realized that it was her pursuit, not my own, and I quit. "Just one, though."

The impish giggles this statement produced did little to reassure me that I'd made the right decision. But before I could back out, Adonis pulled me close and began to swing me around to the beginning notes of a sensuous song. The ethereal music seemed to rise out of thin air all around me. Where was it coming from? A radio behind a tree? I didn't think so. I could hear the alluring notes in my head, as though I were humming the song myself.

Our whirling picked up speed and we spun around and around until my mind grew dizzy and my heart light. My feet were no longer touching the ground, or so I imagined. My partner had submitted to the will of the dance, no longer fighting against our union. His warm skin pressed against my cheek and I heard him singing softly in my ear, his tone nostalgic and longing. We were melting into each other, becoming one, until a cry shattered the dream.

"*Stop!*"

And everything did. I was suddenly alone, my head still full of breathless joy. The shotgun word echoed off tree trunks and stones and I felt myself falling. I closed my eyes just as strong arms caught me and laid me gently on the ground.

"I will kill each and every one of them." The sound of Gabriel's voice cut through me like a scalpel. My eyes flew open. He was balanced on one knee, leaning over me, breathing hard. "I will tear them to pieces!"

"We were just dancing," I whispered into the silence of the forest.

"That was not a simple dance. They will die for their presumption. You are *mine*."

I sat up suddenly, my face only inches from his. "I am not *yours*, Gabriel. And don't you dare try to tell me what I can and can't do. If I want to dance, I will!"

His anger waned like the outgoing tide and he looked amused. "Do you think that anything you do in this place is your choice?"

I nodded slowly. "When you wanted me to go with you the other day, I chose not to."

"I let you go." His erratic tone and clenched jaw told me that I'd hit upon something. "They were taking you, you know. They were using your life force to increase their own."

"What are you talking about?" I looked around. The sky was darker than it should be. "What time is it?"

He shrugged. "Time is not something I bother with."

I stared at him. Hadn't Bessie said something like that? "I have to go." I jumped to my feet.

"Wait!" he called out, grabbing my arm and rising with me. "Stay with me, Eve."

"I can't."

A growl came from deep within his chest. He sounded exactly like Bones. "When will you come back?"

"I don't know. Tomorrow, perhaps."

"The others will not harm you anymore. I will make sure of that."

My heart sped up. "You're not *really* going to kill them, are you?" At the moment he looked capable of doing so.

"Not today, but they will suffer."

I shivered. "Not on my account, I hope." Them?

"They have defied me. There is always a price to be paid for that."

"Please, Gabriel. You could get hurt. There are so many of them—" But only one who had danced with me.

The back of his hand brushed my cheek and he smiled jubilantly at me, as though he had won. Then he pushed me toward the edge of the woods. I began to run, but once free of the forest's confines, I stopped and turned around. Gabriel was nowhere to be seen, not staying to watch me go this time. He was keen on revenge.

Run, Adonis! I shouted in my mind.

Then I ran myself.

Chapter Fourteen

*

Bloody Mary

My feet flew over the bridge as I glanced down at my watch. Five o'clock. I consulted the sky, which was now completely devoid of clouds, and swallowed hard. Over seven hours of my life were missing, as though time had skipped right over them. Worse, this wasn't the first time I'd lost hours in those woods. What was going on? Had I fallen that first night and hit my head? Maybe I had a tumor. The idea haunted me as I sprinted down the road toward Filmore.

No car waited for me in the driveway. Nate hadn't set a time and I dearly hoped I'd have at least half an hour to get ready, enough time to change into something more adult-like than jeans, sneakers, and an argyle sweater. Maybe something more attractive, too.

Mother may have been a tartar when it came to the impression she wanted me to make on the world, but I was starting to see a little bit of sense in some of the advice she'd passed along to me. "Every woman should own a little black dress. Black goes with anything. And unless you're a complete whale, it's very slimming." All this advice giving was usually followed by an up and down scan of my assets to drive home her point that someone like me could always use that kind of help. Still, I wasn't a total failure in her eyes, for what good that did me. If I were a 'complete whale' (which, in her irrational mind, was probably a size eight or higher), she wouldn't have bothered buying me the dress. In retrospect, it seemed an awful way to be deemed a success.

After a quick shower, I shimmied into a daringly low-cut dress, whose skirt dropped like black rose petals from a fitted bodice. Afterwards I pulled on sheer, black stockings and slipped into matching pumps. A black coat, trimmed with red lining, completed the ensemble, though I would don it only if on the verge of hypothermia. I wanted Nate to see my dress in all its glory, and maybe rate me just as glorious.

The curling iron and a dash of fire-red lipstick freshened up what they could. Flushed cheeks from my rush made me look passably alive. With one last check in the mirror and a few swipes of mascara, I finally allowed myself to leave the room, heart thumping as fast as the tapping of my short-heeled pumps carrying me down the stairs.

I'd just closed the outside door behind me when Priscilla and Kelli roared up the drive. Before they could see me, I slipped behind one of the thick shrubs skirting the front of the house, careful to avoid snagging my stockings on the rough branches.

"Move it!" Kelli snapped, as the car pulled up in front of the house, one wheel digging up the grass as it skidded to a stop. "He'll be here any second now!" That Priscilla did not tell Kelli what to do with her bossiness showed how worried she was. "We can put her in the attic," Kelli went on, as she pounded up the steps, several of her parts heaving wildly about. Her mad dash was entertaining to watch, though I had to bite the inside of my cheek to stifle a snort of laughter. She was going to knock herself out if she wasn't careful.

"I'd have to clear it out first," Priscilla breathed, following close behind. "I stored all of Edmund's things in there."

"Then do it, you prongy git. Damnit, I told you to burn that stuff!"

The heavy door slammed behind them. No surprise, they had been planning to lock me up again. For the first time in my life, I hoped when it came to a moral compass that my genetics leaned more toward my mother's side than my father's.

Which goes to show how desperate I was feeling right then.

Just as my knees threatened to lock into a permanent crouching position, a car came speeding down the driveway. I popped my head up, saw that it was Nate, and hurried out to meet him. His look of relief was gratifying to see.

"They ended the meeting early," he explained, as he stepped out of the sporty, black car. Dressed in a dark dinner jacket over a pinstriped shirt, he looked as debonair as a 1920s film star. When he put his hand on the small of my back to guide me into the car, I shivered. "I'd stepped out to take a call from…from a friend, and when I came back, your aunts were gone."

I slid into the smooth, black interior, smiling wryly. Oh, those two were wicked, indeed. I almost admired them for their clever thinking. If only they weren't trying to do such unpleasant things to me.

"They were going to put me in the attic this time," I told him.

He didn't say anything, only revved the engine four or five times. A moment later, the aunts flew out of the house like witches on brooms, looking both furious and stunned. When they were within a couple feet of the car, Nate took off, spraying gravel in a wide arc. "That should even the score between us," he shouted over the roaring engine. "Though I don't know what I'm going to do about their kidnapping exploits. Something horrid, I reckon."

"I hope so." I grinned.

At the bridge he slowed down, then glanced over at me. "You look different."

"I'm wearing a dress," I pointed out.

"I don't mean that, although you do look lovely. There's something different about you today." He gazed at me, his eyes intense, curious, *interested*. He casually placed his left hand over mine.

I blushed and looked away, but my hand did not move. His fingers filled the spaces between mine perfectly. "So you have a car like this and yet you take the train?" As I said this I realized he had discarded the muddy Jeep. I liked the idea that he was trying to impress me, even though I'd have been fine with the Jeep.

"I need to lower my carbon footprint."

"Oh." I hadn't figured him to be conscientious. "Good idea. I suppose I could improve in that department myself. I have a bad habit of leaving all the lights on when my parents aren't home. But I do take public transportation whenever I can." I thought it important to point this out. I don't know why.

He smiled at me. "I'm not a saint. It's sort of a job requirement."

"What do you do?"

"I'm an environmental architect."

"That sounds impressive. What does an environmental architect do?"

"I design buildings that are better for the environment. Wherever possible, my designs incorporate solar panels, wind-power, and natural, renewable materials."

I gazed at his profile, impressed and nonplussed. Such a noble job for an English snob.

We turned onto his road and soon after entered a tunnel created by two rows of trees growing on either side of the drive. After a few minutes, the trees cleared and we emerged to the sight of a castle standing atop the moor like a lighthouse. The building, about twice the size of Filmore Manor, was surrounded by a crenellated wall, and resembled a small fortress. Its five towers rose up like mountain peaks and scores of leaded windows winked in the late afternoon sun.

We crossed the drawbridge and I glimpsed orange flashes in the dark water of the moat—koi, I thought, or redheaded Trolls. As we passed through the massive entrance, I glanced up to see the sharp spikes of the gate, which has been raised. Once inside, Nate parked and turned off the car. A shiver of anticipation vibrated in my chest as I gazed up at the massive stone edifice. I'd always wanted to visit a real English castle. It even came with its own ruin, way off on the right side of the courtyard. All that remained of the broken down building were a few stone pillars overgrown by vines, the outlines of a window, and a small bit of vaulted ceiling.

"That was the chapel," Nate said, noting my interest. "The Queen's guard burned it down during Bloody Mary's reign."

"That's terrible. I hope no one was in it at the time."

"My family was fortunate to have received advance warning of the plot, as was the vicar, who escaped. Queen Mary and her mad ideas about religion caused a lot of trouble for my ancestors. She's one of the reasons for that gate you saw."

"I've read that Queen Mary wasn't all that stable." I was a bit of a monarchy buff and had studied England's royal family thoroughly. I loved all the intrigue and plots, the scheming and politics, though I suppose I wouldn't have wanted to live through any of that. "I feel sorry for her, actually. For what she had to go through."

He turned on me, his hand abandoning mine on the seat. "You feel sorry for a murderer? I suppose you think Jack the Ripper deserves clemency as well?"

I shrugged. "I'm not sure about him. I don't know his story, and neither do you," I interrupted his protest, "since nobody knows who he was or why he did what he did. Anyway, I like to think that there are two sides to every story. If we look at it from Mary's perspective, we might feel more lenient toward her. Her father and role model was King Henry VIII, as you know. The man killed two of his wives because he wanted to remarry to either beget a male heir or because his wife defied him. He separated Mary from her mother, Catherine of Aragon, and at one time he even declared her a bastard, refusing to acknowledge her claim to the throne even though she was his daughter. That might affect a person a little, don't you think?"

"He had them executed."

"What?"

"King Henry VIII had his wives executed. He didn't kill them himself."

"Oh, please! He wanted them dead; he simply had others do his dirty work for him. He didn't swing the ax, but he ordered it to be swung."

"If that's your argument, the same could be said of Mary. Even though she had others do her work for her, she was responsible for killing innocent people all because of how they worshipped God!"

"But only because she thought she had to," I argued. "In reconciling with Rome and the Pope, which also restored the legitimacy of her birth, England's heresy laws were thereby invoked. As ruler, she was held by her country's own laws to rout out and punish heretical offenders. She had a physically weak and emotionally unstable constitution, as well, both of which affected her good judgment. She believed she was pregnant two different times, despite evidence to the contrary. She wasn't evil, she was delusional—messed up."

"You don't think some people can be truly evil?"

"If a being is truly evil, then I don't think he or she is human. I think all humans possess both good and bad attributes. We are all capable of doing evil, just as we are all capable of doing good."

He sat there for a moment, looking up at one of the towers, his hands gripping the steering wheel as though afraid to let go. "Perhaps you're right. But by your argument, we should acquit Henry for his actions, too. He was a victim of his birth and of his times, acting for what he thought was the good of the country."

"Hold on there. I never said to acquit *anybody*. I simply think we need to understand what drives people to do the things they do, or we are just as guilty of wrongdoing as they are."

"Okay, but there are degrees of wrongdoing. Some deeds are obviously worse than others. Many people truly *mean* to do harm. They enjoy it."

"I agree. But in the end, does it matter what their motives are? What if there was no motive at all? Maybe I stole the cookies because they were there and only afterwards thought it through, like a child might."

"The judicial system thinks motives matter. Degrees of crime were established for that very reason."

"That's because humans can be merciful. No matter what the motive was, however, the outcome is still the same. The victim is dead, or the church is destroyed, or the cookies are gone. So, I'll ask you again, Nate. Does a person's motivation matter?"

"Yes," he admitted. "It does."

I smiled at him. "Mary's motivation wasn't to harm, but to uphold a law. Knowing this, I believe we should show her mercy."

"As we should toward your aunts," he turned back on me with a smirk...just when I thought I had him. "They don't really want to hurt you, they only want to keep you away from me!"

"Touché." I laughed. It was fun sparring with Nate. He was very quick.

He relaxed his grip on the wheel and climbed out of the low-slung car to meet me on the other side. I think he might have opened the door for me if I'd let him, but I was too quick, scrambling out on my own. I wanted to see the inside of that castle.

Leaving the car by the wall, we strolled through the large courtyard. Behind us a series of buildings ran along the wall. One looked like a garage of sorts, another, with its wooden door pulled aside to reveal a pile of hay, had to be the stable, where Heathcliff resided. One corner of the courtyard was dedicated to a vegetable garden just beginning to sprout seedlings in the black dirt. Shrubs, rose bushes, and apple trees, some old and gnarled, others fresh and young, landscaped the rest of the court. Small cobbled paths laced the area like a spider web. It was an unusual set-up.

"My father was an amateur gardener," Nate explained. "He loved spending time outdoors, especially after my mother died."

"Oh…I'm sorry. How long ago did she die?"

"When I was six. She had lung cancer."

My heart flipped precariously. "Six? You were so young…"

The grove of apple trees drew his attention. "I had a good nanny, Miss Ames. That helped." He turned and gave me a rueful smile, hoping to cover the pain in his eyes, and failing miserably. "My father was never the same after her death. He came out here to escape his pain. I look very much like her, you see, though our personalities couldn't have been more different. She was bright and happy and outgoing. Perhaps if I'd been more like her Father might have wanted to spend more time with me."

"You can't think like that, Nate. My mother is always getting on my case to be perfect. But I'm never going to be perfect." Too bad I couldn't truly grasp the meaning behind my own words of wisdom. "And you will never be your mother, nor should anyone expect you to be."

"Your mother is that bad?" He looked skeptical. "What about your father? Didn't he take your side on anything?"

"My father is a Filmore. What do you think?"

"I'm beginning to think I was better off with my nanny."

We both laughed, a little bit of it aimed at our own private wounds, how seriously we took them. Our laughter followed us indoors, echoing in the Great Hall where we now stood. Despite the cool air outside, it was surprisingly light and warm in the lofty stone room decorated in a medieval theme that probably had been gracing the room since the Dark Ages. The faint smell of cigarette smoke lingered and I wondered if Nate smoked.

Both Kelli and Priscilla smoked.

"It's so light in here."

"Modern conveniences." Nate gestured at the walls. "I placed six so-lar panels at the back of the building. I also hired a company to install over a hundred tubular skylights throughout the castle. Actu-ally...they're a modified version that my friend invented so you can run the tubes through a wall, not just through the ceiling." The small circles, relatively unobtrusive, let in quite a bit of light, more so than the arched windows of thick, bubbled glass set here and there.

"So how do you keep it so dry and warm in here? I always thought of castles as damp and cold."

"Thorndike Hold, as we call the old dump, used to be frigid, but I've made a few changes to the heating system, plus the solar panels help out. England isn't exactly known for its sunny days, but we have enough of the panels to help cut our fuel consumption by a third."

"You haven't given up on doing things the old-fashioned way, ei-ther," I noted, indicating the tapestries hanging on the walls. Several were old and worn, their color faded, but a few were new, and thicker and heavier than the old ones.

"This is the room where people once gathered to eat and drink," he explained. "It's easier to heat a single room than multiple ones, espe-cially when you have a grand old fireplace that takes up half a wall. However, back then they had a lot more wood to burn." A fire was burning in the fireplace now, a modest one, but bright and cheery all the same. I could smell a hint of apple. Two place settings sat on one end of the long table that occupied a large part of the room. A silver candelabra and lovely china made the table look regal.

"I like it here."

"I'm glad. Would you like to see the rest of the house?" he asked casually, though his expression betrayed a slight apprehension.

I nodded eagerly. "I'd love to. I think a lot of American girls dream of living in a castle. I always have, anyway."

A smile lit up his face. "Even if the castle were draughty and full of cobwebs and ghosts?"

"*Especially* if the castle were draughty and full of cobwebs and ghosts." He laughed. "So where are the dogs?" I asked.

"I locked them up. I didn't think you'd want them around after your last experience with the vicious brutes."

"Oh, I don't mind having them. As long as they don't eat my din-ner."

He looked pleased. "They're in the library. I'll let them out when we go up there."

At the top of a flight of stairs, a long, wide hall big enough to fit a semi-truck stretched before us. Tall windows flanked one wall, on the other hung portraits six feet in height. Nate talked a little about each of the family pictures, which dated back to the 1300s. The evolution in artistry was obvious—from figures resembling wooden puppets to images that looked so real I thought they might step down from the wall and say cheers.

"My parents' portraits hang in my sitting room," Nate answered before I could ask. "I haven't had mine done."

Both parents? I wondered. Wouldn't Nate's father want to see his beloved wife's painting? I didn't dare ask Nate about it, though. Maybe later when we knew each other better, and after I met his distant father, whose presence seemed strangely absent from the place.

From the gallery, we headed to the library and were greeted joyfully by the dogs. After they settled down, I looked around. It was a lived-in, much loved sort of room. A messy desk, surrounded by three easels displaying blueprints, huddled in a corner. Nate showed me a few of the buildings he was working on and I lingered over the delicate drawings, understanding at last his ink-stained fingers. He seemed to really know what he was doing, although when I said this he pointed out that he was considered a rookie in the field and had a long way to go to earn the respect of his colleagues. His modesty surprised me. On the train, I'd figured him to be the type who didn't give a damn what anyone thought of him. He possessed that confidence so often born and bred into aristocrats, and usually, sadly lacking in us plebeians.

After discussing the finer points of Gothic architecture—I thought it was spooky and cool, Nate concurred—we ended up in the music room across the hall, dogs obediently following. An ornate grand piano took center stage, though there were several other instruments—three violins, six guitars, and two shiny flutes, which graced corners, hung on walls, or sat on chairs. For such an uptight guy, Nate was surprisingly messy.

He seemed to read my mind. "I don't like keeping a lot of servants, and I really don't like wasting my time straightening up. It only gets messed up again. I do have a housekeeper, my ex-nanny, in fact—Miss Ames. I mentioned her before. She retired from her nanny position just last year," he joked, his eyes lighting up. I smiled and he grinned, looking at the moment like the boy he'd once been. "Anyway, she's getting old and she's terribly frail and she's been with us forever. I can't keep taxing her with my bad habits. I'd rather she spent her time knitting and watching the telly, and she is quite happy to oblige me."

I nodded at a coffee cup perched precariously on a teetering stack of books next to the piano. "That would drive me nuts." A spiraling series of brown rings from visits by other sloshy mugs decorated the top book cover.

He shrugged. "Yes, well, I'm not sure I like it, either, but I can't seem to bring myself to care more than that."

"Maybe some afternoon I'll come over and do some cleaning for you."

"Oh no, you don't! I'd have to pay you and that would make me your employer." He shook his head. "No. Too awkward."

"You don't have to pay me, Nate. I like straightening things up. There's a certain sense of satisfaction in a clean house."

"People don't do things for free, Evie."

"Tell that to my parents." I smiled to show I was only joking, kind of.

Strangely, at these words, a shadow passed over his face. I quickly pulled out the scarred piano bench and sat down, wanting to drive his frown away. I preferred him smiling. "I take it you play." Someone did, judging by the reams of music sheets scattered all over the place.

"Whenever I can."

"Play me something."

He looked at me for a moment, then sat down on the bench. The three dogs spread themselves out under the piano. His arm brushed against mine as he rearranged a few sheets, penciled notations on each one marking various spots in the music. In the end, though, he never once looked at the pages as he roared through a piece by Bach and then pounded out Rachmaninoff. After that he played, with an unexpectedly delicate touch, a haunting melody I didn't recognize.

When he finished, I sat with my eyes closed a moment longer—I could never fully hear music with them open. My body still breathed the notes and I didn't want the feeling to end. But it did, as all good things do. I opened my eyes to find Nate studying me.

"Do you play?" he asked hoarsely. His fingers tapped the keys restlessly, though not enough to produce sound.

I pecked out *Mary Had a Little Lamb* for him. "I never could quite make it work," I told him as he chuckled. "But I love to listen. Music makes me feel…"

"Real?"

I nodded. "Yes! And connected to others, like I'm not the only one, that I'm not alone in dreaming of a better life. Music takes me away from everything, better than a magical flying carpet could."

"Yes," he breathed. His eyes searched mine, entreating me. He wanted something from me at that moment, but I didn't know what it was. I held his gaze, waiting to find out.

"Are you hungry?" he asked.

I blinked. Not what I'd expected to hear, but I quickly rallied. "Starving."

We stood at the same time, heading back to the Great Hall on unsteady legs. We were both troubled by each other; I could feel that. But what could it be that was troubling us?

Back in the large room, Nate motioned me to take the place at the head of the table. He pulled out the carved wooden chair for me and I sat down, feeling quite grand. The dogs disappeared under the table, Sadie laying her chin on my foot. After ringing a tiny silver bell, he poured me a glass of Merlot, the color of melted rubies, then sat down next to me. A moment later, a distinguished, middle-aged man with silver wings gracing his temples entered the room bearing a tray of delectable appetizers. He set the tray on the table and with a short bow, left us alone.

"That was Benjamin," Nate explained, as he expertly eyed the Merlot in his wine glass. "He's been very good to me. I would have introduced you, but Ben prefers to maintain the illusion of aristocracy—that I am the master and he is the faithful butler. It's a role he strives to maintain, right down to the uniform. I hate to disappoint him so I play along."

"How very good of you."

He grinned. "I try."

I perused the various fare on offer—smoked salmon, chunks of cheddar, green and red grapes, tiny crackers, olives, and canapés. I took a bit of everything, except the olives, which I hated. They reminded me of weird little heads.

Nate took a pile of them.

"So what did you do today?" he asked, thoughtfully chewing on an olive as he watched me with hooded eyes. "Or, should I ask, what did you do that changed you?"

Chapter Fifteen

✳

It Might Have Been the Wind

"I want to know," Nate pressed when I neglected to answer him. I was busy eating, but more importantly, I didn't want to tell him about what had happened in the woods. I'd been hoping—all for naught—that he'd forgotten the observation he'd made in the car about how I looked different today.

"I went for a walk."

"You went into those woods again, didn't you?" I didn't deny it. "Bloody hell, Evie!" He banged his fist on the table, accidentally squashing an olive. He ignored the green mess.

"I can't seem to help myself," I whispered, then took a gulp of Merlot. The strong drink caught at my throat and I wheezed and coughed like an idiot. With the exception of the sherry episode and some wine tasting I'd done when Mother decided I needed to know my vintages, I was not accustomed to drinking alcohol.

He waited impatiently for me to recover. When I finally did, he started again. "There's something you need to know...about why I'm so against your going into the forest."

I fingered a salty, oval cracker. "I'm listening."

"My father disappeared in those woods. I have little doubt he's dead."

I took a few moments to catch my breath and think. It came to me how Nate always referred to his father in the past tense. "I'm so sorry, Nate," I said at last, my eyes tearing up. I hated hearing about anyone dying, about anyone suffering. He looked away from me, focusing on the fire flickering in the fireplace. He did not want my pity. "How did it happen?"

"A year to the day my mother died, my father walked into those woods and never returned. I think he went in there on purpose—to die. That's the worst part of it, I think. He knew the woods, its reputation, but he went anyway."

Some people do the wrong thing with their pain. He had said that on the train...

"That's awful, Nate." I hesitantly put my hand on his. He looked down at it. My sympathetic gesture seemed as foreign to him as it did to me. But my hand stayed put, and so did his.

"I was only seven, but I knew what he'd done. I don't blame him, though, for leaving me. I blame them."

"What do you mean *them*?" I breathed, remembering that Bessie had spoken of *them*. "What is going on with these woods?"

His sentimental moment ended; he was angry now. His hand slipped out from under mine and reached desperately for his wine. He took a drink before continuing in a cool monotone, "The belief in the village is that supernatural creatures live in those woods, and they do not like trespassers. Those who dare to enter the Wrath are punished, one way or another."

"And you think your father was punished…"

"I know he was. They took him."

"They," I echoed.

"It's not really the forest the villagers fear, it's what rules the forest."

"It?" One-syllable words were all I could seem to manage at the moment.

Nate turned troubled eyes on me. "I'm not really sure what they are, Evie. There are old legends…about creatures who share our world, but who are different from us. If you cross them, they will eliminate you simply because they can."

"Are we talking mythical creatures?" I pushed out. "Fairies? Elves?"

"I don't think either of those terms captures what these beings are. Human, yet not. Fairy, yet not. I don't really know. All I know is that these creatures, whatever they are, are very powerful and quick to anger. They are vengeful and merciless. They are greedy and protective. You talked about evil beings earlier. Well, from everything I've heard, I believe these creatures to be evil."

I tried to swallow the mouthful of smoked fish trapped in my mouth, dried to sawdust now. It stuck in my throat and my muscles convulsed. I took a sip of water and barely managed to swallow the whole mess. "Do you have proof of their existence? Has anyone seen them?"

"According to stories that go way back, centuries even, they often take our form, appearing as human as you and I. We've had very little reliable information to go on. People, if they're fortunate enough to make it out, tend not to remember what they've seen in the forest. With one exception. Not long before my father disappeared, Harry Willoughby, a local sheep farmer encountered these creatures. And although he had to be eighty years old if he was a day, he was about as stolid and believable as they come. His dog, Ralphie, an otherwise great sheepdog and loyal companion, had one bad habit; he liked to chase deer. One afternoon Ralphie spotted a large buck at the edge of the woods and tore after it. Harry didn't even think—he raced after the dog, shouting for him to stop. The dog returned in a few hours, none the worse for wear, but it wasn't until two days later, when all hope was lost, that Harry stumbled from the woods and onto our property. My father, working in his garden, found him and helped him into the house. I'll never forget seeing Harry, bruised and battered, his eyes wild and full of fear, as he managed to tell us a few details of what had happened to him. While searching for his dog, he came across a group of beautiful young men and women, fey and beguiling as sirens, and they asked him to dance with them." I set my wine glass on the table before I dropped it. "'They look human, but they ain't,'" Nate quoted, his accent taking on the tone and cadence of an old man. "'If ye look in their eyes, ye'll see the difference. They baint be one of us.' Harry was never the same after that, insisting again and again that he was only in the woods for a few hours at most. Day after miserable day his mind slowly slipped away. He died not long after."

"I'm so sorry to hear that," I managed to push out through dry lips. "Thanks for the warning, Nate. I'll certainly be more careful from here on out."

My contrite words, though sincere, didn't convince him to back off. "I saw an odd look in your eyes this afternoon, Evie, and was re-minded of how old Harry Willoughby looked after what he went through. That's why I need to know what happened to you today."

I ducked my head, feeling like a naughty child, and a very dense one. "I just wanted to see if the stories were true. I wanted my own proof."

"And..."

"I went into the woods, and I met some young people. They asked me to dance."

He pulled back, face drawn. "And did you dance with them?" The tension in the air, like a smoke-filled room, made it hard to breathe.

"I didn't want to, but I did. One of them was nice to me. He danced with me."

"Good Lord, Evie!" Nate slammed his fist on the table again. His wine sloshed, spilling onto the table like fresh blood. "You could've been taken. You could've been killed!"

They were using your life force to increase their own. "But nothing happened. I got out!"

His face turned to stone. "How, Evie? How did you escape the woods unharmed when no one ever has?"

"Mr. Willoughby got out." I was being willfully obtuse.

"And not long after that he went mad, then died!"

I stared at Nate. Now was the time to tell him about Gabriel, but I couldn't get the words out. Gabriel was mine. I wouldn't share him. I'd never had anyone, or anything, in my life I could call my own. Besides, he had saved me from Gwyn and the others. He wasn't one of them. *They* were the problem. Not Gabriel.

"All these stories about evil creatures, about going mad. You're scaring me, Nate."

"I *want* to scare you, damnit!"

My cheeks burned and my fingers twisted the white linen napkin in my lap. "I don't feel very well," I forced out, though it was the absolute truth. "Maybe you should take me home."

His entire body worked to control the rage he was feeling. "Back to that place? No way." He leaned toward me, his face only inches from mine. "You should pack your bags, Evie, and head back to the States. Tonight...*now*."

"Back to what? And why, Nate? My parents sent me here. They paid for this trip." My conversation with Mother came to mind—the part about discovering what the aunts were up to. I owed it to her, and to myself, to find out what was going on. "I can't go home. Not yet," I finished lamely. Nevertheless, a small part of me wanted to do what he said...pack up and leave, not get involved, stay safe.

"I would invite you to stay here," he said quietly. "But there is a complication."

"Just take me back to the manor," I repeated firmly, if somewhat morosely, as I wondered what, or *who*, his complication was. There would be no going back home to the States now, my mind determined. "Why don't you say something to the aunts? Let them know you're aware of what they're trying to do. Give me some time to work this out and then I'll return home, find a place of my own. You won't have to worry about me after that."

"Work *what* out, Evie?"

"What it is those two want with me."

Nate's eyes darkened. "Why do you think they want something with you? Where did you get that idea?"

"From them. Originally they wanted my father to come, but my parents sent me instead."

He pulled back, falling against his chair. "I don't understand. This isn't about jealousy?"

"Jealousy?" I echoed. "Oh, you mean because they both want you and don't like any competition for your affections, whether it's real or not?" He nodded, warily. He'd picked up on the sarcasm. "That's a part of it, but I know they're up to something else. I heard them talking."

He leaned forward again, his lips pale and tight. "What did they say? Exactly!"

"You're shouting again."

"Sorry." He didn't look sorry.

"Something about using me instead of him."

"What else?"

"On one of my first nights here, I overheard Priscilla telling Kelli, 'She has his blood in her,' and then, 'I mean to finish what we started. Whatever the cost.' I don't understand any of that in the least, though it doesn't sound promising."

"I'm not letting you go back there."

"I have nowhere else to go, Nate. I have no choice." I pushed back my chair and stood up. "Please take me back to Filmore."

"Sit down!"

"Don't tell me what to do!"

He looked genuinely surprised, but no more than I felt. I wondered how often anyone crossed him. Probably rarely. And I, myself, typically never crossed anyone. Living with the aunts was certainly teaching me something—good, or otherwise, I'd yet to determine. "We haven't finished dinner."

"I'm not hungry. Just take me home."

"I won't." He crossed his arms, looking like a mix of bulldog and stubborn toddler.

"Then I'll walk." I gently slid my foot out from under Sadie's chin and left the table. As quickly as I could, I crossed the Great Hall, my tapping heels mocking each step I took. Before I made it to the door, he caught up to me, grabbing my arm and spinning me around. I felt the air leave my lungs in dismay.

We stood staring at each other, both breathing hard, Nate refusing to let go. The dogs trotted over to us and sat down, watching. Nate looked as though he wanted to shake me, or some sense into me, as he would see it. He was struggling inside, just as I was. I could see the fight in his wild eyes, in his flushed cheeks and furrowed brow. I stared back at him, defiantly.

Cursing, he dropped my arms and took a step back. "Walk, then. See if I care."

It was a fist to the stomach. "I will." I opened the heavy door and slid out through the crack. I wanted to run, but I couldn't. I was wearing these stupid heels, painful reminders of my wishful thinking. Moving as quickly as I could, I glanced back only once. He stood in the doorway, a shadowy figure outlined by the light from within, dogs sitting on either side of him. Swallowing hard, I turned back around and made my way out of the castle and down the long, tunneled driveway with my back erect and head held proud. I would not slink away, and I would not cry.

My slow progress grew increasingly exasperating and I plucked off my heels and went in stocking feet, sticking to the cool grass growing alongside the road. Dusk had arrived, but the impending dark didn't scare me. The people around me frightened me more than the night did. The aunts and their schemes. Nate and his anger. My nearly falling for his pseudo-concern. My naiveté scared me more than anything—how easily I could be taken in. Nathaniel Thorndike was a fake, I determined. A real gentleman would never have let me walk home alone.

My fingers curled, one by one, into tight fists. How dare he treat me this way! I'd done nothing wrong. He was the one who'd wanted nothing to do with me; he was the one with a massive chip on his shoulder. I should've been the one kicking him out of my grand estate instead of being the chump walking home on sharp rocks and tearing her nylons to pieces.

I hate them all.

The words revived me, filling me with a strange throb of energy. Much better. I was so sick and tired of letting others push me around. This had to stop. Always being kind and good and courteous. How tedious, how *boring*. I didn't want to be boring.

Before I knew it, I was back at the manor house, having spent the entire two miles plotting revenge. My ideas—pushing him into a mud puddle, letting out the air in his fancy car's tires, pantsing him in the street—were petty and childish, but by this point I didn't care. I wanted to be childish. Childish was so much more fun.

I was passing the stretch of woods closest to the lawn when I heard Gabriel's voice calling out to me. I kept walking. "He followed you," he warned. A thrill fluttered in my chest. Nate had followed me? Anger lifted off my shoulders like an emotional cloak and I felt light again. Was forgiveness that easy? "Pretend to go into the house and then come back to me. I want to speak to you."

I had a good mind to tell him to stick it in his ear. Instead I slipped my shoes back on and headed for the house. I made a show of opening the door to the manor and stepping inside. Luckily the entry was dark tonight and I was able to close the door without actually entering the house. While I waited in the shadows, I spotted the movement I was hoping to see—a figure surrounded by trotting dogs. He stopped for a moment and stared at the house. A minute later, he turned about and walked back down the road. Nate. Heart pounding, I felt a strong urge to chase after him. I scurried down the steps, onto the drive.

"Come to me, Eve." My eyes shifted over to the trees. Gabriel was calling. When I looked back to the drive, Nate was gone. "You're beautiful," he said when I approached him. The fading sunlight spotlighted him—he was leaning against a tree, arms folded, watching me. When I was within two steps of him, he uncrossed his arms and held out his hands to me. I took them. They were warm, welcoming, deliciously sensuous.

"Thank you," I murmured, mentally comparing his words to Nate's earlier compliment and finding Nate's definitely the more wanting of the two.

"What did he want?"

"He invited me to dinner."

"An invitation to dinner is never just an invitation to dinner, Eve."

"What do you mean?" His thumb was caressing the palm of my hand in a maddening manner. I looked around the woods, suddenly realizing how dark it had grown. How still. If only an owl would hoot softly, or a cricket chirp, then I might relax. Instead I couldn't get Nate's story out of my head—about the dancers and poor Harry Willoughby.

"I'm sure that he wanted something from you." Insinuation slithered in and around each letter of the word, *something*.

"He doesn't even like me all that much," I protested. "He made that clear when we first met. And thanks for reminding me about that painful memory, Gabriel."

He laughed. "I'm not speaking of attraction, though you're *very* tempting, Eve. He wants to control you."

"So do you," I charged recklessly.

"But I have your best interests at heart. He is too wrapped up in himself, his family history."

My teeth worked at my lip. "Why would you, a stranger to me, have my best interests at heart?"

The thumb stopped its rhythmic stroke. "Because I do."

"That's not an answer, Gabriel. I want to know why."

"I don't really know, Eve. You may not like that answer, but it's the truth. The truth is not a value I hold dearly, but this time I honor it."

"He asked me to stay out of the woods. He wanted to protect me."

"That sounds like someone telling you what to do. Doesn't that bother you?"

"It was a suggestion," I replied, feeling strangely defensive of Nate. Where was Gabriel going with this?

"*Really*?" Sarcasm soaked through his tone like oil on a rag.

"He was nice about it." *Sort of...*

"And what if you'd said no, Eve?"

"I didn't." The words came out sharp, hard.

"Humor me..."

"Why do you care about what happened between me and Nate?" I cried. I wasn't sure why I was getting so emotional about Gabriel's accusations, but I was...and it felt good.

"Because I think you shouldn't let others tell you what to do," he answered, his voice growing as loud as mine, his eyes tempestuous. "I *never* would."

"Then you're a paragon of self-esteem, Gabriel."

The laughter was deeper and lasted longer this time. "You really do amuse me, Eve."

I dismissed this. "I'm my own person, Gabriel. I didn't say no to Nate, and I didn't say yes, because I will do what I think is best for me." I paused for a moment, thinking on my words. It seemed that with Gabriel I forgot who I was. I forgot that I was easily led, like sheep. I forgot to be Evalina Filmore. "Though you must admit after what happened to me this afternoon that his warning was a good one."

Gabriel looked down at the ground and I almost believed he was about to acknowledge I was right. But then his chin swung up and his intense sea eyes fastened on mine. "*Almost* happened. You were never in any real danger, Eve."

"I didn't think so, not at the time, but you and Nate did, *do*. I saw your face, Gabriel. You were ready to kill them right then and there."

"They went too far and they paid the price. You are safe now."

"Funny how I don't really believe you, Gabriel." He actually had the gall to look surprised. "You *were* the one who told me you didn't value the truth."

"I value you, Eve, and so I shall attempt to always speak the truth to you. No guarantees that I'll succeed, of course." He smiled charmingly.

I gently pulled my hands from his. "I should go in. The aunts might be wondering where I am."

"Those two mean you harm. I would keep you safe from them, from others. Always."

"I'll be fine, Gabriel. I agree that they're up to something, but I need to find out what it is first."

"Forget all that. You would be safer if you were to leave them."

"Nate said the same thing," I muttered. When he bristled at the implied connection, I ignored it. "Anyway, where would I go?"

"You can stay with me."

I paused. In that dark house in the woods? A place that wasn't supposed to exist? With an eccentric man nobody seemed to know? "Nate made the same offer," I said, this time purposely provoking him.

"Your Nate is an opportunistic prig," he snapped, taking the bait. I felt an alluring sense of power surge up inside me.

"Why don't you like Nate?"

"I should think that would be obvious. Now I'm warning you never to mention me in the same breath as him again or I'll have to see that the next time Thorndike and I cross paths, he will regret it."

A sudden gust of wind blew past me. "Okay, okay," I replied hastily, mentally taking note not to make that mistake again. "It doesn't matter. I'm not staying with either of you. I'm staying with my aunts."

"If those two harm you, I will have to do something."

"I still don't understand why you care, Gabriel. We've only just met. You barely know me."

One shoulder lifted in a shrug. "I told you, I don't really understand it myself. But isn't that the nature of such things?"

"What things?" I asked cautiously.

"Attraction. Passion. Desire."

I shivered. "I really must go, Gabriel. Perhaps I'll see you tomorrow."

"Oh, you will." His absolute certainty could have been considered arrogance, but I didn't think that it was. Somewhere along the way he'd staked his claim to superiority. "I'll make it happen."

"Unless the aunts actually do lock me in the attic, then no one can reach me."

"Eve..."

"I'm just kidding. I think it's time the aunts and I had a little talk."

He smiled in the darkness, and I could sense his approval. "I believe you're right."

"Goodbye, Gabriel." I turned to go.

"You are mine, Eve," I thought I heard him whisper as I walked away.

Though it might have been the wind.

Chapter Sixteen

✳

Trapped

Iapproached the house, not with fear, but with a growing fury. With dramatic vigor, I rehearsed the threat I would make if the aunts tried to lock me in my room again. Those two were not going to win this battle.

I was quick to learn how wrong I was.

They lay in wait for me in the shadows at the top of the staircase leading to my bedroom. Before I could react, each grabbed an arm and dragged me down the hall and into my room, heaving me onto the bed as though I were a child. When I turned over, I found them looming over me, glaring at me fiercely. Bones padded in behind them and plopped down in front of the door like a dragon protecting his lair. They had me trapped.

I struggled to sit up but Kelli shoved me back. "You don't move until I tell you to move."

"What do you think you're doing?" I demanded angrily, though I felt a cold chill filling my chest.

"Shut your mouth," Priscilla ordered. "You might think you've out-smarted us, Evalina, but you haven't. You're dealing with something you know nothing about, so I suggest you stay quiet and listen to me."

I decided to obey. Perhaps she meant to tell me what was going on. And besides that, I was frightened. I wasn't sure I could speak if I wanted to.

Satisfied with my compliance, she went on. "You're not to leave this house. You are our ward and we are responsible for you. You have defied me and gone into the woods when I told you not to. That is why we have to lock you in your room. For your own good. We cannot have you getting lost. Your father owes us something, Evalina, and I've decided it's time we collect. We thought to use you in place of him, but upon further reflection, I don't think that's going to work. So we've decided to use you as bait. If your father wants to see his darling daughter again, he'll have to come home."

I sucked in air, trembling with an insane urge to correct her. My father wouldn't come to my rescue. He'd fled from England without telling his sisters where he was going and he hadn't returned since. He wouldn't make an exception for me, not at the risk of his own hide.

How could Priscilla not know this about him? She was obviously desperate and not thinking clearly. But I certainly wasn't about to point out her error. Doing so would only make me irrelevant.

"You won't be seeing Nathaniel, you won't be going into the woods, and you'll not be leaving this room until we get what we want. Do you hear me?" When I didn't answer, she slapped me hard. The fierce look on her face could not mask her pleasure in the act, and my stomach threatened to revolt. "Do you hear me?"

"I hear you," I whispered. My own anger died away. In fact, the emotion fled so rapidly that I wondered if it had been mine in the first place. I was back to being Evalina Filmore again—spineless and afraid.

"You'd better hear her," Kelli spat, twisting my arm. My skin burned and my muscles protested. I tried to fight back but she twisted harder and I whimpered in pain. "We're in charge, you prat, and you do what we say."

"I will make you suffer," I uttered, my voice low, more like breathing than speaking, "until you are dead, dead, *dead*." My anger had not gone away, merely solidified, like molten lava cooling into rock. I welcomed it.

Kelli dropped my arm and backed away. "What did you say?"

"I'll burn down this house."

"You'll burn yourself, you git," she hissed back at me.

"So be it. I'm not afraid. Besides, do you honestly think you can keep me in here? I got myself out before, I'll do it again."

She went pale.

"She's bluffing, Kelli," Priscilla said. "She's as gutless as her father."

"I'm getting out of here," her sister huffed, heading for the door without turning her back on me.

"I'm nothing like my father," I told Priscilla, pushing myself up against the headboard. "Not anymore."

"Words," she scoffed, her pale blue eyes hard and cold. "He handed them out like sweets to children and they all meant nothing."

"And with those words he convinced you to do something you didn't want to do." It was a guess. An accurate one. Her whole body jerked as though something had slammed into her from behind.

"What did he tell you?"

"I'll burn down this house," I repeated, as Kelli flung open the door and hurried out of the room. "With everyone in it," I said louder. "I'll take you both down with me."

"You wouldn't do that to Bessie." Priscilla moved backward toward the door, her hands behind her to grasp the doorknob.

"An unfortunate casualty."

She gave me one last, long look, then slipped out the door, slamming it shut and locking it with quick, precise movements. I had scared her. Of course I hadn't really meant that about Bessie. I wasn't the daughter of actors for nothing. But Priscilla didn't know I was bluffing.

Alone, I undressed and got ready for bed. Strangely enough, I was no longer frightened of my situation. Yes, I was a prisoner, but not for long. I would find a way out, like last time. For now I would sleep; in the morning, I would plan.

Despite my lack of fear, I didn't fall immediately to sleep. A movie reel of everything I'd encountered here in England unwound in my head, from losing time in the woods to dancing with the Adonis to touring Nate's castle. Thinking of that disastrous visit reminded me of Nate's father and what he'd done. How miserable he must have been to go against our specie's natural inclination to survive. Things had not been going well for me lately, yet still I couldn't quite comprehend taking that final step no matter how miserable I felt. Of course, I hadn't lost anyone I loved. Even so, I didn't think that would drive me to the point of choosing death over life.

Then again, had I ever really loved anyone that intensely? The startling answer was *no. Not ever.* Not my parents, not any of my friends or the occasional boyfriend, not my crushes, no one. Neither Mother nor Father wanted or needed me to love them. Bessie might be someone that I could grow to care about. I didn't love her, but I might come to over time. I did rather enjoy my home-ec teacher, Mrs. Bonner, and wished the best for her, which was encouraging. But while I was capable of liking others, did I have it in me to love someone?

I wasn't sure how to answer that.

What about the feelings I had for Gabriel? Could they be called love, or even like? I didn't think so. Whatever they were, they were tantalizing, and probably why I went to him despite my better judgment. He intrigued me more than I cared to admit.

Then there was Nate. I think, like Gabriel, I found him compelling. But did I like him? Was there a chance for love? I couldn't say, not when I got so angry with him all the time. Admittedly there were moments when we connected—while discussing his work or joking about his Great-Great-Great Aunt Hildy, who might have been happier if she'd been born a male, but especially when he played the piano with such passion that it made me want to cry.

The difficulty was his officious manner—it really got in the way of things. And when I'd told him that I thought the aunts wanted something from me, he'd reacted like someone who knew more than he was letting on. My heart sank. I wished he'd just tell me what was going on. The more I knew, the better I'd be able to face what I needed to face.

Unless, of course, he was involved with their schemes.

The thought chilled me and ignited another round of questions. Was there anyone who wasn't caught up in this? Bessie, perhaps? She lived at Filmore Manor, though; she must know what was going on. She might be old and going blind, but she wasn't stupid. And what about Gabriel? Where did he fit into this? He wanted to protect me, but at the same time I had the feeling he wanted to own me.

I glanced down at my trembling hands and finally allowed myself to feel truly worried about what might happen to me. Priscilla did own a shotgun, after all. And there was Bones to finish me off if she only managed to wing me. Ridiculous thinking, of course. Still…maybe I *should* go home. I could find a small apartment in the city and attend college in the fall like I'd planned; Mother would loan me some money to get me started, anything to get me to move out. Having me around, she often bemoaned, aged her considerably.

I was suddenly struck by how alone I was. In some ways, I'd been given no choice in the matter, as with my parents and their emotional detachment. But in other cases, I could have behaved differently and not purposely kept people at such a distance. "Make no attachments," seemed to be my motto. It kept me from getting hurt, but in the end I had no one to love me and look out for me because I hadn't been prepared to offer the same.

On this note, I drifted off to sleep, hugging my pillow tightly to my chest.

~

When I awoke the next morning, my muscles ached and my tongue felt shriveled as a raisin. I'd dreamed of being chased through the woods— this time the aunts were brandishing torches and screaming, "Take her instead!" as they hunted me down. Their eyes were little fires and their mouths split wide with rage. The dream followed me into consciousness, clinging to me like evil barnacles. Before climbing out of bed, I mentally booted each aunt to the moon—my personal way of dealing with nightmares. I wished the method worked in real life.

Pulling on my blue suede slippers, I shuffled over to the door, feeling bruised as though I'd been attacked. It was still locked. How disappointing. For some reason I'd expected it to be open, that someone— possibly Gabriel—had learned of my plight and had found a way to free me. Or that maybe the aunts had recovered their temporarily lost sanity. Wouldn't that be nice?

I was about to turn away when something on the floor caught my eye—a battered, wooden tray, bearing toast, strawberry jam, and a pot of tea. Had Bessie prepared this? Judging by the paucity of food, I guessed the aunts had told her I was sick again, suffering from a relapse, no doubt. Still, there was enough sustenance to tide me over for a short while. That she had been party to locking the door disturbed me, though. She could very well have left it unlocked as a favor to me.

At the risk of her job? a little voice whispered worriedly in my head. She'd told me this position was all she had in the world. Other than the failing Aunt Grear, who couldn't be relied on to die any time soon, she had nothing to fall back on. I couldn't expect her to sacrifice her place here on my account. I simply couldn't count on Bessie, or even ask her to help me out; it wouldn't be fair.

You can't count on anyone, Evalina. No one cares anything about you, remember? They'd abandon you as quickly and lightly as a used-up rag. You're nothing to them except a good bit of gossip. They should be nothing to you.

The bitterness of the words startled me. I was used to berating myself for my mistakes—any bit of weight gain, no matter how small, receiving a grade lower than an A, stumbling while walking down the hall in school—but never in such a dark manner.

There are ways to set things right, you know. There are ways to even the score.

Anxiety quivered through me, sapping the last bit of moisture from my mouth. Thirsty and scared, I quickly poured myself a cup of tea. I sat and ate my sad breakfast, chugging down two cups more quickly than I should have and had to hurry to the loo. On returning to bed, the world tilted and I had to catch myself against the bathroom doorframe. Blinking slowly, my sight blurred and a dark shadow filled my head. Before I knew what was happening, I was on my knees crawling to the bed. After a struggle, I managed to climb up onto it. My body collapsed in on itself and I sunk deep into a black hole of sleep.

"She actually is sick," I heard someone murmur through a foggy haze. My brain was spinning, or was it the room? "I be wonderin' about that. Dunna know why they feel the need to lock her in. It's not like she's goin' to escape in this condition. She looks one foot in the grave to me."

"They did say she'd been sleepwalking the other night," a different voice answered.

"Hmm...I still think I should be lettin' Mr. Thorndike know. He called early this mornin' and they told him she was too sick to see anyone. That she'd been tryin' to be brave last night and had got herself sick again."

"But she obviously *is* sick, Bessie. Look at her."

"I know, I know, but this don't hold right. Those two be up to somethin', I'm sure of it."

I wanted to shout that she was right, but I couldn't make my mouth work. What was wrong with me? Maybe I really was ill. My only comfort, and it was a surprisingly big one, was that Bessie hadn't been conspiring with the aunts.

"I wouldn't be making too much of a row about it," the other voice warned, and I thought it sounded familiar. "You know how their kind are. They'll give you the shaft."

"I know," Bessie grumbled, and I felt my heart sink.

Like an overheated engine, my mind shut down again and I slept. When I awoke, it was dark outside. A sliver of moonlight shone through the window, painting a patch of silver on the quilt. My mind had cleared a little, though I still felt terribly weak. The lock rattled and I realized someone was trying to get into my room. I feigned sleep once more.

"She's still sleeping," a voice hissed. Kelli, of course. She had a voice like a murder of crows.

"How much of that stuff did you put in her drink?"

"I don't know. I kind of lost count, beastly little pills. Maybe eight or nine Valiums? A lot, anyway. I take four a day, so I thought I'd double the dose to knock her out. You said to be sure she didn't try to get out again. You know, because she was acting so completely bonkers, threatening to burn down the house and all."

"Eight or nine all at once! You're lucky you didn't kill her. She shouldn't still be like this." A cold finger and thumb clasped my wrist and lifted it to let it drop again. I pretended my arm was a cooked noodle, letting it flop, then lie still. "Good Lord, Kelli, she's completely out of it, even her lips are blue."

"I did what you told me, Prissy," her sister snapped. "If it was a bodge job, that's thanks to you. Anyway, less trouble for us when she's like this. *I* don't want to be burned in my bed."

"I think you mean it was a *botched* job, and it was you who completely messed this up. Next time I'll give her the dose."

"Fine. But put it in the tea. Liquid will get the drugs into her system faster."

"Well, aren't you the expert?" came the snide reply.

"I learned everything I know from you, you hypocritical wanker."

"Lock the door behind you," Priscilla ordered, her voice growing dim.

"I ought to lock you in here with her," Kelli grumbled, as she shut the door.

They were gone and I was left with the chilling knowledge that I'd been drugged. I had never really believed people did that kind of thing, only in novels or made-for-TV movies. Real people, especially family, shouldn't be capable of committing such horrid acts. Then again, those related to us are often the ones who hurt us the most.

Bloody Queen Mary knew that all too well.

I drifted off once more, only to awake in the morning to another tray, sitting on my bed this time. A note was tucked under a plate of scones. "Dearest Evalina, We hope you're feeling better. Drink up your tea, luv. You need your liquids! Auntie Priscilla."

I nearly gagged. Who was she trying to impress? More importantly, would they believe her act? She'd fooled me in the beginning—maybe fooled everyone...except Bessie.

Still feeling out of it—my head pounded and my stomach roiled—I devoured the scones smothered with fresh cream and raspberry jam. They were obviously Dunton scones, and I felt better knowing Miss Dunton had baked them. I was pretty sure the drug was only in the tea, though I wasn't absolutely certain. Still, I needed sustenance and would have to take my chances.

Besides, I really couldn't resist those scones.

After I finished eating, I lay back and waited. After about twenty minutes, I began to feel better, but I was still groggy. Limbs shaking, I picked up the delicate pot and poured a little bit of the tea into the tea-cup. Then, teapot still in hand, I slid off the bed, taking great care not to move too fast. In the bathroom, I tipped most of the contents of the pot into the sink. The orange-brown tea stained the white ceramic like dye, before disappearing down the drain. Using my hand for a cup, I sipped metallic water from the faucet. When my thirst was replete, I regarded myself in the mirror, taking in the dark circles weighing down the delicate skin beneath my bloodshot eyes, and my cracked, feverish lips. I looked as terrible as I felt.

My entire body quivered from the effort as I made my way back to bed. More acting would be required for when the aunts returned, whenever that might be. I didn't want them to know I was awake. Teapot restored to the tray, I crawled under the covers and started to breathe deeply. As luck would have it, I fell asleep. When I awoke, the light was bright between the cracks in the curtains and the tray had been refreshed, this time with cucumber sandwiches, hunks of cheese, and another pot of tea. Ginseng, this time, if my senses were correct. I cleaned off most of my plate, dumped half the tea, and climbed back into bed. Just in time, for there were angry voices outside my door.

"I don't know why I have to come with you every time," Kelli complained. "I'm totally knackered after going out last night. I need a kip."

"I've already told you why you need to be here—in case the drugs don't work. It's been known to happen. Don't forget that she escaped from a locked room once already, and she's also been eating an awful lot for someone who's been drugged."

Too late, I realized the mistake of clearing my plate. As much as Mother wanted me thin, she also couldn't fight her upbringing, which demanded that you clear your plate or don't leave the table until you do. "She's only just got the munchies!" Kelli giggled and I thanked her idiocy for giving me a good excuse.

"Yes, well, I'd still like to be sure. I don't trust her. She is Edmund's spawn, after all."

The key turned in the lock and the door swung open. I relaxed my whole body, mouth gaping slightly as I pretended unconsciousness. My tongue pushed out a little drool for good measure.

"Lord, look at her!" Kelli laughed. "Talk about knackered. She's totally out of it!"

"Yes, well, she should be. Between what you gave her and what I put in that teapot, she should be comatose for a while."

"You don't think she's faking it?" Kelli wondered. "Maybe we should check her to be sure. I could pinch her."

Crap. Leave it to Kelli to think the worst of people. Going on sheer instinct, I sat up suddenly, gazing blankly ahead. Both women jumped back, startled. "I'm so hungry," I mumbled, feeling blindly around for the last bit of cheese on the plate. "So hungry." Finding it, I shoved it into my mouth. "Why can't I have more, Mommy?" I pleaded, once I swallowed the morsel and lay back down. "The nurse at school said I'm not fat, so I don't need to diet anymore, and I'm so hungry all the time!" That last part was either over the top, or a stroke of genius.

"Bloody hell!" Kelli swore. "Did you see that? She thinks she's a kid again. Her mum must have starved her. That woman is a nasty bit of work."

"I hope so. Edmund doesn't deserve any better."

Kelli shivered. "Let's get out of here. She's creeping me out, chewing in her sleep like that. Like an old crony. Blimey! She's drooling again!"

"Grab the tray," Priscilla ordered.

The bedcovers shifted, there was a light breeze, a click in the lock, and the aunts were gone like thieves in the night. I waited a few minutes, then sat up. I needed to clear my head and lying down wasn't helping. Had Kelli actually put eight or nine Valium in the teapot? Was that enough to do permanent damage? Mother took an occasional Valium at two milligrams a pill, which was a low dose. I had the feeling Kelli had more than likely built up enough tolerance to kill an elephant, making her pill dose much stronger. I shuddered at the thought.

When my head stopped spinning, I slid out of bed. Feet flat on the floor I again waited several moments for the world to settle down. When I felt better, I pushed away from the bed and took a step, then another one, lights flashing in my head. The last time I'd felt this weak and out of sorts was when I'd had the stomach flu for a week. Mother had been preparing for her play's opening night and said she couldn't afford to get sick and so couldn't care for me. Father, citing a weak immune system, stayed at a hotel until I got better. In the meantime, I was left on my own, though only after being reminded to dial 911 if I thought I might be dying. Which, after puking until my ribs hurt and resting my hot and pasty cheek on the cool toilet seat between bouts of diarrhea and dry heaves, seemed a strong possibility.

You know, I really ought to off those two.

On my second trek around the room, my big toe caught against a corner of the hearth and I fell heavily against the wall. A loud creak startled me as the panel gave way. With a shriek, I fell forward through open air and landed hard on the floor. Before I could right myself, there was a whooshing noise and the light blinked out.

Darkness dropped over me like a blanket.

Chapter Seventeen

✳

A Visitor

It took my foggy brain several moments to figure out that I'd just discovered a secret room. Hidden rooms, or priest holes, as they are sometimes called, were not a rarity in mansions or castles built during those times when a person could be carted off simply for having a different opinion than those in power.

To actually find a secret door, however, seemed unreal. To be stuck behind one was even more bizarre. What if a latch had clicked into place, trapping me? How was I going to find it in this absolute darkness? Heart pounding, I stayed where I was and tried to orient myself to my surroundings. The absence of light was oppressive, as was the stale smell of age and neglect. An overwhelming urge to scream welled up in my chest. I clapped a hand over my mouth and forced myself to think good thoughts while I breathed slowly in and out through dilated nostrils.

When the desire to panic faded a bit, I pushed myself up on my hands and knees and searched for walls. I found one soon enough, patted it, turned 180 degrees and patted again. Cold stone, both times. I put my arms straight out like a T and touched both walls. Then I reached forward and found wood. When I reached behind me, my fingertips met only air. The wood panel had to be the wall to my bedroom. So far, so good.

When I tried pushing against the panel, it didn't budge. I tried again, and again. Finally I slammed my whole body against it. When nothing happened, except for bruising my shoulder, I started searching for a lever. My palms frantically patted the walls and floor; nausea spilled into my stomach like a tipped over bottle of poison. I didn't like it in here. Something felt wrong, as though other souls were trapped with me, their terror invading my body and further igniting my horror.

Stop it right this instant, Evalina Filmore! I admonished myself. *Keep your head about you and find a way out of this mess.*

Despite sounding suspiciously like my mother, it was good advice. I turned around and crawled several feet without meeting any impediment. There was a passageway here. But it was so dark and I was already so tired from my exertions that I gave up on the idea of trying to follow it. Dazed and exhausted, I'd likely only get myself lost. I turned and crawled back to the paneling, my fear returning. Death seemed entirely real and close to me at that moment, and more than likely to occur in such a macabre setting. My constricting heart threatened to finish off the suffocation the rank air had already started, and I fell forward in despair. As I reached out to catch myself, a small, round stone, an inch high, dug into my palm. Like a button, it sank beneath my hand and the secret door sprang open, nearly knocking against my head.

With a speed inspired by terror, I scrabbled through the opening and collapsed on the hearthrug as the door clicked shut behind me. My eyes ended up level with the bit of hearth where my foot had connected when I'd tripped. I reached out and pushed against the corner piece. It moved slightly, but the door remained closed. I pressed again, this time using my foot to shove against the wall. The door clicked open. I let it fall shut again. I was too tired to explore any further, but felt hopeful that I'd found a way out of my room, one that also wouldn't involve Bones.

After climbing into bed, I slept, and again I dreamed. I was in the woods and the air was heavy with mist as I crept through the trees, searching. She was out there somewhere, I knew, I'd seen her. There she was! But wait. What was this? A trick. An awful, horrible trick! Disgusted, I turned to go back only to find I couldn't retreat. Something was out there, something awful. I turned and ran.

Light footsteps and secretive whispers behind me pushed me forward and I sensed I was heading deeper into danger. Still, I kept moving; I didn't trust going back the way I'd come. Winded, I stopped near a jagged outcrop to catch my breath. The sound of pursuit—a rushing, hissing noise—grew louder. I didn't know where to turn; I didn't know where to run. The elusive threat seemed to be everywhere in the thickening fog, a mist that had taken on a life of its own.

At first I was terribly frightened, then, as though in a trance, I came to accept my fate. Climbing up onto the rocky ledge, I found what I was looking for—a gaping black hole the size of a small car. Moments later, dark figures burst out of the fog like a pack of wolves and I let myself fall backward.

I awoke before impact.

Lying in bed, I tried to calm the panicked rhythm of my breathing. My sense of smell in the dream, sharpened by fear and instinct, had picked up my pursuer's scent—the greasy odor of greed, the tangy scent of excitement, even a touch of fright, metallic and heavy, found my nose, and all these odors remained in my memory, plaguing me. My skin prickled under my bedclothes, my mouth felt as dry as though I'd been licking a salt block. Yet not once had I been under the impression that I was the person in my dream, the one who was searching for a lost someone, who'd been tricked before falling into the dark hole. As vivid as the images shone in my mind, I felt as though I were an actor playing a part. I'd been a peculiar witness to a stranger's death, whether his or her demise was real or imagined, I didn't know.

The absence of light slipping around the edges of the curtains told me it was nighttime again. Today was Thursday. Soon it would be Saturday, the day of the Solstice Festival, and the aunts would make their move. If they planned to wait until then...

Another tray sat on my bed, deposited not long before I had awakened; the muffins were still warm. After eating and dumping most of the tea into the sink, I decided to return to the secret passage. Time was running out. If I didn't make some kind of move now, trouble would seek me out. Besides, it wouldn't take long for the aunts to guess I was acting. Kelli might think I was naïve, but enough to continue drinking drugged tea? That was pushing things a bit.

Sliding out of bed I was surprised at how woozy I still felt. My bare feet on the wood floor felt cold and heavy as bricks. An overdose on sleeping pills, combined with hours of lying flat on my back, had weakened me. I hoped that eating something would restore me. I felt almost completely enervated, like a cooked noodle covered in wet cement.

The door resisted opening despite several weak kicks at the hearth, until I remembered there was a trick to it and shoved against the wall with my shoulder at the same time I kicked. The panel finally gave way, the hinges squeaking loudly. I waited, panting, to see if anyone had heard the strange noises coming from my room. After a couple minutes, when no one sounded the alarm, I entered the dark corridor.

As soon as the door closed behind me, I regretted my decision. My stomach gurgled and I wished I'd eaten more slowly. Shivering in my thin nightgown, I felt my way along the dank passage, icy fingers trailing along the damp stone wall. My imagination dredged up giant spiders sinking oversized fangs into my flesh, and I cursed my overactive mind.

After taking about a hundred steps, I was presented with a choice to turn left or right. I decided to turn left. To avoid getting lost I continued this pattern and made two more left turns. With any luck I'd find my way out of here. That is, if I remembered to take all right turns on my way back.

After the last turn I heard a voice.

"Don't you ever knock?"

My knees grew weak.

"Bessie said you were looking for me." I leaned against the wall, re-lieved. Kelli was the trespasser, not me.

"You could still knock."

A rapping noise echoed down the passage. "Happy now?"

"I am. But not because of your childish antics." Priscilla sounded as triumphant as a human glacier could sound. "Edmund is coming."

"What! When?"

"I finally tracked down his number, and he actually answered the telephone, first try. I told him his daughter was very ill and wouldn't 'recover,' if he didn't come. When that threat didn't work, I finally fig-ured out what would. I said the Wrath was displeased with him and had the power to reverse the command if some kind of agreement couldn't be made."

"That's a lie! The Wrath is as trapped as we are. 'One cannot get what he or she wants without the presence of the others,'" Kelli said, as though quoting, "...and that includes the Wrath!"

"Yes, I know, idiot. I *am* the one who worded the agreement. Unfor-tunately, Edmund disappeared on us. He's managed to hide out for twenty years now, though I can't imagine how a man with the intelli-gence of a rock managed to fool me for so long."

"Changing his name helped the little rat immensely," Kelli growled. "Who would've thought he'd be so damn clever? So when does the eejit arrive?"

"The night of the Solstice Festival."

"Can we keep her knocked out until then? Nat is becoming a prob-lem. He actually stopped me in the village and asked about her."

"We need to do something about him."

"I can distract him," Kelli volunteered, her tone dripping salaciously.

"Oh, good Lord, calm down. And no, you may not distract him. We'll have to do something more than that. He's showing very poor judgment, Kelli. I cannot abide poor judgment."

"Don't you touch him, Prissy. He's mine. You're just jealous because he feels sorry for the brat."

"I think that bothers you more than it does me."

"He's always been a pushover for lost causes, you know, and our niece is a lost cause if I've ever seen one. And don't you dare pretend this doesn't make you potty, Priss. You've been hot for Nat since the moment you set your beady little eyes on him. It's why you did what you did."

"Why we *all* did what we did. I did not act alone."

The board that I was leaning against suddenly shifted and fell to the floor. I silently cursed it, beads of cold sweat popping up on my forehead like goose pimples.

"What was that?" Priscilla demanded.

Footsteps crossed the floor. I stood still, in a cold sweat, unwilling—*unable*—to move. Judging by the increasingly muted sounds, the aunts were moving away from the wall, toward the bedroom door. A creak sounded, then a few seconds later, the door slammed closed.

"Oh, Bones. Go lie down," Priscilla ordered.

My breath eased out of my lungs. Bones had saved me.

The aunts' conversation turned to the mundane, the festival's food line-up, the entertainment, the various booths. They sounded so normal I almost doubted that moments before I'd heard them plotting against my father and myself.

Gathering my strength, I stepped backward along the narrow corridor, inch by painful inch. My head pounded like a drumbeat, but my mind was alert enough to do some fast thinking. I would return to my room and pretend I'd never left it. No sense letting the aunts know I could get out. Then I'd make my escape when neither of them was around to give chase. Kelli, I could outrun. Bones and Priscilla and her shotgun, on the other hand...

When I finally reached my room I spent ten minutes cleaning myself up, anxious and worried they'd come into the room at any time. Dust smudges splotched my face like a coal miner after a long day, and abandoned cobwebs caught in my hair gave me a mad air.

I was toweling off my face when I heard voices. Like a drunken dog I galloped across the floor and leaped into bed, feigning sleep as soon as my head hit the pillow.

"What's going on, Bessie?" *Nate*. My heart thrilled at the sound of his voice. I told it to knock it off. I had yet to forgive him for thinking he could boss me around.

"I dunna know. That's why I called you. Maybe you can straighten those two out. They're up to somethin', you can be sure of that."

The doorknob rattled, then came heavy pounding on the door. "Evie?" he called out. "Are you all right in there?"

I was about to croak that I was fine, let me out, when more voices came hurrying down the hallway. "Nathaniel! What a pleasure to see you. Come to visit Evalina? She's quite out of it at the moment."

"Why the locked door, Priscilla?"

"I didn't want her to get out and hurt herself. She sleepwalks, remember?"

"I don't think she does."

"Well, it doesn't matter," she said dismissively. "She's been acting delirious enough lately to do so. A fever of 104 will do that. I thought she was getting better the other night, but she took a fast turn for the worst. I don't know what she has, the flu, I suppose, but it's probably pretty contagious. That's why I've been taking up her tray rather than having Bessie do it. I have the constitution of an ox. I never get sick."

"I'd still like to see her," he insisted, and my foolish heart fluttered again. "I brought her coat and I'd like to give it to her."

"It's your funeral," Kelli sneered. "I'll stay out here, thank you very much. Whatever she has, I don't want to catch it. I can't get sick, not with the festival coming up, right Nat?"

He murmured something I didn't catch.

"I'll join you, Nathaniel," Priscilla said, giving him little choice in the matter. The door swung open, letting the hall light in. If I had any ideas of appealing to Nate to save me, I gave them up. I still wasn't entirely sure where he stood with the aunts. Plus, he wanted to send me back to the States. Further, though I would love to be rescued, I knew I had to figure out what all this was about. Call me crazy, call me suicidal, but I had to know.

Their footsteps tapped across the wood floor and I made myself breathe low and deep. "As you can see, she's out completely." I could feel Priscilla hovering at the foot of the bed like a vulture. "You can put her coat on that chair and we can go."

There was a movement by my side and then I sensed someone leaning over me, followed by a weight on the bed. I smelled Nate's cologne and felt the warmth radiating from his body. The back of his hand pressed gently against my forehead and I stayed still as best I could, though all I wanted to do was heave a big sigh as I reveled in his touch. His hand stayed for a moment, resting on my skin, then moved away. One finger gently lifted my eyelid.

"She doesn't have a fever, but she looks like she's been drugged. Her pupils are no bigger than a pencil tip."

"It's quite possible. You know how Americans are. Spoiled rotten, wanting their quick fixes the way they do." Priscilla said all this casually, and I hated her in that moment. She was quite willing to tromp all over my good name to get what she wanted.

"You're saying she does drugs? That's why she's like this?" Did Nate sound disbelieving? I couldn't tell. *Don't believe her Nate!*

"I'm only saying it's a possibility," Priscilla wisely backed off. "I thought drugs might be one explanation when I first met her—her story about leaving her luggage behind, then finding it on the ground only feet away from her. Very odd."

"There could be other reasons for that, Priscilla, as you know quite well."

My breath caught. He *did* know something! But what, and how much?

"She lost track of *hours* the other night, Nathaniel. You found her wandering in the woods after repeated warnings to stay out of them. Something is not right with her."

He sighed and rose from the bed. My body, which had rolled toward the edge, settled back into the middle. "I see that she's eating. How's that possible, being that she's so sick?"

"Well, it makes perfect sense, if you consider my theory," Priscilla replied. "Certain drugs make you want to eat more, isn't that right, Kelli?" she called out the door.

Kelli, for once, chose not to say a word.

"She doesn't strike me as the type of person who would do drugs," Nate persisted.

"Most people don't. At any rate, at least she's getting some nourishment in her. She needs to keep her strength up for the battle ahead." I heard foreshadowing behind those words and fought against an urge to shudder.

"What are you talking about, Priscilla? It's not like she's going to war." Nate had caught the warning, too.

"Of course not. I merely meant that her father is coming to visit. I get the feeling the two of them don't exactly get along."

"Edmund's coming home?" Nate sounded shocked. "Are you sure?"

"He'll be here Saturday."

"I never thought he'd come back." His voice was astounded, confused. "One day he's here and the next he's gone without so much as a goodbye. A few of the villagers even wondered if he was a victim of the Wrath, until Frank Ames said he saw him leaving on the train to London. So where's he been? What's he been up to?"

"He lives in the States, working as an actor, of all things. I've always known where he was and when he'd come back," she lied smoothly. "He was the one who wanted to get away from everyone, from the pressure, and he asked me and Kelli not to tell anyone where he'd gone. But he has obligations here now. He simply needed to be re-minded of them, and he agreed to return."

During this exchange, I'd been pondering whether or not to suddenly wake and announce that I was recovered. I finally decided against such a rash move. Unless Nate was willing to whisk me away immediately, I'd have blown my cover for nothing. I also still wasn't absolutely sure I could trust him. No, better to let them all keep believing that I was drugged. Then I'd have the opportunity to search Priscilla's bedroom via the secret passageway before I made my escape.

"Well, let him know that I want to see him. I looked up to him when I was young."

"I will, Nathaniel. We'll be seeing you at the meeting tomorrow morning, of course."

Perfect. I could make my search while she was gone.

"Are you sure you should be leaving Evie alone? She looks awfully sick to me, like she should be in hospital."

"Bessie will be here, won't you, Bessie?"

"I told you, Miss," Bessie called through the doorway. "I have to go see me Auntie Grear. She's failin' fast." It occurred to me that Bessie hadn't entered the room and I wondered why. Was Kelli somehow holding her back? It was possible—either through meaningless conver-sation, or with her substantial bulk. Or maybe, heaven forbid, Bessie believed Priscilla's lies about me doing drugs and had decided to steer clear of me.

I didn't like that at all. In fact, just the idea of it made me feel sick. Her opinion had become quite important to me over the past few days.

"Oh, yes. You did say that, didn't you, Bessie dear? I've been so wor-ried about Evalina that I forgot." A disbelieving snort came from the hall, which Priscilla blithely ignored. "I'll look into finding someone else to watch her."

"Are you sure?" Nate sounded doubtful. "I could stay with her. You ladies don't need me at the meeting."

"We need your expertise on where to place the booths," Priscilla re-marked smoothly. "You're the only one who knows anything about that sort of stuff. Don't worry, Nathaniel. I have a few ideas of who to call. I'll take care of it."

"Well, all right," Nate replied, sounding reluctant. His concern warmed me down to my toes. I tried not to think what this might mean. "As long as she's not alone."

But I would be alone. Priscilla was lying to him. She wouldn't dare call anyone. They might learn something she didn't want them to know. "I'll take care of everything, Nathaniel," she assured him again in a low, caressing tone, like he was ice cream and all she wanted to do was lick him. I knew in that moment that she'd been lying to Kelli, as well. Priscilla was in love with Nate and he either had no idea or chose not to acknowledge her feelings or…well, I didn't want to consider the third option.

Nate lightly touched my cheek one last time, then left the room. The lock turned with a loud click, and I was alone. Time to plan. First, I would need to be sure to wake early. That shouldn't be too hard; I felt better with each passing moment. When the aunts were gone, a visit to Priscilla's bedroom was in order. Afterwards, I intended to head down to the kitchen, via her bedroom door, to gather food, the old flashlight I'd used in the attic, a knife, and whatever else I could find.

I had to be quick about it. I had no idea how long the meeting would run and the aunts undoubtedly wouldn't want to leave me alone for any length of time. I could not be caught outside my room. There was no way I'd be able to talk my way out of getting through a locked door without a key, twice, and this time, while supposedly comatose.

Despite my heightened anxiety, I fell asleep quickly. When I awoke, it was still early. Six a.m. I didn't dare go back to sleep for fear of missing the aunts' departure.

For the next few hours time dragged by. I made several trips to the window on tiptoe, soon learning all the creaky spots in the floor, to peek out from behind the curtain to be sure I hadn't missed anything. While I looked for the aunts, I also searched for Gabriel, but he didn't appear. Where had he gone? Was he in the least concerned that I hadn't shown up these last couple days?

I was scanning the woods when I heard footsteps. A diving leap got me into bed in time, but I'd broken out in a sweat. I lay still, hoping Priscilla, who was sure to be delivering my drugged pot of tea and food, wouldn't notice. Once inside the room she set the tray down at the end of the bed and stared at me for several seconds—I could feel her cold, blue eyes on me like ice daggers. I sweated some more.

"I can't tell you how much I look forward to exacting my revenge on your father, Evalina. Twenty long years he had. Well, now it's my turn. It's really too bad you're an innocent bystander in all this. At first I thought you might be spared, but not anymore. You see, Nathaniel is mine. When someone tries to take what's mine, I get rid of them. I'm sure you understand."

After she finished her speech, the door closed with a confident click on her dark form. Did she know that I was awake and faking it? I

didn't think so. She'd spoken as though she believed I was safe to con-
fide in because I was unconscious. Little did she know… Still, what she
had said, whether she'd expected me to hear her or not, was more than
disturbing. She meant to get rid of me. But did that mean murder? It
didn't seem possible. If caught, she stood to lose her freedom, possibly
her own life. Maybe she believed, like a psychopath would, that she
wouldn't get caught. Maybe she'd reached the point of no return and
was willing to take the risk of going to prison to exact revenge on my
father. What, I wondered worriedly, had he done to her to provoke
such hatred, such wrath?

Wrath.

There was that word again. The whole town was filled with it; they'd
even named a forest and the creatures that lived there after it. Maybe
Priscilla was one of those creatures. Even though she hadn't been with
Gwyn and the others, it was a possibility my mind couldn't dismiss,
and I began to feel uncertain once more. While the Wrath had done
nothing to hurt me, according to Gabriel, they had fully intended to.

My mind was made up. I had to get out of this house today. I'd been
foolish to wait around this long. I had stayed because I wanted to believe this was one of my gothic adventures; that I was the lovely and
irresistible heroine who would solve the mystery just in the nick of
time and make everyone love me. I'd been stupid on both counts.

At ten o'clock, the aunts finally left the house. Bessie had gone an
hour before, glancing over her shoulder several times before climbing
into a squat, white van waiting for her in the drive. Dunton's Teashop
and Bakery was written in flowery script on the side, so I was quite
sure who her ride was. I also figured out who the familiar sounding
visitor with Bessie had been—the secretive Miss Dunton. Bessie threw
one last myopic look up at my window, sending me ducking behind
the curtain, then struggled into the van. It scooted down the road at a
fast clip, disappearing around the corner like a cop car in hot pursuit.

I watched them go with mixed feelings. I wasn't exactly thrilled with
Miss Dunton, not after what she'd said during my visit to the teashop,
nor did I especially trust her. So seeing Bessie leave with her made my
chest ache and my eyes sting. Was Bessie a part of this whole scheme?
Was I just kidding myself that she was on my side?

An hour later, the aunts left the house in a hurry. Priscilla wore her
typical, wraith-like black, whereas Kelli had dressed in a pink miniskirt,
red, low-cut blouse and matching stilettos with heels spiky enough to
be classified as weapons. She was literally dressed to kill. Poor Nate.

Afraid I might accidentally drink the tea in my distraction I dumped the teapot first thing. After rinsing the teacup out a few times, I filled it with water and gulped the contents to quench the uncanny thirst drying my mouth like a wasteland. I ate with a haste that was sure to give me a stomachache later, but I didn't care. My fear had become something alive, its greedy tentacles creeping through my veins like searching creatures. I was afraid for my life and my body took the brunt of it. I wanted to gag, hide in a corner, and run, all at the same time.

I chose to run. Earlier I'd packed my backpack with essential clothes, my passport, and all my money, though I was forced to leave behind my beloved books and two suitcases of clothes. I hid them instead in the secret passage. A search of the wardrobe turned up a musty wool blanket, which I rolled up and shoved under the covers to resemble a sleeping figure. The charade might afford me precious time to get away, or so I hoped. I also checked the door, just in case it wasn't locked. It was.

After pulling my quickly washed hair back into a ponytail, I dressed in jeans, a short-sleeved blouse, and a brown hoodie. Thick, warm socks and my leather boots cinched tight, and I was ready to begin my search.

Bag strapped to my back, I flew down the hidden hallway toward Priscilla's room as quickly as I could in the dark. When I came to the end of the last corridor, it took me several precious minutes to locate the lever for her door. Unlike mine, the opening mechanism was stuck in a corner. When I pressed the protrusion, the door popped open without a sound, as though someone kept it oiled on a regular basis. Maybe Priscilla knew more about this house than I thought.

Her room, when I flicked on the light, was hardly a surprise. I'd expected an arctic décor of all whites and angles and hard surfaces and that's what I found. She was someone who kept all her secrets close to what little heart she might have, fearing to let anything of her personality show, even in her choice of furniture. Or maybe she had nothing in her to share. That emptiness, I think, scared me more than anything.

I rooted through dresser drawers filled with neatly folded camisoles and underwear and t-shirts, carefully straightening everything as I went, wasting precious time, but I couldn't let on that I'd been there. My caution might be irrational, but in my defense, everything about this whole mess was irrational.

Between the thick mattress and box spring, under rugs, beneath chairs, the sides of chair cushions, all were thoroughly explored— nothing escaped my attention. I glanced at my watch to find that an hour and a half had passed since I'd left my room. I was stunned. I hadn't meant to spend so long searching, especially when I hadn't found anything worthwhile or revealing. My shaking fingers and weighted limbs had slowed me down, making me clumsy.

Desperate now, I tried places where no one would hide anything important, like the drawers in the nightstand. I pulled open the top drawer, spotted a tiny, silver handgun, and promptly shut it again. Nothing important, hm? Feeling shaky, I glanced inside the lower drawer, spotted the Filmore stationery with its ostentatious crest, and was about to move on when something struck me as odd. A Bible. Somehow my aunt didn't seem the religious type. I pulled out the black, leather-bound book and it fell open at the beginning of Revelations, where Priscilla had stuck a sealed envelope. What an interesting spot to place it, I thought. Hopefully her choice was not a prophetic one, at least in the apocalyptic sense.

Curious about what the envelope contained, but also worried about the time, I tucked it into the front pocket of my backpack. At the door of the bedroom, I paused and listened, and when I didn't hear anything I turned the bolt, swung open the door, and stepped into the hall. A low growl greeted me.

Bones.

Chapter Eighteen

✳

Escape

The two of us stared at each other like wary cowboys in a standoff. The question was, who would win? I had more to lose. At most, my life. At the very least, several digits. Bones only stood to lose a little dignity, maybe a tooth while chewing on my femur. It appeared that I was going to have to make the first move.

I drew myself up, making my body seem bigger than it was. "Back off, Bones! I need to get through."

Instead of backing off, Bones stood with an effort and stuck his enormous face into mine. Blood rushed through my veins and my heart seemed to swell up to twice its normal size. "I mean—" I gasped. "Please let me through." Bones stuck his cold nose in my ear; his panting was harsh and wet and hungry. It was too late to retreat, and now he was going to chew me up and spit me out. I squeezed my eyes shut and waited for his fangs to pierce my exposed throat.

A cool breeze startled my eyes into popping open. Bones had stepped aside, creating a path for me to slip by. I stared at him in wonder. Was this some kind of dog trick? Fool your victim into thinking everything was forgiven, then attack from behind? Or was he a Mosie in disguise?

Either way, I had little choice but to make a move. If I wanted to escape from my room, this was the way to do it. Pretending a nonchalance I in no way felt, I shut the door behind me and took a step forward. Then another. The floorboards creaked beneath the weight of my tentative feet, which wished nothing more than to be flying down the hall.

I heard Bones panting. I heard teeth gnashing and drool dripping. But no pounding paws. Not yet. Finally, I came to the end of the hall. When I looked back, Bones lay on the floor in front of Priscilla's bedroom snuffling at a paw, seemingly having forgotten my presence.

I released the sanction on my feet and they clattered swiftly down the stairs and toward the kitchen. I imagined at any moment the sound of a dog bent on dinner galloping toward me. He never came, but he still might. I had to move fast.

My watch now read a quarter to twelve. With no Bessie to fill the kitchen with her cantankerous presence, the room seemed less homey and warm. I grabbed the battered flashlight from the shelf, and then, while rummaging through the cupboards searching for food, I heard a noise outside the window. A car door slammed and voices drifted toward me.

I froze. The aunts were back. Startled, I glanced out the window. I could see nothing of them, suddenly remembering that the window did not overlook the front drive. The voices grew louder as they entered the house. Trapped, I ran for the nearest opening and plunged through it, catching myself just in time to keep from plummeting down a flight of stairs leading into the cellar.

Should I backtrack? Too late. The voices were coming toward the kitchen. Going forward was my only chance for escape. My feet took on a life of their own, carrying me down the rickety stairs into the dark labyrinth. There had to be another way out of the cellar, and I had to find it soon. I felt trapped, much more so than in the hidden corridors upstairs. Ghosts of the past seemed to rule down here, and I was loath to meet them.

I flicked on the flashlight and the bright light only made matters worse. Things I would've missed running blind, were now all caught in the flashlight's spotlight—spider webs and their creepy, eight-legged residents, moving shadows, rats.

It didn't take long for me to get lost. After a few minutes of running into dead ends and backtracking, I stopped and bent over, gasping for breath. If only I'd kept my head I might have figured out that I needed to stay along the outside wall. You can't get out of a house when you're in the middle of it.

Gabriel, help me!

As soon as my mind shouted the words, I knew I'd made a mistake, but despite my unease I repeated my call. I didn't like asking for help, probably because whenever I did my mother either laughed at my audacity, shrugged off my request, or got irritated with me for bothering her—telling me I could do it myself. Which was why I was able to cook, clean, make appointments, find transportation to school events, and pay the bills, all by the age of ten. Her callousness had made me very self-sufficient. I'd never point that out to her, though.

She'd make me thank her for it.

A beacon glimmered off to my left and I raced toward it. It turned out to be daylight struggling to shine through a casement window, filthy to the point of being opaque. My heart leaped. I'd not only found an outside wall, I'd found a way out. As I studied the two-by-three foot space, I reassured myself that I wasn't nearly as fat as Mother would have me believe and could fit through it. The tricky part would be reaching the window, which was six feet up. I could jump six feet, even grab hold of the sill, but I wouldn't be able to pull myself up and out.

Luckily the cellar was full of things to climb up on. After finding a ladder-backed chair, I dragged it over to the wall, climbed up on it, and struggled to open the rusty latches. As I fought with them, my rickety perch teetered to the left, then to the right, threatening to tip. Despite the risk, I kept on working until I sliced my finger on a jagged piece of metal near the latch. I cursed loudly. Suddenly a bang echoed down the hall and I froze, my teeth gripping my lower lip. The aunts. They must have discovered that I'd been in the kitchen and had fled to the cellar.

No longer worried about being heard, I pounded on the wooden casement with my flashlight. Bits of white paint flaked off with each thud, coating my arm like snow, until at last, with one tremendous assault, the window gave in. Breathing hard now, I pushed outward and the rusty hinges screeched in protest. Cool air rushed past me and I inhaled deeply before tossing my flashlight out and pulling myself up.

My head and shoulders were soon through the opening, but I couldn't seem to make the rest of me fit. Mother, damn her eternal soul, was right—I was too fat.

The sounds grew louder—two voices, hurrying footsteps. The aunts were heading my way, probably following my footprints in the dust. I might as well have left breadcrumbs or arrows drawn on the floor. Disgusted with my own stupidity, I went back to work on freeing myself. I wiggled and shifted, trying to squeeze my body through the opening, but I couldn't move forward.

Then I remembered something. I was still wearing my backpack, *damnit!* My searching foot found the rickety chair once again. The ancient piece of furniture wobbled, but held, though a loud crack warned me of its imminent demise.

Trying to stay balanced, I fought to pry the straps off my shoulders, which was as difficult as removing a toddler who didn't want to stop playing piggyback. Finally, with a strong tug the pack was off and flung through the window. The effort was too much for the chair. With a snap, one of the legs broke and I dropped to the ground like a brick. The window slammed shut. My elbows met the stone floor and I nearly cried out, muffling my pained groan with the sleeve of my pullover.

Pushing myself to my feet, I looked around and spotted a wooden wine crate. I wasn't sure it was high enough to get me out, but it would have to do. There was nothing else around that was tall enough. Sliding it into place beneath the window, I stepped onto the narrow box and jerked the window open.

Be strong, I told my arms, as I pulled myself up, *and be quick*.

The voices were just around the corner.

I'm not sure how I did it, but a burst of energy flashed through my limbs and I lifted myself up like an Olympic gymnast. With a quick wiggle, I was through and on the ground. The window closed behind me with a muffled bang. Not waiting to see how close my aunts were, I grabbed my backpack and flashlight and dashed toward the woods, threatening at any second to lose my footing on the damp grass.

Finally I broke through the line of trees, but I kept running, deeper and deeper through the darkening maze of trunks and stones, until at last I collapsed onto a rounded, moss-covered rock. I couldn't run any longer. I could only hope they hadn't followed me into the woods, or sent Bones to do their dirty work.

Several moments passed before I stopped wheezing, and then several more before I felt strong enough to look around. Nothing was familiar, of course. I'd never been to this area of the forest, and I was completely lost, which was more than a little worrying. I had no idea how many acres these woods encompassed, and having been interrupted in the kitchen, I had nothing to eat.

Maybe if I lay on the stone long enough, Gabriel would come to me. He had offered to let me stay with him before, maybe he would again. If he could find me. Even in midday, the woods were dark and foreboding, full of whispers and odd screeches. Rustlings in the undergrowth made my head jerk back and forth like windshield wipers, searching for their source. Was it an elk, or a forest deer? Maybe the strange dancers…

But no animal appeared, and neither did Gabriel.

Cold and exhausted, my eyes started to droop, despite my fear. It seemed I still hadn't fully recovered from being drugged. I should rest a bit, I thought, try to regain my energy. Flashlight in hand, I wrapped my arms around my quivering torso and lay down on the velvety moss.

I'll only rest for a few minutes, I told myself. *Then I'll find Gabriel…*

I felt the chilling presence of others watching me, waiting for me to drop off, but I couldn't fight the sleep that descended upon me like death. My eyes closed and I was out.

~

I awoke to firelight and shadows. I was no longer lying on a cold, hard rock but in a large bed beneath crisp, white sheets, my head resting on a soft, down pillow. My eyes flew about the grand room, wary and searching. Where was I? Despite the fire, the room looked and felt un-lived in, as though I were its first sentient occupant.

"Hello?" I called softly.

"You're awake." A figure sitting by my bed leaned forward.

"Gabriel," I breathed. He was wearing his loose, white shirt, the first few buttons undone to reveal his medallion.

"I heard your call."

"The aunts... They almost caught me and I ran and I cut myself and I've probably bled all over your sheets." I pulled my hand out from beneath the covers. A thorough inspection of all ten digits, front and back, revealed not even a scratch. "But I would swear..."

Gabriel leaned closer. His face caught the glow of the fire, and flames flickered in his eyes. I saw him smile. "Perhaps you're a fast healer."

"I'm not," I declared. "Not any more than usual." Had I dreamed the injury, the flight? The voices, the blood? "Where did you find me?"

"In the woods, lying on Roundstone."

"Do you name all the rocks in the woods?"

He chuckled. "Only the important ones."

"How did you find me?"

"It wasn't hard. I'm drawn to you, Eve. Haven't you realized that by now?"

I plucked at the sheet, feeling both uncomfortable and warily in-trigued by his words, even flattered. "Where am I now?" I asked, not responding to his comment. He might elaborate and tell me something that wasn't nearly as flattering.

"You're in my house."

"Is this the place where I first met you? When I can remember first meeting you, that is."

"It is." His eyes were currents, pulling me in.

"I won't stay long," I babbled, looking away from his intense gaze. "Only until I can come up with a plan. The aunts wanted to use me as bait to lure my father here."

Gabriel's shoulders pulled back. "Your father is coming home?"

"Yes. They tricked him into it."

"I somehow missed that. They never said..."

I glanced over at him, puzzled. "Who never said?"

"Oh," he laughed. "My little spies. They tell me what goes on in the village."

"Of all the people I've met so far, no one has mentioned you. So who would act as your spy?"

"Anyone who owes me a favor."

I didn't like the sound of that. "Why don't you just go to the village yourself?"

"I don't particularly like...other people."

"Gabriel, *I'm* other people."

His eyes glinted. "You are not like the others, Eve. There's something different about you."

"I can't see what." My words sounded modest, but really they meant, *do* go on. He was the first person ever to say anything like that to me.

"I feel you inside my mind, in my blood, and in every breath that I take. Yet I cannot see into you, Eve. I try very hard, but you elude me."

"If you're trying to charm me, Gabriel..." ...*it's working*, I finished in my mind.

He smiled. "I wouldn't think of insulting your intelligence."

Flustered, I returned to my original thought. "I won't stay long."

"Stay as long as you like." He reached out and settled his hand on my arm. His skin was warm as the fire's flames, though I was cold as a tombstone. I absorbed his heat, storing it like a bear during its last days of summer. "When is your father coming?"

"The day of the festival, I believe. I think the aunts want to use him for something. Some kind of business deal to do with the house, I'm guessing."

"Or they want to use him as a sacrifice."

He'd read my mind. "I can't imagine that."

"You'd be surprised." He squeezed my arm, watching his own fingers thoughtfully as he continued to press the soft flesh. His movements matched my heartbeat.

"I should warn Nate. He can help."

His grip tightened, each finger a miniature boa constrictor. "Are you sure that your *Nate* can be trusted?"

"He's not *my* Nate," I muttered irritably, though I wasn't sure why this statement should rub me the wrong way. "Why do you ask that?"

"The feud between your families comes to mind."

"He told me the feud started because my family double-crossed his during Queen Mary's reign."

"And you believe him?"

"Well, yes. I do."

"Even when his story makes your family look irredeemably guilty?"

"After having met Aunt Priscilla and Aunt Kelli, and knowing my father as I do, I don't doubt that my ancestors were guilty of betraying the Thorndikes."

"Maybe the Thorndikes brought it on themselves. Maybe they told stories about the Filmores. Being wronged, having falsehoods told against you, has a way of infiltrating your being, warping and twisting *everything.*"

I considered this. "You're saying that his family lied about my family, and that made my family seek revenge?" He nodded and I frowned. "Even if that were true, which I doubt, that still doesn't excuse my ancestors. Everyone has choices in life. You choose to be bad or good."

"Are you certain we're not born that way?" The corner of his mouth tilted impishly.

"I think we're born with certain traits and we choose what to do with those traits."

"What about your complaisance, Eve? How will you overcome your inherent desire to do what others tell you to do?"

I didn't like him pointing out my faults, and I yanked my arm away from his proprietary grasp. *I make them pay,* a voice in my mind answered him. "I don't think following advice is a terrible weakness, and I am getting better at standing up for myself."

"I don't see that."

"You can't see anything beyond your own nose," I growled at him, shocked at the sound, like I had the devil inside me. I coughed, hoping to shake the beast loose.

He pulled back, raising a golden eyebrow. "I stand corrected."

"You can *sit* corrected for all I care. I don't have time for this, Gabriel. I have to do something about my aunts before they do something about me." *Destroy before you are destroyed.* "And even though I'm angry with my father, I can't let them hurt him."

"You have nothing to worry about, Eve. I will help you."

"Nothing personal, Gabriel, but what can *you* do?"

"You'd be surprised. I hold more power in this village than you might think."

"The villagers don't even know who you are."

"Oh, they know me. They just don't talk about me."

"Why's that?"

He gave an innocent shrug. "Who knows?"

I didn't believe him, nor did I think he expected me to. "I'll handle this myself," I told him. I was about to climb out of bed when I realized that my jeans and hoodie, my damp boots and socks, even the rubber band in my hair, which felt clean and soft as though someone had brushed it with great reverence, had been removed. I was now wearing a gossamer white gown, delicate as spider's silk and wispy as mist. I blushed, revealing my youth and inexperience like a beacon in the night.

"Do you like it?"

"How did it come to be on me?"

"Magic," he teased. "A little sleight of hand."

I fought an urge to shiver at the image his words conjured up in my mind. He was intensely adept at the charm game and I wanted to let myself fall hard for him. Oh, did I want to. But I had to keep my head clear to plan what I needed to do next. I didn't want him to know he had me under his spell. I refused to give him that power.

"Did you like what you saw?"

"Oh, yes."

"Good. Next time keep your hands to yourself."

He raised them in the air with a little shrug as if to say, I cannot control them, you see. "Your clothes are drying by the fire." He stood and walked to the door. He wore tan breeches with his white shirt, and black boots up to his knees. He looked like a gentleman from another century. "What I could do to help you, Eve, I do not think you would want. But my door is always open to you. Come and go as you please. When this is over, I'll be waiting for you."

He left the room, his straight back turned toward me like a wall dividing us. A darkness flooded my body and my blood grew sluggish with the silt of disappointment. Gabriel had left me on my own.

Isn't that what you wanted? my practical side demanded. I shook my head as I stared at the closed door. *I'm sick of being alone,* my sentimental half sighed. *I'm tired of always having to do things on my own, of doing everything for others. Just this once, I wouldn't mind being the one getting rescued.*

But he did not come back.

Fighting an urge to dissolve into tears of self-pity, I slid out of bed. Standing in front of the fire, which gave off surprisingly little heat for its size, I felt reluctant to take off my lovely nightdress. I twirled like a ballerina, feeling magically light. I fingered the soft material and sighed. I felt so resistant to removing my gown that I returned to bed to avoid doing so. Halfway there, an image flitted into my mind. It was Gabriel, standing on the other side of the door, waiting for me to give in. He would help me, I realized, but only if I acquiesced, only if I became his. I could climb back into bed, he would treat me like a queen, and he would own me.

Promptly turning about, I quickly dressed in my own clothes, then grabbed my backpack sitting near the door. I may have wanted to be rescued, but not at such a sacrifice. I wasn't that desperate. Not yet. I did not want to be owned.

The hallway was empty when I entered it. He had not been waiting for me, after all. I quickly stifled the sharp burn of regret piercing my chest. Pulling on my backpack, I followed the ghostly passage, which led to a grand staircase, and descended swiftly, as though running for my life. *This house is not real*, I told myself. *None of this is real.*

Once outside, I realized that another day had passed. The morning sun shone brightly on the wild garden, dewdrops shimmered in the light breeze. I smelled sweet roses and honeysuckle and inhaled more deeply. Just as I was losing myself to the garden's allure, I caught another scent—one much less pleasing, and as invasive as maggots. I blinked rapidly several times. The smell was horrible, like rotten meat and vomit, and refused to be ignored.

Frightened, I hurried along the path toward the woods, eager to escape this place, hoping fervently that I wasn't leaving behind a decomposing body, or about to add my own.

The last time I'd come this way had been through fog, yet I easily found the stream where I had picnicked days earlier—seemingly centuries ago. The water burbled happily despite the heavy mood in the air, pitching in a rush over the edge. I stood for a moment and watched the water, which had no choice but to fall.

Leaving the stream, I crossed the fragrant moors along a narrow path, fighting a strong wind whipping over the horizon. I entered the small patch of woods where I'd seen Nate emerge, riding his horse. My intention was not to see him, or be seen by him. I was only coming this way because I knew his property led to the road to the village. Ellwood, believe it or not, was where I was headed.

I was looking for answers.

This time I better find some.

Chapter Nineteen

*

Learning the Hard Way

Despite the glorious weather outside, the road into town was empty. No mothers worked outdoors in their gardens, no children played hopscotch or tossed a colored ball back and forth. There wasn't even a sheep to be found. They must all be preparing for the Solstice Festival, I told myself. Still, I pulled up my hood and prepared to hide behind a tree or a stone wall just in case the aunts were on the prowl.

I spotted the sign to Dunton's and inhaled as I neared it, but didn't go inside. The fewer people involved in this, *with you, Evie*, a little voice insisted, the better. Besides, who in there would help me? Unless Bessie had stopped by for a cup of tea, there was no one, certainly not Miss Dunton. And, anyway, I didn't want Bessie getting hurt.

No, I was on my own. Darkness permeated this village as deeply as ink on a white cotton dress, and I felt, despite fervent debate from my rational side, that I was meant to be the one to root it out.

Even though it's in you, too? That little voice did persist. I turned a deaf ear to it. I had every right to be angry about what was happening here with my aunts, and about what had happened in my past, as well. With Mother and Father, and two ex-boyfriends who had cheated on me. With Gabriel's proprietary attitude toward me and Nate's high-handedness. There wasn't darkness in me; my feelings were perfectly normal. Healthy, even.

I will make them suffer until they are dead, dead, dead...

Perfectly normal, my mind insisted. I shook my head and walked on.

The pub across from the bakery, commonly known as an excellent source of information, was my destination. The building was squat, tucked at the end of a row of similarly low buildings. Atop the pub's slated roof, double chimneys rose up, one on each side like devil's horns. The sign, hanging from a metal hook above the door, displayed a surprisingly artistic drawing of a pale, winding path—the underbelly of a snake—leading into dark woods where an even darker figure stood waiting. Underneath read, "The Wrath's Path." Someone around here had a sense of humor, though a dark one.

Staples held a sheaf of papers to the pub's door. I ripped off one of the pages and read what turned out to be a schedule of events for the

Solstice Festival, ending with a bonfire at dusk. I folded up the paper and tucked it into my pants pocket for later.

I tried hard to ignore the stares as I entered the dark cave of The Wrath's Path and pulled off my hood. A man and a woman sat huddled in a corner booth, hands desperately clutching glasses of ale. Seeing her partner staring, the woman turned completely about to look at the newcomer and her eyes never left me as I crossed to the bar. Another man, old and grizzled, sat at the far end of the counter, gripping the local paper, but reading me over its pages.

Square tables spread themselves haphazardly around the room, as though by their own drunken arrangement. Mottled red cushions softened the dark wood chairs encircling each table. Eight red-seated booths, like the one where the desolate couple sat, filled the space along the outside wall.

Empty wine casks lined a gray, wooden shelf high above an old fireplace constructed of light and dark gray stones in various sizes. A dark mantel topped the pit, large black nails protruding from its beaten wood like porcupine quills. Mugs hung from two of the nails, a few copper pieces and a kerosene lamp, took care of the rest.

The warm room smelled richly of yeast and smoke—wood, cigarette, and pipe. The latter two were not my favorite scents, but here in the pub they seemed both necessary and appealing. One almost couldn't relax and enjoy a pint without the smell of smoke. Pretending a nonchalance I certainly didn't feel, I moseyed up to the mahogany bar and claimed a stool. I'd never been in a bar before, being only eighteen, but eighteen was legal drinking age in England, so really I shouldn't feel as pleasurably guilty as I did. It might be prudent to erase the cheesy grin from my face, though.

Resting my feet on the burnished brass foot rail, I waited for the blond man, built like a construction worker, but dressed in a classy, white button-up shirt and black pants, to come to me. He was wiping out sturdy glass mugs with a white terrycloth towel, running on automatic, his mind anywhere but on his mundane task. While he worked I let my eyes wander over the hundreds of colorful liquor bottles packed on the open shelves behind him.

"Let me guess, lass," he greeted me at last, one of his sparkling blue eyes giving me a wink. "You just turned eighteen today." He had a rich Irish accent that sounded like a flute.

"I bet you say that to all the girls…especially the ones over thirty."

He let loose a big guffaw. "Clever. Only a bona fide adult would have a quick tongue like that." He set a mug upside down on a silver tray lined with a towel. "I'm Frederick O'Callaghan, proud manager of this here fine establishment. You can call me Rick. So what can I get you?"

Mindful of what drugs might be remaining in my system and not having eaten for quite some time, I thought I'd better forego any alcohol, much as I wouldn't mind downing a few shots of liquid courage. "I'm Evie." He wiped his hand on the towel and we shook hands. "Can I get something to eat?"

"I'll warn you, the cook's in a mood, but as long as it isn't anything too complicated, go right ahead."

"Bangers and mash?" I ventured, the foreign words savory in my mouth. "And a big glass of milk."

"I can handle that. Not a pint, then?"

"I'm not much of a drinker."

"Try a bit of this cider ale." He pulled a dusty brown jug from under the counter and poured out half a mug of golden liquid. "It's light. Just the right thing to go with your bangers and mash." He left the bar, disappearing through a small, dark door off to my right, which likely led to the kitchen, to hand along my order.

I took the cool glass in my warm hands—the pub was toasty from the fire, which judging by its languid air, must always burn. The spicy sweet smell of apples and cinnamon teased my nose and I took a sip of the cider. Not bad, I decided. Not bad at all. I took another sip.

Behind me the other two patrons spoke in low tones. Far from depressed as I'd first diagnosed upon entering the pub, their voices sounded excited, almost frenetic. The door swung open behind me letting in a gust that riffled my hair. The door closed, then opened once more, and the voices grew more animated with each occurrence. This ritual repeated itself exactly ten more times—I was counting—as I waited for my meal. Despite the nearly continuous breezes coming in, I found myself growing warmer. Each time the door clicked shut felt like another strike against me, as though I were about to engage in a battle I knew nothing about. I drank deeply of the cider, looking for fortification.

Rick returned with my glass of milk, plunking it down on the counter. A bit of white liquid spilled onto the dark wood. He swiped it away with his towel. "Thirsty, were you?" He nodded at the empty mug, then scanned the bar with a practiced eye. He frowned.

"A bit." I wanted to turn around and see what had made those blue eyes turn glacial, but I didn't dare acknowledge *them*—the ones who had gathered behind me like an angry mob.

"So are you passing through?"

"You might say that."

"Not her." Newspaper forgotten, the man at the end of the bar, now facing me directly and looking accusing, had spoken. His large, bushy eyebrows nearly covered his deeply sunken eyes, which were like pits in a rough, worn face gritted with a salt and pepper beard. "You're the American, come to visit your aunts."

The bartender eyed me differently now, his ruddy complexion coloring a bit. "You're the one who entered the Wrath's Path and survived?"

"I'm hoping I'll survive this one as well." I smiled weakly.

He didn't return the smile as I hoped he would, and thereby alleviate my fears that I might become victim to the rabble forming behind me. He simply continued to study me like the glass mug he'd recently dried and polished, looking for flaws. I squirmed. The door opened once more. Chairs scraped over the wood floor as several new customers found seats. I wished for a mirror behind the bar so that I could see what was going on. I felt so vulnerable—so *surrounded*.

"Are you one of them, then?" the nosy parker asked. I noticed he had moved closer to me during the latest influx of people. Only one stool separated us now. He smelled of rank sweat, tobacco, alcohol, and hopelessness. I noticed how quiet it was in the bar now. Once again I resisted the urge to turn around. I had come in here for information and was determined to get it, harassment or not.

"One of who?" I asked, determined not to give an inch.

"The Wrath, of course," he sneered, equally determined.

Hand shaking, I set my glass of milk back down on the counter. It didn't look very appealing at the moment, more like curdled cream on the verge of spoiling. "I'm not sure I even know what a Wrath is."

"You're a *Filmore*." He said the name with startling vehemence, spittle flying from his thin lips like snake venom. "Your aunts would have told you something."

I looked back and forth between him and Rick. He was staring at me, waiting for my answer; gone was the cheerful bartender. "I know they're as scared of the Wrath as all of you seem to be. They steer clear of the woods."

"But *you* don't."

I realized that I'd made a strategic error. Not only was I a foreigner, I had entered the Wrath without incurring harm. Instantly I became one of the enemies, one of *them*.

"I didn't mean to go into the woods." *Well, not the first two times, anyway.*

"You were lured, then?"

I looked over at Rick, who had asked the question. He was attending to my every word, square chin on hand, elbow on bar. I imagined everyone behind me was equally attentive, though in their case, their arms were crossed defensively and their faces blighted by scowls.

"I might have been. I don't remember anything that happened the first time."

"They want something from her," George insisted. "Taking her in and letting her go like that. If we gave her to them, maybe they'd leave the rest of us alone. Maybe they'd finally stop taking what's ours."

"Shut up, George," Rick snapped, surprising me with his defense. "She's not the trouble, can't you see that?"

"I see that something strange is going on," George growled.

"Strange things have been going on long before she got here," another voice put in. It was an older woman, I sensed, her accent thick as Devonshire cream. I felt grateful to her. "Sounds like they're toying with her, that's what I think."

"But why her?" George again. "I think they're up to something. She's their bait, and she's meant to lure more of us into the forest."

"I came in here," I spoke up over the rising babble of voices that threatened to drown me out, "to find out what's going on. My aunts tell me nothing. They're determined to get something out of me, but I don't know what it is. I was hoping you could help me."

Taking a deep breath, I turned around and faced the people of Ellwood. Young and old and in-between, they crammed into the little room, thick as minnows in a bucket, arms crossed and dubious expressions, as I'd guessed. They were all looking at me, and not in a kindly manner. "Can't you see that I only want to know what's going on? That I'm just as scared as you are?"

It was the wrong thing to say. No stranger would ever understand what they'd been through. Certainly not an American one.

Rick leaned over the bar. "You'd best be leaving," he whispered in my ear. "Come through the kitchen. You can make your order takeaway."

I slowly slid off the barstool. Absolute silence reigned, so deeply that I thought for one brief moment my hearing had gone.

"Where're you going?" George demanded, disabusing me of the notion.

"To use the loo," Rick told him. With a hand gripping my arm, he brought me around the bar and through the swinging door into the hot, steamy kitchen. The sound of vociferous voices rose up behind me. "Make it takeaway, Bridget, and make it quick."

Bridget, the cook, was a woman in her late twenties. She had the slender body of a girl and a cigarette with a half-inch long ash gripped between her teeth. I had a feeling the wild-haired, frizzy blond didn't give a damn about all the health codes she was currently breaking. "I suppose you heard everything," he said to her. "It's getting ugly out there."

Bridget plucked the cigarette from her mouth and threw it to the floor, grounding it out with the toe of her lime green, high-top sneaker. "With that lot, it's always ugly out there."

Rick smiled.

She grabbed a Styrofoam carton from high on a metal shelf, standing on her tiptoes to reach it, and set it on the stainless steel counter. "I lost my brother to the Wrath." She sounded bitter and I thought she might throw one of the thick, juicy sausages she gripped with tongs at me. She surprised me, though. "Did you see him? Was he there?" Her voice, harsh as a grinding stone, was pleading.

I swallowed. "What does your brother look like?"

"Not like me. He were beautiful, Charlie were. Ten years ago he left home and didn't come back. Everyone thought it was because of our pa, but it weren't. Charlie would've told me. We told each other everything." She plopped two large dollops of creamy mashed potatoes next to the bangers.

Something clicked in my mind. "Does Charlie have straight blond hair, a little on the long sides, and light green eyes? About this tall?" I showed her with a hand over my head. I had a feeling Charlie was my Adonis.

Her tired brown eyes teared up. "That were him."

"I think I saw him, but..." I paused, confused. "It's been ten years, you say? But he looked my age."

Her smoke-cracked lips puckered as she shoved my carton into a paper bag along with a plastic spork and knife. "That be their way, so the stories go, anyways. Keep 'em young and fresh, never aging. He's as good as gone, then." She started to turn away from me, her skinny shoulders hunched in defeat.

"He was kind to me, Bridget. He acted like he didn't want to be there."

She spun back around and in her eyes I saw, for perhaps the first time in my life, what real love looked like. "So Charlie's holding his own? He's not giving in to them?"

I nodded enthusiastically, wanting to give her something to keep that fierce love alive. "He was defying the Wrath as best he could."

"What were they like? What did they say to you? How did you get away?" The three questions came at me like gunfire.

In coming here, it seemed I was providing the answers instead of finding them. "They were young, pushy, and very beautiful. They wanted me to dance with them. I was close to the edge of the woods and I ran away." Not the whole truth, but close enough. I didn't want her to know about Gabriel. I needed to keep him out of this; otherwise people might get the wrong idea about him, about me.

Without replying, she scurried over to the fridge and pulled a thermos out, pushing it into the bag. She shoved the bag into my hand. "Go on, Miss. Get yourself out of here. If you need my help down the line, you know where to find me. I practically live at this dump."

"Thank you, Bridget, for the food." I held up the bag. "If I can do anything to help Charlie, I will."

She nodded, turning away to hide her hopefulness, her tears. She strode over to the bar door, gripping her spatula like a sword. "I'll head the others off. Now get yourself moving!" She opened the door. "Mind your own business, you sodding drunks!" she yelled, as Rick steered me toward the back of the building and out a small door.

"I don't mean to come across so dramatic-like, Evie, nipping you out the back way. Most folks in the village aren't like old George. He lost his wife forty years ago to the Wrath and it soured him. I think it was for the best, though. From what I heard, she was never much good anyway, always flirting with other blokes, spending all the poor chap's wages, but he couldn't see it."

I thought maybe I knew which one she was.

"I left my aunts," I confessed. "I'm kind of hiding out right now." I'm not sure why I had told him this, but he seemed a trustworthy and solid sort of guy. Maybe it was all those freckles spattering the bridge of his nose and the kind warmth in his bright eyes. Or perhaps because he was helping me now. His lovely accent didn't hurt his case, either.

He looked both ways before motioning for me to leave the doorway. I stepped outside. We were at the back of the pub, and I saw, and smelled, a dumpster a few feet away, nearly overflowing. Farther on trees rose up, dark and silent. "I know those aunts of yours. They're bad news." He blushed unexpectedly. Kelli had probably gotten her hooks into him—Priscilla wouldn't have looked twice at a bartender, not even once, actually. Right through him, more like.

I patted him on the arm. "I imagine that when my aunt puts her mind to it, she can be very charming."

He gave me a cockeyed grin. "Very charming, indeed."

"Thanks for your help, Rick."

He shrugged. "I know what it's like to be the outsider. You've a place to stay?"

I nodded, not wanting to give away too much. "I'll be all right. Oh, and Rick… I want you to tell the people inside something for me."

"What's that, luv?"

"Tell them my father is coming home."

His mouth dropped open. "I heard of him! Disappeared, didn't he? He was quite the star of Ellwood, from what's said about all his grand exploits. I'll happily tell the others. Gossiping about your da should get them off your back for a bit and make you seem a little less threatening, being his daughter. Now you best get moving. Bridget's a real firebrand, but I'm not sure even she can hold them off much longer."

We waved to each other, and food in hand I scurried back the way I'd come, staying low and heading toward Nate's land. At last, I turned onto his drive and walked along it for a few minutes, my ears alert to the sound of a car. Along the edge of the woods, near where his drive broke free of the tree tunnel, I found a rock outcrop and headed toward it. Once there, I climbed it to the top and sat down between two larger stones, where I could see everything around me, yet remain somewhat hidden to enemy eyes. There I ate my excellent lunch, the smells of which had been driving me crazy during my walk. The bangers were succulent and spicy, the mash creamy and flavored with rich butter and a hint of garlic. Bridget really knew her way around a kitchen. Even the milk tasted better than I'd expected, though I'd have to return the thermos to her somehow. Maybe that's why she'd given it to me, so that when I brought it back she could further question me about her brother, Charlie.

While I ate, I took in the splendor of Nate's property—rolling green lawns, majestic trees, low stone walls edging the property, the castle walls—and enjoyed the delicious food, not giving my mind a chance to dwell on anything that had happened so far. I didn't want to think, to be reminded that I was running from my crazy aunts or that my father was coming to Ellwood, but not for my sake.

Using the flimsy knife I sawed off a piece of sausage and popped it into my mouth. Maybe he'd been fooling Aunt Priscilla, pretending not to care what happened to me so she'd leave me alone. He was an actor, after all. And perhaps he'd concocted a plan and meant to save me. I spooned up some mashed potato and slid the pile into my mouth. Perhaps I'd been wrong to get mad at him. He apparently possessed hidden depths, ones I'd never guessed at. He'd fled the aunts twenty years ago because they were insane, but now he was willing to face them again to come rescue me. The idea gave me hope and my heart grew lighter.

Finished with my lunch, I began to pack my bag, my eyes on the castle as I worked. I was zipping up a side pocket when I spotted a feminine silhouette in one of the tower windows; bright light from behind emphasized her every curve. Was she a maid? But Nate didn't do housekeepers. Then I remembered him mentioning his old nanny, Miss Ames. I shaded my squinting eyes and studied the figure more closely. Judging by her languid pose and bonny curves, this woman was much younger and more sophisticated than a spinster nanny.

Who was she, then, and what was she doing in Nate's house? A couple times he had mentioned a prior commitment, one that kept him from seeing me. And then there was the 'complication' he'd brought up that prevented my staying at Thorndike Hold. Was this woman his complication? If so, she likely was a girlfriend, perhaps even his fiancée, and one he kept hidden like a skeleton in a closet from both the aunts and myself. A bitter taste filled my mouth. I should've known there was someone else.

Why do you care? I demanded ruthlessly. *You aren't interested in him anyway. In fact, you despised him at first, and only tolerated him later. Just because he has those fascinating eyes and a face that one could stare at forever doesn't mean anything. Just because he came to see if you were all right and eats olives like they're popcorn—*

I stopped abruptly. Oh, dear Lord. I liked Nate.

I *really* liked him.

Chapter Twenty

✳

Love and Loss

How had this happened? I watched the woman leave the window and disappear into the shadowed world behind her. How had I come to care about Nathaniel Thorndike? Every other crush I'd nurtured had been so obvious to me, and looking back, probably to everyone around me. When I thought a man was attractive, my heart beat a little harder, my stomach flip-flopped at the sight of him. I blushed a lot and grew dreamy. Romantic fantasies constantly distracted me. None of this had happened with Nate. If I thought of him—well, I did think about him a *lot*—it was usually with disdain or confusion or frustration, not love.

And in such a short time? I didn't believe in love at first sight. Or at second sight. Though, come to think of it, my reaction to him on the train…when I'd first seen him…had been a bit telling.

Giving a little groan, I shoved my agitated hands into my pockets. I couldn't think about this now. I had things to do, plans to make, conspiracies to break open. I'd think about this complication later, when I had a moment. Until then, I had work to do. Tomorrow was the Solstice Festival and I planned on attending it. When the time was right, when everyone could witness it, I would confront my aunts.

But would they tell me anything in front of all those people? It was doubtful…unless I used torture. As appealing an idea as that was, I wasn't about to stoop to Kelli and Priscilla's level. Yes, I was feeling angry and vindictive lately, but all that negativity was likely just a phase. I'd never gone through a rebellious stage, not even once. Perhaps I was overdue. Still, I didn't want the aunts to suffer, did I? The thought that I might was disturbing, and perhaps a little tantalizing. I was not a naturally violent person. If I were, I would've killed my mother long ago. No, I was simply releasing pent-up frustrations. I was *not* a vengeful person. I was *not* like my aunts. I would never hurt someone like they had.

I couldn't. I wouldn't.

Why not? They locked you up and drugged you, told you lies and threatened you. Priscilla as good as told you that she wanted you out of the way.

She might only have meant sending me home, I argued with myself. She didn't need me around anymore now that she'd convinced my dad to come. Besides, murder wasn't something people did. Well, it was, but not on an everyday basis. Okay, scratch that. I was doing a horrible job proving my own point. I needed to clear my mind. I needed to think reasonably and rationally. There were questions demanding to be answered: What was I going to do about this mess my parents had landed me in? What was I going to do about Priscilla?

Kill her before she kills you.

I let the words filter through my mind before dismissing them with a shudder. When all this was over, I wanted to be able to walk away from Ellwood with a clean slate. In the fall I would attend college where I could be myself, or at least discover who myself was supposed to be, without my mother hovering over me. She still lived in my head—a nagging voice of doubt—but voices were only sounds. I could handle sounds. And if all else failed, a lobotomy would rid me of her once and for all.

Growing warm, I stood and pulled off my hoodie, then tied it around my waist. I was stretching in the hot sun when frenzied barking startled me. I immediately ducked low and scanned the horizon. I caught sight of Sadie, Nate's Irish setter. She had spotted me, too, *crap*, but now looked confused at my sudden disappearance. Her black nose bobbed up and down, working to catch my scent. Snout to the ground, she scooted several steps to the right, then several steps to the left. Flat on my stomach, I reached for my backpack and slowly slithered backward. I needed to get off this rock and into the woods before Sadie tracked me.

I was nearly to the edge of the outcrop when the uncomfortable sensation that I was no longer alone hit me. Tiny needles of fear climbed up my spine and along the base of my skull, where they settled in to do their destructive work. I froze.

"I've been looking for you all night." His voice was hoarse. I rolled over onto my back and sat up. Nate towered over me, his dark eyebrows lowered like storm clouds.

"*You* have? Why?"

"You're asking me *why*?" His anger deflated and he dropped down into a crouch. "I came to the house looking for you, Evie. You weren't there. *That's* why."

"How'd you get into the house?" Did it really matter? Did the aunts even lock the door?

"Bessie was with me. She had a key."

"But she's visiting her Aunt Grear, the one who's dying."

He looked away. "She made that up, the visit part. We planned it that way. Miss Dunton came at the end of the meeting with free pasties and scones to distract your aunts and I made my escape then."

They had both planned to rescue me? My heart soared with joy and I said stupidly, "But the door to my room is locked."

He laughed. "There isn't a lock I can't pick, at least not in an old house."

"You can pick locks?"

He frowned. "Yes, and I can change a light bulb and unplug the lavatory if need be. I just don't like cleaning. Now can I get back to what I was saying?" He stared pointedly at me and I clamped my mouth shut and nodded. "When we couldn't find you, I didn't know what to do. When we arrived, I sent Bessie to the kitchen to rest—we really dashed from the meeting—and then I quickly searched your room. When I found it empty, I headed to the kitchen after Bessie, thinking you somehow had got out and were hungry. We heard something in the cellar, but it was only an old chair that had fallen over."

"That was me," I whispered. "I thought you were the aunts coming after me. I panicked and I ran."

He slid a tired hand over his face. "We just missed each other."

I smiled broadly at him. He *must* care for me to take such a risk. Bessie, too! "Thank you for trying, Nate. It's nice having someone care about what happens to me. I've never had that before." My smile returned, bigger this time.

He gave me a strange look. "I would've come earlier, but I thought you were getting back at me for the other night. You know, avoiding me after our little disagreement. Then Bessie called. She was worried about you. Still is."

I couldn't stop smiling. "I've never had anyone *worry* about me, either."

"She isn't the only one who worries about you," he murmured, his fingers jumping to pick at a tuft of grass sprouting from a split in the rock. "Where did you spend the night?"

I hesitated, unsure of what to share with him. I appreciated that he'd come looking for me, more than I could say, but knowing that he had someone else, a significant other of the feminine persuasion, knowing that I might care about him a little too much, made me cautious and my smile faded. "Near the woods," I decided.

He let out a breath. "I'm glad to see you're all right, Evie."

"I'm glad I made it out of that house alive. They drugged my tea. I figured it out after the first time and only pretended to drink it after that."

"I thought it was something like that." His fingers curled into white fists. "I could kill them."

"Do they even know I'm gone?"

"They do now. I confronted them this morning. They still claim you're sick and must be delirious. I asked them how you got out of the room when it was locked." He waited expectantly.

"I found a secret passageway."

He laughed out loud and I just wanted to grab hold of him and hug him tight. "I'll wager they hadn't counted on that."

"No, but if they get a hold of me again, they'll find another way to keep me locked up."

"We'll go to the constable. He'll know what to do. He'll keep you safe, at least."

This sounded all well and good, and very tempting, too, but I didn't think the locals would believe my side of the story. Not after the way they'd acted at the tavern. "I'd rather not."

He studied me for a moment. "Then stay here with me," he urged. "At Thorndike Hold. There are plenty of rooms. Miss Ames can be our chaperone, if that worries you. She'll be back soon from her annual excursion with her book club. They visit famous authors' homes, you see."

The figure had definitely not been Miss Ames, then. "What about the complication?" I tried to ask the question lightly, but jealousy colored my words despite my best efforts.

He looked puzzled. "Complication?"

"Last time we talked you said I couldn't stay with you because of a complication."

His expression grew hard. "That can be dealt with."

He didn't deny that there was a complication; didn't even make the attempt. I swallowed the heated tears desperate to burst out of me. "It's a tempting offer, Nate," I said, as calmly as I could, though I know my voice quavered like a cracked note when I spoke his name. "But I think I'm best on my own. I'm taking your advice, you know. I'm heading back to the States." If I expected him to look happy about my news—advice he'd given only days ago—I was mistaken. He looked thunderous. My heart gave a little flutter.

"You can't go back now, Evie." He glanced at the castle, his eyes troubled, then he turned back to face me. "You said there was unfinished business. You said you needed to find out what your aunts were up to. We can do that together."

"I do plan to see this through, but on my terms, and *alone*," I added. "Anyway, I'm sure the 'complication' needs you more than I do." Throwing that in there was spiteful and petty, but I was feeling spiteful and petty.

He looked pained, torn. "I want to help you, Evie."

My pride was a stubborn beast; I didn't even try to subdue it. "Don't bother. I'll be fine, Nate."

"Where will you stay?"

I shrugged, an honest response. I wasn't sure I wanted to return to Gabriel's house. I had a feeling that this time I wouldn't want to leave. Much as I needed to solve the mystery and go home, Gabriel might prove too tempting to walk away from. "I'll find somewhere to stay. Don't worry about me."

"I *will* worry about you. I…" he paused. "I owe you," he finished, though I thought, *hoped*, that he'd meant to say something else. Wishful thinking, of course. Girls like me specialize in wishful thinking.

"You don't owe me anything, Nate. This isn't personal against you, you know." Tiny white lie. "I simply don't want to get anyone else involved."

"I'm already involved, Evie. More than you can imagine. This whole town is involved."

"What do you mean? This concerns my aunts and my father and myself. This has nothing to do with anyone else."

"Your father wouldn't agree."

"What are you saying? How well did you know my father?"

He turned away irritably. "He was quite a bit older than me, but I knew about him, nearly worshipped him." Worshipped him. Well, that wasn't a surprise. All his fans did.

"What did he look like?" I whispered, feeling a chill crawling up along the bare skin behind my ears. I hadn't realized, should have made the connection—Nate would know what my father looked like when he was young. He possessed within his childhood memory the answer to one of my questions. And all this time it hadn't once occurred to me to ask him. Or Bessie. She would know, too. Good thing I didn't plan on being a detective. My deductive skills were awful.

"He wasn't—" The sound of a car barreling down the dirt drive interrupted him. I flattened back between the two rocks, feeling their stony fingernails prodding at my skin. He didn't move quickly enough and the dogs started barking. A car horn sounded a greeting.

"It's your aunt. Stay down, and don't move," he ordered, as he stood up. He skirted around me, down the rocky bluff, to meet her. "Priscilla. What brings you to Thorndike Hold?" he asked, his tone all affected joviality. He was a terrible actor, a fact that heartened me greatly.

"Have you found her yet?" Priscilla demanded, then softened her tone. "I need her back, Nathaniel. Did she come to you?"

"I haven't seen her." The words were dull, forced. He wasn't a very good liar, either.

"What have you told her?" Suspicion poisoned every word.

"What are you talking about?"

"About the Wrath, damnit! What have you told her about the Wrath?"

"Nothing! She doesn't much believe anything I say anyway. I warned her against going in the woods. That's it."

"Her father is coming. He's going to kill me if he finds her gone."

"That's what you're worried about? Edmund being upset with you?"

"Oh, don't take my words out of context," she snapped. "You know I'm worried about the girl. She's not well, Nathaniel. I've heard that her mother has *issues*." Quote marks emphasized the word, making her meaning loud and clear, even from here. When Nate didn't react, she clarified, "*Mental* issues."

"Have you looked for her in the woods, Priscilla?"

"That's why I came over. I thought you might give it another try for me."

"You think so? Even after I lost my father to them?"

There was a long silence, filled only with the purring of the Mercedes' sleek, powerful engine. It was a sound I would later come to dread.

"Your father wanted to die, Nathaniel."

"My father was mourning his wife."

"For a whole year, Nathaniel? Spare me! His disappearing was probably the best thing for everybody involved."

"Oh really, Priscilla? And how would you know?" I'd never heard Nate angry like this. His voice rumbled like the beginning of an avalanche, cold and destructive and building up power with each passing second.

"Oh, Nathaniel! Don't play the innocent with me. Your father was destroying the estate with his grand schemes, his debts. He was going mad. It's just as well that he died when he did."

"Because his death made me the heir, made me Lord Thorndike."

Lord Thorndike?

"Yes, well, those are two very good things that came out of the whole miserable affair."

Nate made a huffing sound, as though someone had kicked him in the gut. "I hope you don't picture yourself becoming the next Lady Filmore, Priscilla," he said coldly, his teeth clenched as though he were in pain, "because I'd die first."

"Well, that can be arranged, you pompous prig!"

The engine roared like a berserk lion and a screeching of tires followed.

"Hey!" Nate shouted. "What the bloody hell are you doing?" My head jerked up just as the black Mercedes smashed into him. He flew through the air and landed hard on the gravel road. Priscilla jammed the stick shift into reverse and tore off, her expression frightful, her eyes bulging like a madwoman. Without thinking, I jumped to my feet and charged down the rock outcrop, not caring if she saw me. The Mercedes headed in the opposite direction of the castle, roaring through the tunnel of trees, followed by a billowing cloud of dust.

Nate lay sprawled on the ground, his leg cocked at an odd angle. He struggled to sit up as I raced toward him. Congregating around their master, the dogs sniffed at his leg and nosed his face worriedly. Sadie tried to lick at the red stain spreading through his gray corduroy pants. "Go on, now. Get!" I pushed them all away.

"She ran me over." His voice was weak with shock. "She bloody well ran me over! Something's broken." Judging by his clenched teeth, I thought it might be a lot of somethings.

"I'll go get Benjamin. Don't move."

All I remember of running to the castle was the stunned, sick look on Nate's face and how nauseous I felt at the memory. Benjamin heard my hysterical cries for help and the frantic barking of the dogs and dashed out the door, his usual composure slightly ruffled, his gray eyes wide, his breath short.

"Call the doctor," I shouted. "He's all right," I added, seeing the distress on his face, "but his leg isn't." I couldn't bear to add that it had been my aunt who'd broken it...with her car.

I didn't wait for him. Luckily the dogs followed Benjamin into the castle as I dashed back to Nate, unable to bear leaving him alone any longer. He was sitting up now, trying to tug his pant leg up to look at the damage. Seeing all the blood on the ground, I thought maybe it would be better if he didn't look at anything.

"You're bleeding," I told him. "Probably just a scrape, but you don't want to get dirt in the wound." I gently detached his fingers from the gray fabric and made him lean against my shoulder. He was breathing hard and sweat rolled steadily down the sides of his face as though someone had dumped a glass of water over his head. By all rights, he should have passed out from the pain by now.

"You stay away from her, Evie," he growled through clenched teeth. "From both of them. Stay at my place."

"I'm going with you," I told him. "To the hospital."

He paused for a moment, then nodded. "Afterwards, then. When we get back..." When I didn't answer right away—I was trying to examine his wound without him seeing what I was doing—he grasped my arm. Pain dilated his pupils. "Promise me, Evie!"

I swallowed. "Of course, Nate. I'll stay. Whatever you want." I would say anything at that point to make his pain go away, or at least lessen his suffering.

"You're not like them, Evie. I regret I ever thought that you were." His warm hand cupped my jaw and he leaned toward me. I thought he might kiss me and my heart beat like crazy. But then he sighed wearily and slumped against me. He had finally passed out, thank goodness. I held him tight, worried, frightened, wanting to do what I could to protect him from all bad things, and knowing that I couldn't.

Oh, I did love him. I did.

As we sat there together, I ran my fingers through his thick, dark hair and lovingly caressed his broad forehead, wiping away beads of sweat. I felt his heartbeat in my chest and thought maybe mine slowed to match his. I'd never felt so in tune with another being in my life.

Benjamin arrived a minute later in Nate's Jeep. "I'll bring the lad to hospital," he told me, as he bent down to examine Nate's wound. "It will be faster." I nodded my approval and after he pulled Nate's pant leg down, we worked together to lift Nate into the back seat. He groaned and fought against us. "There, there, Nate," I murmured. "You're going to be all right," and Ben, his usually posh voice gruff, soothed, "We've got you, lad, don't you fret." And Nate quieted once more.

While Benjamin hurried in his dignified manner around to the front of the Jeep, I reached down to touch Nate's wounded leg. I had to see what Priscilla had done to him. My fingers shook as I lifted the blood-soaked material. When I saw the angry red skin, the blood, the massive bruise spreading like a purple storm cloud, and then the jagged bone, hot tears flooded my vision. Taking a deep breath, I placed my palm on the wound and closed my blurred eyes. When I finished saying a fervent prayer for Nate, I pulled his pant leg back down and shut the car door.

I was about to climb into the front seat when I remembered my backpack and what was in it. Priscilla's envelope—possible evidence to use against her. I was determined to make her pay for this crime. "I have to get my bag," I told Benjamin. "I'll only be a moment."

I dashed to the rock outcrop. My pack should've been right near the top, but I couldn't see it anywhere. Not wanting Nate to wait any longer, I was about to head back when I spotted a red lump sitting at the edge of the woods. My feet flew toward the bag, my only thoughts to grab it and be gone. That's why I didn't see them. That's why I was such easy prey.

Chapter Twenty-One

✳

Nat the Rat

"Cover that screeching mouth, will you?" One member of the group did as he was ordered, his smooth white hand smothering my open mouth with swift efficiency. I tried to bite him, but he was too wily for me, pressing hard against my teeth every time I tried.

With one easy movement, two of the others grabbed me under the armpits and dragged me through the woods like an old log. I could hear Benjamin honking the horn in the distance, then the noise stopped, followed by the sound of the car's motor. He would think that I'd run off. I'd already done it to Nate once before; it wouldn't surprise Benjamin that I'd done it again.

The boy gagging me dropped his hand, wiping my saliva off on his brown pant leg. This could only mean he was no longer worried someone would hear me.

"Where are we taking her, Gwyn?" Lizzie, Gwyn's toady, wanted to know.

"Wherever I please."

"Oh, he's going to be angry. *Very* angry!"

"Oh, pish and tosh, Lizzie!" Gwyn tossed her head defiantly and her brown braids swung up to slap her in the face. She knocked them away.

"He threw you into the stream when you went against him this last time."

A pause. "Oh, that's just him having a bit of a laugh."

"I don't want any part of this. I don't like getting wet. You know what it does—how it burns."

"Come on, Lizzie. We're all doing it. He can't get mad at all of us, can he?"

"Oh yes, he can!"

"I'll take the blame, like I did for Charlie last time."

"He likes her, Gwyn. He really does. Leave her be. We'll go find someone else."

There was a snort. "She's just a passing fancy," Gwyn replied, ignoring Lizzie's advice. "He takes them from time to time. This too will pass, more quickly if I help it along by getting rid of the object of his affections." If I weren't mistaken, they were talking about Gabriel.

He'd told me I was safe from Gwyn and her groupies, but he had been wrong. And now I was going to pay the price for believing him. I struggled to escape but my captors hung on tight.

"Don't bother trying to get away," Gwyn warned me. "The last one who made the attempt ended up bashing his head on a rock." Grinning, she threw her hands up, fingers spread. "Splat! Split open like a melon. Made my week."

Frightened by the pleasure she took in someone else's pain, I glanced swiftly around the gathering, looking for help. Hanging back was the boy I thought might be Charlie, my dance partner. His pale green eyes shifted up to catch mine, then swiftly flew back down again like a startled bird. I was ready when he glanced back up again, mouthing one word, "Bridget."

The effect was like an electric shock, his cheeks flushed, his eyes grew hectic. "Bridget?" he mouthed back at me.

I nodded slowly, not wanting the others around me to see what I was doing. "Misses you."

He blinked and bit his lip to regain control. "Me, too." His lips formed the words with a slow, poignant delicacy.

"Should we do the chase?" Lizzie offered up her suggestion like a gift. She sounded excited, her fear of Gabriel obviously overcome. *But why so easily?* I wondered. Maybe Gabriel wasn't the one with the true power. Maybe Gwyn was. But if that were true, then why had Gabriel made it sound like he would punish her for trying to take me? Just looking at her now, it was quite clear he hadn't done much, if anything, to her. Perhaps she was in love with him, and so put up with his ego, making the others believe he had more power over her than he did.

But that still didn't answer the question of who these people were. *A harmless gang of bored teenagers?* I guessed. *Who never age?* my mind countered cynically, remembering what Bridget had said about them. *And who live in the woods and kidnap people?* That was the conundrum, I realized, these quirky little details that didn't add up. Still, to believe they were anything but human seemed misguided, naïve. Then again, even Nate thought they weren't human.

The idea brought me up short. Nate didn't strike me as the type to fall for much of anything. He was, in fact, someone of quite the opposite nature. His reaction to me on the train showed a man distrustful to the point of paranoia. And according to Bessie he kept to himself in Ellwood, further confirming his antipathy toward other people.

Yet he now seems to believe the best of me.

He shouldn't, I thought guiltily. I had my own demons. Told my own lies.

Gwyn stopped suddenly, raising her hand to halt the others. "You know, I think a chase is an excellent idea, Lizzie. So glad I took you. You've almost made my life better."

Lizzie giggled. "I'd do anything for you, Gwyn. You know that."

"Then stop questioning me, all right, git? Gabriel doesn't rule me, I rule him." I shivered. I'd been right about her and Gabriel, and that scared me a lot.

"Of course, Gwyn." She ducked her head low, like an animal showing submission.

The supporting hands under my armpits lifted me up, pinching the delicate skin, and set me on my feet, neither of which wanted to support me. I swayed, then righted myself through sheer will. I was determined not to let Gwyn see any weakness.

She did anyway, and began to circle me like a predator before the kill. "You're very stupid, Eve. Did you think Gabriel would really be interested in someone like you? That's a laugh. You're quite plain, some might even say ordinary looking." She sounded exactly like my mother, and that was her first mistake. She gazed up at the sky, her brown eyes speculative. "Do you know how long I've been here, Eve?"

"Forty years," I replied. I had already guessed who she was—bitter George's missing wife.

Her thin lips shriveled angrily. "Who told you that?" The others in the group looked away. Her head tilted to one side as she regarded me with eyes of fire and melted steel. "A very long time," she said. "Longer than anyone here." She waved her arm at the group. "Do you know what that means?"

"That you're an old woman?" Crud. I was going to get myself a smashed skull.

"That I have more *power* than any of these gits!" she hissed, warm spittle flecking my cheeks. "Would you like a taste of it?" she asked in a quieter voice. A deadly voice.

I didn't respond. She was going to give me a sample whether I wanted one or not. I watched her prowl about me, my alert eyes drying out with each pass. After the third turn, she disappeared. I blinked rapidly. Where was she? The person was gone, but now a bright light hovered in front of me. At first I thought it was a firefly. Then I realized that the glowing figure was Gywn. She was much smaller, with tiny wings and sharp teeth. Her eyes glowed red.

Harry Willoughby had told Nate, "They baint be one of us." Then what *be* they? Elves? Fairies? Something fey, that was for sure, which would explain the strange time lapses I'd experienced, the kidnappings of the villagers, Gwyn's invitation to dance with the intention of stealing my soul. Strange as it sounded, the fey theory made a certain sort of sense, more than any other, actually.

Gwyn quickly returned to her larger form, perhaps reading in my expression the desire to slap her down like a pesky gnat. "There aren't any fireflies in England," she informed me, smug as a child. "Only glowworms. How stupid of you not to know that."

"Is this a biology lesson, Gwyn?" I asked, crossing my arms and staring her down. "Because it's getting boring. No, wait. It started out boring and now it's just plain mind numbing, like watching paint dry." I wasn't being entirely moronic, baiting her like this. Lizzie had mentioned a chase and I thought running might be my best chance of escaping. I wanted to provoke Gwyn, make her angry. Angry people make mistakes. I just hoped angry fey creatures did, too.

The petal thin skin beneath her left eye twitched as she pulled back out of her stalking mode. "I think a hunt sounds just the thing, don't you?" She turned to the crowd, which huddled together in small cliques. A half-hearted murmur of response came from a few members of the gang. Only Lizzie clapped her hands excitedly, making her strawberry curls bounce. Gwyn might have the power, but it was given to her grudgingly by most of the group.

"You have to run," Lizzie explained with a fervor that boded ill for me. I didn't like the fanatic glow in her blue eyes.

I turned to Gwyn. "You can't *make* me run." I had to anger her, make her clumsy with it.

Gwyn laughed. "I sense a challenge."

I saw the shower of light before I felt it—burning bits of ash landed on my skin, instantly searing the top layer and leaving behind pink polka dots of agony. The pain was so intense that my feet were moving before my brain had a chance to register what had happened.

I heard Gwyn's laugh behind me, a hollow echo of evil. "We'll give you a head start, little Eve, then the hunt begins."

Unsure what sense they used to track down their prey—smell, sound, sight—I ran straight ahead. The thought occurred to me to hide, but that might prove to be a death sentence. I didn't know for sure what to do and I couldn't think, so I followed my instincts and kept running.

As though conjured up by sleight of hand, a wide, shallow stream appeared unexpectedly in front of me. I skidded to a stop, my left foot sliding into the cold water. I didn't move. For a moment, all was quiet. But only for a moment. I heard the whispering at the same time I felt the others close in. The voices came from all around me, taunting me.

"Why don't you run, Eve?"

"Gabriel can't save you now, Eve."

Where was Gabriel? Had they gotten him, too? Was that why he wasn't helping me?

I began running again, splashing across the stream like a frightened deer. A pile of stones emerged from the darkness of the woods like a whale's snout. I knew those stones; I'd dreamed about them. Someone had died there, and that was where I was being led. My mind made the connection before my body did and I veered to the right of the fifteen-foot high pile.

The whispering grew angry. I had outmaneuvered the Wrath for the moment, but the hunt was still on.

Run, Eve. You must get out of the woods!

I gasped and looked around. Someone was talking to me in my head. Could I trust him? Maybe not, but the advice made sense. The Wrath owned the woods, but maybe the woods owned them, as well. Maybe they couldn't leave it. People only disappeared when they entered the forest. No one, as far as I knew, had ever been taken from the village or the road.

Knowing the stream would lead me out of the woods, I doubled back toward it and raced along its banks. Behind me, the sounds of the hunt grew like the wind of an approaching storm. Fingers entwined in my hair, yanking it hard, branches whipped at me, attempting to knock me backward. Each time, something pried loose the fingers; each time, something caught hold of the branch. One of the Wrath was helping me. It had to be the one who'd told me to get out of the forest.

The way ahead grew lighter and I pumped my arms harder, praying for speed, praying for deliverance. I was nearly to the edge of the woods when a thunderous crack shook the air. I spun around, expecting to see a cannonball flying at me. But it wasn't a cannonball. A mass of bright light bore down on me...accompanied by a figure. Charlie.

"I'll hold them off!" His feet flew over the ground, hardly touching it, and his golden hair parted over his forehead like a horse's mane.

But I didn't run. I couldn't. They meant to trample us both, to crush us in their stampede. My head spun, my body swayed, and my ears rung. I was going to pass out. Here, in the forest, when I was so nearly out of the Wrath's reach, fear paralyzed me. My drugged body could take no more.

Charlie raced past me, grabbing my hand as he went. The force yanked me around, immediately clearing my mind.

"Charlie!" Gwyn screeched. "What do you think you're doing? She's *mine!*"

Hand in hand, Charlie and I sprinted toward the wood's edge. I knew if we reached it, we'd be safe. We were only a couple feet from it when Charlie tripped—or someone made him trip—and he crashed to the ground. He let go of my hand as he fell, releasing me to keep running. "Go, Eve," he gasped, clutching his mid-section. "Save yourself!"

But I couldn't just leave him. Not to the Wrath, not to Gwyn. I turned back around to see a glowing orb hurtling toward me like a meteor. I pulled my arm back and swung it forward. The palm of my hand connected to the ball of light like a bat and sent it flying into a tree. The light transformed back into Lizzie and she howled furiously at me as she cradled her injured arm.

Snatching at Charlie's hand, I pulled him to his feet and dragged him with me. Only a few steps to go.

The Wrath's roar behind us deafened me, then as though a door had slammed, it ceased as we broke through the line of trees, out onto the open moor. We didn't stop running for several more seconds, but finally, exhausted, we stopped and turned around. Just inside the borders of the forest, the remaining Wrath hovered like hungry villagers locked outside the castle gate.

Many looked envious, but Gwyn was furious. We had escaped the woods, and her. With a shriek, she took off, back into its depths, and the others followed after her, unable to do anything else.

I turned and looked at Charlie. He seemed older now. Lines fanned out from the corners of his eyes and wisdom hardened his beautiful features. Grief overwhelmed his face as he watched the Wrath go. "I'm free," he whispered to the woods. "I can't believe it."

"You should all be free," I panted, still winded. "The ones that want to be free. Why don't more of you just leave?"

He ran a shaky hand over his face. "We've tried. Many times. There is a barrier that we cannot pass, like a stone wall that rises from hell to heaven."

"But today you could."

He shook his head in amazement. "And only me. Several of the others tried...I saw them. Yet I was the only one who made it through."

"Maybe it was your time."

He stiffened, his face pained as though wracked with guilt. He glanced at the woods again. "We should leave now." He didn't want to tempt fate any longer, perhaps felt he could get lured back into the woods as he had before. He reached up and pulled off two black straps looped over his shoulders. It was my backpack. "Here," he said, handing it to me with a tired smile.

I took it from him and pulled it on. "We'll go to the pub, where Bridget works. She's probably there now."

"A pub?" he echoed. "Bridget?"

We began to run. "That surprises you?"

"She wanted to become a chef, work in a fancy restaurant. Make something of herself."

"She's a great cook."

"But she's not a chef," he said sadly. "She stayed behind for me."

"Well, now you can both leave here. You're still young. There's time."

The road to the village was nearly empty. Growing dark and close to dinnertime, the villagers had retreated indoors. Whenever we saw anyone, we slipped behind a hedge or a tree. At the pub, I brought Charlie around back and knocked on the door. He hid behind the dumpster in case someone other than his sister answered the door.

"Couldn't you have picked a better time for deliveries, O'Grady?" Bridget yelled, then saw me. "Back for more food?" She laughed and pulled a drag from her cigarette as she flipped a spatula into the air with a nail-bitten hand.

"I've got Charlie."

The spatula dropped to the ground, bouncing off the doormat. "You must be bloody mad, messing with my head like this." She glared at me furiously, her body tense as though she were considering attacking me.

"Bridget." Charlie stepped out from behind the dumpster. "She got me out."

The stunned look on Bridget's face was both painful and wonderful to see. "Can it really be you, Charlie?" She touched his cheek and her shaking fingers trailed down to his chin like water. Her hand fell, then her arms shot around him, pulling him to her in a hug that melded them together.

"Thanks to Eve!" he laughed through his sobs, hugging her back.

"Evie," I corrected him. "Listen, I've got to get going now. Keep him safe, Bridget. Lay low until this is over."

"Will it ever be over?" she asked, talking into Charlie's shoulder, clutching him hard. One hand kept the burning cigarette away from his hair.

"It has to end."

"It doesn't have to, Evie. Some things never end."

"This will…" I said coolly. "Because I'm going to end it myself."

Charlie pulled back from his sister, one arm still about her as he held out his hand to me. I took it. "Good luck, Evie. I'd help you, but…"

"You just aged ten years in ten seconds, Charlie. I think you're done for today."

The brother and sister laughed together; the sound tinged with relief.

"Thanks, Evie," Bridget said and flicked her cigarette to the ground before looking me in the eye.

"My pleasure. Hey, maybe I could get a sandwich to go?"

"The potpie is better."

"Then I'll take one of those." She smiled.

A noise sounded in the kitchen behind her. She spun toward the door, her eyes wary. "Sorry, Evie, but it'll have to wait. That's Elise. You'd better run along before she sees you."

"Got it. I'll see you later." I left them with a quick wave, darting back along the road. When I was nearly at Nate's drive, I saw headlights coming down the road, bobbing up and down as the tires met potholes. Without thinking, I ducked into the ditch. When the lights turned onto Nate's drive, I glanced up, wondering who it could be. The complication? I couldn't resist lifting my head a little higher to get a better look, though it was probably only Benjamin returning from the hospital. I could flag him down and ask him to take me to see Nate. I wanted to be with him, tell him everything that had happened. About being kidnapped. About Charlie getting free. And if he was feeling better, I'd grill him about the 'complication' in his life and maybe convince him she wasn't such a great catch; that I would be better for him. Bold confrontation was not exactly my style, but I'd just have to suck it up if I wanted a chance with him.

Feeling a little giddy at the thought of seeing him, I straightened up to wave, then promptly ducked back down again, sick to my stomach.

Nate was at the wheel and he was laughing. Benjamin sat in the passenger seat. I swallowed hard. Nate wasn't hurt, had never been hurt. I'd been tricked.

Chapter Twenty-Two

※

The Truth

Despite what I'd just seen, I decided to spend the night in the loft of Nate's garage. He'd left the gate to the castle open after driving in, and I was able to slip in after him. I needed somewhere to sleep and this was the only place I could think of.

I tried to settle on the pile of old tarps that served as my bed, but I couldn't relax. Nate's betrayal had stuck itself in my mind like a burr. He'd done such a good job fooling me. His concern for my welfare at the aunts' house could only have been a ruse to make sure that I wasn't let out of anyone's sight. He'd known what the aunts were up to, had always known. In fact, he could very well be the one in charge; he could actually *be* the Wrath. My mind returned to the brief resemblance I'd noted between him and Gabriel. Nate had once said the Wrath could alter their appearance. Perhaps he and Gabriel were the same person? Nate *had* been able to come and go in the forest without anything happening to him. Unfortunately, I'd forgotten to interrogate him on that point. Maybe if I'd remembered, I wouldn't be in this situation. I'd know for sure whether or not Gabriel and Nate were the same person and could move on from there.

Of course, if they were one and the same, that left me with *no* one to trust.

I lay there in misery, my heart thudding dully, my stomach tight with hunger and pain. Just when I'd realized that I was capable of love, I lost my claim to it. Tears threatened, but I refused to give in to them. I couldn't afford sentiments right now, least of all self-pity. Anger would be so much more practical.

I will make them suffer until they are dead, dead, dead.

I understood those words completely now. Once they had frightened and baffled me. Not anymore. Anger was powerful, and so was knowledge. No one knew where I was, nor would they guess that I had figured them out. The aunts were arrogant enough to believe their secret was safe; Nate didn't know I'd caught him out. Gabriel—I still wasn't sure who or even what he was—so I wouldn't trust him.

I couldn't.

My backpack was my pillow and I shifted, trying to get comfortable. My little burns stung and strange outdoor sounds kept disturbing me. But at last I slept, thankfully without dreaming.

Hours later, my hip and shoulder throbbing, I drowsily turned over onto my other side. A crackling noise filled my ear and I sat up, suddenly awake. It was the envelope I'd found in Priscilla's room—I hadn't looked at it yet.

Dawn was breaking, allowing enough light through a nearby dusty window to read. I dug out the white rectangle of paper, then hesitated, not entirely sure I wanted to know what Priscilla's deepest, darkest secret was. But it was the only way I was going to get revenge for all the things she'd done to me. I tore it open.

I soon discovered that it wasn't my aunt's secret at all. It was my father's. I stared down at a photograph of him when he was about seventeen or eighteen. If I hadn't read the caption on the back, I would never have guessed that this boy was my father, not at first glance, anyway.

The teen in front of me was quite ordinary looking. Some might even say homely. He had big ears and a gap between his front teeth, and his chin was as weak as a villain's minion. Only the blue eyes were familiar to me. This stranger was my dad all right, just not the one I knew. Either he had developed like the proverbial ugly duckling into a swan, or he'd had a lot of plastic surgery.

The striking difference between Edmund Filmore, then and now, was most likely what had kept him away from Ellwood. The villagers, his upper crust friends, all would know immediately that he'd gone under the knife. He had left an idol; he would not want that image to be tarnished. Lots of actors changed their names, but now my father's decision to do so made sense. He was hiding from judgment.

But why come back now? What did his sisters hold over his head that would bring him home to face censure, maybe even ridicule?

I felt more determined than ever to solve this mystery. I stared at the photo for a while longer, searching for an answer. True, there was some resemblance between us, but not much. I looked more like my mother than I'd realized—or cared to admit. Still, there was something there...the tilt of his head, the shape of his mouth. Whether I liked it or not, I was this man's daughter. I was a Filmore.

I put the photo away. I needed to eat something soon, and I knew just where to go.

Ducking low, I scurried toward the gate, which was still open, and stealthily made my way into town. The back door to the tavern was unlocked, as I hoped it would be. After getting her brother back, Bridget would've been distracted, forgetting such trivial matters as locking up. At least, that's what I'd been counting on, and for once, luck was on my side.

Inside, the kitchen was dark and empty, and I stubbed my toe on the cast-iron stove as I groped my way toward the refrigerator. A quick search revealed plenty of food to choose from. I wolfed down a leftover slice of shepherd's pie and a piece of chocolate cake, followed by a glass of milk. The light from the refrigerator helped me find a Styrofoam container and I shoved a ham and cheese sandwich and some chips into it, then stuck the container, along with a bottle of cranberry juice, into my backpack. Two ten-pound notes, slapped on the counter, along with Bridget's thermos, and I was all set.

As I turned to go, a flash of light startled me. A large man was standing in the back doorway, scanning the room. Luckily I saw him before he saw me. I ducked behind the island, berating myself for being careless. I should have taken the food and run, rather than eat it here like a starving animal. I hadn't been that desperately hungry.

"You might as well show yourself," the man remarked. "I can see your pack."

Rick. I stood up. "I was hungry. I paid for it." I indicated the notes. "And for yesterday, too."

He slammed the door behind him and rushed over to me. "Evie!" He gripped my shoulders and looked me up and down. "You're okay, then?" I nodded. "Oh, lass. You don't know what you've done!"

I blinked nervously. What *had* I done? "Was that your shepherd's pie I ate?"

He laughed, a delighted roar. "No, no! You've given me back my girl!"

I might have done well in school, but that didn't mean I was always the quickest on the uptake. "Who's your girl?"

"Bridget, of course! She was as trapped as Charlie, but now that he's back she can live again. I asked her to marry me and she said yes."

I felt a rush of pleasure. "That's great, Rick! I'm so happy for you."

He grinned. "I owe it all to you, saving Charlie as you did."

I shook my head. "It wasn't me. Charlie and I helped each other get out..." Something worrisome occurred to me. "Does anyone else know about Charlie?"

Rick's face darkened. "Well, that's the problem, see. George spotted him going into the pub and demanded he come out and show himself. At first the villagers were happy to see the lad, but then George's spiteful tongue started flapping and stirred up folks' suspicions. We had to take Charlie home."

My hands started to shake. "He won't let it go, will he? Not easily. You'll have to leave town for a while. Let this blow over."

Rick grinned, surprising me. "You're a smart lass, and I know that because I was thinking the same thing. Bridget and Charlie are returning with me to Dublin. A mate of mine has a restaurant he's starting up. Bridget'll be head chef, I'll tend to the drinks, and Charlie will do whatever he sees fit. Jack Thomson will take over running The Wrath's Path."

"That's perfect, Rick." I smiled, relieved. I'd only just met the guy, but already I was rooting for him. "You'd have a hard time convincing the whole village that Charlie isn't out to trick them, not with George around."

"Too right," he agreed, then his expression turned sour. "Your aunts will find out, to be sure."

Nate, too. And Gabriel, if his spies hadn't already told him.

Rick brightened. "Why don't you come with us? Just until things blow over, as you said."

I smiled. "Thanks for the offer, Rick, but for the moment I think I'll stick with laying low. There are some things I need to figure out first." I couldn't tell him my plan; the less he knew about it the better.

"Ah yes, your da…he'll be here soon, won't he?"

"Any time now."

"You'll be all right, then. He'll watch out for you."

"Hmmm…" I replied noncommittally, as I went around him to the door. With my hand on the knob, I turned back to face him. "Rick?"

"Yes, lass?"

"Tell Bridget I said congratulations. She's got herself a good man."
One of the rare few.

He winked. "With pleasure."

Before he could say more, I ducked out the door and into the shrubbery. The village had filled with shopkeepers setting up colorful tents and booths; cars were parking alongside the road. Judging by the blue sky, lit now by the rising sun, it was going to be a rare and beautiful day. Everybody would be out to celebrate the festival, including Nate and my aunts.

I had no desire to meet any of them. I had already decided that I wouldn't make my move until dark. I would be going to the bonfire, but not to see my dad. I meant to confront my aunts and Nate. I meant to show the villagers the photograph of my dad and demand that they answer my questions.

If they didn't, then I would be forced to kill them.

What the hell? Where had that come from? It was one thing to repeat a vague expression to ward off feelings of powerlessness; it was another to plot murder. *I've been around Kelli and Priscilla too long,* I decided, pushing the thought away as though it were laden with arsenic.

The attic of Nate's garage served as my hiding place once more. The day passed slowly, though I managed to make my provisions last until dusk, which wasn't easy. I was nervous and hungry and the food tasted delicious; I just wanted to wolf everything down like Sadie had done to my scone.

A small window gave me a good view of the moor where a giant pile of wood, off to my left, and in the direction of the waterfall, waited to be ignited. As the sun lowered in the pale blue sky, a battered, red pickup truck chugged up the hill, blue smoke puffing from its tailpipe. A farmer in faded blue overalls parked by the bonfire and climbed out of the truck. After lighting a cloth-bound torch, he methodically set about igniting the pile, moving from left to right, thrusting his torch into spots high and low, waiting for the wood to catch with a rush of flame, then moving on.

The moment the bonfire really caught hold, a slow, steady trickle of villagers began to make its way up the hill toward the bonfire, like ants heading for home. The sky darkened. The time had come.

Backpack stashed behind a pile of old tires, and my father's photo stowed in my pocket, I left the castle grounds. Hood pulled up, I joined the other villagers on the trek to the bonfire. Most were dressed in period costume—the men in tights and tunics, the women in flowing dresses with flowers woven in their hair. Luckily, enough of the teenagers wore their everyday clothes, and I easily blended in with them. We were all on a pilgrimage. I, to discover the truth; they, to avoid it for a while.

As I approached the bonfire, tendrils of heat reached out to warm me, tempting me to come closer. But I had other plans. A large boulder fifty feet from the crowd beckoned and I split from the group and headed toward it. It would serve as my hiding place until the moment came to make my move. I climbed to the top and lay on my belly, watching the crowd expand.

The number of people was impressive. I hadn't thought Ellwood held so many people. Scanning the crowd, I quickly spotted George looking about with hungry eyes. Searching for Charlie, maybe? Or me?

Surely he'd want to know if we'd seen his wife, if we could tell him anything. His whole body bent forward as though yearning for something, anything, to take away the bitter pain of his loss. I felt a little sorry for the man, to be mourning a woman who would have chewed him up and spit him out had she stuck around. Gwyn was so awful that she soured his life even when she wasn't in it.

Most of the villagers had laid out colorful blankets and quilts on the grassy ground, far enough from the fire to watch the spectacle without danger of getting showered in sparks. A smaller bonfire about twenty feet away had been set up for the children. The villagers chatted and laughed while roasting nuts in pans, and bread, sausages, and marshmallows on sticks. Some of the children danced around the fire, mimicking the adults whirling like pagan worshippers around the larger one. A small band provided the music. A flute, a fiddle, a Bodhrán, and a short, dark-haired young woman singing a Celtic tune were the instruments.

The atmosphere was festive, yet I wasn't fooled by it. Beneath the joviality lurked an air of waiting. More than a few adults cast furtive glances over the crowd, as though searching for someone, likely Charlie or myself. And if they found one of us, there wouldn't be a welcome. These people were afraid, rightly so, and would sound the alarm so that we couldn't escape. Like George, they wanted answers. I was glad I'd decided to bide my time.

My father crossed my view before I realized that it was him, even though he looked exactly the same as I'd always known him. He moved with an ease he'd never shown with me, smiling at the swarm of villagers surrounding him. "You're too kind!" he exclaimed loudly, his rich actor's voice carrying far. "Such a welcome! Don't you think, Prissy? Kelli?"

The aunts trailed after him, looking both sour and furious. I had a feeling this reunion was not going according to plan. Not once did Father's expression appear worried or searching. I had thought maybe he'd come for me, to rescue me, but no, Priscilla had been telling the truth. He'd come because she'd threatened him.

"I'd be delighted, Mayor Walsh," he continued when a tiny, potbellied man scurried up to him and spoke to him tremulously. "I've always wanted to make the introduction for our little Solstice Festival. It would be an honor." Fearing my father might change his mind, the balding man grabbed him by the elbow and pulled him to stand up on the small stage the music makers occupied. Here he introduced my father as "Ellwood's own, Edmund Filmore." Father stepped forward and was met by raucous applause and whistles.

Priscilla and Kelli stood behind him, sticking close as though worried he might escape. Kelli no longer looked nearly as furious as Priscilla, who gave the impression that she'd swallowed a bottle of liquefied loathing. Kelli waved to the crowd, giggling and simpering like a little girl, with the exception of the flashes of cleavage she seemed intent on displaying.

My father addressed the rapt audience. "Citizens of Ellwood, my beloved childhood home, I am honored to be standing here before you. You have been most welcoming. I should not have stayed away so long." A cheer rose up and Priscilla's lips curled into a snarl. Bones, standing by her side, looked poised to attack. Only her thin fingers tangled in his fur held him back. Unwillingly, was my guess.

"I join you in celebrating another year of good fortune in Ellwood. I myself have been greatly rewarded in this life. I finally grew into my ears!" They all laughed. I realized with dismay that they had accepted him as he was even though he looked so outrageously different. Perhaps to them it only made sense that someone so talented, so upper class and rich, should 'become' attractive, too. "Seriously, though, I thank you all for your kind words and to those of you who have remained my loyal fans from all those years ago. And now, without further ado, let the festivities begin!"

He raised a bejeweled gold goblet, shoved into his hands by the beaming Mayor, high into the air and the crowd shouted and cheered. When my father lowered the cup and drank from it, emerging from behind it with a wide grin, they cheered again. I found myself getting pulled into the spirit of the celebration and mentally shook myself. I had to remember who this person was. He was not the lord of the manor; he was only playing at it. Even so, if he had played this role with me, I might have been more forgiving of him, or at least more enchanted by him.

But he hadn't even tried.

Laughing and smiling, my father stepped down from the makeshift dais. A flash of silver in the firelight caught my eye. Father froze for a second, then nodded smoothly. Priscilla leaned hard on him, her hand in one pocket, her elbow sticking out at an odd angle. Bones had circled around to Father's other side with Kelli closing ranks at the back. She was pouting, upset she had to leave the adoration of the crowd behind, even though none of it had been directed at her.

Waving at the crowd, smiling as though nothing was wrong, my father walked, along with his sisters, away from the bonfire, away from the people of Ellwood.

The Filmore family slowly, nonchalantly, made their way toward the woods. A series of fireworks filled the sky, distracting the villagers, and the aunts and my father moved more quickly. I slid off the boulder and hurried after them.

Just as they reached the line of trees, a tall figure closed the distance between them. Nate. My breathing turned ragged. All this time I'd been hoping that I had made a mistake—that Nate wasn't involved in this. Turns out I'd only been fooling myself. He was definitely a part of the scheme, if not the leader of it. Perhaps he felt some vendetta against my father and wanted revenge. Or maybe, despite his protests, he really was in love with Priscilla and was helping her out.

Anger spurred me on. I would make him suffer; I would make them all suffer for treating me like dirt. For once in my life I was going to stand up for myself. For once in my life, I refused to give up and go away. Today I would be a fighter. My show of bravery might get me killed, but what did I have to live for anyway? The whole world was filled with traitors and demons.

My mouth watered in anticipation as I entered the dark wood. I was the hunter now. Revenge would give me power; it would keep me safe, at least long enough to do what I needed to do. Nothing would stop me now. Not my aunts, not my father, not the Wrath. I was determined to win this war.

Destroy before you are destroyed.

Up ahead, Kelli led the way with a flashlight. The shadowy trees made way for the group, perhaps sensing it best to simply get out of their way.

"You've got it all wrong, Prissy," my father protested. "I meant to return, but every time I tried something would come up."

"No, Edmund, *you've* got it all wrong. You think that by making excuses I will spare your pitiful life. I won't. Once I get what's rightfully mine I'm going to kill you, and I'm going to enjoy doing it."

"Hey now, Priss! Settle down. We can work this out. There's no need to make threats."

"That isn't a threat, Eddie," Kelli spat over her shoulder. "It's a promise."

"You stay out of it," he warned.

"I will not! I've suffered just as much as anyone. Now it's *my* turn. I want what's been promised to me, and I intend to get it."

"You're a slut, Kelli. Do you really think having beauty will change that part of you? Beauty won't make you any less common."

I swallowed, hardly able to believe my ears.

"I'm not a slut, you bastard!"

"You've been one since the day you started toddling about, always hanging on men. Rubbing against them, taking their hands, even as a child. You disgust me; you've always disgusted me." His elegant voice somehow made the words more hurtful.

"Says the paragon." Kelli would not be easily silenced. "Says the man whose vanity started this hell in the first place!"

"Shut up, you two," Priscilla snapped. "We don't want to draw any more attention—"

I didn't hear the rest. A large hand clapped over my mouth and an arm as strong as a boa constrictor wrapped around my waist, yanking me backward to sit on the ground. I found myself leaning back against a warm, solid body.

"Don't move," a low voice threatened.

I couldn't anyway. Whoever had me was relentlessly strong and his grip was tight. When the others disappeared into the shadows my attacker removed his hand and came around on his knees to face me.

"Gabriel!" I breathed, thrilled to see him, all my doubts swept away. "What are you doing here? Come on. We need to follow them!"

He rose to his feet. "You will not miss anything." He laughed, pulling me up. He spun me around in a circle, a joyful pirouette. His golden hair and sea blue eyes glowed, as did his skin in contrast to the all-black outfit he wore. He dropped my hands and leaned forward to peer into my eyes. His nearness sent a shudder through me. "You are different tonight, Eve. More powerful than ever, I fear. You won't use your powers on me, will you?"

"What are you talking about?"

"I heard about your adventure. How you found the long-lost Charlie."

"He was with the Wrath, Gabriel. They took him and they weren't going to let him go. That Gwyn is the worst of the lot. Did she hurt you to keep you away from me? I was wondering where you were, why you didn't come."

Gabriel didn't answer. Despite the darkness I could see his excited face. He seemed to shine from within. Suddenly he grabbed my hand, his grip strong and warm. "Do you want to know everything?"

"Of course, I do. That's why I'm here."

"Do you like my place?" The question, so seemingly out of context, was casual, though his expectant air as he leaned forward to hear my answer lent it weight.

"Your house?"

"No. That is…just a stopover. I mean, this place. All around you. The woods. This land. It is all mine."

I considered what he said. "You own the Wrath?"

"I *am* the Wrath."

Chapter Twenty-Three

✳

A Wish Comes True

I felt a tremor quake through me, shaking me to the core. "No, you're Gabriel."

"I told you I had another name. *You* chose Gabriel."

"I don't understand. *You're* the one the villagers fear? The one who hurts people or makes them disappear?" I couldn't have known this already, could I? I couldn't have been so blind.

He waved a dismissive hand. "If you knew the stories behind each event you'd see that what I do is always justified."

A part of me rebelled—Charlie wasn't a debt to settle—yet a darker figment felt a thrill. "You're telling me you're a vigilante?"

He pondered the word, rolled it around in his mouth like a dram of whiskey. "You might say that." He smiled. "So now you know my real name, Eve. Does that please you?"

"Wait a second. You're honestly telling me your name is Wrath?" He must be making fun of me. He had to be. "Did you pick that out of a dictionary?"

His golden brows pulled together, nearly touching. "*I* did not choose the name, Eve. It was chosen for me. My christening happened long ago. The Wrath is a name that aptly describes what I do. Once it was bestowed upon me, I kept it."

"I'm not sure I can call you that." That would give him too much power.

He looked stunned, then angry. "You have no choice, Eve."

"I have every choice, *Gabriel.* It's just a name."

"Names are powerful, Eve. They can invoke pleasure, recognition...fear. Are you afraid of me at last, Eve?"

"I might be. Though if I could understand what you really are..."—certifiably mad, utterly sane? For some reason, the latter seemed more frightening—"...I would feel better."

"I told you. I am the Wrath."

"And the others?" I whispered, thinking of Gwyn and her followers.

He grew still. "I warned them once about you. People wrong me, you know. They say I show no mercy, that I don't even understand the concept." The hand holding mine squeezed hard and one of my knuckles cracked. "Even after they tried to take what is mine, I still gave them another chance. Now I'm afraid I will have to get rid of them. What a waste."

"They aren't all bad," I said, as I wiggled my hand about, trying to loosen his painful grip.

"Like Charlie?" His voice was quiet, baiting me.

"Yes, and most of the others, too. Gwyn makes them do what she says. They're innocent."

"Nobody's innocent, Eve. No one is without sin." *Not even you*, his tone implied.

"That doesn't mean you should punish them with death. People make mistakes."

"What if I told you they were all dead already? Would you feel avenged?"

I shook my head, feeling sick. "*No*. I wouldn't want that." I hoped I didn't want that.

"And your aunts who treat you like an imbecilic child? Your father who treats you no better than a worthless dog? What do they deserve?"

"I don't want them to die, Gabriel!"

"Of course, you do. What other punishment would serve after what they did to you?"

"They could go to prison."

"You've no proof against the aunts, and your father hasn't broken any law. Cruelty violates no decree. They are all free to go. Now do you understand why I do what I do?"

I refused to answer that. "You didn't really kill the others, did you?"

He shrugged. "What if I did? Why do you care?" He turned abruptly and pulled me along behind him. "Come. We have business to attend to."

In a flash, we were at his house—his manor in the woods. I felt as though he had snapped off the lights, then turned them back on only to find that we were standing in a different room, without so much as taking a step.

All the lights in the manor glowed brightly. The sight was not welcoming, the light was sterile and cold as an asylum's operating room. The odor from the garden, the rotting stench, was stronger now. Death thrived here like a living thing, like a merciless weed determined to take over the garden, overcoming all the other plants with its ruthless patience.

The others were here already, I knew. My father, Priscilla, Kelli, and Nate—the schemers.

Gabriel waved his hand and the door opened before us. Bones was lying on the top step, but he ignored us. Gabriel pushed me inside ahead of him and I stumbled into the room. The bright light hurt my eyes and it took a moment for my vision to adjust. When I could see, I discovered that I had been wrong. Everyone was here but Nate. He was nowhere to be seen.

Priscilla regarded me suspiciously and Kelli rolled her eyes in disgust. "What's *she* doing here?"

"Evalina!" my father cried. "What a relief to see you!" He rushed to greet me, arms spread like the wings of a swooping hawk. I stared at him in shock, and stayed stone still while he hugged me—it was the first time I remember him ever making the attempt. "I need your help," he whispered in my ear. "Your aunts are bloody mad. They tricked me into coming here, saying they were going to harm you. I came as soon as I could."

I struggled out of his arms. "Aunt Priscilla said you wouldn't come until she threatened you with the Wrath."

He stepped back from me, chuckling nervously. "The Wrath? What do you know about the Wrath?"

"She knows enough." Gabriel made his presence known then, stepping into the house to stand directly behind me. I felt his warmth through my clothes.

"Wrath!" Father gasped, then quickly recovered. "It's good to see you, old mate!"

Gabriel blinked slowly. "I can't imagine that it is, Edmund. You have stayed away too long."

"They told me you were going to reverse the spell. I had to see, make sure..."

I faced him, stunned. "You *knew*, Father? You knew what my aunts wanted and you sent me anyway? You were prepared to sacrifice me? What kind of monster are you?"

He cringed. "I'm sorry, Evalina. I didn't know what else to do! If I came back, Wrath would have taken everything from me. Your mother would have left me. I would've had nothing."

"You would've had *me*." My hand pressed against my chest and I could feel my own heart beating madly.

He looked surprised at the idea, then gave a shuddering hiccup...a sigh. "That's not enough, Evalina."

Make him suffer until he is dead, dead, dead.

The words swirled in my mind. My breath came in short gasps. "You *betrayed* me, Father."

Suffer, suffer, suffer.

"That was never my intention, Evalina."

"Never? Your betrayal started the moment I was born. You never talked to me, held me, took me for walks. I know nothing about you. You're my father yet it's like you're a stranger to me. I never asked for much. I only wanted a bit of your time, some of your love and affection. A fond pat on the head, even."

"There was so little time, Evalina," he protested, his blue eyes tearing up. "I was doing everything I could to make money to support our family!"

Dead, dead, dead.

"He's trying to fool you, Evalina," Priscilla sneered. "Just as he fooled us."

"Why did you do it?" I cried.

He struggled to put his excuses into words.

Kelli beat him to it. "He was always the most conceited prat! He was so vain, worrying about his Dumbo ears and his nonexistent chin and his stupid, fat nose, that he destroyed every photo of himself. Prissy and I took care of the recent ones." She gave a satisfied smile. That explained all the missing and altered photos I'd found in the attic. "It was his vanity that got us into this mess. One night, after downing a pint too many at the Solstice Festival, we made the mistake of going into the woods. Someone probably made a dare. Sure enough, we met the Wrath. We were bloody well scared out of our knickers! Until we found out that he wanted something from us. In return, he would give us whatever we asked for. Then, after Prissy and I did the dirty work, Eddie goes and reaps all the rewards. We'd have ours too, *Eddie*," she spat, "but you had to go and run off because you were afraid your new looks would be taken from you!"

"You were the ones who worded the bargain so foolishly," Gabriel spoke up. "'One cannot get his or her wish without the presence of the others.'"

"I don't understand," I said. "Why didn't you just give Priscilla and Kelli what they wanted?"

"You're not listening, Eve. They all needed to be together. That's how these things work. Humans always include some little detail in their wishes that makes my life so much more difficult than it needs to be. Edmund got his wish and then he left on the pretense that he was feeling rather odd and that he wanted to be sure the wish was safe before his sisters got theirs. Very wily, Edmund."

My father beamed. He thought he was being admired, and I thought his foolishness one of the sadder episodes of this whole awful experience.

"Well, we're all together now," Kelli breathed. "I want—"

"Don't do it, Kelli!" my father shouted, his brow beading with drops of sweat. A vein on his forehead bulged with panicking blood. "You don't understand what it is you're wishing for."

Her heavy eyes regarded him coolly. "Oh, I know exactly what I'm wishing for, Eddie. There is only one thing that I desire. I wish for Nathaniel Thorndike to be mine!"

The Wrath smiled, either pleased with her choice, or amused. He brandished his hand, like royalty waving to its legions. I was to find out the reason for his satisfied expression moments later when the door opened and Nate walked through, his presence refuting once and for all my theory that he and Gabriel were one and the same. He looked dazed as he marched like a soldier over to Kelli's side. She took his arm and beamed up at him, blithely ignoring the fact that he was staring straight ahead, seeing nothing.

"You can't have him!" Priscilla howled, rushing at Kelli, claws out. "He's mine!"

"Stop her, Nat," Kelli ordered. He obediently turned and stood between Priscilla and Kelli, receiving the blows intended for his master while he did nothing to defend himself. There was something very wrong with him. Kelli owned his body, but not his soul. His spirit had fled.

Panting, Priscilla straightened up, regaining her composure, breath by ragged breath. "You haven't won, Kelli. I still have *my* wish to make."

Kelli's smug eyes flickered. "Don't you mess with what's already mine, Prissy. Be a good girl now and give it up."

Maybe if Kelli hadn't insisted on calling her sister Prissy things might have turned out differently. Instead, Priscilla's blue eyes iced over and she ground out, "I wish that Kelli were dead."

Gabriel threw back his head and laughed. "What do you think about that, Eve? Your aunts are doing your work for you!" Eyes wild and bright as skies above a roiling sea, he threw both hands into the air. "Your wish has been granted, Priscilla Filmore. I hope it pleases you."

Chapter Twenty-Four

✳

The Discovery of a Lifetime

Kelli's eyes widened in alarm, then she gagged and turned a harsh blue. I ran over and pounded on her soft, fleshy back, hoping to dislodge whatever was choking her. She ran from me, thinking I was attacking her, clutching her throat and wheezing. In a corner of the empty room, she collapsed to her knees. Nate did not move to help her; his face remained untouched.

"Stop it, Gabriel!" I shouted. "She's dying!"

He shrugged. "The wish has been made. I cannot undo it. I'm powerful, but not that powerful." He tried to look regretful, but couldn't quite pull it off. His turbulent eyes observed her struggles, her painful spasms, as avidly as a predator. He was enjoying the show.

Priscilla and my father watched their sister dying and only looked mildly repulsed by the whole scene. Observing them, I realized something momentous. Most of my life, I'd done as my mother had told me to do and hated myself for it, but I had made a *choice* to live like that. Following orders always gave me someone to blame if things went wrong. Perhaps even more critical, I realized that if I didn't make a change now, I'd never do it. I'd never break free and become my own person. And I'd never be happy. I'd be like everyone else in my family—a blight on anyone who came into contact with them.

"Save her," I said to Gabriel. "Save her, and do nothing to harm the others in this room, and I will do what you wish."

He frowned. "You don't even like her, Eve, and she is suffering greatly. Isn't that what you want?"

I swallowed. "Not this way."

"You must follow your family motto, 'Destroy before you are destroyed.'"

I didn't bother to ask how he knew about it. "It's not *my* motto. I don't want her to die."

"Death is only a transition. Nothing to fear."

"She looks scared to me."

"Scared to death?" His smile urged me to join in his amusement.

"Gabriel!" I shouted. Kelli's eyes had rolled back into her head; her face was purple as a grape. "Fix this!"

He tilted his perfect head. "Oh, fine." He flicked his hand and Kelli sucked in air; her chest rose and fell in great billowing heaves. She was alive.

Priscilla swung on Gabriel. "You can't undo my wish!"

Nate looked around him, confused. "What's going on? How'd I get in here?" Kelli, struggling to sit up, somehow dredged up the energy to jut out her lower lip. Her slave was himself again and no longer hers.

I glanced at my father. He had changed, too. His features, like those in the old photograph of him, were plain, almost ugly, and much older now. Catching me staring at him in shock, his hands flew up to his face.

"No!" he screamed, his fingers discovering the unwanted truth.

All the wishes had been undone, and I was the one who'd made it happen.

"You can't do this, Wrath!" Priscilla shouted angrily. She looked like she wanted to attack him and only just managed to hold herself back. "We had a deal!"

"I did my part. Wishes granted for all." He pointed to me. "And *she* undid them."

Priscilla turned on me, her expression a smear of ugliness. My stomach dropped and I knew at last what it meant to take a stand, to take responsibility. I wasn't sure I liked it. "*You!*" she hissed. "You ruined everything!" She pointed her gun at me and fired six times before I could even think to duck. The roar echoed throughout the room. Stunned, I looked down. There wasn't a mark on me. I spun around. The wall was riddled with bullets, at the same level as my heart. I turned back, blinking and wide-mouthed.

Kelli cackled hoarsely. "I thought you were a crack shot, Prissy! Guess now you're just cracked."

Priscilla's face was a livid red. "You're a disgrace to the name Filmore," she spat at me.

"Oh, I think Eve has been a true Filmore today," Gabriel corrected with a smirk, and I stared at him sickly. He held out his arm to me. "It's time I collect on that promise you made, Eve." He looked up at the ceiling for a moment, directly at the vengeful man in the painting. "What I wish for is you, Eve. Even now I cannot predict what you will do next. You had a chance for revenge and you declined. How intriguing." He smiled to himself. "Come along, then." He held out his arm to me.

I hesitated, glancing back at Nate. He was taking in his surroundings, his eyes dark with disbelief. "Evie? What are you doing here?"

I nodded at Gabriel. "He brought me. But I have to go now."

"Don't go with *him*!"

"I made a promise, Nate. I won't be like the rest of them." I aimed my words at my cowering father. "I won't go back on my word." I wanted to. I wanted to run and not look back. But I had to do this, whatever the consequences.

"I won't let you go." He stepped forward.

Gabriel laughed. "Then come with us, Thorndike. Join my little group."

"*Your* little group?" I repeated dumbly. "Gwyn is not the leader?" *No, no, no.*

"Is that what you thought? How naïve of you, Eve." He did not sound pleased by my mistake, even though he had been the one to encourage it. "I just told you I was the Wrath."

"But *you* tell the others what to do?" I had thought he worked alone. I could *not* accept that he led them, gave them orders. It meant that he was as bad as they were, worse even, and it also meant that I was more easily deceived than a child. I felt sick from the humiliation and frightened by my own ignorance.

He sighed. "They say that humans see only what they want to see. In that, you are predictable, Eve. You wanted me to be good and so I was, but not too good, you didn't want that, either."

He was right. I had wanted to be fooled.

"You wanted me to see things that way, Gabriel!" I shouted, suddenly making the connection. "Otherwise you would've been honest with me from the beginning."

He shrugged. "Perhaps. But I've always believed honesty is overrated, Eve."

"You trick everyone, is that it?"

"I don't need to."

"What about Charlie, then?"

"Charlie came to me of his own free will."

"I don't believe that."

Gabriel's lips thinned. "You should. He hated his home, his father. He wanted to teach the man a lesson. So he came to me."

I remembered the look of guilt on Charlie's face. I had thought it was survivor's guilt, now I felt some doubt. "But he changed his mind."

Gabriel gave me a scornful look. "I couldn't simply let him go again, Eve." His tone was patronizing. "He understood the deal we'd made. Once you're in, it's for life. I cannot have others going about the country blabbing about me. They so often present me in a bad light."

"Some people make choices before they fully understand the consequences," I argued, thinking of myself more than Charlie.

"That's not my problem. Charlie was mine. I wasn't about to let him go simply because he had made an *error in judgment*."

"Fine," I conceded. "But if you didn't let him go, then how was he able to escape?"

"That, my dear Eve," his eyes met mine, "is exactly what I would like to know."

"What about them?" I waved my hand toward the others standing beneath the dome, appearing defeated or livid, depending on who I was looking at. Sunlight shone through the windows. Daytime had arrived faster than it should have. We were living on fey time.

"They will return to their pathetic lives, although things could have gone much worse for them considering the troubles the Filmores have caused me."

"What? How has all this affected *you*?"

His eyes shifted away from mine. "Let's just say I have suffered as a result of their actions. But, I have completed my half of the bargain— Don't look at me like that, Eve. I do have some honor, just not your sort. They will have to suffer the consequences of angering me, though."

"They will suffer your *wrath*," I said slowly. The truth was glaringly obvious now; my blind eyes miraculously cured. All that mindless following of orders had created a simpleton. What a silly girl I'd been! If I wanted to survive this, I was going to have to do much better from now on.

His eyes lit up. "Exactly! I will make them suffer until they are *dead, dead, dead*." His laughter chilled my skin. "Though I won't kill them like I did your grandparents. I tried to get them to reverse the curse and they refused, so they had to go. But I'll keep your family around for you, Eve." He winked at me, then turned to Nate, who was listening to our conversation with a strange expression on his face. "Come along, Thorndike. There is something I want to show you."

Nate looked back and forth between us. I shook my head. "Don't come, Nate."

"Yes, stay here, Nathaniel!" Priscilla commanded through clenched teeth, her hands curled into fists as she looked at me, then back at him.

His eyes, cold and furious, turned toward her. "You tried to kill me, Priscilla. You ran me over with your car."

What was this? He hadn't been faking? Or was this still part of some elaborate charade? I wanted to believe the best in him, but maybe that was part of my problem. I wanted to believe the best in everyone and they took full advantage of it.

"That was an accident." Her cool demeanor melted and grew soggy with despair and desperation. "I got mad. I'm sorry."

"I'm going with Evie. She's the only one in all this madness who's been honest with me."

"You don't mean that!" she cried. "I've loved you since we were children, Nathaniel. I did all this for you. I wanted to be beautiful for you!"

"I don't want any part of your schemes, Priscilla. I don't want any part of you."

Her face crumpled into sullen planes. "I should've killed you when I had the chance. I wish I'd pressed the gas pedal harder!"

Gabriel laughed. "That is one wish I cannot grant, more's the pity." Looking jubilant, he strode out of the building and I followed after him as though tied to him by a rope. Nate caught up to me, his face grim. Gabriel left us alone to talk as he led the way at a rapid pace. He was on a mission, I sensed, obsessed with it, and nothing was about to slow him down as long as we kept up.

Nate leaned low to murmur in my ear. "What happened to you?" His arm pressed warmly against mine.

"What do you mean?"

"Benjamin said you disappeared on us. That you went to fetch your bag and never came back. I thought maybe your aunts had caught you. That's why I was following them tonight. I was looking for you." *He was looking for me.*

"Gabriel's goons kidnapped me when I got too close to the woods. There was evidence in my backpack—I wanted to use it against Aunt Priscilla after she hurt you. But you were never really hurt." My voice wavered despite my best efforts to stay cool and composed.

"I *was*," he insisted. "I thought I was, anyway. As soon as the car started moving, I regained consciousness. When I couldn't find you, I told Ben to stop the bloody vehicle, but he wouldn't. He said I needed a doctor. But I didn't. There was nothing wrong with me. Dr. Carter couldn't even find where the blood had come from. She was, to say the least, a little perplexed about the whole incident. Fortunately, she's been my doctor all my life, so she knew I wasn't playing a trick on her."

Like Dr. Carter, I was having a hard time believing his story. Even so, I found I wanted to. "You're saying you simply recovered from a compound fracture? I saw the bone sticking out of your leg, Nate."

"That's what I'm saying! So what happened out there, Evie? What did you do to me?"

"What did *I* do to you? What are you talking about? I wasn't there. I was getting my bag, remember?"

"Ben saw you touching my leg, just before you left the car."

I remembered suddenly. "I did. I touched you. That's all I did, and I said a little prayer. Nothing more."

Gabriel was suddenly between us, pushing us apart. Nate stumbled away and caught himself against a mossy tree trunk. Gabriel's arm pressed against mine, insistent, electric. "We're here."

I glanced about. A stream ran nearby and a mound of stones pushed out of the earth next to it. The place of my dreams. Gabriel left my side to climb the pile. Stopping at the top, he peered down. "This is where your father has gone, Thorndike."

"What do you mean, *gone?*" Nate asked sharply. "Gone where?"

Gabriel shrugged. Caught in the stream of sunlight breaking through the dark treetops, he looked as angelic as the chosen one. His golden hair glowed like a halo; his black shirt glistened like raven wings. "Wherever it is you go when you're no longer here." He leaned over. "Oh, wait. There he is. It seems he was never really gone after all."

"What are you saying?" Nate demanded. He rushed up the pile. "That he's down there, in that hole?" His voice, bleak as the death of hope, trembled and broke. "*No.*" The single word was soft, pleading. He turned on Gabriel. "You did this to him?"

"Oh, not me, personally. The others. They are such scamps."

"You bloody bastard!" Nate shouted and charged at Gabriel. With an amused smile, Gabriel flung out his arm, sending Nate skidding backward, an invisible hand flinging him away. "Let me go!" Nate cried. "Fight like a man."

Gabriel's smile deepened, chilling me. "But I am not a man, so I shall fight as I wish." Still, he drew back the invisible hand, freeing Nate from its power. Feeling himself released, Nate launched himself at Gabriel, face hard and determined. His fist connected with Gabriel's cheekbone, whipping his head around. Gabriel slowly turned back to face Nate. He was no longer smiling. Nate swung again and Gabriel caught his fist with one hand, holding it tight as Nate fought against him, his entire body shaking with the effort. Gabriel looked at me. "Do you care about this man, Eve?"

"Yes! Don't hurt him, Gabriel. Please. I'll do whatever you say, just let him go!"

"As you wish." Gabriel pushed Nate's fist away, sending him flying off the pile. Nate tumbled down the rocks. Close to the bottom, his head smashed against a flat stone and he crashed to the ground. He lay still, blood pouring from the wound on his brow.

"Nate!" I raced over to him, but Gabriel jumped down between us, knocking me backward. Nate didn't move as I struggled to get to him. Gabriel held me off, his strong hands gripping my wrists like talons. I couldn't tell if Nate was alive; I couldn't reach him. I felt a scream building up inside me. "What have you done to him?" I lunged again.

"Which one are you referring to? The irritating father, or the equally annoying son?"

"The father and the son," I croaked, my body hiccupping with sobs.

"The others hunted the senior Thorndike and he fell and bashed his head in, and the son became something of an issue between you and me, so I did something about him. He might live, though I doubt it."

I couldn't breathe. I realized too late that I should never have declared my feelings for Nate. In doing so, I'd signed his death warrant. My sobs died, leaving only tears running down my cheeks. "You killed Nate because he annoyed you, and the others sacrificed Nate's father *just because?*"

"Sacrificed?" He gave a chilling little laugh. "What need have we of sacrifice when we can simply take what we want?"

Good Lord, what had I done? My conscience fevered to make this right, to reverse events, to stop time. "Why did they kill Nate's father, then?"

"For a bit of fun. There is so damned little to do around here. I did take them, after all, so I have an obligation to keep them occupied. And anyway, life would be much worse for the good citizens of Ellwood if I didn't."

The horrid words barely registered. I needed to know how my family had gotten involved with him and how we could get out of it. "What was my father's role in all this? With you, and his wish?"

"Oh, he never really did anything but promise not to tell anyone. Priscilla did most of the dirty work. She wanted Thorndike junior. Well, she wanted his title, anyway. Her greed made her reckless. She agreed to lure the elder Thorndike into the woods in exchange for a wish. My little Pucks did the rest."

I did my best to control the disgust shuddering through my body. I couldn't afford to make him angry with me. Not yet. "Why did you encourage her to do that?"

"I had a score to settle with the Filmores." He bent down and picked up a stick. "Some centuries ago I informed the Queen's guard about the Thorndikes, who insisted on practicing their heretical beliefs despite the law of the land, then I put the blame for my action on the Filmores. Of course, when the Filmores found out what I'd done, they took revenge on me." He cracked the stick through the air as though whipping a passing horse. "Somehow they learned of a way to trap me within the confines of the forest. And I've been here ever since." He sighed. "At the time my scheme seemed like such a good idea, but I was younger then, and less willing to think things through to their proper end." He shook his head. "But now I'm free to come and go as I please once more." He looked delighted as he broke the stick in half and threw it into the stream.

All the pieces crashed into place, like a broken teacup in reverse. "So you struck a bargain with my father and my aunts—if you granted their wishes, then the Filmore family curse on you would be lifted. You said you tried to get my grandparents to lift it and when they didn't, you killed them. But Priscilla was more wily than they were. She's the one who made the agreement so that she got something out of it, too."

"You're very clever, Eve." He looked the tiniest bit disgruntled that I had figured it all out.

"So did Nate's father really need to die?"

He blinked slowly, then spun away to face the rock pile. "His death was necessary to keep Priscilla and the other two in line. Possessing a murderer's secret is an excellent bargaining tool. I highly recommend keeping one in your back pocket at all times."

"So what did my ancestors do to trap you here in the woods?" I asked quickly.

He pivoted on one heel to face me again. "Eve, Eve! Now really, why would I tell you that?"

"So *you* started this whole disaster, and yet *you* wanted revenge for being rightfully punished?"

His eyes twinkled. "Why not?"

"You're a monster." A beautiful monster, who pulled me to him despite everything I'd heard.

"Monster is one of the many names I've been called, though Gabriel has been my favorite, Eve." He moved toward me, each step slow and deliberate. My breathing quickened. "You are very astute...calling me by the name of your God's avenging angel. We are of like minds." He stopped within inches of where I stood, wrapped his arm around my waist, and pulled me to him. He felt warm and alive. The back of his hand rose and stroked my cheek softly, slowly. My traitorous body stirred to his touch. He leaned toward me, his full lips parted, his breath hot and sweet.

"Gabriel is also known as an angel of mercy," I managed to push through trembling lips that nearly touched his.

"I told you I could be merciful," he murmured. "I'd do that for you, Eve."

I jerked backward. "No, not for me. *Never* for me." Then he would own me for sure.

"I suppose you really do like the dull one." I didn't answer. "I heard what you said, about touching his wound, about him healing at your touch."

"I must have imagined seeing the broken bone."

Gabriel slid a warm, strong finger beneath my chin, tilting my head back. He peered deeply into my eyes, then released a delighted sigh. "How could I have missed it? You're one of us, Eve! That's how you saved Charlie. That's why I felt so determined to lure you into the woods when I spotted you with that horrid driver, the one I enchanted to get him to bring you to me. I am beginning to understand so much now." The smile on his triumphant face spread slowly, like the light of a rising sun. "Your effect on me, how you unlocked a locked door, how you healed the dull one, how you escaped unscathed from a round of bullets aimed directly at your heart. We are kindred spirits."

I pulled myself out of his arms, taking several steps backward. He reached out to grab me and I skirted around him, leaping up onto the pile of stones. "Stop it, Gabriel!" I shouted when I reached the top. "You're making this up to get me to stay with you."

"I quite often make things up, Eve. But not this time. I can see the Wrath in your beautiful blue eyes. You have our powers, you are part of us, and I claim you!"

"I would never join you, Gabriel. I would rather die." Did I mean that? I could still feel his caress on my cheek.

"But you must join me, Eve." He was calm, frustratingly sure of himself. "You are one of my own. I'm not sure what happened to make this come about. Perhaps your father passed something along to you, who knows? This passing of power has never happened before—not as far as I know, anyway. It's all very intriguing, I must say. None of that matters, though. We made a bargain, and we must abide by it."

"You broke that bargain when you hurt Nate," I accused. "He was part of our agreement, don't you remember? You were to leave all of them alone and I would be yours."

"Eve, Eve. What I remember is that you once despised him as he surely despises you. He hates all Filmores, as he should. As far as he knows, your ancestors double-crossed his."

"*You* did that, and I'll tell him so. He'll believe me." Gabriel only smiled at me with condescension. I swiped at the air in frustration. "What does it matter, anyway? All that hatred is in the past. It happened so long ago. It's time to let it go."

The smile dried up. "You must *never* let anything go, Eve. How else will you fuel your powers? Revenge is yours for the taking. Revenge must be had on your aunts, on your father. That's why I let them live, so that you could dispose of them as you wished. They were not only cruel to you, they were willing to sacrifice you for their own interests. Your own family, Eve! How can you bear it?"

I swallowed, feeling confused. He was right. When had they ever treated me well? When had anyone in my family been kind to me, offered to help me, without wanting something in return? "Prove to me that I'm one of you," I whispered.

"Make something happen. Make the wind blow."

"You're saying that if I want something to happen all I have to do is wish it?"

"That's all there is to it, Eve."

"And what if I wish for you to once more be bound to this forest?"

He didn't look worried in the least. "You wouldn't do that. You don't want to. You like me." He grinned. "And you are *like* me."

"Perhaps." I glanced over at Nate. He hadn't moved. "One last question, Gabriel. What will happen to Gwyn?"

He looked irritated. "I'll take care of her."

"How?"

"She won't bother you again, Eve, if that's what's bothering you."

"Are you going to kill her?"

"I don't need to. Now that I know you are one of us, Eve, your safety is guaranteed for eternity. Join us, Eve," he continued, skillfully evading my question. "Our world is so beautiful. You will have such power here; you will have your revenge. Anything you want will be yours. You could even have your nobility back."

My fists clenched tightly as I struggled with my desire to believe him, to do as I was told. Old habits die hard. "I can't join you. I can't let you tell me what to do. You said I let others do that too much."

"But I'm not like the others, Eve. What I want for you is what is best for you."

I wanted to believe him. He represented everything I desired to be—beautiful, powerful, my own master. If I went to him, I could have those things, just like he did. Nobody would treat me like dirt ever again. My mother and father would love me at last. Life would be perfect.

And then I remembered something he'd said to me, *Honesty is overrated, Eve.* He was lying. No way would he give me what he had. Because then we would be equals.

I took a deep breath, knowing what I had to do, even though I wasn't entirely sure it was the right thing. "What I want, Gabriel—*Wrath*—is for you to stay here in this forest. I wish it."

"Eve!" For the first time since we'd met he looked uneasy. "What are you doing?"

"I'm making my own decisions for once."

"Don't do this, Eve! You'll regret it!"

My fingers curled into determined fists. "No, I don't think I will."

"Eve…" He began to move backward down the rock pile and into the woods, retreating from me like fog from a wind. A violent gust kicked up suddenly. "Undo your wish, Eve!" he shouted.

"Never!"

"This isn't over!" He flew backwards, his hands reaching out for me. Just before he disappeared, one hand whipped upward.

A thick branch over my head snapped and a loud crack reverberated through the woods. I reared back to avoid getting hit and my foot slipped. Before I could steady myself, I fell backward, into the hole that held Mr. Thorndike's long dead body. My head struck stone and I was gone.

Chapter Twenty-Five

*

The Complication

It was terribly dark. I felt like I had a freight train roaring through my head and my entire body burned with pain. I wanted to go back to sleep, back to the agony-free darkness of unconsciousness, but at that moment, a desperate whisper filled my ear.

"Tell him. Tell my Nathaniel that I was coming back to him." The words were blurred and broad. "Tell him that I was going to live for him."

Evie...

"Tell him I was coming back. Please!" I turned my head toward the voice. A man lay beside me, his light brown hair matted with blood. He looked odd, crumpled, really, as though the fall had crushed him like a paper bag. His image faded in and out as my mind fought consciousness.

Come back, Evie!

"I saw her, and I followed her," he went on. "I thought it was my beloved Jessica. But it was only *her*. She turned about, tore off her wig, and laughed at me. That's when *they* came. I didn't want to go. I wouldn't ever have left him like that." He began to sob, a wretched, keening sound.

"I'll tell him," I whispered, then louder. "I'll tell him."

"You must tell him I love him," he insisted. "He doesn't know."

"I'll tell Nate everything," I assured the man, reaching over to pat his hand.

A smile lit up his pained face as he faded away, flesh gone to dust quick as a lightning flash. I blinked and my hand dropped to rest on bone.

"Evie!" The voice, a different one, came from above.

"I'm down here," I moaned. My mouth tasted of copper and salt.

"Thank God! I'm going for help. Don't move."

A classic line, and I laughed helplessly and silently, perhaps a little hysterically, too. "I won't." Then I passed out.

~

I awoke in a bedroom, feeling warm and cozy. A fire crackled in the nearby fireplace. *I must have hit my head awfully hard*, I thought muzzily. I could see my mother. She sat by the bed, curled up in a chair, legs tucked beneath her. She was watching me.

"She's awake," she announced, sounding just like her favorite stage character, Mrs. Eloise—a no-nonsense woman who didn't have time for emotions. She was too busy ordering people about. This was a role made for my mother.

"I see that." Nate. I turned my head toward the other side of the bed, both thrilled and relieved to hear his voice. He was smiling, though he looked worried, half his forehead furrowed like a newly plowed field. A large white bandage covered the other half.

I tried to smile back, but gave up the attempt. My teeth hurt.

"She's a hallucination?" I managed, waving a wobbly arm in my mother's direction.

He laughed and despite my battered state, I felt my stomach quiver warmly. "She's really here."

"When did she get here? How long have I been out?"

"Oh, for Heaven's sake, Evie!" my mother exclaimed in disgust and my head pivoted toward her again. I instantly regretted the move. "I flew into London only a few hours after you did. I wanted to know what your father was hiding from me. A man doesn't leave his country and never return without good reason. Besides, I wasn't going to let those aunts of yours decide whether or not I could come."

"*Plus* you were worried about me," I added.

"Of course, I was. Your aunts are lunatics. I would never have abandoned you to them."

I wasn't so sure about that.

"Your mother knew my mother, you see," Nate explained.

"I scared the crap out of him at first." Mother laughed. "He had no idea who I was. I met his mother when she was only sixteen and visiting the States as an exchange student. Jessie auditioned for a play I was in and we became instant friends. But after she returned home, I never saw her again until I flew to England for her funeral." She paused for a moment, as though collecting herself. She actually seemed to be truly sad, not just acting as she usually did. "That's why when I showed up at the Hold a week ago, Nate actually recognized me. But he didn't remember why until I explained. I also met Jessie's husband, Augustine, at the funeral. I was sorry to hear of his death. He'd been very kind to me."

Augustine—the Augustine Affair. He must be the one Priscilla had referred to in the letter to my father. It made sense now. She was alluding to his murder, which they had all conspired to commit.

"Anyway, Nate relaxed after I told him everything. I shared enough of our story to get him interested, leaving out the part about me checking up on your father. I simply told him I was worried about you staying with the aunts and, as they didn't like me, asked if he'd check up on you."

"Meeting my mother, is that when you changed your mind about me?" I croaked to Nate.

I wished one of them would migrate to the other side of the bed so I could stop moving my head. "There was never anything to change," he protested, leaning forward. "I liked you from the start...on the train. Watching you fighting off that bloke's giant elbow was thoroughly entertaining, and strangely charming. You should've seen your face." He smiled, as though remembering. "And then, you were so still and quiet looking out the window at the landscape passing by, yet your expression never stopped changing. I wanted to know what was going on in your mind. I still do."

"And what would your girlfriend think of that?" The words were stupidly expressed, but my head hurt and I needed to say something.

"My girlfriend?"

"Your other engagement. Your complication." He stared at me, not understanding. "I saw her standing at the window..."

"You idiot!" my mother guffawed, and I turned to look at her, closing my eyes for a moment as the pain washed over me. "That was *me*." She stabbed at her chest. "I would think you'd have made that connection by now, being such a good student. I guess book learning isn't all it's cracked up to be. Not that I ever gave it much credence. *I'm* Nate's complication, his other engagement. The poor thing felt as though he had an obligation to me, as his guest and as your mother." She gave him a surprisingly fond look.

"You?" That explained the smell of cigarette smoke in the house. The relief made me giddy. I looked over at Nate, then back at my mother. "You can go now," I told her. "I'm sick of moving my head. But before you leave, might I remind you that I most likely have a concussion. I'm not making *any* connections right now."

She smirked, and perhaps looked a little approving. "I told you she was a fighter, Nate. She just needed something to fight for." She sashayed out the door, putting on her best pageant walk.

When she was gone, Nate took my hand. "You're all right, then?"

I nodded, glancing at his bandage. "How's your head? You hit it pretty hard. I actually thought you might be dead, you looked so awful."

"Did that worry you?"

"A little bit."

His smile was wry. "I'm fine, actually, though I did hit my head pretty hard." He fingered the edge of the bandage. "Got quite a bump, and I was out for a few moments. When I came to, I planned to jump Gabriel, but he ran off and just sort of disappeared. Right after that you fell into the pit. That wasn't very smart of you…falling into a hole like that."

"I didn't try to—" He grinned. "Very funny, wise guy." I paused, feeling suddenly sober. Now was the time to tell him what had happened to me down there. "Nate…when I was down in that hole I saw your dad."

His face crumpled. "I know. The Wrath was telling the truth. We found Father's remains when the rescue team pulled you out. I recognized his clothes, what was left of them anyway." He paused, gathered himself. "He must have fallen and died in that horrid place, all alone."

"No, I mean, I saw him as a…as a ghost, I guess. He wanted me to tell you something." I put my hand on his arm.

He frowned. "What do you mean?"

"He wanted you to know that he was coming back to you, that he wanted to live for you. But they chased him and he fell and he died down in that hole." Nate's features hardened with anger. "He wanted you to know that he loved you very much."

"How could you…?" He stopped himself. "You saw him…?" he tried again.

"I'll tell you everything some time, when you're ready to hear more."

"I want to hear it now—" He broke off when he saw my face. "Yes, all right. I'll wait." He was working hard to control his fury, though his hands trembled. "Why did the Wrath run off, Evie? What did you do? I hope you didn't promise him anything."

"You wouldn't believe me if I told you."

"Try me." He was close to me now, his face inches from my own. I could feel his warm breath on my neck as he bowed over me. I could count his eyelashes, each soft and vulnerable curl. He was so warm and solid I wanted to put my arms around him and hang on forever.

Instead, I found the courage to say, "Gabriel, the Wrath, told me that I was one of them."

"Say that again?"

"He thinks I'm like him, that when I was conceived the spell or magic that changed my father was passed along to me. Crazy, huh?" Nate said nothing. "I'm not one of them," I stated loudly and firmly.

"Gabriel told me that he didn't particularly like telling the truth. He was just lying to get me to stay with him."

Nate stared at the wall over my head. "It would explain why you remained unharmed when you passed through the forest," he said quietly into the tense air between us.

"You passed unharmed, too."

"I know. I've wondered about that. I think it was because of you. That you kept me safe."

"How? I didn't do anything special."

"You survived a 15-foot fall onto your back, and while in the woods, none of the rescue team came to harm." I shrugged helplessly. "How were you able to help Charlie escape, then?" he pushed on. "How did you heal my leg?"

"None of that was me," I insisted, gripping the blue duvet in my cold hands. "It was all just a strange coincidence."

"I don't think so. I think it was you." I shook my head stubbornly. "Well, it's something you're going to have to consider, Evie. Promise me you'll do that."

"Why? I'm leaving here. Once I'm gone, it won't matter one way or the other whether he was telling the truth. I'll go back home." I had to leave England. A fragment of myself had enjoyed Gabriel's wickedness a little too much, and maybe still did. What kind of person did that make me? Besides, I wasn't sure I was strong enough yet to test my newly acquired backbone—not with so much on the line.

Nate pulled back, taking his warmth with him. "You can't *leave*, Evie."

"I can only stay so long, Nate. There are rules." The thought made me sad and I felt myself tearing up, even though going home was my only way to escape this nightmare.

"You can stay here as long as you like, Evie. Your father is an English citizen. That makes you an English citizen, as well. You'll just need to fill out a few forms. I'll help you with that."

"Really?" My heart swelled at the possibility, and I realized that I really didn't want to go, even though staying would be a challenge, maybe even one that could change me for the worse. Still, I had determined I needed to make a change, even if it meant failing, even if it meant taking responsibility for failing.

"Stay a while. Here in my home. I'll show you around, give you a better view of England than what your aunts gave you. We're a mad lot, us Brits, but most of us won't be out to imprison you and kill your father."

I smiled wryly. "So what happened to the aunts?"

"They went home and cried their little eyes out."

"Over losing you?" I teased, though inside I was relieved they were still alive. Feeling brutally angry was one thing; acting on that feeling was a whole other kettle of fish—dead, rotten fish. I disliked my aunts—neither, it seemed, had matured beyond that day when they'd struck their selfish bargain with the Wrath. I especially disliked Priscilla, but I couldn't condone her murder. Which was why I hadn't yet told Nate what she had done to his father. I might not want revenge, but Nate surely would. For his father first, then for himself. He had lots of scores to settle with the Filmore family. I would have to think long and hard before I told him anything more.

"Over losing their wishes," he corrected.

"And my father?"

"I don't know what he's doing. Probably hiding out somewhere."

"He looks so different now."

"He looks exactly how I and the whole village remember him, plus twenty years."

"I wish he'd never changed himself. He might have been more likeable if he'd stayed as he was. I'm glad he turned back."

"Well, I'm glad that in looks you take after your mother."

I laughed. "Don't let her hear you say that. You'll give her a big head."

"Too late." Mother strode into the room as though walking on stage. She had fixed her hair and make-up, even changed her outfit.

My eyes widened at Nate as if to say 'see?' and he winked. I liked that wink—a signal that he was on my side. "I'll leave you two to talk." I watched him walk out the door with a heavy feeling in my chest. I didn't especially want to talk to my mother. Talking with her usually involved her tearing me down.

"I'm leaving your father," she stated without preamble.

It took me a moment to adjust to this unexpected announcement. "I suppose you're leaving because he lost his looks, not to mention his job. Or *will* lose his job, soon enough."

"Neither help his cause, but no, not for those reasons. I'm leaving him because he's a self-centered prig. I tried to keep this from you, you know. How terrible he was."

She'd done nothing of the sort. "You weren't exactly maternal yourself, Mother."

"Why do you think I stopped having kids?" She sighed. "I never meant to have any in the first place. But your father was a wild, desperate man in those early days and I wasn't as careful as I should've been. We had a whirlwind romance, you might say." She shook her head. "Turns out I was only a means to a green card for him." She didn't truly believe that, I noted, otherwise she'd have been furious right now. "I did my best with you, Evie, which wasn't much, I suppose. But I kept you. That's got to count for something."

"It means more to me that you see it as a compliment that I look like you."

"I do. You're gorgeous, darling, and I'm horribly jealous. Lucky you that I didn't eat you when you were young."

"Is that why you were always telling me I was ugly?"

She waved her hand. "Don't be dramatic. I was simply preparing you for life. People are harsh, they judge. I wanted you to be ready. It's a rough world out there and I figured it was my job to teach you that. Besides, arrogance is so annoying and I didn't want you to get obsessed with your looks like your father was."

Mission accomplished. "So what are you going to do now?"

She smiled, her whole face lighting up as best it could through the Botox. "Baby, you won't believe this! Well, it's me, so maybe you will. I've got a role in a new TV series on cable called *Life Bites!* I'll be playing a vampire mother." Here she frowned. "But a sexy one. I get to be bitchy and mean and full of life…so to speak."

"So you won't really be acting."

"Not at all!"

"I'm happy for you, Mother." Surprisingly, I was.

She looked at me from beneath fake lashes. "Really? Because I was under the impression that you hated me. I did send you into the lion's den, after all. But in my defense, I didn't realize those two were homicidal maniacs."

"I used to hate you. But I've gotten over that." And my fear of her. Not once had my fingers sought each other out, staying still and calm in her presence. Well, mostly, anyway.

She stood up. "Good. Now I can die in peace." Our precious moment was over. "Stay here with Nate for a while. Forget about college for the moment. Just relax and live a little. You're going to need all the recovery time you can get before you show that face in public. You look like a grape."

"Mother!"

She waved this aside. "Nate is a babe and a *Lord*—not that I care about that sort of thing. But if I were ten years younger…"

I threw my pillow at her. She neatly sidestepped it. "I'm flying out tonight. We start filming in a couple days and I want to look my best." Halfway out the door, she stopped. "You'll be all right?" She hadn't wanted to ask the question, having no desire to hear a negative answer, but she had asked it. I'll give her that.

"I'll be fine. Knock 'em dead, Mom."

She smiled. "Call me Katherine, why don't you? Mom makes me sound old."

I heard her laughing all the way down the hall.

Nate's face was bemused when he returned. "Your mum just pinched my bum."

"She must approve of you."

He grinned, the smile dissolving years layered on by the grief he'd worn for so long. He sat and took my hand. His own was warm, soothing me, making me believe in possibilities. "So are you going to stay?"

I certainly wanted to, but I also didn't want to be dependent on anyone right now. Relying on myself during my stay with the aunts had been liberating. "Is there a place I could rent around here?"

"I told you that you could stay here at the Hold, Evie."

"But oh how the neighbors would talk." I smiled and touched his hand. "Well?"

"I'm sure there's a flat somewhere in the village," he finally conceded. "If that's what you want."

"It is." For the most part, anyway. I needed to show myself that I could do things on my own, live by myself, hold down a job. But I also didn't want Nate thinking I was only interested in him because he was a lord. Though, admittedly, Lord Thorndike had a nice ring to it.

"All right, then. I'll help you find a place." He looked grim at the thought.

"Thank you, Nate."

"Get some sleep now." He stood to go, giving me one last, searching look, thinking thoughts I could not guess at, before leaving me alone. I watched him go and felt instantly adrift. I had wanted to be on my own, and now I was.

Chapter Twenty-Six

✳

Doubt

Aweek passed. I was, for the most part, recovered, and Nate was about to drive me to my new flat situated above Miss Dunton's Teashop. According to Nate, six or seven years ago she'd bought a large home on the other side of the forest and no longer had use for the extra space. Rick had rented the room before me, but now he was gone to Ireland in the night, much to the villagers' consternation. Likely they'd turn to me for answers now, but as long as they didn't turn on me, I'd cope.

I was to begin work at the bakery tomorrow, mopping, washing dishes, serving customers. Not a glamorous job, and it certainly wasn't intellectually challenging, but it was all mine, and it was a place to start. Eventually I might convince Miss Dunton to let me bake, a job Mother abhorred and thought too domestically demeaning to pursue, but I liked baking and I'd discovered I was good at it. I couldn't wait to start.

Nate was packing my suitcases, which he'd fetched from the aunts. Bessie had provided the keys to get in the house. Going by my instructions, he found the secret passage in my room, explored it for a bit, then snuck all my stuff out through a back door.

Bessie was now happily 'working' for Nate and had promptly gone about making friends with Miss Ames. He even set up an appointment for her with an eye doctor, at my request, since I figured she'd be willing to go for him. "I told you Nate was a good 'un," she'd crowed while serving me soup the first day of my confinement. "And I'm glad *you* got him and not the Misses Muck and Cluck." We both had a good laugh at that one, even though I wasn't entirely sure what 'Muck' and 'Cluck' meant.

I enjoyed the attention immensely—for the first day. But after that, when she started checking every five minutes to see if I was still breathing, often waking me to do so, I told her to go find something else to do or I'd strangle her. She happily acquiesced. Right now the two women were in the kitchen discussing scone recipes, their rheumatism, and their favorite shows on the telly. I was glad for Bessie, and grateful to Nate for taking her in. Her 'dying' aunt was being difficult, clinging to life with both clawed hands, so Bessie had nowhere else to go.

"After they found out I'd helped Nate," she explained, "I got the boot. I wouldna have stayed there anyhow. They're a couple of be-soms, they are, and they dunna deserve someone like me." She cackled mischievously, but I agreed wholeheartedly.

While Nate fussed over the arrangement of luggage—he had to re-move several dilapidated, overfilled cardboard boxes from the back seat to make room—I wandered over to a dark stretch of woods bor-dering the lawn and stood there looking into the cool retreat.

As I contemplated the beauty of the lush forest, I thought about the person I had become. I had come a long way from the naïve, young girl I'd been when I first arrived. I felt stronger and more confident now and thrilled to find that there was a bit of something in me, after all. I'd learned that if I wanted to grow I had to take risks, stand up for myself—not *let* people be rude to me. I'd also learned that I could sur-vive people not liking me, and that included my family.

Coming to England, I realized, had helped me tap into an inner core of strength I might never have discovered otherwise. I suppose I had Mother to thank for that. She had sent me here, after all. I imagine, though, that if I was smart about it, I'd never get around to acknowl-edging her role in my positive development.

Of course, in coming here, I'd also discovered another part of my personality that wasn't so appealing. I had a dark side, it seemed, a frightening, destructive temper I never knew existed. Whether that part of me had come about due to Gabriel's influence, my upbringing, or my ancestors, I had yet to figure out. In the meantime, I thought I had better watch myself. Because if what Gabriel had said was true—that I had some element of the Wrath in me—then I had an unusual and dif-ficult battle ahead of me.

Thinking of Gabriel—something I'd been doing a lot of since our last encounter—I wondered where he was right at this moment, what he was doing, what he was thinking. Then I wondered why I still cared about him. Twenty or thirty times a day, I searched my mind for ways to absolve him of wrongdoing. Sometimes I thought maybe he was the Queen Mary of my argument—not truly evil, simply misjudged, and I considered whether I should give him another chance. I shook my head, confused. What was I thinking? Of course, I shouldn't let him off the hook. He had meant to do everything he'd done. Queen Mary had had choices and so had Gabriel. Shouldn't they both be held ac-countable for them?

Come to me, Eve.

I gasped in fright. The wind. It had to be the wind.

I will make him suffer until he is dead, dead, dead.

I took a step backward.

I want you, Eve. More than life. More than revenge! Come back to me...

I whirled about, flying right into Nate's arms. He steadied me, holding me tight as he peered into my eyes. "Are you all right?"

I nodded. "I'm ready to go."

"Not just yet. There's something I started with you, Evie. Something that I didn't finish."

I frowned, trying to think what it was. "I'm not sure—"

His hands cupped my face and his lips found mine and then he was kissing me with an intensity that made my head spin.

"I won't let you go back to him," he breathed in my ear, his forehead pressed against mine in feverish connection. I clung to him.

I knew that he meant it; that he would try. But Gabriel was strong. I would have to fight him.

I wasn't sure that I could.

I wasn't entirely sure that I wanted to.

About the Author

When author, Kristina Schram, was growing up she wanted to be a star. When that didn't turn out quite like she expected, she turned her mind to achieving other goals: Earning her Ph.D. in Counseling Psychology, working as an Artist-in-Residence at local schools, being a free-lance editor and reader, coaching parks & rec basketball, and publishing her first novel, a YA fantasy called The Chronicles of Anaedor: The Prophecies (Book One).

Knowing what it's like to struggle with self-doubt and lack of confidence, her biggest dream (in addition to owning a castle) is to stamp out low self-esteem for everyone, especially young people. "Feeling bad about yourself is the number one deterrent to achieving happiness," she says. "So for the sake of a better world, it's got to go." She lives in New Hampshire with her husband, three boys, her mother and various pets, and can also throw a tomahawk, if need be. For more information, visit her website: www.kristinaschram.com. She's also on Facebook and Twitter.

Other Books by Kristina Schram

Mayhem at Nepenthe Manor: A Pandora Belfry Adventure
(Book One)

Precocious and morbidly obsessed with death, Pandora Belfry has spent her entire life at Nepenthe Manor, a dark, Gothic mansion also known as the local loony bin. Recently turned fourteen and growing exasperated with her stifling life, Pandora wants two things more than anything else in the world—to make her escape from the asylum, and to get her mom to finally act like a real mom. Until these wishes are granted, she acts as self-imposed ringleader to a wayward posse of inmates. Known amongst themselves as the Secret Six, Pandora and her friends spend their time at Nepenthe Manor stirring up trouble—holding weekly Midnight Meetings to concoct schemes, sneaking into places like the Nepenthe family cemetery and the forbidden attic, and generally doing everything they can to avoid the curse of living a mundane life. But when a mysterious new inmate arrives at the manor, things change for Pandora, and not for the better. In retaliation for a trick she plays on him, the charming and handsome Xavier connives to take over the posse, threatens to divulge one of Pandora's biggest secrets, and refuses to tell her what he did to get himself locked up. This boy is obviously hiding something, and it's up to Pandora to use whatever nefarious means necessary to find out what it is, before he destroys the only world she's ever known.

The Labyrinth of Lunacy: A Pandora Belfry Adventure
(Book Two)

Pandora Belfry, along with the eccentric members of her posse, is back, and looking for trouble. The posse's first order of business is to break into the off-limits labyrinth, even though they can't find its door. Against her mother's wishes, Pandora also works to solve the mystery of her father's identity. Perhaps he's a staff member, or maybe he's the stranger haunting the beach late at night. Topping the list of possible dad candidates is the new therapist, Dr. Steele, who keeps popping up in Pandora's life like an annoying, but handsome, nanny. To add to her problems, Pandora's date with the slimy, but oddly fascinating, Dougie Daft, is fast approaching. She isn't sure how to get out of it, or even if she dares to. Her new acquaintance, Giganticus, certainly doesn't want her to go, but if she doesn't, she'll be obligated to Dougie Daft, and that's the last thing any sane person would want...

The Chronicles of Anaedor: The Prophecies (Book One)

Strange things happen to fifteen-year-old Lavida Mors. Maybe that's why her father sends her to Portal Manor, a mysterious family estate she never knew existed. Lavida quickly discovers that not everything at Portal Manor is as it seems when she stumbles across a secret passage to a hidden world—Anaedor. Long ago, humans drove the Anaedorians, a civilization of magical and strange beings, into the dark world of huge caverns, frigid rivers, and bottomless pits deep within the earth. Malevolent forces, led by the evil Malvado, seek to control all of Anaedor, but an ancient prophecy tells of a hero who will save them from destruction. While trying to escape the dark realm, Lavida must battle overgrown leeches, survive a poisoned arrow, and outwit a giant, all while trying to convince the hopeful populace of Anaedor that she is not the savior they believe her to be.

The Chronicles of Anaedor: The Return to Anaedor (Book Two)

After escaping from Anaedor, fifteen-year-old Lavida Mors starts a training course with her guardian, Mrs. Keeper, in hopes of improving her magic skills before the dreaded Malvado returns. But while trying out a new spell, something awful happens, and she vows never to do magic again. When an unexpected discovery forces her to return to Anaedor, she is faced with her most terrifying challenges yet. Strife reigns in the hidden underground world as lootings and burnings break out, and numerous enemies conspire to capture Lavida, fight her, even kill her. Without magic, how can she possibly flee from dragons, escape the Goblins, outwit the ruthless Frio, and fight a duel with a young rebel intent on proving she's not the One? Time is running out. If Lavida doesn't learn to trust herself and her skills, a series of catastrophic events will ensure that she and her friends never make it out of Anaedor again.

The Chronicles of Anaedor: The Lost Ones (Book Three)

Sixteen-year-old Lavida Mors is in for a long, hot summer. With no way into Anaedor, the Lost Ones seeking refuge at Portal Manor are taking over the house, creating havoc and misery. Lavida is overwhelmed trying to keep up with her chores, learning magic, and fighting off the Pixies—tiny creatures who have made it their mission to harass Lavida at every turn. Meanwhile, unbeknownst to the residents of Portal Manor, the AAK is hard at work opening a Portal to the Upland. They are successful at last, and the twins, Loria and Darian, on the run from Malvado, and the AAK leader, Trey, manage to make it through the opening only to have it collapse behind them. With no way back into Anaedor, they are forced to take refuge at Portal Manor. As they try to settle into this strange new life, tensions between the humans and the Anaedorians grow, creating rifts between Lavida and her friends. To make matters worse, Frio, Amoral Hunter Leader, is hiding out in the Upland, and when he goes after Lavida, he starts in motion a series of events that could end up costing Lavida her life.

The Chronicles of Anaedor: The Uprising (Book Four)

In this final book of the Anaedor series, sixteen-year-old Lavida Mors is placed in grave danger when a group of young Anaedorians infiltrates the Upland. Their orders are to eliminate the evil one, whom they believe is Lavida, and then launch an Uprising to take over the Upland. Disguising themselves as humans, they befriend the unwitting Lavida and her friends, allowing them easy access to Portal Manor. Darian and Loria, Blendar twins and Lavida's friends, and Trey, ex-AAK rebel leader, have come to the Upland to warn Lavida about the intruders. But before they can, Darian learns something about Lavida's past that turns him against her. Surrounded by betrayal and danger, and faced with an astonishing revelation that makes her question everything about her existence, Lavida feels increasingly alone and afraid. If she cannot convince Darian and the others that she is not the evil being they think she is, she will lose everything to the Uprising.

The Battle to Become an Author:
When Great Expectations Go Awry

Are you looking to find an agent and/or get published? Are you a published author frustrated with the whole process? Or have you simply heard the horror stories and are looking for a ray of light before plunging into the fray? In this short booklet, author Kristina Schram discusses how one's unrealistic expectations about becoming an author can contribute to feelings of negativity and isolation. Dr. Schram offers a real-world discussion of this growing issue, humorously incorporating her own experiences throughout. She also offers insights and ways to cope with the increasingly difficult battle to become a published author. Come prepared to challenge your own expectations, to laugh and to cry, and to battle against the forces conspiring to keep you from reaching your writing potential!

www.ingramcontent.com/pod-product-compliance
Lightning Source LLC
Chambersburg PA
CBHW021244260626
47155CB00004BA/1300